SHE H

"Can I as his
tea to the ta

"Fair's fair." He gave her a lopsided smile. "I plan to ask you a couple."

"I figured as much. Why did you come here this morning, instead of going home to catch up on your sleep?"

"Why didn't you tell me you dreamed of this bombing?"

A bitter, incredulous laugh escaped her. "Why didn't I tell you! Where do you get the nerve to ask me that?"

Donovan retreated, both literally and figuratively. "Okay. You're right. I'm—"

"Do you think I enjoy being ridiculed and insulted? Called a liar—or worse, psychotic?"

"I never called you a liar! Or psychotic either, for God's sake."

"Not out loud, maybe, but you thought it! Screwball, that's what you said."

As soon as the words left her mouth, a horrified chill swept over her, dampening her anger. She watched the realization creep up on him, saw his brief attempt to deny it. The wary suspicion in his eyes gave way to disbelief, startled comprehension, and finally something that looked very much like fear. It wasn't the first time Faith had seen that look; it probably wouldn't be the last. But the pain it caused never diminished.

"No," he said, his deep resonant voice reduced to a harsh whisper. "I only thought it."

Praise for Lynn Turner's *Race Against Time*

"A magical, high-spirited tale that combines humor with plenty of action. One of the most intriguing time-travel novels to date. Don't miss it!"

—*Romantic Times*

DANGEROUS GAMES (0-7860-0270-0, $4.99)
by Amanda Scott

When Nicholas Barrington, eldest son of the Earl of Ulcombe, first met Melissa Seacort, the desperation he sensed beneath her well-bred beauty haunted him. He didn't realize how desperate Melissa really was . . . until he found her again at a Newmarket gambling club—being auctioned off by her father to the highest bidder. So, Nick bought himself a wife. With a villain hot on their heels, and a fortune and their lives at stake, they would gamble everything on the most dangerous game of all: love.

A TOUCH OF PARADISE (0-7860-0271-9, $4.99)
by Alexa Smart

As a confidence man and scam runner in 1880s America, Malcolm Northrup has amassed a fortune. Now, posing as the eminent Sir John Abbot—scholar, and possible discoverer of the lost continent of Atlantis—he's taking his act on the road with a lecture tour, seeking funds for a scientific experiment he has no intention of making. But scholar Halia Davenport is determined to accompany Malcolm on his "expedition" . . . even if she must kidnap him!

LYNN TURNER

DREAMER'S HEART

PINNACLE BOOKS
KENSINGTON PUBLISHING CORP.

PINNACLE BOOKS are published by

Kensington Publishing Corp.
850 Third Avenue
New York, NY 10022

First Printing: August, 1996

Printed in the United States of America

10 9 8 7 6 5 4 3 2 1

Dear Reader,

Have you ever had a dream come true? I have. It scared the daylights out of me. Fortunately, it's only happened once.

What would it be like to know that your nightmares were prophetic? That your dreams were actually glimpses into the future—a future you had the power to change, if only you could convince others to believe in your dreams?

What about telepathy? Is direct mind-to-mind communication an ability you'd like to have, for just a day? (Haven't you wished, at least once, that you knew what someone else was thinking—your boss, for instance, or your child?) And then there's psychokinesis, the apparent ability to influence physical objects with the mind. Sure would make washing those dirty second-story windows easier, wouldn't it?

Assuming such extrasensory powers exist, would they be gifts or curses? Would you exercise them openly, maybe even flaunt them? Use them to settle old scores, or win the lottery? Or would you try to keep them secret?

These are some of the questions I played with when I started thinking about this story. I began with the premise that a woman had started dreaming about a series of crimes that hadn't yet taken place. When she realized that her dreams were precognitive, what would she do? Go to the police? A psychiatrist? Start overloading her system with caffeine every night?

The woman is Faith McRae, the heroine of this book. Poor Faith. I saddled her with a veritable cornucopia of psychic abilities, a traumatic past, a psychotic villain . . . oh, yes, and a sexy, cynical, hardheaded police detective to provoke and harass and totally captivate her. And then, as almost always happens, things sort of snowballed. Faith is psychic, but I'm not; at times I wasn't entirely sure what was around the next corner, behind the next door. But, hey, life's an adventure. So is each new book. I hope you enjoy this one.

Lynn Turner

Chapter One

In the beginning everything had been so beautiful. Breathtakingly so. Fantastic, yes, obviously beyond the realm of possibility; yet *real* in the way dreams often are.

She was flying, which she frequently did in dreams—sailing through the balmy night, soaring so high it seemed she could, if she wanted, reach out and touch the stars. They were like enormous, glittering slabs of ice, with every hue of every rainbow from the beginning of time frozen inside, waiting for the chance to burst free and fill the cold, vast emptiness of space with color and light.

But then suddenly the stars became flickering pinpoints of light in an endless indigo sky, and she was back on Earth. A little above it, actually, skimming the tops of the trees in a small, moonlit park. Branches swayed and dipped to the silent rhythm of a gentle breeze, their silvered leaves whispering ancient secrets. A chorus of insects chirruped and whirred. A small animal—squirrel? cat?—scampered across a graveled path.

When she reached the edge of the park she descended again to glide along a city street. The aroma of still-warm asphalt enveloped her, a pungent combination of tar and motor oil and exhaust fumes. The distant bass drone of large trucks replaced the soprano notes of the insect choir. An amber streetlamp at the end of the block illuminated nearby buildings with unnatural yellow-orange light.

Faith realized that she was headed straight toward one of the buildings—an ugly, two-story pile of mud brown bricks that squatted at the rear of a corner lot as if it knew how unattractive it was and would like to sink into the ground. The owners had tried to dress it up by planting flowering shrubs along the two sides that faced the streets, then added a black wrought-iron fence between the shrubbery and the sidewalk. The aesthetic touches only drew attention to the building's complete lack of architectural grace or style—sort of like stuffing a wart hog into a ruffled pinafore.

What was this place? Faith wondered as she drifted closer. The cloying scent of honeysuckle wafted from the corner where the sections of fence converged and appeared to be held together by a snarl of vines and delicate tulip-shaped petals. Cheap toilet water, on top of the ruffled pinafore. Insult added to injury. Poor, homely building.

An instant later she found herself on the other side of the nearest ugly brick wall. She was simply *there*—inside the building—with no idea how she'd got there. She certainly hadn't transported herself, flown through an open window or door. She didn't think there *was* an open window or door; at least, she hadn't seen one. One second she'd been gliding, weightless and free, over the street outside, studying the building from a dozen yards away . . . and the next she was standing on the hard cement floor, flanked by rows of packing boxes stacked eight or ten feet high.

And she was so dizzy that for a moment she was afraid she would topple into one of the cardboard towers and send boxes flying in every direction.

She closed her eyes and inhaled a deep, steadying breath. The rush of vertigo was both a physical reaction—the result of having been brought to earth so abruptly—

and an emotional response to being zapped across forty feet and through a brick wall in about two seconds flat. Faith made herself count to ten, slowly, before she opened her eyes. By then, she'd partially adjusted to the almost total darkness. What *was* this place? More to the point, what was she doing here?

Despite the absence of light and her own disorientation, she registered two things right away: first, that the building was a large warehouse; and second, that she wasn't the only person in it.

At the end of the corridor created by the stacked boxes, she could just make out a dark, amorphous figure scuttling back and forth between two large wooden crates. His hunched form and gleaming eyes invoked the image of a large scavenging rodent, though in the shadow-filled gloom the eyes were his only recognizable feature. They glinted with a feral light as he scurried to and fro. At first his furtive movements seemed random, haphazard. But as Faith watched, she became aware of an economy and taut control that telegraphed purpose and intent.

Without consciously deciding to get a closer look, she began to creep forward. She was too far away to tell what he was doing, but faint smells and sounds drifted to her—the mingled aromas of sawdust, human sweat and machine oil, plus a sharp, acrid scent that was vaguely familiar.

Faith stopped when she was still roughly a dozen feet away, closed her eyes and waited, hoping the smells would trigger an image, a picture, some clue about what the man was doing.

Nothing. She wished she could identify that dry, slightly scorched odor . . . Charred wood? The charcoal ashes from a barbecue grill? Maybe he was just some poor homeless man who'd slipped into the warehouse to cook a few hot dogs for his supper. But no. If he'd been roasting weenies—or anything else—the smell of seared flesh would have eclipsed everything else.

So what the hell *was* he doing here?

The sounds were more helpful. The scrape of a hard

rubber heel against the concrete floor and the whisper of a screw being tightened were barely audible, but Faith instantly *saw* the actions that produced them, in her mind. And then, in his haste, the man allowed the blade of a screwdriver to tap against a metal surface. She saw the tool move in his hand at the same instant she heard the soft, tinny *clink*. The man froze, then slowly lifted his shaggy head to glance around fearfully.

For a second or two the mottled shadows beneath his eyes started to resolve into individual features. Faith could almost make out a face—long nose, wide mouth, squared chin. . . . But then he ducked his head, turning away to collect something from the floor, and the inchoate image dissolved.

Faith sighed in frustration. At least he hadn't seen her spying on him.

When he'd finished his work—whatever it was—he gathered his tools and crept stealthily to a heavy steel door, then out into an alley that was only a little more well-lit than the interior of the warehouse. Faith followed, curiosity tugging her along as he hurried toward a small graveled parking lot behind the building.

The lot was inadequately illuminated by an ancient dusk-to-dawn fixture on the far side, at the entrance from the street. Unfortunately the man wasn't moving toward the light. Almost jogging now, he headed for a pickup truck parked in the impenetrable shadows beside the warehouse wall. Once he was inside the truck, Faith knew she wouldn't be able to see his face.

Impulsively, almost instinctively, she willed herself to rise. Not to take flight—this was entirely different from the aimless, sailing-among-the-stars flying she'd experienced earlier. This was better. Much better, because she didn't have to wait and hope it would happen. She could *make* it happen, whenever and wherever she wanted.

It had been so long, years, since she'd allowed herself to even remember, much less test the ability, yet it still required no more effort than breathing. She immediately began to ascend, her consciousness slipping free of her corporal form, an invisible, intangible presence that rose through the still, humid air until she willed herself to halt. Hovering about ten feet above the ground, she took a moment to assess her condition. She was a little nervous, a little excited. More than a little fearful. As always, there was no tactile sensation, but all her other senses were functioning perfectly. She could see the circle of pale, washed-out yellow at the base of the dusk-to-dawn light; smell the diesel exhaust from a nearby expressway; hear the yap of a small, insistent dog.

Relief buoyed her. The fear and nervousness fell away, but the excitement remained. She'd forgotten what a glorious, intoxicating experience it was to float free of her body. Like being let out of prison. The feeling of release—no, *deliverance*—overwhelmed her and for several exultant seconds she reveled in it, soaring high to look down on the gritty, abandoned streets; spinning and whirling giddily, like a leaf seized by a whirlwind; swooping low to study her own motionless body and vacant expression.

Until she suddenly realized that the man had reached the truck, was opening the driver's door.

Faith sent herself racing toward him. She had to catch him, see his face, if only for a moment. Her rational mind couldn't provide an explanation for the powerful compulsion. She still didn't know what he'd been doing in the warehouse, but she sensed it was something sinister. Darkness and menace surrounded him, shrouding both his identity and his purpose.

She reached the truck just as he ducked behind the steering wheel. She caught only a fleeting glimpse—a head of dark, longish hair, a few inches of grimy blue sleeve—before he pulled the door closed.

No!

Frustration and defeat almost sent her spinning out of control. By the time she recovered her equilibrium, the truck had passed beneath the dusk-to-dawn light and turned onto the empty side street.

Faith awoke from the dream before she could decide whether to leave her physical self behind and pursue the man. She lay on her back, eyes open but unfocused, her body heavy and sluggish, heart thundering against her ribs. The scent of honeysuckle drifted through the open bedroom window, momentarily snaring her in a cloud of confusion. Was she really awake, or still dreaming? Then she realized she was staring at the blades of the ceiling fan, turning slowly overhead. She closed her eyes and released a long, shuddering sigh.

It was only a dream. It doesn't mean anything. It was only a dream.

She recited the words silently and then aloud, her voice a tentative whisper, trying to make them an affirmation. The trouble was, she couldn't quite convince herself. Her dreams had never been *only* dreams. They always meant something. Especially the waking dreams.

Fear seized her in an icy grip, making her shiver uncontrollably.

"Stop it," she muttered through clenched teeth. "This wasn't one of those. You don't have those anymore. It was just a bad dream, period. Everybody has bad dreams now and then."

Yes. Absolutely right. Everybody has bad dreams. Of course she wasn't the same as everybody else, but that didn't mean she couldn't have an ordinary, run-of-the-mill nightmare. She shouldn't have eaten that second bowl of pistachio almond ice cream. Or stayed up to watch that campy old sci-fi movie. Never mind that it had been more farcical than scary; obviously the bad actors in the chintzy rubber Martian costumes had had some effect on her subconscious.

Well, more likely it had been the ice cream. And maybe the damned honeysuckle dripping from a trellis in her neighbor's backyard. She got up and closed the window.

Her mouth tilted in a rueful smile as she climbed back into bed and punched her pillow into shape. She made herself remember scenes from the awful movie, and soon slipped into a sound sleep.

If she had any more dreams, she didn't remember them when the alarm went off at 6:30. A tepid shower got the day off to an inauspicious start. After a quick detour to the utility room to reset the circuit breaker for the water heater, Faith unlocked and opened the front door to collect the morning paper. It wasn't on the porch, or on the sidewalk leading to the porch, or in the overgrown hydrangea bush next to the porch. She closed the door and heaved a frustrated sigh. Damn it. First no hot water, and now no *Dilbert* or *Garfield.*

The last English muffin in the package fell apart when she tried to split it in half. She dropped the pieces into the toaster anyway, then discovered she was out of both tea bags and orange juice. She was sniffing a week-old carton of skim milk—the only other beverage in the fridge was an almost-empty bottle of Gatorade—when she smelled something burning and glanced over her shoulder.

The toaster was discharging spirals of thick black smoke. Faith thrust the carton of milk in the general direction of the table with a muttered "Shit!" and lunged to yank the toaster's cord out of the wall.

Her reach was a little short. The carton hit the floor. Milk splattered over her bare feet and ankles. She stared down at the mess and gave serious consideration to going back to bed and pulling the covers over her head.

By the time she finished cleaning the floor and herself, she only had time to guzzle what was left of the Gatorade before grabbing her purse and the lunch she had, thank God, packed the night before.

She arrived at the physiotherapy department at 7:55, and discovered that she'd been assigned two new patients in addition to the three who were already scheduled: a high school football player recovering from arthroscopic knee surgery, and a businessman who'd broken his collarbone and an elbow Rollerblading with his son.

She got the running back settled in one of the whirlpools and started Mrs. Hooper, who was recovering from hip replacement surgery, on a treadmill before taking a minute to scan the businessman's paperwork. His name was Alvin Baylor and he would be coming in daily for the next four weeks, primarily for range of motion exercises.

Faith hoped the orthopedic surgeons she worked for would wait a few hours before sending down anyone else. Having their own PT department in the basement of the building was wonderfully convenient, but sometimes her employers forgot that there were only three physiotherapists at their disposal, not a dozen.

At 12:30 she escaped to the break room to wolf down her lunch—a turkey sandwich, an apple, a carton of yogurt and a single-serving bottle of tea. She saved the apple for last, munching it while she read the funnies section of the morning paper. At 12:45 on the dot, Rollie Peters rose from his seat across the table.

"Back to the salt mines," he murmured, wadding an empty bag of corn chips and the wrapper from his microwaveable burger into a ball.

Faith looked up long enough to give him a sympathetic smile. Dirk Malloy entered the break room a minute or so after Rollie left, and went to collect his lunch from the small refrigerator.

"Are you done with the front section?" Dirk said as he dropped into the chair Rollie had vacated.

Faith took another bite of apple and pushed the bulk of the newspaper across the table while she finished reading *Dilbert*. She hadn't even glanced at the front section, being in no mood for depressing headlines about crime and the national deficit today.

"How's Tommy Carver doing?" she asked between bites of apple.

"Terrific. He'll be ready to start chipping away at Gretsky's records by the time hockey season starts."

"That's great," she said sincerely. Tommy was fourteen, and a sweetheart of a kid. Hockey was his life. During the youth league's championship game he'd been charging down the ice, on the way to scoring the winning goal, when a hard cross check dumped him on his head and sent him sliding unconscious into the boards. He'd sustained a severe concussion, a separated shoulder, and a compound fracture of the right ankle. Faith hated to think what his injuries might have been if he hadn't been wearing the required protective padding.

"Well, that's typical," Dirk muttered around a mouthful of sandwich. "The cops still don't have any leads on that bombing."

"You mean at the software company? It's only been, what, two days? Besides, from what I saw on TV there couldn't have been much evidence to collect. The lot that building used to stand on looked more like downtown Sarajevo than Louisville, Kentucky."

"A classic case of overkill," Dirk agreed. "Still, there's always something—the detonator or a trace of whatever explosive was used, at least. You'd think they'd have a few suspects by now, a list of disgruntled employees or dissatisfied customers."

"Maybe they do, but they just aren't ready to make any announcements."

He shook his head in disgust. "Says here they have no leads and no suspects. The company made medical software. Mostly for private practices, accounting and patient records, that kind of thing. Aha, but here's something interesting—they were supposed to start shipping a new program for hematology labs next week. This software alone is expected to generate several million in sales the first year. I bet that's it."

"That's what?" Faith asked as she stuck the core of her apple in the empty yogurt container.

"The motive for the bombing. Five'll get you ten one of their competitors had it done so the company wouldn't be able to ship this new software on schedule."

Faith stood and gathered her trash. "One of their competitors?" she scoffed. "Like who, Bill Gates? Get real,

Dirk. Software companies don't bomb their competition out of existence, they just buy up all the stock in a nice, clean corporate takeover. If somebody did hire some schmuck to bomb the building, it's more likely to have been a real estate developer who coveted the company's prime location."

Dirk's face had started to cloud with displeasure. He didn't like being contradicted. "I know you're being snide, but that's a possibility."

"Could be," Faith murmured. Experience had taught her not to let Dirk draw her into an argument. Once he'd taken a stand, he was constitutionally incapable of backing down from it, and 90 percent of the time she ended up agreeing just to shut him up.

She dropped her sandwich bag and yogurt carton into the wastebasket and rinsed out the empty tea bottle, which she deposited in the appropriate bin for recycling.

"Darn it, the aluminum cans are spilling out on the floor again. Would it kill you guys to bag 'em when the bin gets full?"

"There are only a couple on the floor. Anyway, Leon will collect all that stuff tonight."

Faith grimaced and opened a cabinet to find a garbage bag. By the time Leon got around to cleaning the break room, the floor would be tacky from spilled cola and juice.

"I saw that," Dirk remarked as she tossed cans into the bag.

Faith didn't look up. "What are you talking about?"

She knew she sounded curt. She didn't care. Dirk and Rollie were responsible for 95 percent of the cans that accumulated, yet neither of them ever offered to bag the damn things. Why? Because there was a woman to do it, of course. Sexist pigs.

"That look, when I mentioned Leon's name. He's not such a bad guy, you know."

"'That look' wasn't about Leon," Faith said dryly.

Either Dirk didn't hear her or decided to pretend he

hadn't. "Okay, I admit his religious views are a little conservative."

"Conservative?" She straightened to glare at him, the half-filled garbage bag in her left hand and a sticky Diet Pepsi can in the right. "He's a fanatic, Dirk, and fanatics are dangerous."

"Oh, c'mon. Just because he preached at you about your makeup—"

"And my clothes, and my hairstyle." She threw the Diet Pepsi can into the bag. "And the fact that I have a career, when I should be keeping house for some studly lord and master and dutifully bearing the fruit of his loins."

Dirk laughed. "All right, so he's *very* conservative. Can't you just shrug it off, consider the source?"

"No, I can't," Faith said tersely.

She turned back to bagging cans, reminding herself that Dirk had no idea what a sensitive subject he'd broached. He wasn't deliberately needling her; he just didn't comprehend how Leon's proselytizing made her skin crawl, or why. And that was exactly the way Faith wanted it. She'd gone to a lot of trouble to conceal the history of her old life from everyone she met in this new one.

"Anyway, why should I just shrug it off?" she demanded as she fastened a twist tie around the garbage bag. "We have laws that are supposed to protect people from harassment in the workplace."

"You really think of Leon's sermons as harassment?"

"I do, they are, and if he keeps it up I'll file a complaint."

Dirk didn't reply, but the look he gave her as she passed him on her way out clearly said he thought she was overreacting.

Was she? Faith asked the question of herself several times during the afternoon. If she were someone else, if she hadn't been so severely traumatized at such an impressionable age, would she be able to dismiss or ignore Leon Perry's evangelical lectures?

Around three o'clock she finally acknowledged that it was one of those unanswerable questions that could only lead to frustration and depression. She'd encountered a lot of those questions over the years. By now she should recognize one when it jumped up and smacked her between the eyes, and have the good sense to turn away from it.

Trying to imagine how she might react if she were someone else—an average, "normal" person—would always be an exercise in futility. She wasn't someone else, she was Faith McRae. At least she had been for the past eight years. And God knew the scared, confused, unhappy girl who'd existed pre-Faith had never fitted anyone's definition of average or normal. In fact, she'd been distinctly *ab*normal. Peculiar. Bizarre. A freak of nature. She knew things, saw things, *did* things that marked her as an aberration and scared the daylights out of everyone who came in contact with her.

Sometimes she'd even frightened herself.

The thought flared in Faith's mind without warning, unbidden and unwelcome. She gave herself a little shake to dislodge it, and went to collect the next patient's file folder.

Damn. She hadn't given in to this kind of morbid introspection in years. She'd put the past behind her, made a new life for herself. A nice, quiet, tediously *ordinary* life. If only Dirk hadn't started her thinking about Leon Perry and his irritating tendency to proselytize. . . .

No, that wasn't fair. To be honest, the reminder of her recent problems with Leon wasn't what had set off this bout of melancholy. It was that unsettling dream she'd had last night. It had been hovering at the edge of her consciousness all day, taunting her, mocking her, challenging her to figure out what it meant.

Because the dream had to mean something. There was no doubt in her mind about that. What she couldn't decide was whether the vaguely ominous images had been merely symbolic, or if she was supposed to interpret them literally. Did the man in the dream really exist, and if he did, what had he been doing in the warehouse? Faith didn't think he'd gone there to steal anything, unless it was the tools that were all he took with him when he left. Of course she couldn't be absolutely sure about that, because he was already *in* the warehouse when she got there.

She wished she'd been able to see what he was doing. Not that seeing would have made any difference, since she'd always been severely mechanically challenged. She could tell a hammer from a screwdriver, but that pretty much covered her expertise.

The last patient left at 4:20. A few minutes later, Dirk, Rollie and Missy Clarence, the PT Department's clerk-receptionist, said good-bye and headed home. Faith stayed behind to catch up on some record-keeping. She couldn't concentrate, though, and gave up when she caught herself making a notation in the wrong patient's file.

She spent the evening on an emotional seesaw, one minute hoping she'd have the dream again so that more details would embed themselves in her memory, and the next minute hoping it never returned. More than anything, she wished she could rid herself of this obsession with the dream and its meaning; dwelling on it reminded her too much of an earlier time, things she'd spent years trying to forget.

But she couldn't let go. The dream *did* mean something, she knew it did. Calling herself a masochistic fool, she settled in front of the television with a double helping of pistachio almond ice cream and tuned in a sixties vampire movie. When she turned off the TV and went to bed at 11:30, she made a solemn promise to herself that if the overdose of sugar and kitsch didn't trigger an exceptionally weird nightmare—either a repeat of last night's or a completely new one—she would take it as an omen and forget about the stupid dream.

At first everything was the same. The same gloomy, cavernous warehouse, the same faint scuffling sound as the man moved across the concrete floor. The same spooky glint as his eyes reflected the murky light that filtered through a row of dirty, dark green windows under the rafters. Faith was still too far away to see what he was doing. And, though she tried, she couldn't get any closer.

It was as if she were encased in an invisible cocoon. She pushed against it as hard as she could, with both her body and her mind, but she could neither break free nor force the cocoon to move with her. That was the first difference she noticed—both her efforts to get close enough to see what he was doing and her inability to do so. A second later she realized that there was another, even more extraordinary difference tonight.

She was aware that she was dreaming.

The insight startled and alarmed her, because it proved that the dream was significant—and certainly not the result of too much ice cream before bed. It had been a dozen years or more since she'd had a lucid dream.

A soft but distinct *clink* drew her attention back to the figure skulking in the shadows between the wooden crates. Faith remembered the sound from the night before. He had almost finished whatever he was doing. Next he would collect his tools and leave.

Which was exactly what he did. And thanks to whatever force was immobilizing her, this time she couldn't follow him. Frustrated anger welled inside her. Evidently she wasn't meant to get a good look at the man. Well, hell, what was the point of this stupid dream, then? Why was she even *here,* if she wasn't supposed to see him? For that matter, why was she still dreaming? Now that he was gone there was nothing happening, so why didn't she wake up, or at least cruise right out of this dream and into another one?

Because you haven't done what you're supposed to do.

The thought flared in her mind like an unexpected flash from a camera. Faith felt herself flinch in reaction. All right. What, exactly, *was* she supposed to do? By now Rat Man had reached his truck and was long gone, so apparently she wasn't supposed to follow or identify him. What else was there?

She willed herself to leave her body, expecting that it would still be impossible, and was so astonished when she started floating up through the musty air that she almost lost control. She bobbled for a second or two, then regained her equilibrium and hovered just above her own head while she tried to decide what to do next. Even in a dream state, she was still rusty at this out-of-body projection. It felt more natural tonight than it had the first time, though. And this time there wasn't so much as an instant's fear.

Okay, her objective wasn't the man. And probably not the warehouse or its contents—if anything of great value was stored here, there would at least have been a night watchman. Rat Man's little project? Was that what she was supposed to investigate? What had he been up to in a grungy, half-empty warehouse in the middle of the night?

Faith concentrated on remembering where that *clink* had come from and started moving toward the spot, but a shimmer of green light near the floor caught her eye before she reached it. Curious, she dropped down for a closer look. The light was being projected through a small hole—about the size of a drinking straw—in the end of a small metal box sitting on the floor. A narrow, pale green beam stretched away from the hole, about four inches above the floor.

A laser? No, she didn't think so. She'd never actually seen a laser, but she had the impression they were much smaller and more concentrated than this, less diffused. Surgeons used lasers as scalpels, after all; this would be more like a butter knife. Drifting effortlessly, she followed the beam of light about fifteen feet until it entered another hole in a second metal box.

What on earth—? For a moment Faith was tempted to return to her body, and try to examine the mysterious apparatus more closely, maybe interrupt the beam to see what would happen. She didn't, though, because she somehow knew that the twin boxes and the green light connecting them weren't what she was supposed to be looking for.

She turned away and once again focused her concentration on locating the source of the metallic sound. She succeeded fairly quickly, but didn't comprehend what she was seeing for several seconds. When she did, she was stunned and horrified.

If the contraption she was looking at was what she thought it was, she knew what Rat Man had been doing in the grungy warehouse in the middle of the night. He'd been assembling a bomb.

Chapter Two

Rhys Donovan ground the heels of his palms against his closed eyes until he conquered the urge to jump out of his chair and vent his frustration by swearing—violently and at the top of his lungs.

It was only 10:15, and already he'd interviewed a half-dozen assorted kooks and publicity freaks. Through the wide doorway opposite his desk, he could see at least a couple of dozen more patiently waiting their turn in the cramped reception area. Rhys would have bet his next paycheck that every last one of them would claim to be the bomber or to know who he was, and that none of them would leave until he or she had dictated a fantastically improbable but meticulously detailed statement.

Rhys was confident about these things because he'd been saddled with this kind of job before. Thanks to an easygoing, normally amicable personality, good instincts, and interviewing skills that had taken the better part of two decades to develop, he was often called upon to winnow genuine leads and probable suspects from the mountains of information that flooded the Louisville P.D. after every major crime.

Which meant that he was now on a first-name basis wit
most of the local nut cases. He also knew about a lot o
neighborhood feuds, since neighbors with an ax to grin
were often among the first in line to point an accusin
finger.

And then of course there were the sad souls whose live
were so barren that they seized on any chance to fee
important, even if only for a few minutes. They tied u
the phone lines or came in person to report every strang
face, unfamiliar vehicle or license plate, suspicious deliver
or service truck. Rhys usually gave them more time an
attention than he should have.

He had a lot less patience for the screwballs, though
Jesus, how had so many people come to be so demented
One of the first statements he'd taken this morning ha
been from a guy who was convinced Martians had plante
the bomb three nights ago.

"They know we'll be sending manned missions to thei
planet in a few years," the space cadet had explaine
gravely. "And then we'll find out that under all thos
poisonous gases, Mars is a mother lode of precious metals.'

"You don't say," Rhys murmured. "I had no idea.'
Neither, he'd bet, did the folks at NASA.

The solemn little man nodded vigorously. "Oh, yeah
it's all there—gold, silver, platinum, not to mention
diamond field the size of Pennsylvania." He glance
around, leaned across the desk, lowered his voice. "See
the Martians are determined to prevent the rape of thei
home world. Can't blame 'em, really."

Rhys pursed his lips and nodded. Christ. If this was a
indication of what the day was going to be like, he'd b
ready for a padded cell himself by the end of it.

"So they decided to come to Earth and destroy th
technology that will make space travel possible. This bomb
ing is just the beginning."

Rhys didn't bother to ask why the Martians had waite
till now, or why they'd picked a small Midwestern compan
that specialized in applications for doctors' offices. As i

was, it took another fifteen minutes to get rid of the looney tune. That interview had set the tone for the rest of the morning. When Rhys took a half-hour lunch break at noon, the cynical thought crossed his mind that if by some miracle a genuine lead did drop into his lap, he probably wouldn't recognize it. His brain had already shifted into dealing-with-screwballs mode: get 'em in, let 'em rant for a few minutes, then hustle 'em out the door.

By four o'clock he was in a foul mood that wasn't improved by a pounding headache. For the first time in weeks he craved a cigarette. Preferably unfiltered. He glared at the untidy pile of papers in the center of his desk, wishing he could feed them to the shredder but knowing he'd have to start sifting through them first thing Monday morning. At least it looked like he'd finished with the screwball brigade, thank God. The last of the wackos had trooped out fifteen minutes ago.

Or so he'd thought.

"Excuse me, are you Detective Donovan?"

The voice was low and throaty. Deliciously sexy. So was the body that went with it, Rhys discovered when he glanced up. The woman standing in front of his desk was petite—no more than five-three or four—with a slender but lusciously proportioned figure. Her straight dark brown hair was cut almost as short as his, but that was the only mannish thing about her. He decided on the spot that she was the most beautiful woman he'd ever seen. In person, anyway.

Rhys's headache miraculously vanished. Maybe the day wasn't going to be a total loss, after all. Belatedly remembering his manners, he rose to his feet, resisting the urge to fasten his top shirt button and slide the knot of his tie back into place.

"At your service." He offered her a smile and gestured toward the wooden chair placed flush against the right side of his desk. "What can I do for you?"

He noticed how gracefully she moved as she came around the corner of the desk and sat down. He wondered for a moment if she was a dancer, or maybe a model, but quickly discarded both notions because of her height. She seemed a little nervous. Being in a police station often had that effect on people. Rhys smiled again, trying to put her at ease as he resumed his seat and folded his hands on the desk blotter. She was carrying a canvas and leather shoulder bag that looked too big for her. Letting the strap slide down her arm, she placed the bag on the floor next to the chair. It sat there like an alert, beautifully trained dog. Rhys watched it for a couple of seconds, expecting it to wilt or fall over.

"The sergeant in the lobby said I should talk to you," she said, reclaiming his attention.

"In regards to . . ." Rhys prompted when several seconds passed and she didn't add anything more.

A delicate flush stained her cheeks. "The bombing. At the software company."

Rhys felt a tingle of premonition, but dismissed the reaction a second later. Her deep brown eyes glinted with intelligence, not imminent psychosis. He reached for a blank statement form.

"You have information about that crime, Ms.—?"

"McRae. Faith McRae." She spelled her last name for him. "Yes. Well, no. That is, I don't know anything about *that* bombing."

Rhys finished printing her name in neat block letters at the top of the form, then stopped writing and looked at her. Damn it. It would be just his luck if the best-looking woman he'd ever met turned out to be missing half her marbles.

"That's the only bombing we're investigating, Ms. McRae. Has there been another one we don't know about?" *Like maybe on Venus?*

"Not that I'm aware of, but I believe there's going to be."

The sober response sent Rhys spinning back in the opposite direction. Maybe she wasn't a member of the screwball brigade after all.

"You've seen or heard something that makes you think there'll be another bombing?"

Her eyes narrowed slightly, her gaze so focused and intent that for a second he had the crazy feeling she knew exactly what he'd been thinking. But then she glanced down at her hands, folded neatly on her lap. They were nice hands. Small, like the rest of her, perfectly formed. No rings. Nails trimmed short and coated with clear polish.

"Yes," she murmured, lifting her eyes to his again. "I saw something. A man, in a warehouse. It was late at night. I think he was setting up some kind of bomb."

She shouldn't have come. She'd known how it would be, what kind of reception the police would give her. She'd argued with herself about what to do all day, seesawing back and forth between a dread that made her sick to her stomach and an overwhelming sense of responsibility. Eventually responsibility won out, but the queasiness stayed with her because she knew all too well what she was letting herself in for.

What she hadn't known was that she would pick up Detective Donovan's disbelief so strongly, or that it would have this effect on her. Surprisingly, she was more angry than anything else. In fact, she was beginning to be really steamed. How dare he dismiss her like this, just write her off as a nut case? She'd felt his resistance even before she told him about the dream, as soon as she mentioned the bombing, in fact.

Of course things only got worse *after* she told him about the dream.

She returned his cool blue gaze with a composed facade, letting his disappointment and disbelief wash over her. Damn him. Damn them all—all the hardheaded, narrow-minded cynics who would only accept what they could see or hear or touch. She knew better than to try to convince him to take her seriously. His mind was closed as tight as a bank vault.

She was suddenly exhausted, both physically and mentally. Despite the incredulity he was broadcasting like a radio transmitter, Detective Donovan had conscientiously taken down every detail of her statement. There was no reason to prolong this unpleasantness; she'd done all she could do. She reached down to collect her purse.

"Well," the handsome detective said as she stood. "Thanks for taking the time to come in."

He made only a token effort to hide his relief that she was leaving. Faith's simmering anger came to a boil.

"For wasting my time and yours, you mean? We both know you don't believe a word I've said. It's a shame you had to waste so much paper and ink writing it all down."

His wide mouth compressed to form a watertight seam, his eyes narrowing in surprise. "It's my job to record whatever information you provide, Ms. McRae."

"It's *Miss,*" Faith said tersely. "Well you should sleep well tonight, knowing you've done your job." She hitched the strap of her bag onto her shoulder and started to leave. But then, purely on impulse, she paused at the door and turned back to add a curt, "And for the record, I'm not a screwball."

She shouldn't have taken that last parting shot. It had been a childish and petty gesture, the kind of impulse she rarely gave in to. But that hateful, pejorative word "screwball" had popped into her mind twice while she was telling him about the dream, and again when she started to leave. The slur had to have come from Donovan; there was no one else nearby. The third time had been the last straw.

It wasn't till a couple of hours later, while she was fixing herself a chef's salad and a cup of instant soup, that the significance of what had happened hit her.

She'd *heard* the word, all three times. As clearly as if he'd muttered it in her ear.

The knife she was using to slice a hard-boiled egg

slipped, nicking her index finger. Faith automatically turned on the faucet and stuck her finger under a stream of cold water. She felt dizzy, light-headed, but not from the cut, which had stopped bleeding by the time she turned off the faucet and dried her hand.

Oh, God. What was happening to her? First the dream, now this. It had been years since she picked up someone else's thoughts. She'd been, what . . . fourteen or fifteen, the last time it happened. She'd assumed that ability was lost—along with the other "gifts" that were actually curses—and had been both relieved and thankful.

Not again. Please, God, don't let it be starting again.

"Stop it," she murmured shakily, trying to quell the panic she could feel rising. "Just calm down and think!"

She hadn't actually *heard* the detective's thoughts—not in clear, distinct phrases and sentences. She'd registered his skepticism and resistance, yes, but any observant person would have; his vivid blue eyes and expressive face betrayed every thought and emotion. The only telepathic message she'd received was that single insulting word.

And maybe there was a sound, logical explanation for why she'd picked it up so clearly. It was probably a word he used often, or at least *thought* often. Or maybe something had brought it to mind just before she showed up. She hadn't gone to the police station until after work. For all she knew, Donovan had been taking statements about Tuesday night's bombing all day. If that were the case, several of the people he'd seen might truly have been—she shied away from even thinking the hateful word—a little out of touch with reality.

By the time she finished eating and had washed the few dishes she'd used, Faith had convinced herself there was no cause for alarm. She hadn't started intercepting other people's thoughts again; the incident with Detective Donovan was just a one-time fluke, an aberration. She conveniently ignored the fact that it had happened three times in the space of fifteen minutes.

Any residual doubts that might have been lurking at the

back of her mind disappeared when she woke at eight o'clock the next morning—it was Saturday, so she hadn't set the alarm—and realized she hadn't had the dream again. Not only had she not had *the* dream, she didn't remember dreaming at all. She felt rested, energized, the previous night's exhaustion and anxiety only dim memories.

While the water heated for tea, Faith went to collect the morning paper from the front porch. She waited to open it till she was back in the kitchen, which was good because there was a chair handy when she got her first look at the front page headline; in fact, there were four. Her knees gave way and she dropped onto the nearest one. The inch-and-a-half boldface roman type shouted up at her: SECOND BOMB DESTROYS WAREHOUSE.

She stared at the words in numb horror until the piercing *shreee* of the teakettle startled her and she dropped the newspaper. A second later the doorbell rang. Faith jumped again, then swore under her breath and got up to turn off the burner under the teakettle.

The doorbell chimed three more times as she hurried down the short hall, checking that her robe was closed and the sash securely tied as she went. She got her second major shock of the morning when she squinted through the peephole and saw Detective Donovan standing on her porch. Judging by the scowl on his handsome face, he wasn't paying a social call or soliciting donations to the Police Athletic League. Faith grimaced as she released the deadbolt. No doubt he'd seen this morning's headline, too.

"Surprise, surprise," she remarked, stepping back in unspoken invitation as she opened the door.

Donovan came in and she closed the door behind him. He was dressed casually today—worn jeans that had to be restricting his circulation and a long-sleeved dark blue Polo shirt, the sleeves of which were pushed up halfway to his elbows. The shirt and the tan bucks on his feet were stylistic touches that Faith appreciated. Most of the men she knew wore T-shirts and running shoes on their days off.

His right eyebrow rose a wry centimeter. "Don't tell me you dreamed I'd show up at your front door this morning."

She shook her head no. "I just brought in the newspaper. I was about to have a cup of tea. Would you care to join me?"

She headed back to the kitchen without waiting for an answer. That crack about dreaming didn't bode well for this visit. Why was he here? Did he think *she'd* planted the second bomb . . . and maybe the first one, too? And then obligingly presented herself at the police station and given him a statement that could later be used against her? Come to think of it, that was probably exactly what he thought. Every cop she'd ever come in contact with was a suspicious cynic through and through.

"Do you have Earl Grey?"

The question surprised her. She would have taken him for a coffee drinker.

"Yes. Have a seat."

He sat at the table and read the lead story on the front page while Faith collected cups and saucers, spoons, tea bags, poured steaming water into the cups . . . trying all the while to give the impression that entertaining a police detective who no doubt suspected her of complicity, at the very least, was something she did every day of the week. In her nightgown and bathrobe, yet. Barefaced and with her hair still uncombed and her teeth unbrushed.

Of course it didn't help a bit that the detective was so damned good-looking, or that he didn't appear to notice the savoir faire she was trying so hard to project.

"Would you like cream or sugar?" she said as she set his tea in front of him. "Sorry, I'm out of lemon."

"This is fine, thanks," he murmured. He didn't look up, leaving the tea bag to steep while he finished reading.

Faith carried her cup to the table and sat across from him. She thought about excusing herself to go get dressed, but decided that would betray her nervousness. Idly dunking her bag of Constant Comment, she inhaled the min gled aromas of orange rind and spices and studie Donovan overtly, while she had the chance.

He was without doubt the most physically attractive mar she'd ever met, but not quite as classically handsome a she'd remembered. His features were even, symmetrica and well-proportioned, but his mouth was a shade too wide and his eyes could be a little bigger. Of course if they were they'd have even more impact, so on second thought the were probably just the right size. Dark brown hair, thic in back and at the sides, starting to thin a bit on top. Grea physique.

"Penny for your thoughts," Donovan murmured out o the blue. He shot her a look as he removed the tea bag from his cup and placed it on the saucer.

Faith had had some experience with policemen wh tried to catch you off guard in order to make you blur out something idiotic or incriminating, so the tactic didn' surprise her.

"I was thinking that you're carrying approximately a hundred and seventy-five pounds on a six-foot, two-inch frame and that, considering your age, you probably main tain that weight with twice-weekly workouts."

His mouth quirked in a reluctant smile. "Three time a week. I forgot, you're a physical therapist, right?"

"Physiotherapist," she corrected. "Same job, newfan gled label."

Donovan nodded and took a drink of tea. "Somehow always imagined a physiotherapist would have to be bigger Don't you have to lift patients in and out of bed, that kind of thing?"

"Some therapists do, but I work primarily with sport injuries and people who've had orthopedic surgery, after they've been released from the hospital. They come in on an outpatient basis. Most of them are ambulatory."

"Still, you probably have to help some of them get in and out of a whirlpool now and then, or onto a table or a piece of exercise equipment."

"Sure. But managing a patient's weight is largely a matter of knowing how and where to apply leverage. Is this conversation headed somewhere?"

He took another drink of tea. "I was just wondering if you're a lot stronger than you look."

"And why, pray tell, were you wondering that?" she asked warily.

He didn't hesitate or hedge. "Because the initial reports indicate the explosive device that leveled the warehouse last night probably weighed between thirty and forty pounds. And whoever put it there had to carry it in."

Faith wrapped both hands around her cup and willed herself to take slow, deep breaths. Damn it, she never should have gone to the police about those dreams.

"Are you saying I'm a suspect?"

"No. At present, you're not a suspect." He allowed her a couple of seconds to enjoy the relief that poured through her, then added, "But only because nobody else has seen the statement you gave me yesterday."

"Every word I said to you was the truth," Faith murmured.

"You saw a man planting the bomb . . . in a dream."

She didn't need extrasensory perception to detect his disbelief; it came through loud and clear in his voice.

"That's right."

"Twice."

"I had the dream two nights in a row, yes."

"But you didn't come in after the first time."

She released an exasperated sigh. "I didn't know what it meant, or even if it meant anything. It might have been just your garden variety nightmare. Besides, I told you, I couldn't tell where the warehouse was, or see the man's face."

"Or the license plate on his truck."

"Or the license plate," she confirmed. "It was too dark. The truck was next to the building, right up against the wall. He probably parked it there deliberately, so no one would be able to read the plate." She lifted a hand and combed restless fingers through her hair. "Look, I realize it's hard for you to accept, but sometimes dreams *are* prophetic. I didn't put the bomb in that warehouse, I only saw what was going to happen."

"Before it happened."

His arid tone told her she hadn't made a dent in his skepticism. Faith massaged her forehead with the pads of her fingers and tried to think of some way to convince him she was telling the truth . . . or at least shake him loose from his stubborn refusal to even consider the possibility. That was always the biggest hurdle—getting people like Donovan to let go of their own rock-solid certainty about what was possible . . . and what wasn't.

"Has this kind of thing happened to you before?"

Of all the things he might have asked her next, she would never have anticipated that question. It was the kind of thing a believer would ask. Or someone who was determined to compile a list of reasons not to believe. Faith hesitated, knowing in her gut she should lie. The trouble was, she'd always been a lousy liar; he would know immediately if she tried.

"Yes." She said it as if she were confessing to a capital crime.

Donovan leaned forward, his gaze sharp and calculating. He looked, she thought, like a hunter who'd just watched a small, unsuspecting animal walk into a trap he'd baited and set. "You've had other dreams that came true?"

"I've had other dreams about things that were going to happen," she corrected.

He cocked his head to one side. His expression didn't soften. "I don't understand the distinction."

Faith shrugged. "Saying that a dream 'came true' implies cause and effect—that something happened *because* someone dreamed it would. It doesn't work that way. Dreams don't influence future events."

Donovan heaved a long-suffering sigh, then picked up his cup and drained the last of the Earl Grey. Faith wasn't trying to read his thoughts, or even his mood. If she'd been tempted—which she absolutely was not—the effort would have been unnecessary. His expressive face told her he was troubled, upset, and she could guess at the reason: there was a tug of war going on inside Detective Donovan between his instincts, which were counseling him to believe her, and the comfort and security of a lifetime's convictions.

"Dreams don't influence future events." He repeated what she'd said slowly, as if he were weighing and considering each word. He hadn't bought the idea, yet, but at least he was mulling it over.

"That's right."

"They just . . . forecast them."

"That's one way to put it. There's a long, well-documented history of precognitive dreams, and most of the people who have them are ordinary citizens, not space cadets or . . . crazies." She almost said "screwballs" but caught herself at the last second.

Donovan's response was a noncommittal grunt. He sat there, arms resting on the table, fingers curled loosely around his empty cup, for what felt like a week, studying her in stoic silence. Faith forced herself to meet his cool blue gaze without squirming or averting her eyes. It wasn't easy. Detective Donovan made her extremely uncomfortable, and not just because he was both a cop and a bull-headed, die-hard cynic.

She was too aware of the long, thick lashes fringing his striking eyes; of the strength evident in his hands, even when they were at rest; of the dark hair visible on his forearms; of the breadth of his shoulders. He was altogether too much man to be sharing her small kitchen with.

"So," he said at length. Rather than easing the tension that had built to an ache inside her, the sound of his deep, resonant voice made it worse. "What were these other dreams about?"

Faith's uncomfortable sexual awareness instantly transformed to stomach-churning dread.

Oh, God.

"I don't see what that has to do—"

"I'm curious. Humor me."

She got up to fetch the teakettle and more tea bags, stalling while she tried to decide how much to tell him . . . and how to go about it. If she didn't handle this just right, he would probably summon a bunch of men in white coats to haul her off for a psychiatric examination. And even if he didn't, she'd spent the past eight years hiding that part of her life. From everyone. To reveal even part of the story to Donovan would be to invite the kind of attention she abhorred.

"Don't tell me you've suddenly turned shy," he murmured dryly.

The sarcasm in his voice was a deliberate goad. Faith felt the skin on her face tighten as she dropped a fresh bag of Earl Grey into his cup and poured scalding water on top of it. She was tempted, for just an instant, to let a few drops fall onto his hand . . . or his lap.

"I suspect you've already made up your mind not to believe anything I tell you," she said as she resumed her seat. "And, if that's the case, I don't see any point in answering your question."

He didn't reply for a full minute. Faith waited him out, knowing he wouldn't be satisfied with a stalemate.

"Maybe if you convince me it's happened before—to you, I mean—it'll be easier to believe it happened this time."

Faith shook her head. "There's no way for you to verify that I've had precognitive dreams in the past."

"Because you never told anybody about them?"

"No. That is, I did tell someone." A team of parapsychologists, as a matter of fact, who had believed every word. Unfortunately, the police officers *they* reported the dreams to hadn't been nearly so open-minded."

"Well, then, couldn't I get in touch with whoever you talked to?"

"There wouldn't be any point," she said tersely. No way

was she going to give him their names. They didn't know where she was, or *who* she was, and that was exactly how she wanted it.

"Don't you understand?" she said, her voice sharpening with frustration. "It always comes down to one person's credibility—the person who claims to have had the dream. Either you accept what I've told you, or you don't."

Donovan's attractive mouth thinned in impatience. "Don't *you* understand what you're asking—how unreasonable you're being, for God's sake? I don't know anything about you. You could be a full-blown psychotic for all I know. You show up out of the blue and spin this fantastic yarn, claim you've been having dreams about a mad bomber and you think he's going to hit a warehouse next—and that very night another bomb goes off, and it's exactly like you said it would be, *Exactly!* The warehouse, the parking lot behind it, the old dusk-to-dawn light next to the street. He even used the safety mechanism from an electric garage door opener as a secondary detonator—the gizmo that keeps the door from closing if something's blocking it."

"The two metal boxes and the beam of green light," Faith murmured.

"Bingo. If somebody had found the bomb before he was ready to detonate it, tried to disarm it—" He broke off, took a deep breath. "The point is, everything was exactly like you said it would be. Jesus, it's as if you were *there,* watching him!"

"In a way, I was," Faith said quietly.

"But you were asleep. Dreaming."

"Yes."

Donovan made a disgusted sound and took a gulp of tea, as if he were trying to rinse away a bad taste.

"Lady, if I try to sell that story to my lieutenant, I'll be working crowd control for the next six months."

"Would it help if I volunteered to take a polygraph test?"

Faith regretted the impulsive offer the second it was out, but he didn't give her a chance to retract it.

"A polygraph?" he barked, instantly snapping to attention. "Great idea! Let's do it."

He was on his feet before she could respond, looking down at her expectantly. She stared up at that relentlessly masculine face, those shrewd, intelligent blue eyes, and wondered if she'd lost her mind.

"Now?"

"You have something else to do this morning, someplace you have to go?"

Faith wished she could think of something, but her mind was an absolute blank. "No. Nothing important."

"Okay then, we might as well do it now, get it over with." He suddenly grinned, displaying a mouthful of even white teeth and a deep dimple in each cheek. "Well, I guess it would be a good idea for you to get dressed first. While you're doing that, I'll phone in a request for a polygraph technician."

He headed for the wall phone, evidently assuming she would hustle her bones down the hall and throw on some clothes. Obviously a man of action, Faith thought with a rueful smile.

She tried not to think about that knee-weakening grin as she pulled on jeans and a T-shirt. Or those dimples. *Dimples,* for pity's sake! Totally inappropriate; dimples didn't belong on such a ruggedly chiseled face. His mesmerizing eyes were enough of an unfair advantage, Lord knew. He had no business owning a pair of dimples, too.

When she returned to the kitchen, he'd washed the cups, saucers and spoons and stacked them on the drainboard. Great. He cleaned up after himself, too.

"Ready?" he asked with a smile.

Faith reflected that his mood had undergone a vast improvement since she offered to take a lie detector test. He was probably an absolute doll so long as things went his way, but watch out if you crossed him. No doubt his present good humor was a direct result of his expectation that she would flunk the polygraph test, big time.

"I guess so," she muttered.

There was no point telling him he was in for a nasty surprise. He'd find out soon enough.

Chapter Three

Rhys didn't believe it. She'd sailed through the polygraph test without a hitch. Without a single blip or suspicious jiggle. Jill Greeley, the technician who'd administered the test, admitted that she was surprised, too. She was nowhere near as surprised as Rhys, though, and a lot more willing to accept the results.

"Maybe she's psychic," Jill said when she'd finished giving him the news.

"Right," he muttered. "And maybe my grandmother will elope with Mel Gibson tomorrow."

Jill grinned. "He's already married, with a passel of kids. I know you don't want to hear this, Rhys, but there *are* people who possess knowledge and abilities the rest of us don't have."

"Give me a break," he jeered. "You can't actually believe it's possible to see into the future."

"Let's just say I have an open mind. I'm not convinced it's possible but I'm not convinced it isn't, either. And you saw the results of her test—she wasn't lying, or even consciously holding back. About that, I'm a hundred percent sure."

Well, he wasn't. People had been known to defeat the machine—psychotics, for example, and a few individuals who'd learned to control their physiological responses through biofeedback. Granted, it didn't happen often, and to his knowledge nobody had ever managed to pull the wool over Jill's eyes. But that didn't mean it wasn't possible.

He thanked Jill for coming in to administer the test, then returned to the large investigations squad room where his desk was located. Faith McRae was waiting patiently.

"You look like somebody just clued you in about the Easter bunny," she said as soon as she saw him. "I assume that means I got an A-plus."

Rhys didn't bother to sit down. He wanted to take her home, get her out of his presence, ASAP. Yet at the same time he felt a sudden, inexplicable compulsion to question her at length about those alleged dreams. Not the ones she'd already told him about; the others, the ones she claimed to have had before. The irrational impulse annoyed him. Whatever she had or hadn't dreamed about in the past was completely irrelevant.

"The technician says you weren't lying," he conceded grudgingly.

"Of course I wasn't lying," she retorted, her tone at least as brusque as his. "What kind of idiot would volunteer to take a polygraph test and then lie, for pity's sake?" She collected her shoulder bag from the floor and stood up. "Don't take it so hard, Donovan. It isn't your fault I passed; no one's going to hold you responsible. Can I go home now?"

Her eagerness to be gone triggered a perverse desire in Rhys to keep her there a while longer. He shook his head and gestured for her to sit back down.

"Not just yet." He strode around the desk and dropped into his chair. "There are a couple of things I'd like to ask you about."

Her full, disturbingly sensual mouth took on a pinched, obstinate look. She remained standing. "I've already told you, there wouldn't be any point in describing precognitive dreams I've had in the past."

Her attitude was really beginning to irritate him, but *what* she said made the hair at the back of his neck stand at attention. It was the same spooky sensation he'd had yesterday, when he wondered for just an instant if she'd been reading his mind. He didn't like the feeling. It made him uncomfortable, off-balance and uncertain. Rhys didn't like feeling uncertain, about anything, which was why he decided to drag the question that had been nagging him since yesterday afternoon out into the open.

"All right," he murmured. He let his body relax into an indifferent slouch, propping his right foot on the opposite knee and folding his hands on his stomach. "If you won't talk about that, why don't you enlighten me about the remark you made on your way out the door yesterday."

He was gratified to see that he'd knocked some of the starch out of her. She slowly sank onto the hard wooden chair. He thought her face paled a little.

"What remark do you mean?"

There was a shade less self-confidence in her voice, but her poise hadn't completely deserted her. She was guarded, wary, her defenses raised and on full alert. Rhys had seen the look many times; it usually indicated guilt.

"You know what I'm talking about. You said, 'for the record, I'm not a screwball.' "

"Yes." She drew the word out, making it more a puzzled query than an affirmation. Her direct gaze didn't waver.

She was good, he'd give her that—a regular iceberg. He was going to have to work for every scrap of information she didn't decide to offer voluntarily.

"So where did that come from?" he pressed. "That 'screwball' comment?"

Her left shoulder lifted in a small, graceful shrug. "It was obvious you weren't taking me seriously. You thought I was either lying or crazy."

Rhys didn't respond to that. What could he say? She had deftly evaded giving him a direct answer, while at the same time managing to put him on the defensive. He remembered noticing the intelligence that shone from her eyes the day before, and wished he'd heeded his own observation, instead of dismissing her as just another crackpot.

But, damn it, *nobody* would have believed such an outlandish story. He still didn't buy it, despite the fact that the second bomb had been planted precisely where and how she'd described. There had to be some other explanation for how she'd known about that bomb—some reasonable, *rational* explanation. There had to be!

"You still do," she said quietly. Her voice held a curious blend of resignation and bitterness.

Rhys frowned in confusion. "I still do what?"

"Think I'm either lying or crazy." By the time she got to "crazy," the resignation was gone from her voice and the bitterness had turned to undisguised resentment. Gold sparks flashed from her deep brown eyes.

Rhys lowered his right foot to the floor and sat up straight. "I know you're not crazy," he said impulsively, and realized the instant it was out how it sounded. She didn't give him the chance to correct his blunder, though.

"I see. You just think I'm a pathological liar."

"No. That isn't what I meant."

"Well then, Detective Donovan, what *do* you believe? Do you think *I* put the bomb in that warehouse?"

Irritated with himself for letting her retake the offensive and stung by her sarcasm, Rhys fired back "Did you?" before he could rein in his own temper.

She inhaled a sharp, stunned breath. The skin of her face tightened over her exquisite bones. He half expected her to jump up and march out of the room. Or else hit him with something. He felt his body tense, instinctively preparing to react to either possibility. But all she did was stare straight into his eyes and declare with icy contempt, "No. I did not."

Rhys was taken aback by the force of her anger. He could actually *feel* it, pouring out of her like steam from a ruptured high-pressure hose. For a split second he had the crazy feeling it was pushing against his chest, pinning him to the back of his chair. The impression passed so quickly that he dismissed it as an overreaction to her unexpected but, he had to admit, completely justified hostility. He leaned forward slightly, lifting one had in a gesture of conciliation.

"Okay," he said on a sigh of regret. "That was out of line. I apologize."

"You know I didn't have anything to do with that bomb," she said as if he hadn't spoken.

Rhys hesitated. Did he know that? His gut said yes; his logical, naturally suspicious mind wasn't ready to concede the point.

"You know it," she insisted. "In your heart, you know everything I've told you has been the truth. Why can't you admit it?"

Rhys slumped back in his chair and heaved another sigh. "Honest to God, Miss McRae, at this second I don't know *what* I believe. I can tell you what I *don't* believe, though. I don't believe in ghosts, flying saucers, that Elvis is still alive, or that people can see into the future. Even in dreams. Sorry, but it just isn't possible. I've come across a lot of weird things in this job, stuff that would curl your hair, but nothing I've ever seen or heard—including what you've told me—has convinced me otherwise."

Her eyes narrowed, and for a moment she seemed about to say something. Evidently she changed her mind, though. She stood up and arranged the strap of her bag over her left shoulder.

"Then I guess we're right back where we started," she said coolly. "Could you please take me home now."

The trip to her nondescript red brick duplex was made in tense, strained silence. Fortunately it lasted less than ten minutes. After she climbed out of the car, Rhys realized that she never had explained that "screwball" remark. He gave the side mirror a quick, impatient glance and accelerated away from the curb too fast, refusing to acknowledge that he felt more relieved than frustrated by the fact.

Faith was shaking all over. A drink. She needed a drink, and not one of those wimpy wine coolers that had been in the fridge since New Year's Eve. Unfortunately, since that was the only alcohol in the house, it would have to suffice.

She gulped the sweet-sour citrusy concoction straight from the bottle, not stopping for breath till she'd drained it. Not half bad; better than she'd remembered, anyway. She collected another bottle and carried it into the living room, where she sank down on one end of the sofa.

Damn that pompous jerk Donovan! Tightassed, bull-headed know-it-all! *"Sorry, but it just isn't possible."*

She'd been tempted, for one terrible, fleeting moment, to give him a demonstration of exactly what *was* possible.

Which was the reason she'd started shaking as soon as she was safely back in her own house.

She chugged down more wine cooler. She seldom drank alcohol in any form, and she could already feel a pleasant warmth spreading through her. Kicking off her canvas shoes, she folded her legs onto the sofa cushions and sagged against the arm.

God, she'd almost lost it, almost let loose something horrendous; something she'd spent the past eight years trying to forget had ever existed.

She didn't even know if it was there anymore, if she could still summon it. She didn't *want* to know. But for several horrible seconds, back in Donovan's office, the temptation had been almost irresistible.

She tipped her head back and took another long pull on the wine cooler. Her hand was still trembling.

All right, calm down. You didn't do anything. Nothing happened. You were tempted, yes, but you didn't act on the temptation. You maintained control.

Control. Yes, that's what was important, what she had

to remember. Control was everything. It had never been the power itself that was so terrifying, but her inability to control it. Once set free it became like a living thing with a will of its own. It ran amok, like an angry, undisciplined child, until it had spent whatever energy fueled it.

When the parapsychologists first learned about the power, they'd constantly urged her to set it free—deliberately provoking her; coaxing her with assurances that this time she'd be able to call it back or stop it; promising that no one would punish her if she couldn't.

In the beginning, she almost never could. They'd kept their promises, though; she'd never been punished, except by her own conscience. And the more she practiced, the more control she was able to exert. Until that last time. Her increasing successes had caused everyone, including Faith, to become dangerously overconfident. Looking back, she could see that. She understood that it had been her own overconfidence, along with her desire to please them, that caused the disaster. The knowledge didn't lessen the pain, though, or relieve her guilt.

Dear God, what might she have done to Donovan, if she'd lost control? Her hand jerked, so violently that she dropped the empty wine cooler bottle. She bent over and picked it up, then lay back and closed her eyes, willing herself to relax. Deep breaths. Find the calm center. Sink into it. Let it swallow you.

It took several minutes, but eventually she reached the cool, dark, tranquil place where nothing and no one could touch her. She let herself drift, just drift, not thinking or feeling, until it was safe to return. Then she stood and stretched luxuriously.

"All right, this day has gotten off to a generally lousy start, but there have to be a few positives among all the negatives," she told herself. "There are always positives. You believe that, you really, truly do. That's why you named yourself Faith, remember?"

Number one, she'd passed the polygraph test. When Donovan filed his report, he would have to include that information. Number two, she'd encountered a hated and feared personal demon from the past and hadn't gone to pieces. That in itself was a huge, positively colossal positive. Not that she was willing to tempt Fate by repeating the experience, but the knowledge that she hadn't lost control gave her self-confidence a tremendous boost.

Only two positives? Well, to be honest, there was a third: Detective Donovan. Despite his hardheaded cynicism and arrogant personality, just being in the same room with him gave her a warm, tingly feeling right down to her toes. Damn, he could be infuriating as hell, but that grin! Those astonishing dimples! Those incredible, penetrating blue eyes . . . that long, hard body . . .

Faith gave herself an impatient little shake, followed by a dry admonition. "And he thinks of you as an iceberg. A deranged iceberg, at that. Forget him, as of now! Put Detective Studly right out of your mind, and pray you never have reason to see him or talk to him again."

It was good advice, and she intended to follow it. But, darn, she wished she'd thought to ask what his first name was. Something that went with Donovan, she'd bet. Maybe Liam, or Sean, or Tim . . .

It was getting harder not to betray the joy and exhilaration that filled him . . . to keep the blazing white light dammed up inside, when it wanted to spill out and blind everyone around him.

He had to keep it hidden, though. The Truth could not—*must not*—be revealed before the time was right. They mustn't know, mustn't see. They weren't ready. Pathetic creatures, stumbling around in their darkness and ignorance. If they knew, if they even guessed, they would try to stop him, or maybe destroy him, foolishly believing that destroying him would destroy the Truth. They were all weak and stupid; they didn't understand that they had to be saved from themselves. And for the time being, only he was strong enough and wise enough to know what must be done.

But it was getting harder every day to conceal his secret knowledge. To pretend he was the same as all of them, to move among them and do his job and remember to never do or say anything that might give away the Truth he carried inside. It was a terrible strain, acting "normal" for their benefit.

He smiled a little to himself. What a ridiculous, impotent word that was. Mother had told him once, years ago, that "normal" was just a setting on the washing machine. That had been the last time they'd called her at work and made her come to the school and take him home. They'd said he couldn't come back again, that he was dangerous to himself and others, not "normal," and a lot of other things, and that she should put him in a school for "disturbed" people. Maybe she should enroll herself in that school, too, Mother had said, because she was sure as hell disturbed about having to leave work at least once every week and having her pay docked, all because some snotty teacher had taken a dislike to her boy. After they left the building, she told him that thing about normal being just a setting on the washing machine, and that since he was sixteen he didn't have to go to school anymore anyway and she could get him a job at the factory if he wanted. He'd said yes, he thought he'd like that.

Of course Lenny had stayed in school. Nobody ever accused Lenny of being a "problem" or "incorrigible," much less "disturbed"; Lenny had always been a model student. That had been the only bad thing about his going to work in the factory. It was the first time in their lives that he and his twin brother weren't together all day, every day.

He didn't want to think about those times, though, or about Lenny. He'd just get mad if he did, and being mad would make him do something to get himself in trouble again.

So he thought about his secret, instead, about the Truth

that only he knew. And he thought about what he would do if somebody found out before he'd finished his work. It didn't take long to decide that he would have to kill that somebody.

He'd rather not. Killing was wrong, the Bible said so. It was right there in the Ten Commandments: *Thou shalt not kill.* That was why he'd been so careful about picking his targets. Even though the people who worked for those places were serving Evil, he couldn't risk accidentally taking an innocent life. He might have to, eventually—he would know if and when it was necessary—but for now he mustn't do anything to bring down God's wrath before his work was finished.

If somebody did find out about the Truth, though, or that he was its messenger, that person would have to die. About that, he was certain. *He* was the Bringer of Truth. No one else was allowed to know. Not until he decided it was time.

A shaft of fear suddenly pierced him, causing him to drop the crescent wrench he'd just taken from his toolbox. But what about the police? There were dozens of policemen working to find out who'd planted the bombs, maybe even hundreds—too many to kill, even if he could think of a way to do it. Had they managed to collect any fingerprints, or microscopic bits of his skin or hair—anything they could use to identify him? He didn't think it was likely; he'd tried to make sure there wouldn't be any evidence for them to sift through. Just in case, though, maybe he should try to find out what they knew.

He didn't have any idea how to go about that, but he was confident something would come to him if he thought about it long enough. In the meantime, he had to decide which of the names on his list would be his next target.

Chapter Four

All day Monday Faith expected Detective Donovan or one of his colleagues to appear and stick her in a police cruiser for a ride "downtown." She was certain that when Donovan's superiors got a look at the statement she'd given him, she'd be in for a heavy-duty grilling at the very least, maybe a second polygraph test. When four o'clock rolled around and no law enforcement types had shown up to collect her, she breathed a heartfelt sigh of relief.

She even allowed herself to hope that the bizarre events of the previous week had been no more than a pothole in the freeway of life—a one-time cosmic anomaly, caused by sunspots or the hole in the ozone layer or something. It helped that she hadn't dreamed—about anything, so far as she could remember—for the past couple of nights. Of course she hadn't tried very hard to remember. Dreams had become something to dread. Again.

Her spirits got an additional boost when she scanned the next day's appointments before she left for home, and spotted Tommy Carver's name. He was such a terrific kid, always optimistic and full of enthusiasm; just being around him cheered her up. She was thinking of Tommy, looking forward to seeing him, when she pushed through the PT department's swinging double doors and found Leon Perry stolidly pushing a mop around the lobby floor.

Her mood, which had been steadily improving, took a sudden downturn. Leon interrupted his work long enough to send a disapproving glance in her direction, but other than that he didn't acknowledge her. Faith almost said hello, then thought better of it. There was no sense tempting Fate.

She regretted the confrontations she'd already had with Leon, even though she knew they weren't her fault. He was certainly entitled to his beliefs, and while those inflexible, extremist beliefs would always be offensive to her, she'd have been happy to live and let live. Unfortunately, Leon didn't share that attitude. Not surprising; fanatacism and tolerance were mutually exclusive traits. A month ago, after he had followed her into the break room twice in one week to proselytize, Faith had complained to the clinic management. She didn't know what action had been taken, but the preaching stopped. In fact now Leon went out of his way to avoid her, which suited her fine.

She hurried past him and onto the elevator for the short ride to the ground floor. Most of the time she took the stairs—it was only one short flight, and jogging up was good cardiovascular exercise—but entering the stairwell just then didn't seem wise. Not that she was afraid Leon would follow her, but why take the chance?

As the elevator door closed with a soft hiss, Leon suddenly lifted his head and looked directly at her. Even from halfway across the lobby, the animosity on his face was unmistakable, and so fierce that Faith took an involuntary step back.

By the time the door opened on the ground floor, she was angry with herself for reacting like that. Damn it, she would *not* be intimidated by a crusading janitor who'd made it his mission in life to persuade her to abandon her wicked, worldly ways, and then apparently decided she was the spawn of Satan when she refused to be persuaded.

If running into Leon hadn't already soured her mood, that malicious look he gave her would have. Faith had had her fill of people like Leon Perry before she was out of her teens. Dour, sanctimonious zealots whose pious fervor so consumed them that there was no room left for joy or compassion . . . even for those they professed to love.

Thank goodness she hadn't intercepted Leon's thoughts the way she'd intercepted Donovan's, she thought an hour later, as she stood in her kitchen feeding spaghetti to a pot of boiling water.

Now that she thought about it, she decided that was an encouraging sign. Whatever Leon had been thinking, his emotions had obviously been intense, highly charged and directed straight at her. She'd seen the antagonism on his swarthy face . . . but that was all. She hadn't *felt* or *heard* anything.

Yes, no question, that was definitely a good sign. Heaven knew she didn't want Leon Perry's bitter, critical thoughts in her head. They would be much more disturbing than Donovan's had been. At least Donovan didn't have anything against her, personally; he had just lumped her with all the other "screwballs" whose statements he'd automatically rejected.

A wistful sigh escaped her. Considering the circumstances, she supposed she shouldn't be upset by his refusal to take her seriously. She was, though, and not just because he was the sexiest, most mouth-watering man she'd ever met or was likely to meet in this lifetime. She was strongly attracted to him, no use trying to kid herself about that, but the attraction wasn't *only* physical. If she could ever get past that hardheaded cynicism, she was sure she'd discover a sharp, intuitive mind . . . and just maybe a tender, generous heart, as well.

Of course she didn't have a snowball's chance of ever finding out if she was right. Now that the dreams had stopped, she doubted she'd ever see Dimples Donovan again. Which, she assured herself as she carried the cooked spaghetti to the sink and dumped it into a colander, was probably for the best.

There was more light this time. She didn't realize at first that it was because she was outdoors. The breeze alerted her. While she couldn't feel the breeze, she did smell the muddy, fishy tang of the river it carried. The sky was an inverted ebony bowl; no moon or stars visible, but there was enough reflected city light to distinguish the shape of the large rectangular structure in front of her and the figure kneeling at its base.

It was him—Rat Man. She knew even before she was close enough to recognize his shape and his quick, furtive movements.

She moved nearer, wanting to see—both his face and what he was doing—yet afraid. Strange, she hadn't been afraid before. Why now? It was silly to be afraid. She was aware that she was dreaming, that whoever he was, he couldn't hurt her. Still, the fear shivered over her and through her.

He was hunched over something. A box, she saw when he shifted a little to the right. Not as large as the metal boxes she'd seen in the warehouse; this one was roughly the size and shape of a cigar box. There were wires sticking out of one end. Now he rose from his knees, holding the wires in one hand and something else in the other. Was it some kind of small tool—a screwdriver? A pocket knife?

Using both hands, he pressed the wires against the front of the big boxy thing. What was it, anyway? A storage shed, maybe; it was the right size and height. There wasn't enough light to see the surface clearly, and even if there had been, Rat Man was blocking her view. Faith impulsively tried to rise, but once again the invisible cocoon restrained her.

Frustration and curiosity overcame her fear. She strained against whatever was holding her, summoning every ounce of mental energy she possessed. It was no use. All she could do was watch, and try to figure out what he was up to. He held the wires in place against the wall of the shed—if it was a shed—with his left hand and did something to them with whatever he held in his right. Then he moved a few inches higher and repeated the procedure.

No metallic clink. No sound at all, in fact. He probably wasn't using a screwdriver, then. What was he doing to the wires? Fastening them to the wall! Yes, that was it. But with what? A hammer or stapler would have made a noise.

And why, if he was placing another bomb, had he picked an outdoor structure, where anyone might happen along and see him?

It belatedly occurred to Faith to examine the area surrounding her. Though she couldn't physically *move,* if she concentrated on directing her vision, she could *see* everything on both sides, and even behind her. She was at the edge of a large, empty parking lot. To the left was a wide street; to the right, nothing but an enormous expanse of cement pavement. A network of cracks—both old, patched seams and raw new fissures—zigzagged across it like a combination of scabbed-over and still bleeding wounds. The nearest streetlight was a block and a half away, beyond the mysterious shed or whatever it was. No, wait; there was a light closer than that, on the corner behind her, but it wasn't working.

Had he done something to the streetlight—shot it out, or caused it to short circuit?

What about buildings? Were there any nearby that she might recognize? It was impossible to see the far end of the parking lot, much less whatever was beyond it. There were buildings across the street, but the only architectural feature she could make out was the murky gleam of glass in a couple of windows.

Her frustration was building to an intolerable level. She turned her attention back to Rat Man. . . .

And discovered that he was gone. Vanished into the night.

"Noooo, damn it!"

Faith lurched upright, fighting the sheet and light flannel blanket that had wrapped themselves around her arms and legs, uncertain whether her angry shout had been part of the dream, or real. Her heart pounded against her ribs; her breath came in quick, shallow gasps.

When she'd extricated herself from the bedclothes, she dropped her head into her hands with a tormented moan.

"No," she whispered in despair. "God, no. Please."

Even as she uttered the prayer, she knew the request was futile. The last eight years had been nothing more than an extended reprieve. She'd been running from something she could never leave behind, because it was part of her.

The warehouse had been used to store UPC bar code scanners and computerized cash registers. Now why the hell would anybody want to destroy electronic equipment intended mostly for supermarkets?

Unable to come up with an answer that made any kind of sense, Rhys tried a different question. Doctors' offices and supermarkets—what did they have in common?

Not a blessed thing. Okay, maybe if he thought of doctors' patients as their customers . . .

But that road led to the same dead end.

He propped both elbows on his desk and raked his hands through his hair. If there was any logic in the bomber's choice of targets, he couldn't see it. Not that he hadn't tried. His head ached from the effort of trying to find some connection—*any* connection. A criminal who had a clear, consistent motive could usually be identified and caught. A criminal who was just plain nuts, on the other hand, wouldn't be caught until he made a major mistake or the cops got lucky.

Rhys was beginning to think this guy was just plain nuts. And as for luck . . . well, the only luck he'd possessed lately had been bad. What else would explain his getting saddled with the screwball brigade, then having Faith McRae show up just as he was about to leave for the day? And *then*—

this had to set some kind of record for disgustingly rotten luck—the damned bomber had struck again, exactly the way she'd said he would.

Of course he had to admit that he'd made his own luck from that point on. He shouldn't have gone to her house Saturday morning; but once he was there, he shouldn't have been so quick to take her up on that offer to undergo a polygraph test. The very fact that she'd volunteered should have set off some kind of alarm.

He scowled down at the clipped-together papers on his desk blotter. What the hell was he going to do with her statement and Jill Greeley's report on the polygraph results? Rhys knew his lieutenant: Buford Jackson would be even less inclined to buy Faith McRae's incredible tale than he'd been. If Rhys passed her statement and Jill's report on to him, Jackson would either rake him over the coals for wasting department time, or order him to bring Faith in for questioning as the prime suspect in the warehouse bombing. Most likely it would be the latter, since there wasn't a legitimate suspect in sight.

Every instinct Rhys possessed told him she hadn't had anything to do with that bombing. So what the hell was he going to do about her statement and Jill's report?

Not giving himself time to second-guess the decision, he picked up the papers, folded them, and stuck them in the inside pocket of his sport coat. Then he gathered up the handful of statements in his out-basket and carried them across the room to Lieutenant Jackson's office.

Tommy wasn't his usual exuberant self today. Faith noticed the difference right away, even though she was busy with another patient when he arrived and so it was Rollie who took him back to the whirlpool. He didn't look glum, exactly, but he seemed subdued, his energy sapped. Most of the time you heard Tommy before you saw him. Today she didn't realize he was there until she happened to see him pass the treatment room where she was guiding a patient through range of motion exercises for a frozen shoulder.

She didn't get a chance to talk to Tommy till he was about to leave, and then he was unusually reticent.

"Hi, Sticky, how's it going?" she asked as she sat beside him on a bench while he tugged on his Converse high tops. He'd told her during one of his first appointments—bragging a little—that his teammates had nicknamed him Sticky Fingers because of his knack for stealing the puck.

Tommy shrugged. "Okay, I guess."

"You don't sound okay. What's the matter, wouldn't Dr. Nance clear you to play roller hockey?"

"No, she said I could start playing in a couple more weeks." His familiar grin flashed briefly, revealing a mouthful of orthodontic appliances. "As long as I wear a helmet."

"Well, I should hope so," Faith said dryly. "You wouldn't want to scramble your brains again before the season even gets started."

Tommy sobered. "Yeah, well, . . ."

"What?" she coaxed softly.

He glanced around, checking to be sure no one else could hear. "I'm worried my brains may still be scrambled. I haven't been sleeping too good, and about a week ago I started having these awful headaches."

"Have you seen the neurosurgeon who treated you in the hospital?" Faith asked.

"Yeah, yesterday. He gave me some medicine for the headaches, and I'm gonna have an MRI tomorrow morning. He said it's probably nothing to worry about, but . . . well, you know."

Faith put her hand on his back, just above his shoulder blades, and gave his tense muscles a quick mini-massage. She was careful to make her touch casual.

"But you can't help worrying a little, until you find out for sure that everything's all right."

Tommy sighed. "I guess it's stupid to be scared just because of some dumb headaches."

"After everything you've been through—including two

weeks in a coma? Trust me, Sticky, even The Golden Brett would be a little worried in your place."

That coaxed another grin from him. Brett Hull was one of his idols.

"Let me know how the MRI turns out, okay?" Faith said as he stood to leave.

"Sure," Tommy agreed. "If I forget, ask me next time I come in."

It was hours later, when she was ironing a pile of blouses, and putting off getting ready for bed, that she made the connection between Tommy's concussion and ensuing coma, his headaches, and his disclosure that "I haven't been sleeping too good."

She finished pressing a blouse, slipped it onto a hanger and then stood motionless, her mind racing. Sometimes people who'd suffered brain injuries later developed psychic abilities. Was it possible—? Tommy had said his headaches started about a week ago, around the time the first bomb exploded at the software company.

Why hadn't he been sleeping well? Because he'd been having strange, frightening, prophetic dreams?

Faith realized she was gripping the hanger so hard that she'd bent it. Forcing her fingers to uncurl, she straightened the wire, hung the blouse on a folding rack and turned off the iron.

"You're overreacting," she told herself firmly. "Don't project what's been happening to you onto poor Tommy."

The kid had suffered a blow to the head that put him in a coma for two weeks, and a couple of months later he was experiencing headaches and insomnia. There was probably a perfectly sound medical explanation for both complaints. The fact that he was fourteen—the age when latent psychic abilities often first manifest themselves—was completely irrelevant.

Still, the next time she saw Tommy, she thought she would find a tactful way to ask if he'd had any weird nightmares lately.

* * *

He was afraid. He could feel the sweat beginning to trickle down his body, inside his shirt. In a few more minutes it would saturate the material under his arms and make dark, damp triangles on his chest and back. People would be able to smell his fear in his sweat. Dear Lord, he didn't want to be here; the desire to get up and run out the door, into the sunshine, was almost too strong to resist. But he had to make himself do this. He had to know.

So he sat on the hard wooden bench and waited, along with the other six people in the room. He wondered why they were there, but he didn't ask. He knew better than to say anything to any of them. They might be spies, or worse. That skinny woman in the brown and green flowered house dress—was she watching him? No, he decided after a minute or so; she was just suspicious. Her eyes kept darting around the room, lighting for no more than a second on each of them in turn.

She was probably crazy. Crazy people's eyes jumped around a lot, just like hers were doing. Sometimes it was because they thought they saw things that weren't really there. It was too bad some people had to be crazy. He felt sorry for them, but he didn't hate them, and he wasn't afraid of them like some were. Mother had taught him and Lenny that people like that were more to be pitied than scorned. Same with blind people, and cripples. They couldn't help the way they were, any more than crazy people could help being crazy.

"Be thankful you have all your faculties," Mother had told them. "As long as you have your health, you'll be richer than ol' King Midas ever thought about being."

And they'd both been healthy all their lives. Neither of them ever had anything worse than a bad cold. Until the night Lenny got a terrible stomachache that felt like a red hot knife being jabbed into him, and they'd had to call old Doc Summers.

But he couldn't start thinking about that. Not now. He had to stay cool, had to remember why he was there.

He'd told his boss he had to take the morning off to go to his cousin's funeral. He'd figured that would cover him until after the lunch hour, but now he was beginning to worry that he would still be sitting on this bench well into the afternoon. He didn't think he could stand to stay that long. Another half an hour, and he'd be as crazy as that skinny woman. Maybe if they didn't get around to him before noon, he should take it as a sign that he wasn't supposed to do this, that he should just leave.

The big round clock on the wall said 11:53 when a tall, dark-haired man in shirtsleeves, the knot of his tie tugged loose, appeared in the doorway and gestured for him to come along. By then he was the only one left of the original seven.

"Sorry you had to sit out there so long," the man apologized as he turned around and walked back into a big room full of desks and people. "Things have been pretty chaotic around here the past week."

"Yes, I can imagine." He was relieved that his voice sounded fine, not nervous or excited. "These bombings have the whole city on edge."

"Especially my superiors," the tall policeman muttered. "Have a seat." Taking his place behind one of a dozen identical desks, he pulled a blank form from an untidy pile of papers and pulled it across the blotter. A brown plastic nameplate that was holding down another stack of papers said Det. Donovan.

"First I need to get some basic information. Your name?"

"Perry. Leon Perry," Leon answered, lowering himself onto a straight-backed chair beside the desk. He was careful to pronounce each syllable distinctly.

Det. Donovan printed his name at the top of the form, then asked for his address, phone number, and place of employment. When he'd finished filling a bunch of spaces with the answers Leon provided, he sat back, rolled his shoulders, and looked at Leon expectantly.

"All right, Mr. Perry, what have you got for me?"

Leon was ready. He'd rehearsed this last night, several times. He leaned forward slightly to make sure he had Det. Donovan's attention.

"I think I might have seen the person who planted that bomb that blew up the warehouse last Friday night."

Rat Man hadn't come to visit Tuesday night, but he was back on Wednesday—still tinkering around at that mysterious shed.

Only now Faith could see that it wasn't a shed at all. It was an automatic teller machine.

And he was rigging another bomb.

Christ, didn't the guy do anything else? she wondered the next morning, while she waited for the teakettle to whistle. He needed a hobby, something that would let him get out and meet people, make a few friends. Maybe if he had a social life, he'd mellow out a little, stop wanting to blow things up all over town. Stop haunting her dreams.

She spent a good fifteen minutes arguing with herself about whether or not to call Donovan. In the end, the coward convinced the responsible citizen not to bother. He still wouldn't believe her, and he was probably every bit as loath to see her again as she was to see him.

Well, to be honest, she would enjoy seeing Donovan again, even knowing he thought she was a fruitcake. But she was afraid to risk telling him about these new dreams. So far nobody had followed up on the statement she'd given him—probably because the entire police department shared Donovan's assessment of it. But God knew what would happen if she went back with a brand new tale about the nocturnal adventures of Rat Man. The cops wouldn't be any more disposed to take her seriously, but somebody might feel obligated to make a show of investigating. And that could lead to all kinds of unpleasant complications.

No, she decided as she sipped at a steaming cup of Constant Comment, it would be best to keep the dreams to herself. At least for now.

Chapter Five

Thursday afternoon two agents from the arson and explosives division of the Bureau of Alcohol, Tobacco and Firearms presented themselves in Lieutenant Jackson's office and announced that they were assuming responsibility for the investigation into the previous week's bombings. During a brief, tense department meeting, the lieutenant ordered his detectives to hand over all pertinent files and give agents Whitley and Hearst their full cooperation. No one objected out loud, but the resentment in the room was palpable.

"Whitley and Hearst," Mort Singer groused, shoving a stack of papers aside and sliding his wide rump onto a corner of Rhys's desk. "Sounds like a friggin' accounting firm. Damn, you'd think they'd have given us a couple weeks to catch the bastard, at least."

Herb Aikers sauntered over from his desk. "Obviously they think he's going to strike again."

Mort snorted. "Hell, any bookie in town could've told 'em that. Let's see these hotshot ATF agents predict where and when, be there to grab him when he plants the bomb. Then I'll be impressed." He slurped coffee from a styrofoam cup, then asked of Rhys, "Turned up any likely suspects?"

Rhys shook his head no. "Just the usual gang of oddballs and misfits."

"The screwball brigade, you mean," Mort said. "Man, I don't know how you do it. If I had to interview those wackos all day long, I'd prob'ly end up blowin' my stack."

"Which is why Rhys got the assignment instead of you," Herb remarked. "He has the temperament to deal with them."

"Most of the time," Rhys amended with a droll smile. "But a couple of the people I interviewed this past week seriously tested my self-control."

One in particular—a petite stunner with a pair of fathomless brown eyes, a ripe, luscious-looking mouth, and an irritating knack for causing him to do and say things that were completely out of character.

"Too bad none of 'em produced any leads," Mort muttered. "I'd love to get this case closed before the damned ATF can work up a good head of steam."

Herb glanced around nervously. "Careful, Mort. You're talking about disobeying a direct order."

"Not necessarily," Rhys murmured. Herb shot him a surprised look. "We were told to turn over all pertinent files and cooperate with their investigation. Jackson didn't say we couldn't follow up if something just happens to drop into our laps."

"If he didn't, it was because he assumed we'd have more sense than to tangle with the Treasury Department," Herb retorted. "I don't know about you, but I'd like to keep this job long enough to collect my pension. Besides, you know damn well there won't be a break in this case unless the bomber makes a major screw-up or some citizen happens to be in the right place at the right time and sees him rigging another bomb."

"And then decides to tell us about it," Mort added sourly. His gaze swung back to Rhys and suddenly sharpened. "You've got something, don't you—something you didn't share with Whitley and Hearst?"

Rhys's casual shrug was all the confirmation the other detectives needed.

"Shit," Herb said under his breath.

Mort braced a pudgy hand on the desk blotter and leaned forward conspiratorially. "A witness?" he guessed, his eyes glittering.

"It better not be," Herb warned. "If you've withheld a witness's statement, and the ATF finds out, they'll have your shield."

"Not to mention your ass for breakfast," Mort added dryly.

"Relax, I gave them everything I had," Rhys said, and immediately thought of the folded papers he'd taken home and locked in his desk the night before. Well, almost everything. "But you know what kind of statements we get from the screwball brigade. Whitley and Hearst will read a few pages, then more than likely pitch the rest. They won't give serious consideration to any of it."

"But maybe they should, is that what you're saying?" Herb asked quietly.

"Maybe."

Mort pushed himself upright and blew a stream of air through pursed lips. "You think one of the wackos actually knows something? Now that'd be a first."

"I think one of the people I interviewed in the past couple of days told me something that's worth following up on," Rhys said. "And I also think Agents Whitley and Hearst will dismiss his statement along with the rest. This guy wasn't one of the serious space cadets, but he was what you might call a little . . . eccentric."

Herb Aikers's mouth tilted in an ironic smile. "So the ATF will probably throw away the only potential lead that's turned up so far."

"Now that would be a damned shame," Mort said soberly. "You can't let that happen, Rhys. You have a duty to the law-abiding citizens of this city to correct the blunder those guys are about to make."

Rhys smiled. "Great minds think alike."

"And misery loves company," Herb put in. "Which is good, because if the two of you tangle with the ATF, Buford Jackson will give you a new appreciation for what the word *misery* means."

Mort flashed a wicked grin. "In other words, we should count you out?"

"Please. Count me way the hell out."

Mort waited till Herb had returned to his desk before assuring Rhys, "I'm with you. Anything I can do to help, let me know. Damn, it frosts me that they can just walk in and take over our case, like we were a bunch of incompetent morons!"

Rhys nodded grimly. If Leon Perry really had seen the bomber early last Friday morning, on his way to the janitorial service where he worked . . . He knew it was a long shot, but at the moment it was all he had.

He'd already sent through a request for a cross-referenced search of the mainframe's database of convicted felons. Mr. Perry, bless his heart, had provided a clear, fairly detailed physical description of the man he'd seen leaving the warehouse at 5:00 A.M. According to the company that owned the building, the place should have been deserted at that hour. With a little luck, the computer would spit out the name and last known address of a fair, balding male Caucasion, approximately six feet and a hundred ninety pounds, who had a tattoo of a red and yellow dragon on his right forearm.

Since Rhys knew better than to count on luck, he decided it would be a good idea to hit the streets, visit a few informants. And he should get Leon Perry together with the sketch artist, too. But, damn it, Whitley and Hearst had the file with Perry's address and telephone number.

Rhys pulled the phone book out of a desk drawer and searched for Perry's name. It wasn't there. Either he didn't have a phone, or the number was unlisted. Okay, sitting

Perry down with the sketch artist would have to wait. The ATF agents would probably decide the file didn't contain any useful information and return it before the weekend; he could call Leon Perry then.

In the meantime, he'd just pray the damned bomber didn't strike again.

Leon managed to hold his laughter inside until he left the office building where he'd spent the afternoon cleaning windows and polishing floors. The cops didn't know anything! They had no evidence at all, not a single clue about who he was!

That Det. Donovan had seemed like an intelligent man, but obviously he wasn't. He'd sat there not three feet away—close enough to reach out and touch the very person he was hunting!—and he hadn't even suspected.

Leon felt as if the weight of the world had been taken off his shoulders. He'd been so scared while he was talking to Donovan, afraid that any second the policeman would look into his eyes and *know.* So he refused to make eye contact, staring at the loosened knot of Donovan's blue and gray striped tie instead. And he'd forced himself to speak slowly, think about what he was going to say before he said it. It had helped that he'd rehearsed the night before, but he was still terrified he'd make a mistake, slip up and say something to give himself away.

He hadn't, though. Donovan had believed every word, wrote it all down, then thanked him and shook his hand before he left. He had a strong grip. Leon liked that. A man's handshake said a lot about him; Donovan's was firm and no-nonsense. Too bad he was going to waste a lot of time looking for a man who didn't exist, Leon thought with a sly smirk. He laughed again as he steered his truck out of the office building's parking lot. Now that he knew he was safe from the police, he could get on with his important work.

* * *

Another Friday night. Another bombing. Another visi
from Detective Dimples Donovan bright and early the nex
morning.

Faith hoped this didn't develop into a weekly routine
If she was going to be seeing the man on a regular basis
it would be nice to now and then have a conversatio
about something other than a sick creep who got his jollie
blowing things up. Or her dreams about said creep. Fo
starters, she could ask Donovan what his first name was
Eventually they might even get around to whether he wa
involved in a relationship, meaningful or otherwise.

Unfortunately, as long as Rat Man was still scurryin
around the city turning buildings into piles of rubble, th
latter subject probably wouldn't make it onto the agenda

At least this morning she was dressed and had read th
front section of the paper before Donovan showed up
Most of it, anyway. So she wasn't really surprised when th
doorbell rang, or when she opened the door to find hin
standing on the porch. She *was* surprised by his appear
ance, though.

"God, you look awful," she blurted before she coul
stop herself.

He grimaced and stepped past her, not waiting to b
invited. "Yeah, well, I have trouble managing bright-eye
and bushy-tailed on less than three hours' sleep."

He was wearing another pair of faded, form-fitting jeans
Though on closer inspection, she thought they might b
the same pair he'd had on last Saturday. The polo shir
had been replaced by a much-washed gray sweatshirt wit
a Commonwealth of Kentucky seal stenciled in blue o
the front and frayed ruffles around the armholes wher
the sleeves had been ripped out. Chunks had peeled of
some of the stenciling, leaving gaps in the seal. Same ta
bucks on his feet. He was still wearing yesterday's fiv
o'clock shadow, his beautiful eyes were red-rimmed an
bloodshot, and his hair looked as though a family o

gophers had tried unsuccessfully to fashion it into some kind of nest.

Faith murmured an embarrassed, "Sorry," then closed the door and gestured toward the kitchen. "I could fix you some breakfast."

Good grief, where had *that* come from? All right, so he could obviously use a hot meal. That was no excuse for turning into a simpering toady. He was probably there to fingerprint her and/or haul her off to jail.

"A cup of Earl Grey would be good," he replied without missing a beat. You'd have thought they'd lived next door to each other all their lives and he made a habit of dropping by for breakfast.

"Okay. Sure," Faith muttered.

He followed her to the kitchen and sat in the same chair he'd occupied the previous Saturday, once again reading the newspaper while she heated water for tea. Faith kept expecting to hear the theme music from *The Twilight Zone* start playing on the radio. Come to think of it, that tune could be the leitmotif for her life.

"Can I ask you a question?" she said as she carried his tea to the table.

"Thanks." He gave her a lopsided smile. "Fair's fair. I plan to ask you a couple."

"I figured as much. What's your first name?"

His eyebrows ascended in surprise. "Rhys."

"Like the peanut butter cup," Faith murmured, her mouth stretching into a spontaneous smile.

"Yeah, coincidentally my favorite candy. But it's not spelled the same."

He spelled his name for her. They both sipped their tea. The silence stretched out, but for once it wasn't strained.

"I wish you hadn't mentioned food," he said eventually. "But since you have . . . twice, now . . ."

She grinned and stood up. "Would you like cereal? Eggs? An oat bran muffin?"

"Yes. Thanks."

Faith's grin evolved into an indulgent chuckle. "The

cereal's up there," she said, indicating a cabinet. "Bowls are next to it. Silverware's in the drawer beside the sink."

He got milk from the fridge and settled down with a bowl of shredded wheat to finish reading the paper, while she took out a skillet and fixed him a couple of scrambled eggs. By the time she brought the eggs and a muffin to the table, he'd rinsed his bowl and poured them each a fresh cup of tea.

Faith couldn't make up her mind whether to feel pleased or resentful that he'd made himself at home so easily and so quickly. She should probably be at least a little resentful, but it was damned hard to dislike anything about the man. Even his name was attractive.

"Have you had any more dreams?"

The question hit her like the proverbial ton of bricks. She felt the blood drain from her face, then rush back as a hot flush suffused her entire body.

"You mean, . . ." she began hesitantly.

He gave her a quick, razor-sharp glance between bites. "Yes. About the bomber."

Faith closed her eyes and inhaled a deep, fortifying breath, struggling to get past her emotional shock and think. Damn him. He'd slipped the question in so smoothly, knowing she didn't expect it, wasn't prepared for it. Was he trying to trick her—trap her somehow? But that didn't make sense. He was a police detective. If he thought she was in cahoots with the bomber—helping him, or withholding information about him—he could take her in for further questioning, or arrest her for suspicion or something. At least she thought he could do that. TV and movie cops did it all the time.

She opened her eyes and focused on his face. "Why are you asking me that? For that matter, why did you come here this morning, instead of going home to catch up on your sleep?"

He pushed the front section of the newspaper across the table as he finished the last forkful of scrambled eggs. Faith frowned down at the laser color photo of a ruined automatic teller machine. Dear God, if someone had been about to make a withdrawal . . .

"I've read it," she said quietly.

Donovan moved his plate aside and leaned forward, arms on the table. "And did you also *see* it? Before it happened?" There was a curt impatience in his voice Faith hadn't heard before. "Come on, it's a simple question," he prodded when she didn't answer fast enough.

"So are the ones I asked you," she replied. Damned if she'd let him bully or intimidate her in her own home—especially after she'd just fed him breakfast.

"Why are you asking me this, now?" She jabbed a finger at the photo. "Why *now,* Donovan? You didn't believe me before. You wrote me off as a wacko, a crackpot. Why are you suddenly so interested in my dreams that you came here straight from the scene of this latest bombing?"

He glared at her in silence for several long, tense seconds. Faith could feel the frustration seething inside him, but there was also a lot of confusion and misgiving. She waited, wary of pushing him any harder.

Finally he heaved a gusty sigh and reached up to rake both hands through his hair.

"We've got nothing on this guy," he said bluntly. "Not a goddamned thing. He doesn't leave any trace evidence, no fingerprints, no fibers from his clothing—The devices have all been built from components any twelve-year-old electronics buff would know how to get. The explosive charges could have come from any one of a hundred sources, including personnel at most of the army bases in the country."

Faith nodded. She'd recently read a couple of exposés and seen a special report on television about the hundreds of pounds of explosives and ammunition that are stolen from the government every year.

"You're desperate," she murmured.

It wasn't just an astute observation. She both heard his desperation in his voice and *felt* it. In fact she was suddenly being bombarded by his emotions. Like tiny, barbed needles, they drilled right through the shell that had protected her for eight years and imbedded themselves in her mind, until it was difficult to be sure whether the feelings tearing at her were his or her own.

"'Desperate' doesn't come close," he said. "If somebody had decided to stop at that ATM on the way home, to get some cash to pay the babysitter, or—"

"I know," Faith interjected. She wrapped both hands around her cup to hide the fact that they were shaking. "Yes. I dreamed about this one, too."

The look in his eyes hurt her. Was it the pain of guilt she felt, or something she was picking up from him? Not a feeling of betrayal, surely?

"Why didn't you tell me?" He made it an accusation.

A bitter, incredulous laugh escaped her. "Why didn't I *tell* you! Where do you get the nerve to ask me that?"

Donovan sat back from the table, retreating both literally and figuratively. "Okay. You're right. I'm—"

"Do you think I *enjoy* being ridiculed and insulted?"

"All right. Just calm down."

But she was too incensed to do any such thing. "Called a liar—or worse, psychotic?"

"I never called you a liar! Or psychotic either, for God's sake."

"Not out loud, maybe, but you thought it! Screwball, that's what you said."

As soon as the last word left her mouth, a horrified chill swept through her, dampening her anger. Every muscle frozen, scarcely breathing, she watched the realization creep up on him, saw his brief attempt to deny it, shut it out of his mind. The wary suspicion in his eyes gave way to disbelief, startled comprehension, and finally something that looked very much like fear. It wasn't the first time Faith had seen that look; it probably wouldn't be the last. But the pain it caused never diminished.

"No," he said, his deep, resonant voice reduced to a harsh whisper. "No, I didn't say it. I only *thought* it."

Faith inhaled a jagged chunk of air. "Yes," she confirmed. She wanted to turn away, avert her eyes, cover her face with her hands, but she made herself hold his stunned gaze, and wait. Each second was agony.

"Jesus." He surged out of his chair, almost knocking it over, and then just stood there, staring at her in shock. "Jesus," he said again. "You *read my mind?*"

Faith winced. He made it sound as if she'd violated him. To be fair, she supposed that was how he must feel.

She shook her head. "No. Not exactly."

"What do you mean, 'not exactly'?" he demanded. "Either you did or you didn't, damn it!"

"I . . . picked up a couple of your thoughts. One thought, actually—one *word.* The same word, three times. That's all."

"That's *all?* You just reached in and snatched a thought out of my head, and you say 'that's all'!"

"No! I didn't—"

Faith shook her head helplessly. She felt battered, and scared, and sick with guilt, but she was also starting to feel just a little ticked off, because she knew she didn't deserve the guilt. She hadn't done anything wrong. In fact, she hadn't *done* anything at all. She hadn't *tried* to read his thoughts; if she'd had any warning it was going to happen, she would have done everything she could think of to prevent it.

"That isn't how it works," she told him. "At least, not with me. It isn't something I *do.*" She released a sigh of exasperation. How could she possibly explain it, especially to him? He didn't believe precognitive dreams were possible; he probably thought only witches or Satan worshippers practiced telepathy.

"It isn't like tuning in a station on the radio. Most of the time I don't have any control over it. Sometimes I just suddenly hear things—words—inside my head. But usually what I pick up is emotions, impressions, other people's moods. Not what they're thinking, not literally. If you'd been thinking 'The world is flat,' or 'I wish I hadn't had that corned beef sandwich for lunch,' I wouldn't have heard it. But apparently this particular word was repeating in your mind, like a scratched record. And there was no question you were associating the word with me."

Rhys planted his hands on his hips and glared at her, his eyes narrowed, mouth grim. She couldn't tell how much of what she'd just said he believed. Assuming he believed any of it. When he spoke, it was as the hard-nosed detective. He started rapping out questions, barely giving her time to answer one before he fired off the next.

"How long have you been able to do this?"

"Since I was a child."

"And the dreams—have you been dreaming about things that haven't happened yet since you were a child?"

"No. I've had precognitive dreams, off and on, since I was thirteen."

"Explain 'off and on.'"

Faith shrugged. She didn't like talking about this. "I had a lot of them until I was sixteen, then they came less and less often. They'd pretty much stopped before I was out of my teens. It was the same with the telepathy. Until that day in your office."

He mulled that over for roughly two seconds. "Before that day, when was the last time you 'heard' what somebody else was thinking?"

She sighed and took a sip of lukewarm tea. "Almost eight years ago."

"And the last time you had one of the dreams?"

Faith hesitated. "I convinced myself they'd stopped about the same time as the telepathic episodes, but I suspect I've had a few since then. I just refused to acknowledge them as precognitive." She managed a sardonic smile. "It's easy to dismiss that kind of thing as nothing more than a spooky coincidence, especially when you don't want to face the fact that you're seeing into the future."

Rhys tilted his head to one side, his expression moderating from grim to quizzical. "A lot of people would give everything they own to be able to do that."

"Ah, but it's never happened to them," she said. "Imagine dreaming about an airplane crash, or a terrible fire, and knowing that it's not *just* a dream, it's really going to happen. People are going to die! But you don't have any idea which plane it is you're seeing, or which apartment building in which city. Or if you do get those kinds of details from the dream, and you try to warn somebody—for instance, the airline company, or the police—you're treated like a deranged lunatic."

He eased back onto the chair he'd vacated so abruptly a couple of minutes ago. "So you've gone to the police before with this kind of information?"

Faith expelled a short, bitter laugh. "Oh, yes."

"That's why you didn't come forward the first time you dreamed about the warehouse."

"Give the man a cigar." A memory suddenly flooded her mind, one of several she'd worked hard to suppress. "When I was fifteen, my guardians took me to the police and had me tell them about a recurring dream I was having, about a man murdering his wife in a drunken rage. Every night, I saw him beat her to death with some kind of club. I described the house they lived in, what they both looked like, even his truck and the clothes he wore to work. The detective I talked to threatened to have the child welfare office take me away from my guardians and put me in a mental institution."

As soon as she finished the story, she dropped her head into her hands, aghast that she'd blurted it out to him.

"God, I shouldn't have told you that."

"Why not?" Rhys murmured.

Faith straightened, pushed her hair out of her face, tried to collect herself. "Because it isn't any of your business," she said, trying to purge her voice of emotion. "And because it's ancient history. It has nothing to do with the sick bastard who's here, now, blowing things to smithereens."

"He killed her, didn't he?" Rhys asked. "His wife. He did it just like you dreamed he would."

Pain sliced through her, so sharp and fierce that she wrapped her arms around her waist. "Yes."

"Because they didn't believe you."

"Yes. *Yes!*"

She closed her eyes, rocking back and forth in response to the pain, the torture of remembering. And then suddenly strong hands were gripping her arms and lifting her out of the chair, pulling her against a hard, warm chest, gently stroking her back.

"It won't happen again," he said into her hair. "I promise you, Faith, it won't happen again. This time I believe you."

Chapter Six

The incredible thing was, he *did* believe her. He knew he shouldn't; what she'd told him was insane. None of it fitted his orderly, rational concept of how the universe worked. Seeing into the future, reading people's minds—that kind of thing wasn't supposed to happen. It defied every natural law. It shouldn't be *possible,* for God's sake.

And yet he believed.

Because he'd heard it from her. Because he knew she wasn't lying, or deranged. He couldn't have explained how he knew; he just did. It was the instinctive kind of knowledge that originated in his gut, rather than in his head. And Rhys had learned years ago to trust his instincts.

Which meant that the question was no longer: Was she lying, or nuts? It now became: What was he going to do with this extraordinary new knowledge?

He sure as hell couldn't take it to Lieutenant Jackson, or to agents Whitley and Hearst. Any of them would probably strap a strait jacket on him and toss him into a padded cell.

But how could he be one hundred percent sure that

wasn't exactly where he belonged? What if Faith McRae *was* crazy, and he'd merely bought into her delusions?

Rhys's desk chair creaked loudly as he leaned back and rubbed his burning eyes. Was that a possibility? He couldn't deny that he was strongly attracted to her, had been from the moment he looked up from the statement he was reviewing and saw her facing him across his desk. Had he allowed himself to be seduced by that attraction—did he believe her fantastic claims because the only alternative was unacceptable?

Both his gut and his mind rejected the idea. At the moment, though, he knew his brain wasn't firing on all cylinders. He'd come directly to the investigations office from Faith's house, hoping to find that the crime scene technicians had managed to collect some evidence from what was left of the ATM. He'd known he wouldn't be able to sleep if he went home; he was still too affected by the extraordinary things Faith had told him.

Unfortunately, the bomber hadn't left any more clues at this site than at the previous two. In fact there were significant differences in the device he'd used this time, which would make it harder to establish that the same person had built all three bombs. Damn it, why couldn't the bastard at least be consistent, if not predictable?

Glancing at the slip of paper lying on the desk blotter, he grimaced in disgust. The search he'd requested of the mainframe's database hadn't produced the name or alias of any known felon who matched the physical description Leon Perry had given him. Adding to his frustration was the ATF agents' failure to return the file containing Perry's statement. Now, along with everything else, Rhys had to worry that Whitley and Hearst might decide to follow up and question Perry themselves, robbing him of his one potential lead.

But maybe if he could get to Leon Perry first, . . .

His already rotten mood deteriorated further when he discovered that he couldn't remember the name of the janitorial service Perry worked for. *Damn* it! He pulled out the phone book and started scanning the Yellow Pages. None of the firms advertised there rang a bell.

"What are you doing here?"

Buford Jackson's suspicious voice boomed down at him from on high, like a vigilant, bad-tempered god. Rhys closed the phone book.

"Just stopped in to see if our man might have screwed up and left some trace evidence this time."

Jackson scowled as he took in Rhys's appearance. "If he did, it'll be turned over to Whitley and Hearst, per my orders. Looks like you spent most of the night at the scene. Did they tell you anything?"

"Not a damned thing," Rhys said sourly.

"Then you know as much as I do. Don't cause me any trouble, Rhys. I've got enough headaches already, without having one of my detectives piss off the ATF."

"I didn't get in their way," Rhys muttered. He couldn't completely purge his voice of resentment.

"Good. See that you don't. If they want our help, they'll ask for it. Now go home and get some sleep."

When Rhys left the building he intended to do exactly that, but as he passed a branch library, inspiration suddenly rose up and smote him right between the eyes. He parked his car in the lot at the side of the building and went inside. The middle-aged woman at the information desk directed him to a congenitally cheerful librarian, who in turn helped him locate four books she said should answer most of his questions. Rhys thanked her, checked out the books, and headed home to educate himself about the group of paranomal phenomena known collectively, the librarian had informed him, as psi. She pronounced it "sigh."

Faith arrived for work Monday morning in a cautiously optimistic frame of mind because Rat Man hadn't visited her dreams for the past two nights. Of course she hadn't heard from Rhys Donovan, either, but she refused to fret about that. She especially refused to wonder if he might be having second thoughts about that huskily sincere "This time I believe you."

She'd promised to get in touch with him if she had another dream, and they'd left it at that. Which put her, she reflected glumly, in a maddening and completely unexpected predicament. She didn't *want* to dream about Rat Man again, heaven knew. But without the dreams, she had no legitimate reason to communicate with Rhys.

"Damned if I do, damned if I don't," she muttered as she began an inventory of the supply closet.

Rollie Peters's amused voice came from directly behind her. "Still haven't made up your mind whether to get a VHS camcorder or an eight millimeter? It really isn't such a monumental decision, you know."

Faith glanced around and smiled. "Morning, Rollie. No, I've pretty much decided to go with VHS. This is a different dilemma."

"Serious?" he asked.

"Compared to world hunger or the depletion of the rain forests, I'd have to say no." She hesitated, but only for a moment. Rollie was the most stable, level-headed person she knew. He could always be counted on for sound, sensible advice. "It concerns a man."

His surprised "Ahhh!" positively resonated with curiosity. Depositing his clipboard on a waist-high counter, he rested his lean hips against the edge and folded his arms across his chest.

"Well, it's about time. In the three years I've known you, we've never had a conversation about a man who wasn't either a patient or a clinic employee."

"That's not true," she murmured in embarrassment.

"Yes, it is," Rollie insisted. "For a while I wondered if maybe you were a lesbian."

Faith felt her mouth drop open.

"Eventually I decided you weren't, because you never talk about women, either."

"You thought—" she began, then broke off and gaped at him, utterly speechless.

"Dirk still does. In fact, he's convinced of it. But I suspect that's because at some point he came on to you and you cut him off at the knees."

Faith's embarrassment was swiftly replaced by indignant anger. Rollie was right. About a year ago, Dirk Malloy had hounded her to go out with him for the better part of a month, until she got tired of inventing excuses and told him bluntly that, while she liked him fine as a co-worker, she wasn't interested in any kind of personal relationship with him. Unfortunately, Dirk was the kind of man who interpreted rejection as a challenge. Eventually Faith's patience ran out and she threatened to file a sexual harassment charge against him with the clinic management. Dirk stopped hitting on her, but the atmosphere in the PT department was strained for several weeks. Until, apparently, Dirk convinced himself that only a lesbian would fail to be bowled over by his charm and scintillating wit.

"That chauvinistic . . . *jackass!*" she fumed.

"That's our Dirk," Rollie drawled. "But forget about him. Dirk's opinions are a dime a dozen, and none of 'em's worth spit. C'mon, tell your Uncle Rollie about this man who's got you talking to yourself. That's definitely a promising sign."

If she'd been in a calm, rational frame of mind, she might have hesitated, at least long enough to consider how much she should tell Rollie. But she wasn't feeling particularly calm or rational at the moment. What she felt was angry, and insulted, and fed up. Damn it, wasn't there a man alive who possessed both the tolerance and the self-confidence to accept her as she was? Rhys Donovan had judged her crazy within ten minutes of meeting her; Dirk had labeled her a lesbian. Even Rollie, without doubt the most decent, open-minded person she'd ever known, thought there was something wrong with her because she didn't entertain him with anecdotes about her sex life during lunch. Okay, so he'd finally decided she wasn't a lesbian, but what *did* he think—that she wasn't interested in men, or that she just didn't have whatever it took to attract one?

"He's a cop," she said as she resumed the inventory. There was just a hint of challenge in her voice. "A detective."

"No kidding. How'd you meet him?"

Still miffed, and encouraged by the genuine interest in his voice, Faith didn't take so much as a second to think about whether she should prevaricate.

"Well, I'd had a couple of dreams. About the man who's been planting the bombs . . ."

Twenty minutes later Rollie knew about Rhys's two visits to her house, the polygraph test she'd volunteered to take, and, incredibly, about the dreams. All of them. In detail. Faith couldn't believe she'd told him that part. She hadn't intended to. It had just come pouring out.

"Christ," Rollie murmured when she stopped talking. He'd listened intently, his expression alternating between amazement and fascination—but never, thank goodness, veering into disbelief—until she ran out of words. "You actually *saw* the guy who's been planting the bombs?"

In the reception area, just around the corner, Missy Clarence laughed at something an arriving patient said. The sound reminded Faith that this private conversation might not be so private. She shook her head and returned to counting elastic bandages and splints.

"Not clearly. I doubt I could identify him from a photo, or a police lineup."

Rollie noticed her sudden constraint and moved a little closer. "But still, seeing him in your dreams, knowing what he was doing—that had to be downright creepy."

Faith nodded silently. Creepy. What adjective would he use to describe picking up someone else's thoughts? she wondered.

"So, what's the deal with this detective? Is he going to try to use your dreams to catch the guy?"

"Assuming I have any more," she murmured, glancing

over her shoulder to make sure no one else was within earshot.

"Ah, so that's what you meant by 'damned if I do, damned if I don't.' You really like this guy, huh? Even though he thought you were cuckoo at first."

"Yes," she admitted with a sigh.

"A lot?"

"A lot."

"But you're convinced he's only coming around because of the dreams—because he thinks you can help him catch the bomber."

Faith jotted down the last of the inventory figures and closed the closet door. "That *is* the only reason, Rollie."

"Wrong!" he said with an indulgent chuckle. "Faith, honey, when was the last time you looked in a mirror?"

"This morning, when I brushed my teeth. And my vision is twenty-twenty, Rollie, so don't try to convince me I'm the personification of every man's secret fantasy."

He shook his head. "A fantasy is something you know isn't and won't ever be *real.* A dream, on the other hand, is something that isn't unattainable, just out of reach for the moment."

She started to point out that she was neither. "Rollie—"

"Faith!" He put his hands on her shoulders and gave her a little shake. "You're a beautiful, desirable woman. Ask Dirk, if you doubt it, or any of the doctors upstairs, or our patients. Hell, if I weren't happily married with a couple of kids . . . and you weren't several shades too pale . . ."

His exaggerated leer was so comical she had to smile.

"I could start using a tanning bed," she teased.

"Yeah, and end up with skin like shoe leather and melanoma ten years down the road. No, sweetheart, you're gorgeous just the way you are. That's what I'm trying to tell you. Everybody else can see it. Why can't you?"

Gorgeous? Beautiful *and* desirable? Faith stared at him blankly, completely at a loss. Rollie wasn't a flatterer; she'd never known him to be less than one hundred percent honest. Why would he say such things . . . unless he meant them?

"It's true!" he murmured. His smile was affectionate, but also a little puzzled. "And you really don't know, do you? You aren't even aware of the way men look at you."

Faith found it hard to believe that anyone, male or female, ever gave her more than a passing glance. There had never been anything special about her, except for the "gifts" she'd developed in childhood. And since most people would consider her some kind of freak if they knew about that part of her life, she'd always been careful to keep it secret. Or so she'd thought.

"What do you mean?" she said suspiciously. "How do men look at me?"

Rollie sighed and shook his head. "Next time you see that detective, pay attention."

Before she could ask what that was supposed to mean, Missy Clarence stuck her head around the corner to alert them that they both had patients waiting. Faith was kept busy the rest of the morning, and she didn't get a chance to corner Rollie that afternoon because he was making his hospital rounds.

As the clinic's chief physiotherapist, he spent one morning and one afternoon each week at the brand new, state of the art hospital across the street, visiting the orthopedic partners' postsurgical patients. He used the visits to explain the follow-up therapy they would need, answer questions and schedule their first outpatient appointments. Rollie had initiated the practice of making rounds right after he was hired, three years ago. It was a good system; patients arrived for their first PT treatment knowing what to expect so most of them were relaxed and eager to begin.

This week, though, Faith wished Rollie's afternoon rounds had been scheduled for another day. What *had* that enigmatic "pay attention" meant? If Rollie only knew—when Rhys Donovan looked at her, the only thing his beautiful, cold blue eyes gave away was suspicion or blatant disbelief.

Except for that last time. When he left her house Saturday morning, there had been something else . . . a softening, almost a tenderness . . .

Disturbed by the direction her thoughts were taking, Faith admonished herself not to be deluded by what had probably been a temporary lapse on Donovan's part. Okay, so he'd finally accepted that her dreams were real, and precognitive. Didn't mean a thing, except that maybe he'd given up the idea that she was somehow aiding and abetting Rat Man. The next time she saw him—*if* she saw him again—she would probably discover that he'd reverted to his stubborn, cynical cop persona.

And even if he hadn't changed his mind about the dreams, she knew better than to hope that he would suddenly start seeing her as a woman—a beautiful, desirable woman, yet!—instead of as a tool. Because, bottom line, that's all she was to him. A tool, something that could be used to help him catch Rat Man.

Faith continued to dispense such pragmatic, cautionary advice to herself after she got home from work, and into the evening. The trouble was, Rollie's words kept repeating in her mind, sometimes drowning out the voice of reason.

Gorgeous, he'd said. Beautiful, desirable. Next time, pay attention.

She put off going to bed until she started to nod off in front of the television.

"Damned if I do, damned if I don't," she muttered as she slipped between the sheets. "Damn *you,* Rollie Peters."

Why had he planted these ideas in her head, thoughts that could only bring her grief? She wasn't like other people; never had been, never would be. She couldn't afford to hope for the things other people hoped for. Rollie had defined the difference between dreams and fantasies very well. And she had accepted years ago that other people's dreams would always be fantasies for her—unreal and unattainable.

Before she fell asleep, she prayed that she wouldn't dream about Rat Man.

The device was the same as the last time—a rectangular container approximately the size and shape of a cigar box, with a pair of slender wires appearing to grow out of one end. The box was partially concealed by a clump of daisies. The wires ran up one side of another automatic teller machine until they disappeared into the bank card slot. They were secured to the ATM with three evenly spaced pieces of electrical tape.

Everything was startlingly clear. Faith could distinguish the individual insulated wires and even the edges of the tape against the matte black of the ATM's metal surface. Her brain had recorded all these details before she suddenly realized why everything was so sharply defined.

She was seeing it in full daylight.

No sooner had the comprehension registered than she was awake. Fully awake and clear-headed, her mind racing. She jerked upright on the bed, then reached down to snag her shoulder bag from the floor. One hand rummaged for the business card Rhys Donovan had given her on Saturday, while the other fumbled for the switch of the lamp on the nightstand and, when she'd found it, the telephone receiver.

He answered with a rusty "Donovan" on the second ring.

"It's Faith. I just had another dream."

There was a beat of charged silence. "I'll be there in fifteen minutes. Start writing down everything you can remember, while it's still fresh in your mind."

"All right," she said, but he'd already hung up.

She met him at the door, blurting, "It's another cash machine," before he could get inside.

She'd pulled on a short kimono over her nightshirt but hadn't taken time to brush her hair, a detail that occurred to her only when he was standing less than two feet away.

Not that there was much of it to brush, but she was suddenly obsessed with the thought that she probably looked like an outraged porcupine was squatting on her head. She waved Rhys down the hall with a self-conscious, "I made some notes. They're on the kitchen table."

As soon as he turned in that direction, she raked her fingers through her hair a couple of times and gave her head a quick little shake for good measure. No doubt about it, she mused as she followed him down the hall, the man was born to wear jeans. Not the fashionably baggy kind, though; they wouldn't have done him justice. The pair he had on, like every pair she'd seen him in, clung fast to his tight, round buttocks and long, muscular legs. Her appreciative gaze drifted down over the soft, faded denim and she noticed that his familiar tan bucks were missing. In his rush to get here, he'd slipped on a pair of tobacco brown deck shoes that had seen as much wear as the jeans. He hadn't taken time to put on socks.

He entered the kitchen, pausing to glance at the steno pad on the table before he moved on to the stove. Without saying a word, he collected the teakettle, filled it, and set it on to heat. Faith took a couple of steps into the room, intending to fetch tea bags from a canister on the counter, but he beat her to it. She gave a mental shrug and took a seat at the table.

"Okay, tell me about the dream," he murmured as he collected cups and saucers. "What did you see?"

"Another cash machine, like I said a minute ago. But this dream was different from the others."

Rhys turned to face her, leaning back against the counter while he waited for the teakettle to whistle. He casually crossed one foot over the other, which drew Faith's attention to his bare ankles. When she looked up, seeking distraction, she encountered his bristled jaw and piercing eyes.

Okay, Rollie, I'm paying attention. Sorry to disappoint you—not to mention myself—but whatever you thought I'd see isn't there. This man has one thing and one thing only on his mind. Unfortunately, the one thing isn't yours truly.

"Different how?" he said tersely.

"The sun was shining. In the other dreams, whatever I saw was happening at night. This time I saw everything as it would look during the day."

"Including a bomb?"

Faith nodded. "Yes. I wrote down what it looked like."

"Good." The teakettle shrieked. Rhys turned to switch off the burner and pour the water. When he'd brought their cups to the table, he asked anxiously, "Were there any people—passersby, somebody getting ready to use the ATM?"

"No. And that's strange, now that I think about it. There was no one, not a single person in sight . . . not even Rat Man."

His eyebrows pushed together in surprise. "Rat Man?"

"That's the name I gave him after the first dream," she explained, a little embarrassed. "Because of the way he scurried around in the dark. He reminded me of a giant rat."

"And he wasn't there this time?"

"No." She hesitated, staring at her teabag as she held the string and twirled it in the water. "I could be wrong, but I think it means he isn't *going to* plant the bomb at the ATM I saw—he already has."

Rhys didn't look at all pleased by that hypothesis. Faith got up and went to the counter for the sugar bowl. When she returned he was reading the details she'd jotted down in the steno pad.

"You didn't take sugar before," he said without looking up.

The observation surprised her. He must be very good at his job. "I can feel my energy level dropping," she replied as she added a couple of spoonfuls to her tea. "In fact, I think I'd better eat something. Otherwise I won't be able to concentrate."

She left him to finish reading her notes and got up again

to fetch a bag of bagels, a pitcher of orange juice, and two glasses. They each gnawed on a bagel as they went over what Faith remembered of the dream.

"I hate to admit it, but I think you're right," Rhys said eventually. "The fact that Rat Man wasn't there, combined with the fact that you saw the ATM during the day, probably means he's already planted the bomb."

Faith didn't comment on his reference to "Rat Man," but it gave her a tiny tingle of pleasure. If she wasn't careful, she'd start thinking of them as a team, partners, and that would be a big mistake. He was the cop; she was just a tool. She mustn't let herself forget that.

Rhys glanced at his watch, then at the window over the sink. "It'll be light soon. What time do you have to be at work?"

"Eight o'clock," she said, realizing at once what he had in mind. "There's no way we could hit every automatic teller machine in town before then."

"No, but we could cover a few. Who knows, we might get lucky. Anyway, we have to start somewhere."

The way he matter-of-factly paired the two of them seriously undermined Faith's resolve to maintain some emotional distance: ". . . *We* might get lucky . . . *we* have to start somewhere." He sure didn't sound as if he only thought of her as a tool.

She nodded eagerly and stood up. "Give me twenty minutes to shower and dress."

Chapter Seven

They took Rhys's car, a four-year-old black Lumina, and headed out to inspect as many ATMs as possible before Faith had to report to work. Rhys said that as soon as the banks opened he would try to get a master list, or a map, and check off the machines they'd already eliminated.

First they covered Faith's neighborhood. Since it was a residential area, there weren't many cash machines. She gave him directions to the three she was familiar with: one in the parking lot of a branch bank; another around the corner from a laundromat; and the third adjoining a building that housed a group of doctors' and dentists' offices.

"That's it?" Rhys said when they'd checked the last machine and returned to his car. It was the only one of the three that had any vegetation growing beneath it. Unfortunately the greenery was a patch of crabgrass, and it wasn't camouflaging a black box with wires sprouting from one end. "Are you sure there aren't more than three machines in the neighborhood?"

Faith finished jotting down the location of the third

ATM and looked up from the steno pad. "There's one at a credit union a few blocks from here and another one at a supermarket, but they're both inside, so I thought—"

"We can skip those two," he agreed. "Okay, we've got a little more than an hour left. Let's see how many we can hit in my neighborhood."

While he skillfully navigated the rush hour traffic, he coaxed her to try to remember any identifying details from her dream. "Did you see a Cirrus logo? Were there bank card emblems stuck on the front, or the name of a specific bank?"

Faith shook her head. "I don't remember any of those things, but that doesn't mean they weren't there. They could have been, and I just didn't notice. My attention was focused on the bomb."

His thoughtful "Mmm," didn't sound critical, but she felt a little guilty all the same. She flipped back to the notes she'd made, concentrating, trying to recall any details from the dream that she might have neglected to write down. Something besides the clump of daisies, the black tape, the wires threaded into the bank card slot . . .

Wait. She *had* seen something else . . . to the right of the slot. What was it? She closed her eyes and tried to reconstruct the image.

"Braille," she said suddenly.

"What?"

"There were three—no, four—small metal plates, beside the buttons you push to tell the machine what kind of transaction you're making. Smooth, shiny strips of metal. Aluminum or stainless steel, with raised dots. It was some kind of Braille menu, so blind people can use the machine."

"That's good," Rhys said. He sounded impressed. "I don't think they've got around to adding Braille menus to all the older machines yet. Write that down."

"I am," Faith murmured as she finished adding the information to her notes.

"I don't understand how this works," he said. "How

come you can remember a detail like that, but you can't remember whether there were any identifying signs on the machine?"

She couldn't tell from his tone whether he was doubting her again or displaying sincere curiosity. She decided to give him the benefit of the doubt. "Like I said, I was concentrating on the bomb . . . and the wires. Obviously I *saw* the plates with the Braille instructions, but only in a peripheral way."

"Out of the corner of your eye, so to speak," Rhys murmured.

"Right. The image was always there, in my memory, but it wasn't close to the surface. I had to work to bring it up."

He nodded. "That happens all the time with people who've witnessed a crime or an accident. The more they go over what they saw, the more details they remember."

He signaled a left turn and pulled into a bank parking lot, then around the building to an ATM enclosed in a large concrete column that supported the roof over three drive-through lanes. Faith gave the machine a quick once-over and shook her head.

"You're sure?" Rhys asked.

"Positive. The one in the dream wasn't set in cement."

"Damn, I wish there was a faster way to do this," he muttered as he steered the car back into traffic. "At this rate, it'll take a week to check every machine."

"Why don't you get some other policemen to help," Faith suggested.

"I can't do that."

The reply was brusque, almost curt. She swiveled to look at him. "Because your tip came from a crazy woman's dream?" she challenged. "All right, so don't tell them that. Just say an anonymous source called you on the phone and told you a bomb had been planted at another automatic teller machine."

Rhys started shaking his head before she finished. "No, that isn't the reason." He darted a sideways glance at her while he waited for a light to change. Faith had the impression he was making up his mind about something.

"Hell, I might as well tell you. I'm not even supposed to be working this case. The Bureau of Alcohol, Tobacco and Firearms took control of it last week. I've been ordered to turn over any leads I get to their agents."

Faith's stomach flip-flopped in reaction. "Last week? Does that mean—Do they have the statement I gave you?"

"No. I took all your paperwork home and locked it in my desk."

The admission astonished her. "You took it home? Why?"

"Damned if I know," Rhys muttered. He suddenly whipped the Lumina into another bank parking lot, taking the right-hand turn so sharply that if Faith hadn't been wearing her seat belt, she'd have landed in his lap.

"You could be in a lot of trouble if anybody finds out, couldn't you?" she said as he braked the car to a halt in front of another ATM.

"If you consider losing my job and being charged with obstruction of justice 'a lot of trouble,' then I guess the answer would have to be yes. Damn it, this one doesn't have Braille signs *or* daisies."

"So why did you withhold my statement?" Faith pressed. She could tell he didn't want to discuss this. In fact, she suspected he already regretted having told her. But the answer was important to her. She couldn't just let it go.

Rhys gripped the steering wheel with both hands and stared straight ahead, his gaze fixed on the Taco Bell across the street as if he expected a group of Mexican fast food bandits to run out of the building any second. She watched the tendons in his wrists flex, saw his stubbled jaw move as if he were grinding his teeth. Just as she decided he was going to ignore the question, he turned his head to look at her. His striking blue eyes were dark and troubled.

"I've been asking myself the same thing since last Monday night," he said with a sardonic smile. "The reason I gave myself at the time isn't good enough, and it sure as hell won't keep either of us out of jail."

"Tell me anyway."

"The minute I passed your statement and the polygraph report on to my lieutenant, you would have become our prime suspect. And, despite how things looked, I couldn't believe you'd had anything to do with the bombings."

Faith tried not to let her disappointment show. "I guess that's something," she murmured. "We'd better get moving. I have to be at work in forty minutes."

Rhys's forehead creased in a frown. " 'I guess that's *something*'?"

He sounded put out. Downright peevish, in fact. How typical, Faith thought. How *male.*

"What did you expect, that I'd throw myself on the floor and kiss your feet in gratitude? You generously absolved me of criminal guilt, but you still wrote me off as a nut case."

"I didn't say that," he retorted. His eyes narrowed in suspicion. "Are you reading my mind again?"

"No!" she denied. "I told you before, that isn't something I do intentionally. But the fact that you asked proves I'm right—you *still* don't entirely believe me about the dreams."

"Now *that's* crazy," Rhys said as he shifted the car into gear. "If I didn't believe you, would I have come running in the middle of the night when you called? Would I be driving all over town looking for an automatic teller machine accessorized with daisies and a Braille menu and a bomb, for crissake?"

"I can do without your sarcasm," she snapped. "If you don't believe the bomb exists, just say so and take me home to get my car."

He pulled out of the bank parking lot without waiting for a break in traffic, cutting between a Datsun station wagon and a bread truck to get to the inside lane. They missed the truck's front bumper by millimeters. Faith gasped in fright, then winced when the truck's driver registered his opinion of Rhys's driving with a blast of his horn.

"Jesus Christ," Rhys muttered. She didn't think the remark was directed at the truck driver. "I *believe!* All right? I believe in the dreams, the bomb, Rat Man—the whole shebang. I wish to God I didn't. My life would be a lot simpler if I could write you off as a charter member of the screwball brigade. But I can't. You've sold me. Didn't I say so on Saturday?"

"Yes, you did. But if you believed me last week, why didn't you give your lieutenant my statement and the polygraph report and try to convince *him?*"

And why in God's name was she arguing with him about this? She didn't *want* the Louisville police department, not to mention the Bureau of Alcohol, Tobacco and Firearms, investigating her; heaven knew what they'd turn up once they started poking and prying. What on earth had come over her?

Rhys didn't respond until they'd driven a dozen blocks and he'd deftly inserted the Lumina into a parking spot that shouldn't have accommodated anything bigger than a motorcycle. Faith glanced around and saw that they'd stopped in front of a large supermarket-drugstore-garden-center complex. She nervously wet her lips with her tongue and tried to figure out how to retract the challenge she'd hurled at him.

"You're right," he said bluntly, preempting her. "When I decided to bury your paperwork, I did think you might be . . ."

"Psychotic?" she suggested.

"Stop putting words in my mouth," he said irritably. "I knew you weren't crazy. A little loopy, maybe, but not certifiably wacko. Still, I had a hard time buying into the precognitive dreams. That was just too unreal."

He switched off the ignition and swiveled to face her, resting his right arm on the back of the bench seat. Faith was suddenly and acutely aware of that sun-bronzed, impressively muscular arm; also that the long, slender fingers at the end of it were less than an inch from her shoulder. The Lumina's interior seemed a lot smaller than it had a minute ago, and Rhys Donovan seemed to fill every inch of it.

"I do believe you now," he said with quiet intensity. "I wasn't lying about that. But I have to tell you, all this stuff makes me *extremely* nervous—dreams that predict the future, reading people's minds . . . frankly, it's spooky as hell."

Surprisingly, Faith felt as if an enormous weight had been lifted from her chest. "I know," she murmured.

The ATM outside the garden center had a Braille menu, but no daisies and no bomb. Rhys drove her back home to collect her car and said he'd call if there was anything to report.

Faith was five minutes late for work. She apologized to Rollie as she stowed her purse in a cabinet, using the construction work still taking place at the new hospital across the street as an excuse for her tardiness.

"Traffic in both directions was blocked this morning while they unloaded a backhoe."

He nodded. "Yeah, they're finishing up the west parking lot and putting in a few big trees. We'd better allow an extra ten minutes or so in the morning the rest of the week, or else detour around."

"You'd think they'd have finished the place before they started admitting patients," Dirk complained. "They didn't even put in the helipad till last week."

"For your information, a lot of hospitals manage to operate without a helipad," Faith replied. She knew by the way both men looked at her that her uncharacteristic sharpness surprised them. The knowing glint in Rollie's eyes said he also understood the reason for it.

"We're not going to have a personnel problem because of what I told you yesterday, are we?" he asked when they shared a ten-minute break later in the morning.

Faith shook her head. "No." She already regretted snapping at Dirk; he wasn't worth wasting emotional energy on. "Sorry. I'm a little out of sorts today. I didn't get much sleep last night."

Rollie gave her a sly look. "Because of your detective?"

"He isn't 'my' detective," she said primly, then got up and left the break room before he could comment on the blush she knew had bloomed on her face.

Rhys spent most of the morning interviewing businessmen about a couple of robberies that had taken place over the weekend. On his lunch hour he swung by the central branch of Louisville's largest bank and picked up a map that showed the location of all the automatic teller machines in the city and surrounding suburbs. He was discouraged by the number of little ATM signs peppering the map. Damn, there must be a hundred of the things, maybe more.

After lunch he collected information on an incident of vandalism. Somebody had broken into a high school science lab and trashed two desktop computers. He was inclined to suspect gang members, until the principal set him straight. The staff counselors and neighborhood religious groups had made a point of reaching out to local gangs, she told him, and as a result the schools and churches had been declared safe zones. Rhys asked if she thought any of the gang members might be willing to give him any information they picked up on the street. The principal said she'd pass on the request, but he wasn't optimistic.

By 3:30 he'd plowed through a mountain of paperwork, including updates to a couple of his ongoing investigations to keep the files current. After first making sure that Buford Jackson was out of the office, he spread the map he'd got from the bank on his desk and used a pen to X out the six cash machines he and Faith had visited that morning. Switching to a red marker, he added an X at the location of each of the three bombings—the software company offices, the warehouse, and the ATM.

There was no discernible pattern, and the bombs had been planted too far apart for him to zero in on a specific area. Which meant he was going to be spending all his spare time in the foreseeable future inspecting automatic teller machines, hoping he'd be able to find the next bomb before it went off; and that if he did, he would also get a lead on Rat Man's identity.

He would also, of necessity, be spending a lot of time with Faith McRae. Rhys took a moment to analyze how he felt about that, and discovered that the prospect excited him. Not good. Not good at all. A purely physical attraction was one thing. He could deal with that; had been, in fact, since the first time he laid eyes on her. But enjoying her company, her conversation—looking forward to just being with her—was something else, a complication he didn't want and couldn't afford.

Who was she? What was she hiding? Why had she refused to tell him about the other dreams she claimed to have had? Except for that one brief lapse, when she let the story about the man beating his wife to death slip out, she'd kept everything about her past locked up tight. He knew where she worked, where she lived and that she lived alone, but that was it.

It wasn't enough. He wanted to know more . . . a lot more. He folded the ATM map and tucked it into the pocket of his sport coat, then took out the telephone directory.

Faith didn't dream about Rat Man or bombs Tuesday night, probably because she was so bushed when she went to bed that not even a precognitive dream could overcome her exhaustion. All day Wednesday she hoped Rhys would call her at the clinic. When he didn't, she hoped there'd be a message from him on the answering machine when she got home. The tape for incoming calls was blank. The intensity of her disappointment was surprising. It was also troubling, because it had little to do with a desire to know whether Rhys had managed to find the second ATM bomb. The truth was, she longed to hear his deep, resonant voice, even if he was only calling to report that he hadn't had any luck.

Damn, she couldn't let herself fall for the man. She *wouldn't,* and that was that. Because she knew exactly what would happen if she did: she'd end up being hurt and disillusioned . . . again. It had happened every time she lowered her guard and formed an emotional attachment, even with people who'd claimed to value and envy her "gifts." Love couldn't exist side by side with fear. And, without exception, every person she had ever loved eventually came to fear her. And rightly so. If their roles had been reversed, she'd have been afraid of someone with such powers, too. Any sane person would be.

"So maybe you should try to find a man who isn't entirely sane," she muttered as she stripped and climbed into the shower. Not somebody who was certifiably wacko, as Rhys put it, but whose perception of reality was skewed by a few degrees, so he wouldn't be thrown if she read his mind now and then, or told him not to take the expressway to work because an oil tanker was going to crash and burn or the overpass was going to collapse.

She closed her eyes and stepped into the spray, letting the warm water pelt the top of her head and cascade over her face. Question was, where would she find such a compliant, accepting soul, outside a mental ward? Well, there was always Leon Perry. Gads, what a thought. Leon would probably chain her to a basement wall while he hunted down an exorcist to drive the demons from her.

Come to think of it, she hadn't seen Leon for several days. Maybe the janitorial service had changed his work schedule or something and he was no longer assigned to the clinic. Now that would be a gift from the gods. Just remembering the way he'd looked at her when she got onto the elevator last week was enough to raise goosebumps on her arms and the back of her neck. She adjusted the water temperature to a hotter setting and resolutely put Leon Perry out of her mind.

She had pulled on her terry robe and was blow-drying her hair when the doorbell rang. When she squinted through the peephole and saw Rhys Donovan standing on the porch, her heart gave an excited little jump. At the same time, the thought crossed her mind that he had a positive knack for catching her undressed. He, on the other hand, was nattily turned out in charcoal gray slacks, a white shirt, navy sport coat and red and gray striped tie. He must have just got off duty.

"Hi," she said as she opened the door. "I hope you've come with good news."

"Only to the extent that no news is good news." He hesitated a moment before stepping inside, taking in the short robe and her bare legs and feet with a single swift glance.

Faith self-consciously pulled the robe's lapels together. "Oh. I hoped . . . Then why—"

"I thought it was about time I fed you."

She blinked owlishly in surprise, which made him smile. "Do you like pizza?"

Did she? The sight of all those pearly whites—not to mention his dimples—made it hard to remember if she'd ever *eaten* pizza. She took a gamble. "Sure, doesn't everybody?"

"Good, 'cause that's what I'm in the mood for. We can check out a few more ATMs after we eat."

He reached up to loosen his tie and unfasten the top two buttons of his shirt. Faith noticed right away that he wasn't wearing an undershirt. While she was trying to nudge her brain back into gear, he turned and walked into the living room. His left arm brushed the front of her robe, directly over her right breast, in passing.

"I'll wait in here while you get dressed. Just throw on something casual. I'm starved."

Mouth dry, her pulse racing, Faith managed to pull

herself together and reply, "Okay, make yourself at home," before escaping to her bedroom.

As if he'd ever needed an invitation, she thought as she searched for a pair of jeans. The only clean ones she could find were as old and faded and tight as the jeans he usually wore. Well, he'd said to throw on something casual. And maybe the fact that she could barely squeeze herself into them would keep her from making a pig of herself. Now, please God, let him still have his coat on when she got to the living room. Considering the state she was already in, and the way the jeans almost pinched her in half, she might literally swoon if he'd exposed another inch of that hard, overwhelmingly male body.

Not only had he removed both his sport coat and tie, he'd unfastened another button and rolled up his shirt-sleeves. Heaven help her. She'd have sworn it wasn't possible for the man to look any better than he did in jeans and a ratty old sweatshirt with ripped out sleeves. She'd have been wrong.

This was terrible. Absolutely pathetic. Hadn't she just made up her mind not to fall for him? What was she, for pity's sake, a woman or a mouse?

He was lounging on the couch, right ankle resting on his left knee, idly flipping through one of her magazines. Looking for home decorating tips, no doubt, or twenty ways to recycle leftover hamburger. A giddy laugh gurgled up in Faith's throat. She choked it off and announced her presence with a panic-stricken, "Ready."

Rhys glanced up, saw her standing in the doorway . . . and underwent an amazing metamorphosis in virtually the blink of an eye. Faith actually watched it happen.

It wasn't just his expression, though anyone who was the least bit observant would have noticed that his spontaneous smile was almost instantly replaced by an alert, slightly wary mask. His body manifested the same transformation: he casually lowered his right foot to the floor, tossed the magazine back on the coffee table, and started to rise. But by the time he was on his feet, his relaxed, even eager, momentum had ossified into a rigidly formal posture.

"Great. Let's go."

He sounded as if he were headed to the dentist's for a root canal, instead of out for pizza. Faith stared in bewilderment as he reached down to collect his sport coat. His neatly folded tie stuck out of the breast pocket.

What was going on here? she wondered as they walked to his car. He briefly rested his hand on the small of her back as he opened the door for her. Even that light, perfunctory touch felt constrained. Uncomfortable.

Something was definitely wrong. He scarcely said two words on the way to the pizza parlor, which turned out to be a cozy family-owned establishment rather than one of the franchise places. Though it was still early, the dining room was already half filled. And, wouldn't you know, not a single person in the place was wearing jeans.

Chapter Eight

Faith tried to bury her self-consciousness as a voluptuous waitress who bore an uncanny resemblance to Sophia Loren led them to a corner booth and gave them each a menu. As she handed Rhys his, she bent over the table to adjust the amber snifter that held a flickering candle, managing in the process to give him an up-close and personal view of the impressive cleavage her white peasant blouse displayed. Her smile was dazzling, and all for Rhys.

Faith looked on in amazement. Good grief, was this the effect he usually had on women? She tore her fascinated gaze from the waitress to check his reaction as the woman backed away from the table. Incredibly, he didn't appear to have noticed that she'd practically shoved her breasts in his face.

"Thanks, Elena," he murmured. "We'll have the deep dish Sicilian. Pile on everything but anchovies, I think." He glanced at Faith in question. She nodded and wondered what the "everything but" would be. Rhys picked up her menu, which she hadn't even looked at, and handed it to the waitress along with his. "And bring us a carafe of house wine with the salads, would you?"

"Of course, Rhys," the woman crooned. "I'll make sure Gino fixes the pie just the way you like."

She gave him another adoring smile before she glided off in the direction of the kitchen. Faith watched her go, admiring the sway of her hips and how the artless, rhythmic movement made her full skirt swirl around her legs. Now why couldn't she walk like that?

"Must be an inherited talent," she muttered enviously.

"What's that?"

Faith sighed and turned her attention back to Rhys. "Nothing. Come here often?"

"Not often enough. The decor isn't exactly elegant, but the food's fantastic."

"I don't doubt it. The smells from the kitchen already have my mouth watering." She used an index finger to idly push her fork back and forth across the red and white checked tablecloth. "Speaking of things that stimulate salivation, are you sure the *decor* isn't as great an attraction as the food?"

His expression was blank for a second or two, then his mouth quirked in a sheepish smile. "I meant the plain wood tables and chairs, the cheap candles . . ."

"The waitress straight out of a Fellini movie. Does she have grape stains between her toes?"

"I wouldn't be a bit surprised," Rhys drawled. His eyes glittered with amusement. "If you're really curious, I can go back to the kitchen and ask her husband."

"Dear Lord. She's married?"

"Very. Her husband's making our pizza. They've got four kids."

Faith shook her head in surprise. "I hope he isn't the jealous type."

"Are you kidding? He's Sicilian. If Gino ever *suspected* Elena was fooling around with another man, he'd commit double murder. She never would, though. She's crazy about him."

Elena appeared with their salads, a carafe of wine and two glasses before Faith could reply, which was probably just as well. She bestowed another brilliant smile on Rhys and assured him their pizza would be ready soon, but she didn't loiter at the table. Faith suspected it was only because two couples had just entered the restaurant. While Rhys poured the wine, she watched Elena greet the new arrivals. She lavished the same flattering attention on the men that she'd given Rhys.

"It's the way she was brought up," he remarked. "Her mother and grandmother taught her that men respond well to that kind of treatment."

"I see. So it's a kind of behavior modification technique—like paper-training a puppy?"

He almost choked on his wine. "I guess that's one way to put it," he allowed, dabbing at his chin with a snowy napkin.

Following his example, Faith ignored her salad and took a sip from her glass. "Mmmm. What I know about wine you could put on the head of a pin, but this is delicious."

"Drink up," he urged. "Maybe it'll put you in a better mood."

She looked at him in surprise. "I'm not in a bad mood. At least I wasn't, until—" She cut herself off and took another sip of wine.

"Until what?"

"Nothing. Never mind."

"Until Elena started flirting?"

Faith gave him an oh-please look, but the assumption annoyed her. He thought she was jealous? What conceit!

"Well then, what?" he persisted. "Something's obviously bugging you."

"Well, let's see. Could it be that I look like somebody you dragged out of a cardboard box and brought here to feed, as your charitable act of the week? No, that couldn't possibly be it."

"What are you talking about?"

He sounded honestly baffled, but he was smiling as he said it, and for some reason that irritated her even more.

She took another healthy gulp of wine. Her salad remained untouched.

"Every other person here, including you, looks like he or she just came from a board meeting. You said I should wear something casual."

"So you're upset because of the way you're dressed? Don't be silly. You look fine."

Faith just stared at him, hard.

"Better than fine," he amended. He was beginning to sound a little annoyed, himself.

She reached for the carafe to top off her glass.

"Uh, maybe you should slow down until you get some food in your stomach."

Faith appreciated that it was good advice, but some perverse streak she hadn't known she possessed made her take another drink.

"What's the matter, afraid everybody will think I'm a wino, too?"

Rhys turned his hands palms-up in resignation and reached for his own glass. "Anything else bothering you, other than your wardrobe?"

"Yes, as a matter of fact. You. Specifically, your Jekyll and Hyde routine."

He opened his mouth, she was sure to argue, but then closed it without saying anything. Just then Elena passed their table and he reached out to lay a hand on her arm. She immediately screeched to a halt.

"Sorry Elena, but we're going to have to leave. Have Gino box the pie to go, would you."

Elena was obviously disappointed, but she only asked if they would also like a bottle of wine.

"I don't think—" Rhys began.

Faith jumped in with a polite, "Yes, please." She gave the waitress her brightest smile. "It's the best wine I've ever had."

Elena had the boxed pizza, a bottle of wine, and the check on their table in record time. Faith could tell Rhys was ticked off, but he maintained a stony silence all the way back to her house.

She led the way to the kitchen and busied herself collecting plates, glasses and flatware. He deposited the pizza and wine on the table, then went to the sink and ripped off a few paper towels to use as napkins. After Faith put his service in front of him, she sat down and heaved a put upon sigh that she knew perfectly well he heard. He pretended he hadn't.

"All right," she said in the most calm, temperate tone she could manage. "Can we talk now?"

"I don't know. Can we?"

The cynical, smartass cop was back. She didn't make another stab at conversation until they'd helped themselves to pizza and wine, using the interval to get her temper under control. If she wanted to find out what was causing his strange behavior, fighting with him probably wasn't the best way to go about it.

"Has something happened since yesterday morning?" she asked. "Did your lieutenant find out about my statement and the polygraph test?"

Rhys shook his head and uttered a terse, "No," as he dug into his pizza.

"Well, then, have *I* said or done something?"

"I don't know. Have you?"

The cryptic response made Faith pause with a forkful of pizza halfway to her mouth. "If I knew the answer to that, I wouldn't be asking, would I?"

She chewed, swallowed, drank some wine. Watched him devour a second portion of pizza, which she had to admit was the best she'd ever tasted. Finished her first piece and took another. Rhys remained maddeningly silent, and he was taking pains to avoid looking directly at her. She began to feel uneasy. In fact, though it didn't make any sense at all, she felt a tiny twinge of something that closely resembled guilt.

"I get it," she said, attempting to lighten the somber

mood that had descended on her cheery kitchen. "We're playing twenty questions, you just forgot to tell me."

Rhys started on his third piece of pie. He took time between bites and sips of wine to give her an enigmatic look that sliced through her like surgical steel.

"*What,* for God's sake? What have I done?"

He laid down his fork, sat back, and wiped his mouth with one of the paper towels. "You tell me—what have you done?"

His damned stoicism was intolerable. "Will you please stop playing these idiotic games and tell me what the hell is wrong!" Faith snapped. "Why are you behaving this way?"

She finally got a reaction, though not one she was in any way prepared for.

"Where did you live, before you came to Louisville eight years ago?" he asked in the same emotionless tone.

Faith went cold, all over. She could only stare at him, numb with shock, unable to think, let alone formulate an answer. Not that he waited for one.

"More to the point, *who* were you? Because you sure as hell weren't Faith McRae. Apparently no such person existed until you enrolled at the university."

For a fleeting moment anger replaced her shock. Damn him. He'd been checking up on her, *investigating* her, as if she were a criminal! She couldn't sustain the outrage, though; it wasn't fair to resent him for being curious, or for following up on that curiosity. He was a cop, after all. Faith slowly laid her fork across her plate.

"I hoped you wouldn't start digging," she murmured. "But I guess I should have known you would. If you're thinking I changed my name because I'm some kind of fugitive, all I can say is that, so far as I know, I've never broken any laws. I just wanted to . . . start over."

She tried to read his expression, but couldn't. Whatever he was thinking, he wasn't letting it show.

"Why?" he said.

"Why did I want to start over?"

He nodded. Faith closed her eyes and expelled a frustrated breath. She really didn't want to give him a blow by blow account of her bizarre, rather sensational personal history. Besides, it was none of his business. None of it had anything to do with what was happening now.

"It's a long, boring story, full of overdone melodrama." Her tone was deliberately cool and discouraging. She should have known Rhys Donovan wasn't easily discouraged.

"I love melodrama, and I don't have to be anywhere till tomorrow morning."

Faith poured herself more wine, stalling. Maybe if she told him just enough to reassure him that she wasn't a criminal on the lam, he'd be satisfied.

"You know that I developed certain psychic abilities when I was a child."

"Precognitive dreams and telepathy."

"Yes." She hesitated, took a sip of wine for courage. "But those weren't the only two."

"I'd wondered," Rhys murmured. She gave him a sharp, surprised look. "I've done some reading on the subject the past few days. People don't usually display only one or two of these abilities. So what others did you have? Recognition—seeing into the past?" He pronounced it correctly, just like precognition, but with the *p* lopped off.

"No. I've tried, but . . ." She trailed off and shrugged.

"Remote viewing?"

Faith nodded. "Yes." She didn't explain that remote viewing required traveling outside your physical body. No doubt he already knew that.

"PK?"

The initials hit her like a sledgehammer. Psychokinesis: the ability to influence matter with the mind. She reached for her wineglass again. Her hand was trembling.

"Well?" Rhys prodded. "Did you ever move something just by willing it to move? Or make a glass break, or set something on fire?"

The glass slipped out of her hand. Fortunately it was

almost empty. Faith jumped up and dashed to the sink for the roll of paper towels. When she returned, Rhys was mopping up with the towels they'd used as napkins.

"Bull's-eye," he murmured. Both his tone and his expression had softened noticeably.

When she'd finished blotting the wine and tossed the soggy towels in the wastebasket, she came back to the table with a wet sponge.

"I almost killed a man." She watched her hand move the sponge over the table, unable to meet his eyes. "It was an accident. I was taking part in an experiment."

"Somebody was testing your powers, you mean."

"Yes."

Rhys suddenly reached out and laid his hand over hers. Faith gave a startled little jerk.

"What happened?"

His voice was so gentle, his touch so comforting, that her eyes filled with tears. She blinked furiously to clear them and, when that didn't work, used the back of her free hand to wipe them away. Flustered, she withdrew the hand he was sort of but not quite holding and took the sponge back to the sink to give herself an extra few seconds.

Rhys didn't ask again; he just waited patiently. When she returned to her place at the table, he'd refilled her glass. Faith tentatively reached out with her mind, scanning for negative emotion—skepticism, suspicion, fear. All she detected was sympathy, and a slightly grudging curiosity. Immensely relieved, she retracted her psychic antennae before she could pick up anything else.

"He was one of the parapsychologists who were studying me. They were fascinated with my psychokinetic abilities. Actually, obsessed by them would be more accurate. They kept coming up with new tests, each one more difficult than the last."

Rhys set her wineglass in front of her. "Such as?"

"Simple stuff, at first." She picked up the glass. One side was sticky. "Making the arrow on a game board turn without touching it, pushing a playing card across a table, turning the pages of an open book."

"You call that simple stuff?" he said in amazement.

"For me it was." Turning the glass so the sticky side was away from her, she took a sip of wine. "Then they started asking me to move things that were heavier, and bigger—dishes, a stack of books, a bag of sugar. Eventually I graduated to furniture. I kept waiting for them to take me outside and ask me to push a car uphill with my mind. I guess they didn't think of it."

"How old were you when all this started?"

"Twelve, almost thirteen."

"Entering puberty," he observed. "That fits the pattern."

"You have been reading up on this, haven't you?"

She no longer needed to scan for his reactions. She could see that he was totally absorbed in the conversation. Not repelled or disturbed, but genuinely interested. A warmth that had nothing to do with the amount of wine she'd consumed spread through her. She picked up her fork to finish the slice of pizza on her plate.

"And at some point they wanted you to try to start fires."

Faith nodded. "Just little ones in the beginning. Trying to light a candle, or an incense cone. I didn't want to do it. I was afraid, but they kept at me. Finally I gave in, just to make them stop pestering me."

"But they didn't."

She looked up in surprise. He'd said it with such certainty, as if he'd been there with her. "No. When they found out I could raise the temperature of an object until it caught fire, they pushed me even harder to do it again."

"And again, and again."

"Don't tell me," Faith said. "You knew about recognition because *you* can see into the past."

He smiled and shook his head. It was only a small, crooked smile, but it felt like a hug. "Not necessary. Anytime somebody displays a special talent—whether it's swimming or writing songs or starting fires with her mind—

jerks will come crawling out of the woodwork to exploit the person and the talent."

"That's so cynical. These people were scientists."

"So? You think scientists can't be as unethical and self-serving as the rest of us? Anybody who would force a child to do the things you're describing—"

"They didn't twist my arm, or lock me in a closet until I did what they wanted."

"But they pressured and manipulated you. 'They kept at me,' that's what you said. Why were you afraid?"

"What?"

He noticed that she'd finished the pizza on her plate and gave her another slice.

"No, I can't eat any more," Faith protested. "These jeans are too tight already."

"So unfasten them, or take 'em off. You said you didn't want to start fires because you were afraid. Why?"

She only hesitated a second before unbuttoning the waist of her jeans. If she finished the pizza he'd just put on her plate, she might have to unzip them, too. What would he think if she did? More intriguing, what would he *do?* The thought crossed her mind that she'd already drunk far too much wine. Trouble was, she'd drunk too much to care. She reached for her glass again.

"I was afraid that once I'd set that power loose, I wouldn't be able to control it, or turn it off." She ate a bite of pizza and washed it down with more wine. "This wasn't like anything I'd done before. If I dropped a bag of sugar or a stack of plates, the worst that happened was somebody had to sweep up the mess. But, Jesus, *fire!*"

Rhys nodded and poured more wine for both of them. "It's an elemental fear, for good reason. Fire is an extraordinarily destructive force. Every animal with a brain bigger than a BB fears it."

Her mouth full, Faith nodded. Leave it to a cop to use a BB as the standard for measuring brain size. How did he estimate breast size, she wondered? Smaller than a cannon ball? Bigger than a grenade? She would fall somewhere between those two. The thought almost made her laugh. Lord, she'd had *way* too much wine. She carefully pushed her glass to the center of the table.

"I think I've reached my limit."

Rhys gave her a shrewd, narrow-eyed look that intensified the concentration of his beautiful blue gaze. "You're not drunk, are you?"

"Of course not," she scoffed. "Tipsy, yep, no doubt about it. But not *drunk.*"

His wide mouth turned down at the corners. "Do you have any coffee in the house?"

"I think there's a jar of the instant stuff above the stove. I thought you were a tea drinker."

"It isn't for me," he said as he stood up.

"I told you, I'm not drunk, just a little tipsy."

Ignoring her, he located the small jar of instant coffee. "God, this stuff is fossilized. How long's it been up here?"

" 'Bout a year. No, closer to two. I bought it to make some mocha frosting. I tell you, I don't need any coffee. Anyway, I hate the stuff. It's too bitter."

"Tough," Rhys muttered as he stabbed at the jar's contents with a steak knife.

"You're not listening to me. I don't *want* any *coffee,* dammit. What're you gonna do, hold my nose and pour it down my throat?"

He took a mug from the cabinet and scraped what looked like half a cup of pulverized charcoal briquettes into it. "If that's what it takes."

She believed him.

"Not only are you a judgmental cynic, you're also an arrogant, bossy pig," she informed him. He didn't respond. "I'll gag if you make me drink that. I'll probably vomit . . . all over you."

Rhys took the mug to the sink and used the steak knife to stir water into the ground charcoal. "Wouldn't be the first time a drunk threw up on me."

He had the nerve to sound amused.

"Almost a whole bottle of wine and pizza with everything

but anchovies,'' Faith pointed out. ''And I am *not* a drunk.'' She stood up, then closed her eyes until a wave of dizziness passed. ''I'm going to my room to change into something more comfortable. Please pour that disgusting gunk down the drain.''

She pretended there was a bright red line painted on the floor and concentrated on placing one foot and then the other smack in the middle of it until she was halfway down the hall. After that she figured he couldn't see her, so she braced a hand against the wall to steady herself the rest of the way to her bedroom.

Damn. Why had she guzzled so much wine? She'd had what—two glasses? three?—at the restaurant, all on an empty stomach, followed by at least that much more here. She hardly ever drank wine, but this stuff tasted so good she'd forgotten it was booze.

As she kicked off her shoes, she heard the high-pitched hum of the microwave from the kitchen. Rhys was heating the two-year-old instant coffee. She managed to wriggle out of her jeans without falling down, then wrestled her T-shirt over her head. He wouldn't actually force her to drink it, would he? She really might throw up if he did. She might anyway, and maybe that would be for the best. If he would just leave, she'd go into the bathroom and stick her finger down her throat.

A soft *ping* alerted her that he was removing the mug from the microwave. Oh, Lord, what if he decided to bring it to her? Faith lunged for the kimono lying across the foot of her bed; but when she tried to pull it on, she discovered that somebody had sneaked in while she was at work and sewn the armholes shut.

''Shit,'' she muttered, jabbing her hand at the fabric where the right sleeve should have been.

''Allow me.''

She hadn't heard Rhys come in. His voice, right behind her, made her jump and give a startled yelp. Before she could collect her wits, his hands were on her bare skin, guiding first one arm and then the other into the appropriate sleeve. When that was accomplished, he reached around her to wrap the front of the kimono and tie the sash. Faith stood paralyzed, staring at his long, nimble fingers as if they were spiders. A tremulous sigh escaped her when he withdrew his hands, but a second later they were on her shoulders, gently turning her to face him.

Her mouth went dry.

"Here you go," he said, releasing her to reach for the mug he'd set on the nightstand. "Drink up."

Faith started to refuse, but then she caught a whiff of the familiar mingled aromas of orange rind and spices. Smiling in relief, she accepted the mug with a heartfelt, "Thank you."

He returned her smile. "You're welcome. The coffee *was* pretty disgusting."

She held his eyes as she took the first grateful sip. Heaven knew what was going to happen when the Constant Comment mixed with the contents of her stomach, but it felt and smelled and tasted wonderful going down. She didn't stop drinking until the mug was empty.

"Good girl," Rhys said, taking it from her. "Now get into bed."

Faith's eyes shot open wide. "What?"

"You, all by your lonesome," he drawled. "I'll let myself out and make sure the front door's locked."

"Oh . . . no," she stammered. "That wasn't—I didn't think—"

"Good." He didn't even try to hide his amusement. "Because I don't take advantage of women who are even just a little tipsy. Not that the idea isn't tempting."

Faith gaped at him. Tempting? He thought *she* was *tempting?*

His unexpected grin and the light tap of his finger against her chin almost stopped her heart. "Close your mouth," he murmured. But then his eyes narrowed and he stepped closer. "No, wait. On second thought, . . ."

His mouth landed on hers before Faith could anticipate the kiss. Not that she would have done anything to prevent it if she'd seen it coming. His lips were warm, smooth, mobile. Obviously he had a lot of experience at this. She was slipping toward insensibility when he eased his mouth from hers.

"Sleep well," he whispered against her lips.

When she managed to pry her eyes open, he was gone.

Chapter Nine

What in God's name had possessed him? Rhys wondered on his way home. Had he temporarily taken leave of his senses? Or, like her, just had too much to drink?

No, that was a cop-out. He couldn't blame the wine for his lapse in judgment. He hadn't drunk that much. Significantly less than Faith had, in fact.

His mouth tilted in a wry smile as he pulled into his space at the rear of the apartment building. She'd started drinking in the first place because she was tense, anxious and uncertain. Mostly because of him. His sudden withdrawal—a purely defensive reaction, though she couldn't have known that—had thrown her off balance.

And maybe she was also a little nervous because they were going out together to do something besides drive around looking for a bomb wired to an ATM.

Rhys locked the car and crossed the sidewalk to the building's rear entrance, telling himself he had no business even thinking such a thing, let alone hoping it was true. It was bad enough that he couldn't be in the same room with her without wanting to pull her into his arms and kiss her deaf, dumb and blind. This entire, bizarre situation was messy enough as it was; God knew what new problems he'd have to deal with if she shared his attraction.

Still, whatever the reasons, he could tell before they left her house that she was confused, off balance. He could almost hear her thinking *What's going on here?* And while he hadn't deliberately set out to rattle her, in the end it had worked to his advantage.

He jogged up one floor to his apartment, let himself in and tossed his sport coat on the sofa. When he'd confronted Faith about changing her identity, her reaction had been a pleasant surprise. He'd seen the flash of anger in her eyes, the slight tightening of her lips. If she'd changed her name to hide something sinister in her past, her first, spontaneous response wouldn't have been anger.

But the anger had faded quickly, and then—finally—she'd opened up about her past. No doubt about it, the wine *was* responsible for that. Rhys was certain she wouldn't have told him so much if she'd been stone cold sober. The wine had relaxed her, caused her to let down her guard and come out from behind that wall she'd built around herself.

He was beginning to understand why she'd put up the wall in the first place. Just thinking about a twelve-year-old Faith being manipulated and tested like a lab rat enraged him all over again.

He tried to convince himself that had been the reason for his impetuous kiss. It didn't have a thing to do with how much wine either of them had consumed, or the fact that when he entered her bedroom she was standing there in nothing but her bra and a pair of bikini panties, trying to find the sleeve of her robe. He'd been overcome by sympathy for the exploited child she had been, that was all.

Bullshit, an internal voice derided. *You know damn well what you were feeling wasn't anything like sympathy. Try sexual desire. Otherwise known as old-fashioned lust.*

Unflattering as that explanation was, Rhys accepted it. Almost gratefully, in fact. Labeling himself a lecher was preferable to exploring the possibility that some other, more tender, emotion might have prompted that kiss.

Making up his mind not to give Faith McRae another thought, he parked himself in front of the television to watch the evening news, just in time to catch an interview with the high school principal he'd spoken to the day before. She was telling the reporter about the vandalism to her science lab's computer. After the interview, the station's anchorwoman reported that a middle school and a private elementary school—both in the near-downtown area—had also been the targets of vandals who'd demolished desktop computers.

Technopunks, Rhys thought in disgust. Assholes with nothing better to do than trash somebody else's property. He remembered, and it hadn't been that long ago, when a vandalism report from a school meant broken windows, overflowing toilets and spray-painted walls. In the past few years the little creeps had graduated to ripping off stereo systems, TVs and VCRs. Once in a while they stole a computer, but he didn't recall a single instance of a PC being deliberately destroyed.

Which made him wonder: Why now?

He scowled at the television without seeing the leggy blonde weather girl or the kaleidoscopic map behind her. Three desktop computers trashed at three different schools. Maybe somebody had a major grudge against IBM or Apple. Or just hated computers in general.

Rhys snapped upright in his cherished brown leather-upholstered recliner as the first half of the weather report ended and the station broke for a commercial.

Computers . . . or computerization.

"Shit!"

He smacked the arm of the recliner in his excitement. That was it—the connection he hadn't been able to see. First a computer software company, then a warehouse where computerized bar code scanners were stored, and now automatic teller machines—basically computers that dispense cash and record bank transactions.

He jumped up and hurried to the phone in the bed
room. Mort Singer was working second shift this week
With any luck, he'd still be at his desk and could get the
paperwork started for another search of the mainframe'
database—this time for known cyberphobes.

Mort wasn't thrilled with the request. "I don't think
that's even a word—'cyberphobe,'" he said dubiously
"Even if I spell it right, how the hell's the computer gonna
know what it means?"

Rhys reined in his impatience, reminding himself tha
Mort was not only at the end of his shift but also happened
to be a bit intimidated by computers himself.

"That isn't what you put on the form. Use an 'and
statement to narrow the search—try 'malicious vandalism
and computers' to start with. If the database doesn't kick
out any names, I'll send through another request."

Mort grumbled about not getting home before 1:00 A.M
three times this week already. He went on to predict tha
one of these nights either his wife or their teenage son
would mistake him for a burglar and blow him to kingdom
come with his own .357 before he could get the front door
unlocked. But in the end he promised to complete the
requisition and put it with the paperwork that would go
out first thing in the morning.

Rhys thanked him and hung up. Now, if he could jus
think of a way to find out whether the computer connec
tion had occurred to agents Whitley and Hearst, and if i
had, what they'd turned up.

The explosion woke her at 2:35 A.M.

At first Faith thought it had been part of a dream. She
lay on her right side, staring at the glowing digital display
of the alarm clock, groggy and disoriented and wondering
what the dream had been about. Funny, she didn't remem
ber anything about it, except for that loud bang at the end
that had jolted her awake.

She was still facing the clock, which now read 2:39, when

she heard the sirens. More than one, so it wasn't a cop going after somebody who'd gambled and run a red light on a deserted street in the middle of the night. Some of the sirens issued long plaintive wails, while others emitted short, excited whoops.

An explosion . . . followed by sirens.

Suddenly wide awake, she scrambled out of bed and tugged on a T-shirt and a pair of sweatpants. A faint orange glow was visible from her bedroom window, between the rooftops and the star-studded sky. A fire. A big one. Only blocks away. Faith shoved her feet into a pair of shoes and grabbed her car keys.

She had to park her Geo Storm so far from the snarl of police cruisers, firetrucks and snaking black hoses that she might as well have left it at home. She approached the chaotic scene with fear and fascination, oblivious to any physical danger until somebody gave her a rough shove and a curt order to stay back.

The spectacle before her was horrifying, a video image transmitted directly from Hell. Flames completely engulfed a small single-story building and leapt ten or more feet above the roof, illuminating the helmeted, heavily cloaked firefighters and their equipment in an eerie red-orange glare. As the men battled to bring the conflagration under control, their urgent shouts were all but drowned out by the roar of the fire and the angry hiss of pressurized water being instantly transformed to billowing clouds of steam.

The asphalt street in front of the building gleamed like black glass, capturing the inferno and the men battling it in a grotesquely distorted mirror image. As the heat intensified, the very air changed, thickened, seemed to take on physical substance. Faith became aware that inhaling required a conscious effort. Her throat and lungs burned as though she were drowning in acid; tears streamed from her eyes. There must be some kind of toxic fumes in the smoke.

But there was something else . . .

She instinctively took a step back, and then another. Something was growing, building . . . something inside the fire. She could feel it. It wasn't just the smoke and the intolerable heat. There was something *here.* Hiding, gathering itself to spring through the flames . . .

She was dimly aware that someone had taken hold of her from behind and was pulling her away from the building, back down the street. She let herself be pulled, neither resisting nor cooperating, her concentration focused on the thing hidden within the fire. Suddenly she felt its energy surge, knew it was about to break free.

"No!"

She heard the hoarse cry as if from a great distance, and a small, detached part of her mind realized the sound had come from her own raw throat. Without thinking, reacting purely on impulse, she reached for the power, dragging it from the dark, forbidden place deep inside her, and sent it at the building. *Threw* it, hard—harder than she'd ever projected it before, hurling a psychic thunderbolt into the heart of the fire.

It had been so long, she'd forgotten the effect such an effort would produce. She could see the current of pure energy streaking away from her—with her mind, rather than with her eyes—but she knew no one else was aware of it. Whatever universal clock controlled the laws of motion seemed to abruptly wind down, so that everything around her appeared to be happening in slow motion. Faith knew it was only an illusion. The firefighters were still moving as quickly as their bulky gear would allow; the water still surged from the hoses with a force that would have knocked a grown man off his feet; the flames continued to leap in a mad, deadly dance.

She felt her body jerk backward, recoiling as the force she'd launched shot away from her through the shimmering air. Expecting to hit the pavement, she was surprised when she collided with a human body instead. The person who'd been dragging her away from the fire, she realized an instant later. She didn't turn to look at him, though, not even when his arms came around her to steady them both.

The thing inside the flames erupted with a ferocious roar a split second before the energy she had sent to crush it reached the building. A split second to Faith; much less to everyone else. The four firemen nearest the front wall lifted into the air as if they'd been scooped up en masse by a giant hand, soared gracefully for a dozen feet or so, then tumbled to the ground. Several others toppled like bowling pins. One of the hoses escaped and whipped back and forth across the narrow street until a uniformed policeman and a firefighter managed to bring it under control.

The fire suddenly multiplied in size and intensity, erupting upward and outward with a violence that made the firemen who were still on their feet scramble to clear the area. But a second later it was extinguished. Completely. Snuffed out as if it had been a candle on a birthday cake.

At first no one moved; the firefighters and policemen just stared in disbelief at the blackened ruins of the building. Then one by one they began to emerge from their shock and bewilderment, and went to assist those who had fallen. No one appeared to be critically injured, a miracle in itself.

"Jesus God," a stunned voice muttered in Faith's ear. It was a voice she knew. "What the hell—?"

She didn't have the strength to speak. She laid her hand on one of the bare arms encircling her waist. Her head fell back against Rhys's chest as exhaustion overcame her. The last thing she remembered hearing was his alarmed voice, saying, "Faith?"

She came around in his car, as he started the engine.

"Just sit still," he said brusquely. "The paramedics have their hands full. I'm taking you to the nearest ER."

"No." She sat up and massaged her temples. She felt utterly drained, her head was pounding and her throat hurt, but her mind was clear. "I'm all right."

He gave her a grim glance as he shifted the transmission into drive. "I'm taking you to a hospital to be checked over, so just sit back and shut up."

His tone made it clear that arguing would be a waste of time, and, anyway, Faith didn't have the energy. She sank back against the seat and closed her eyes.

The nearest hospital happened to be the brand new Gaines Memorial, just across the street from the clinic where she worked. Almost an hour and a half later—after enduring needless poking and prodding, having a vial of blood drawn and a couple of X rays taken—she was given a couple of acetaminophen tablets and instructed to go home and get into bed. It was advice she desperately wanted to follow, but first Rhys had to take her back to collect her car.

"This place is really something," he remarked as they left the hospital.

"The cutting edge of medical technology," Faith mumbled, quoting from one of the brochures she'd seen. The acetaminophen wasn't making much of a dent in her headache, not that she'd expected it to. This kind of headache didn't have a physical origin.

"Wonder how much it cost."

"Somewhere in the neighborhood of two hundred million, give or take a couple mil."

"Ritzy neighborhood," Rhys said dryly. "I was surprised how fast they got everything done. Usually you can count on a visit to the ER taking four or five hours."

"Everything's computerized at Gaines. Blood work, X rays, the patient's medical history—all analyzed and processed by the mainframe. It increases efficiency by reducing the amount of time the staff has to spend with each patient. Of course it also means less human contact."

"The price of progress, I guess." He pulled in behind her car and shifted into park, but didn't cut the engine. "You sure you're okay to drive home?"

Faith nodded, and instantly regretted the gesture when pain hammered her temples. "It's only a few blocks."

She got out of the Lumina and fished her keys from the pocket of her sweatpants. She wasn't surprised when Rhys followed her, but was when he stepped in close and put a hand under her chin, turning her face into the glare of his car's headlights.

"You look like death warmed over."

Faith grimaced. "Thank you."

"I think I should take you back to the hospital. Maybe their cutting edge computers missed something."

She knew better than to shake her head again, so she settled for reaching up and pushing his hand away. "No. I appreciate your concern, but except for a killer headache I'm fine."

"But—"

"No," she repeated firmly as she unlocked her car door and gingerly eased behind the wheel. "All I need is a good night's sleep."

She realized that had been the wrong thing to say when he followed her around the corner at the end of the block. Damn. No doubt the reference to a good night's sleep had reminded him of Rat Man, and that they'd just witnessed the result of his most recent handiwork. Which Rhys would probably want to talk about. At any other time she'd have welcomed his company, but not now. She was too disturbed by what she'd done back at the fire; she needed some time alone to think about it, sort out how she felt about it. She was much too vulnerable to deal with Detective Donovan just now.

"I don't need a babysitter or a nurse," she told him when he got out of his car and joined her on the front porch.

He didn't respond, following her inside before she could close the door. "Go get in the shower," he said quietly. "Make it as hot as you can stand it."

Faith would have argued, but it was what she'd intended to do anyway; besides, he'd already turned away and was heading for the kitchen.

The hot shower did make her feel immeasurably better,

though she was still weak and shaky—both physically and emotionally. The prospect of another question and answer session about her latest dream made her briefly consider locking herself in the bathroom till morning. The trouble with that idea was, Rhys was so stubborn he might decide to either break down the door or park himself on the other side of it and wait her out.

She pulled on her thick terry-cloth robe, grabbed a towel to finish drying her hair and crept down the hall to her bedroom. If she could get into a nightshirt and under the covers before he showed up with tea or hot milk, she'd pretend to be asleep. Surely he wouldn't so hardhearted as to wake her.

He was sitting, barefoot and cross-legged, on the middle of her bed, studying the steno pad she'd been using to keep track of the stuff she remembered from the last dream and the locations of the ATMs they'd visited.

He hadn't brought hot milk, or tea, but there was a glass of wine on the nightstand.

He put the notebook aside. "I thought you could use a drink."

"You're not supposed to combine alcohol with acetaminophen," Faith said. "But what the hell."

She draped the towel around her neck and picked up the glass, downing half the wine in a couple of nervous gulps, then closed her eyes and released a long, soughing breath. The next thing she knew, Rhys had slipped an arm around her waist and was guiding her to sit on the edge of the bed. She clutched the wineglass and prayed the belt of her robe wouldn't come untied.

He settled himself behind her, his back against the headboard, and lifted the towel from her shoulders. "You shouldn't go to bed with wet hair."

Yes, she'd heard that. She gulped more wine, then hurriedly set the glass back on the nightstand when he started rubbing the towel over her head.

"I can do that."

"Hush. How's your headache?"

Faith fought to keep her breathing steady. Headache?

"Umm, it's almost gone."

"Good."

His right hand moved to her shoulder, urging her around and back until she was leaning against his chest. When he resumed drying her hair, she couldn't keep her eyes from drifting closed.

"In case you were wondering," he murmured next to her ear, "the ATM next to that building was just installed last Friday. There's no reason you should have known about it."

He had the sexiest voice she'd ever heard, sexier even than Patrick Stewart's. Faith tried to concentrate on what he was saying, instead of the effect his voice had on her libido.

"What kind of business was it?" What she really wanted to know was, what was inside the building, but she didn't feel safe asking.

"A store that sells photographic equipment and supplies. One of the patrolmen said the fire got out of control so fast because of all the chemicals they stocked."

Faith nodded. Incendiary chemicals. That would explain both the toxic fumes and the horrendous explosion she'd anticipated seconds before it happened.

"Unfortunately the heat of the blaze destroyed any evidence Rat Man might have left—assuming he screwed up just this once and left any evidence."

He stopped rubbing her head and tossed the towel to the floor. Faith missed the sensual massage so much she wanted to complain when it ended, but a second later she felt his fingers in her hair.

"Almost dry."

Had she imagined the husky rasp in his voice, or that his touch was more caress than matter-of-fact inspection?

"Thank you." Her throat and chest felt so constricted that she barely got the words out.

Rhys's fingers continued to sift through her hair.

"You're welcome."

His face was so close to hers that she felt his breath on her cheek. And she hadn't imagined the slight rasp. Could he feel how her heart was pounding, hear the way her breath quavered in her throat? If she opened her eyes, would he interpret it as an invitation? Or might he think that anyway if she kept them closed?

His mouth brushed her temple, soft and warm and gentle. Faith stopped breathing altogether for an endless, agonizing moment . . . until she felt his lips graze her cheek—not kissing, or exerting even the lightest pressure, but serving notice nonetheless. Giving her the time and the opportunity to turn away, or push him away, or tell him to cease and desist. She didn't do any of those things.

When he reached the corner of her mouth, he stopped.

Lingered.

Waited.

A dozen seconds passed while Faith floundered in a morass of doubt and apprehension. Finally, acutely aware of the risk she was taking, she turned her head to close the inch of space that separated them.

At first the kiss was tentative. He coaxed; she responded, but timidly. His arms slipped around her, one hand cradling the back of her head while he carefully rearranged them until they were lying face to face. And then that first, experimental kiss quickly evolved into a series of eager little kisses. He sipped at her lips, rubbed his mouth over her throat, nibbled at her chin, stirring sensations that left Faith giddy and breathless.

Her hands fluttered against his shirt before they found their way to his hair. So soft and cool and silky. She buried her fingers in it, let it slide between them . . . massaging his scalp, caressing the back of his neck, delighting in the crisp line where his hair ended and his warm flesh began.

His mouth—open now, hungry and relentless—sought hers again. This kiss was long and deep and wet, an all-out assault on her defenses. His soft moan and the sudden, shocking stroke of his tongue obliterated any thought of resistance. For a moment Faith was afraid she would faint.

Before she could regain her equilibrium, his hand was at the front of her robe, tugging on the belt, pushing the fabric aside to expose her breasts. He touched her and she gasped with pleasure. Her fingers curled spasmodically, driving her nails into his shoulders. The involuntary response sent a shudder through his body that she felt in every cell of hers.

Still, nothing prepared her for the swift, consuming rush of desire when he abandoned her mouth for her breast. The first flick of his tongue across her nipple wrung a sharp cry from her throat. Her hands clutched at him frantically, one clenching in his hair, the other clawing at the material of his shirt. Rhys rolled away long enough to remove the shirt, then he was back, lifting her from the bed, dragging the robe from her. His breathing was harsh and ragged. His hands and arms trembled as he lowered her to the quilt and eased himself on top of her.

"I've been fighting this since the first time I saw you," he said hoarsely.

The feel of his erection, pushing against her through his jeans, temporarily stole her breath. "You have?" she whispered, hardly daring to believe him.

"Day and night." He took her mouth again, ravishing with lips and tongue, at the same time slowly rocking his hips from side to side.

Faith's helpless moan ended on a sob.

"You dream about a mad bomber," he muttered between voracious kisses. "I dream about you. About touching you . . ."

He caressed her breasts, stroking her nipples with his thumbs until tears leaked from her eyes, then skimmed his palms down her sides to grasp her hips and lift her into his restrained thrust.

". . . about how it would feel to be inside you . . ."

One of his hands moved between her legs, found the wet, aching center of her being.

"God! Rhys!"

She reached out blindly, working her hands between

them, fumbling with the snap of his jeans. Rhys groaned into her mouth, a desperate, wordless sound that set her blood on fire. A second later he pulled away to rid himself of the rest of his clothing and, with it, the last of his restraint.

They came together in an urgent frenzy—hands caressing, stroking, kneading; mouths inflicting pleasure so intense it crossed over into pain. The passionate moans Rhys didn't even try to hold back mingled with Faith's, stoking the flames, driving her to the brink of madness.

But as she teetered precariously between ecstasy and delirium, something incredible happened. She literally *felt* herself expanding . . . unfolding, like a tightly closed bud suddenly thrust into the heat and light of the sun. And not only her body, but her mind and heart, her very essence.

It was the most extraordinary sensation—a little like floating free of her body, but different. Better. A thousand times better.

She felt Rhys pressing against her, hot and hard, the entire length of his body taut with need, and she reached down to guide him. From his first deep, gliding stroke she was lost, swept away. Completely out of control. The sensation of opening like a flower intensified, until her most private thoughts and impressions were exposed and her mind was as naked and vulnerable as her body. Everything she felt—every tingle and quiver and explosion of indescribable pleasure—was laid bare. She might have been frightened, if there'd been room for any emotion as bland as fear. Her final, shattering climax was unlike anything she'd ever experienced before, lifting her to a plane of existence she'd never known or dreamed of.

Sometime later she drifted back to full awareness and realized that Rhys had moved to lie beside her. Faith turned her head to look at him, knowing the wonder she still felt must surely show on her face. He propped himself over her on an elbow and reached out to tenderly caress her cheek.

"All right?"

Faith nodded, not sure she'd be able to speak just yet, or what she would say if she could. The bright glitter in his eyes and the tremor she felt in his fingers betrayed that he was also shaken. But it was the bemused—no, *dazed*—expression on his handsome face that caused her stomach to knot with anxiety.

"That was . . ." He trailed off, shook his head, exhaled a shuddering breath.

Faith watched him and waited, almost afraid to breathe. A torrent of emotions poured from him—confusion, amazement, incredulity. He felt as if he'd been sucked into a whirlpool, or snatched up by a tornado, and whisked away to some strange realm where nothing was familiar and the laws of physics had all been suspended. She knew this because his chaotic, disconnected thoughts were chasing each other through *her* mind. What she couldn't know was how he would react when the shock and disorientation wore off and he started to think clearly.

Which happened sooner than she expected.

He abruptly pushed away from her, his dazed expression vanishing as he sat up and fixed her with a stare as sharp and focused as a laser.

"What in God's name was that?" he demanded.

Chapter Ten

He sounded astounded, rattled, but not—thank God—even a little afraid. Faith's anxiety loosened its grip.

"That wasn't—Was that what I think it was? I could swear—" Rhys broke off and raked an agitated hand through his hair. "Holy Christ, was I reading your mind?"

Faith looked around and spotted her robe on the carpet beside the bed, next to the damp towel. She leaned over to retrieve it and started pulling it on. Intensely aware of his piercing gaze, she forced herself to move slowly and deliberately.

"I think so."

"That's how it felt—like I was inside your head!"

She nodded silently as she secured the robe's belt with a double knot. Rhys's emotions continued to swirl in her mind like a cloud of gnats, but they weren't nearly so overwhelming or chaotic now. She thought that was a good sign. She *hoped* it was.

"I didn't intend for it to happen," she murmured, wanting to get that straight right away. She couldn't bring herself to meet his eyes.

"Is that what it's like for you . . . when you pick up other people's thoughts, what they're feeling?"

"Yes . . . but . . ." Faith felt herself blushing. "Most of the time it isn't nearly that intense."

"Intense!" Rhys surprised her with an astonished laugh. "God, Faith, *intense* doesn't begin to describe it!"

She finally looked at him. Really looked. What she saw—what she *felt*—caused a slow, delicious warmth to spread through her.

"You aren't . . . upset?"

Understanding flared in his eyes. His expression softened, his lips curving in a tender smile.

"Upset?" he repeated as he slipped a hand around to the back of her head. "As in pissed off?" His lips covered hers warmly. "Or as in stunned . . . dazed and confused . . ." He sipped at her mouth, tantalizing and reassuring at the same time. ". . . bewitched, bothered, and bewildered?"

Faith released a shivery sigh and leaned into him. "Any or all of the above."

His soft laugh filled her mouth. His emotional ardor filled her mind. His tender concern filled the dark, hollow places in her heart. It was just as well her lips and tongue were occupied, because Faith couldn't have spoken if her life had depended on it. She knew the doubts would creep in later—fear that this miraculous feeling couldn't last, that after he left her the shock and horror would take hold of him—but for now she let his acceptance envelop her and refused to think about the future.

After a while he eased away and they arranged the pillows behind them to sit against the headboard. When Rhys belatedly noticed that she'd put on her robe, he gave her a disapproving look and shifted his attention to the double knot she'd tied in the belt.

"So that's how it feels," he murmured.

Judging by the tone of his voice, his amazement hadn't started to wear off. Faith smiled at the top of his head.

"As I said, it isn't usually that intense."

He glanced up. "No, I meant the sex. So that's what it's like for a woman."

"Oh." She bit her lip in chagrin, but a second later an impish smile took possession of her mouth. "Like I said, it isn't usually that . . . intense."

Rhys finished working the knot loose and slid his arms inside the robe to pull her against him. "Good," he murmured as he reclaimed her mouth.

It was the last intelligible word either of them spoke until Faith's alarm clock went off forty minutes later.

Leon was overjoyed with his latest success. The results had been far greater than he'd dared hope for. It was a sign; it had to be. Fire was the universal cleanser. God's disinfectant.

A sign, yes. Of recognition. No, of approval!

It was time to increase his efforts, time to move on to bigger and better things.

It had been a rush to get to work on time, what with having to share first the bathroom and then the kitchen with Rhys. Did all working couples have to perform this kind of unchoreographed two-step every morning? Faith wondered as she pulled into a vacant parking space at the clinic. If so, it was no wonder the divorce statistics were so high. He was always where she had to be, taking up space she needed to occupy, and vice versa.

Of course his physical proximity had resulted in a lot of pleasurable, often downright intimate contact. That part of the two-step she could get used to without any trouble at all.

She was smiling as she entered the stairwell and started down to the PT department. The smile lasted until she came out into the lobby and almost collided with Leon Perry, who was on his way to the elevator.

"Oh! Excuse me," Faith blurted as she dodged out of his way.

Leon muttered an inaudible reply and hurried into the elevator. He seemed preoccupied, didn't even glance at her, which was fine with Faith. The less interaction she had with Leon, the better.

Her first patient arrived at eight on the dot and she was busy the rest of the morning. At a few minutes past eleven Missy Clarence came to the treatment room where she was finishing up with a high school student who'd broken his collarbone when he rode his motorcycle into a telephone pole. She had a phone call. Faith's pulse fluttered wildly. No one ever called her at work.

Hoping it was Rhys, but just in case it wasn't, she picked up the phone at Missy's desk and identified herself with a brisk, "Faith McRae speaking."

"If I didn't know better, I'd think I was talking to an IRS auditor wearing a pinstripe suit and a girdle," Rhys replied. "Quick, say something sexy so I can get that revolting image out of my mind."

Faith turned away so the patients in the waiting room wouldn't see her giddy smile.

"Sorry, that won't be possible."

"Too many people around, huh? Okay, *think* something sexy."

"What?"

"I want to test this connection or bond or whatever the hell you call it, find out if it works over the phone."

"I'm fairly sure it doesn't," she murmured. It was almost impossible to maintain a businesslike tone. The instant she'd heard that "think something sexy" her mind had flashed back to her bedroom. Specifically, to what the two of them had done there in the hour or so before her alarm went off.

"Oh, ye of little faith," Rhys drawled. "Wait, I'm starting to get a picture. It's a little fuzzy around the edges, but I think . . . Oh, yes, that's definitely us. One of us is moaning, but I can't tell whether it's you or me. Concentrate harder."

Faith shot a panicky glance at Missy, saw that she was tapping away at the computer keyboard. "You're not getting that from *me,*" she said under her breath. "My mind is a complete blank."

His soft, throaty "Liar," sent tremors of arousal coursing through her body. She closed her eyes and inhaled a deep, steadying breath. Lord help her. How could he do this to her when they weren't even in the same building?

"I know exactly what you're thinking," that deep, sexy voice insisted. "Want me to describe it, in detail?"

"That sounds . . . interesting, but it'll have to wait. I have to get back to work."

"When's your lunch break?"

Faith's heart executed a double somersault. "Uh, 11:45, I think. It's Thursday, isn't it?"

"All day. So you'll be free to leave in half an hour?"

She didn't ask what he had in mind. Her mouth suddenly felt like the Mojave Desert at high noon.

"Yes. But only for forty-five minutes."

"Okay. See you then."

He hung up before she could say anything. Faith carefully replaced the phone's handset and turned to collect the next patient's chart. As if everything were perfectly normal. As if her entire world hadn't been turned upside-down and inside-out in the past few hours. As if the crêpe soles of her shoes were actually touching the tiled floor.

Rhys sat at his desk, staring at the phone, aware of the goofy grin on his face and wondering at his own behavior. What the hell was happening to him? It was as if he'd turned into a different person during the past twenty-four hours.

It wasn't just that he'd made love with Faith, though the way it happened had been completely out of character. He never gave into impulse like that. Nowadays having indiscriminate sex was equivalent to playing Russian roulette.

And it wasn't just the telepathy or mind-melding or whatever the hell had happened while they were making love, though God knew he still hadn't come to terms with that. He'd never been an especially spiritual person, but the complete and unreserved *sharing* he'd experienced had made a believer of him. A believer in what? was the question.

In Faith, for sure. He knew now, if he'd had any lingering doubts, that everything about her was real, and honest. She was often guarded, yes, but considering what he knew about her past, that was understandable. He remembered how he'd first reacted to her story about precognitive dreams, and felt embarrassment and shame. How many times over the years had she endured that same mocking disbelief?

No wonder she'd put up walls. The wondrous thing was the way she'd let them crumble this morning. And there wasn't a shred of doubt in his mind that she had *let* it happen. He was humbled by the courage that must have taken.

He stood and collected his coat from the back of his chair. Yes, he believed in Faith. And for now that was more than enough.

He was waiting for her in the lobby, standing to one side of the elevator. Faith's heart did a little tap dance against her rib cage when she saw him.

"I wasn't sure which door you'd use," he said. "So I decided to wait inside."

"How long have you been here?"

His mouth tilted in a crooked smile that made her knees go weak. "Seventeen minutes."

Faith knew she'd come through the swinging double doors at eleven forty-five on the dot, which meant he must have left the police station within a minute or two after he hung up the phone. Ignoring the elevator, she started toward the stairwell door instead.

"I usually take the stairs."

"I should've known," Rhys said as he followed her. "I bet you're an exercise nut."

He let her get to the small corner landing halfway up and then suddenly took her elbow from behind, stepped up beside her, swung her around and backed her against the wall—all in one smooth, swift movement.

Faith heard the latch of the basement door snap into place as his mouth fastened greedily on hers. He pressed her against the wall with the entire length of his body, his hands gripping her hips, anchoring her to him. Even more devastating, he assaulted her with a flood of images and emotions, filling her mind with his desire for her . . . his desperate, driving *need.* She didn't know whether she'd become more receptive to his thoughts or if he was doing it deliberately, but the effect was shattering. When he finally released her mouth they were both trembling and gasping for breath. He held her pinned to the wall with his body.

"I just need to know one thing," he muttered. "Does this scare you as much as it scares me? Because I have to tell you, as exciting as it is, it scares the bejesus out of me."

Faith nodded. "Me, too."

He released a pent-up breath and took a step back. The instant he put some physical space between them, she felt his presence also recede from her mind. "That's good to know. Let's go get some lunch."

To her surprise, that was exactly what they did. After that no-holds-barred kiss, she'd expected him to drive straight to her house—or his—so they could spend the next half hour or so in frenzied lovemaking. Instead, he took her to a nearby Burger King.

"We need to talk," he said when they were seated at a corner booth.

Faith had started to unwrap her burger. She paused to glance at him in question. "About Rat Man? Or about us?"

"Both." A small, wry smile flitted across his mouth. "But

since we only have forty-five minutes, let's take one subject at a time."

She lifted her burger and prepared to bite into it. "Should I guess what the first subject will be?"

"Would you have to guess?"

Her mouth full, Faith nodded in reply.

"Then that answers one big question. I've been wondering if this telepathic connection will be a constant thing from now on, or if it'll only happen . . ." He trailed off, glanced around to be sure nobody was eavesdropping.

Faith swallowed and took a sip of Coke. She was a little amused by his discomfort. "If it will only happen when we're making love? I don't know. It's never happened to me before. That someone else could read *my* thoughts, I mean. Or if it has, I never knew about it."

"But based on your own experience and gut instinct, you must have an opinion."

She hesitated. "Maybe. Let me ask you a question. Just now, back at the clinic, were you consciously transmitting your thoughts to me?"

Rhys's eyebrows rose in surprise. "Consciously? No, I—" He glanced around again. Faith wondered if he was regretting that he'd brought her to such a public place. "To tell the truth, I wasn't *thinking,* period. Christ, anybody could have come along!"

"And did you pick up what I was thinking or feeling?"

A resurgent flare of desire in his eyes told her he had.

"Describe it," she asked. "Try to remember. Be specific."

"Here?" he said with a startled laugh. "Now? Jesus, Faith, we're sitting in a Burger King, surrounded by a couple dozen people."

"Nobody's paying any attention to us, and even if they were, they couldn't hear what we're saying. Tell me, what was I feeling?"

When he saw that she was serious, he set his burger on its wrapper and leaned forward. "Surprise, at first." He was careful to keep his voice low. "But only for a second.

Then I put my hands on you and pinned you against the wall, and you felt like you'd been hit by a freight train." His voice had hoarsened. "It was that fast, and that powerful—the wanting. By the time I pulled away . . ."

. . . you were wet.

Faith jerked back against the vinyl-upholstered bench. He hadn't said that last aloud. She knew he hadn't; she'd been watching his mouth, transfixed by the sensuous movement of his lips as he spoke.

"Oh my God," she breathed.

Rhys froze. "You heard that?"

She nodded mutely.

He closed his eyes for a moment, sat back, drew a deep breath and released in it a rush. "Oh, man. This is—All right, let's just stay calm, think about this rationally."

Rationally? Faith thought with a touch of hysteria. He couldn't be serious. Why had she insisted on hearing what he'd picked up from her back in that stairwell? Well, obviously, she hadn't had any idea what she was in for. Lord, had he really known—

She cut off the thought, concentrated on making her mind a blank slate.

"I guess that answers my question," Rhys said with a trace of dry humor. "Obviously we don't have to be actually making love."

"Just thinking about it," Faith muttered.

"Maybe not. Maybe we just have to be close—in terms of physical space, I mean."

She stared down at her hands rather than meet his intense blue gaze. There was an excitement in his eyes and his voice that disturbed her, though she wasn't sure why. Maybe because it wasn't the sort of reaction she was accustomed to. It certainly wasn't what she'd expected from him. In her experience, the discovery that another person could read your most private thoughts didn't provoke an enthusiastic response, or even intellectual curiosity. Most people were appalled, if not horrified. For the first time in her life, she could empathize with that reaction.

When had she clasped her hands together? The bones of her knuckles showed white through the skin. She forced her fingers to relax.

"Well?" Rhys prodded. "What do you think? We're close now, only a couple of feet apart. Let's try—"

"No!" She reinforced the refusal by throwing up an imaginary wall in her mind; a barrier to keep her thoughts in and his out.

"Why not?" Rhys's puzzled voice penetrated the barrier. "Faith? Don't do this."

His hands settled over hers, his touch light, yet firm enough that she couldn't ignore it.

"I can't." She wouldn't—couldn't—look at him. "You don't understand. I've spent the last eight years denying that part of myself, trying to forget it ever existed. I thought I'd buried it so deep I'd never have to worry that it would come back, and now—" Her voice wavered; she broke off until she could regain control.

"All this is new and exciting to you. You see it as some kind of wonderful . . . adventure. You don't have any idea what a nightmare it can be. You've only experienced a couple of episodes of telepathy, with one other person."

Rhys squeezed her hands, hard. "With one other very special person. Look at me."

She slowly lifted her gaze, trying to steel herself; for what, she wasn't sure. When she encountered the warmth and compassion in his eyes, relief poured through her, unlocking the tension that had her tied in knots.

"You're right, it is all new and exciting to me," he murmured. "But it's you who doesn't understand—Faith, *you're* the reason it's an adventure. It's sharing the adventure with *you* that makes it exciting. Christ, the idea of somebody else—*anybody* else—reading my mind would make me crazy! Remember how I reacted the first time I realized you could do it?"

Faith nodded. They'd been sitting at her kitchen table. He'd jumped out of his chair, an expression of absolute horror on his face.

"At first I felt . . . I don't know if I can describe it. Like I'd been mentally raped. But then you started explaining, and I realized you weren't reading my mind then . . . that you couldn't do it whenever you wanted, and that even if you could, you wouldn't. And after awhile the idea didn't seem so—"

"Abhorrent."

"Frightening," he corrected. "In fact, once I accepted that it was possible, my curiosity kicked in. That's when I started reading about paranormal phenomena. Some of the stuff I've read still seems . . ." He trailed off with a shake of his head.

"Spooky?"

"To put it mildly. But after what happened this morning—God, it was the most incredible experience of my life. You have to believe that. It was as if, for those few minutes, we actually became one person."

Faith didn't question his sincerity. The fervor in his voice would have convinced her, even if the passionate emotion bombarding her hadn't already demolished the barrier she'd sought to hide behind. And she understood perfectly what he was trying to express: a feeling so profound that it couldn't be described or explained, it could only be experienced.

Rhys leaned across the table until their faces were inches apart. "You admitted this has never happened to you before, that no one else has ever read *your* thoughts. Doesn't that tell you something?"

She didn't have an answer to that. In truth, she'd been afraid to let herself speculate about what it might mean.

"What's happening between us is special," he said, with a conviction that made her fears seem foolish. "I don't have a clue how it's happening, or why, but every instinct I've got is telling me not to fight it. Trust your own instincts, Faith. What are they telling you?"

Trust her instincts? That wasn't something that came

easily. Instinct couldn't be controlled or explained or understood. Like her psychic abilities, it just *was*. She'd spent years suppressing her instinctive side. Could she just throw caution to the winds now and go with what *felt* right?

Why not? If Rhys could set aside his doubts and let himself be guided by instinct, why shouldn't she?

Because he didn't have as much at stake. The risks for him weren't nearly as great.

"You're wrong," he said. He spoke quietly, with such conviction that Faith felt only mild surprise when she realized he'd been eavesdropping on her internal debate.

"I've lost my faith in the rules that made the world a familiar, if not always predictable or safe, place," he said in the same calm tone. "Suddenly there are no rules. I've got nothing to believe in . . . nothing except you, and us . . . what's happening between us. If I thought about it too long it would scare the hell out of me. But it's all I've *got* to believe in now, and my instincts are telling me that's all right, that everything will work out."

He gave her a small, coaxing smile. "If you're afraid to trust your own instincts, how about trusting mine? Could you do that, you think—try trusting me to decide what's right for both of us?"

Faith only hesitated a moment before she sent a nervous but emphatic *Yes* into his mind.

Leon sat in his truck in the parking lot, his work shirt darkened front and back with sweat, hands clenched on the steering wheel. He'd been sitting there, paralyzed by fear and confusion, for almost twenty minutes—ever since he saw Detective Donovan come out of the clinic and drive off with Faith McRae.

What was Donovan doing here? At first Leon thought the detective must have come for him—somehow the police had discovered that the statement he gave them was a pack of lies; or, worse, they'd turned up something that connected him to the bombings—and he'd almost thrown up right there in the parking lot. But then he noticed the way Donovan was looking at Faith, the familiar way his hand rested on her waist as they walked to his car, and realized the man wasn't there for him after all.

Of course, she might have complained to the police that he was harassing her, like she'd threatened to do a few months ago. But Leon didn't think she had. After the clinic manager warned him to leave her alone or risk losing his job, he'd been careful to stay out of her way. Besides, he could tell just by looking at the two of them that they didn't have police business or clinic business or any other kind of business on their minds.

Lust, that was what they had on their minds. No doubt they'd gone off together to spend their lunch hour fornicating like wild animals.

Leon's apprehension metamorphosed to scorn and simmering anger. He was disappointed in Faith McRae. When he was first assigned to the clinic, he'd seen the goodness in her, the decency. But he'd also seen that at some point she'd taken a wrong turn and was headed down the road to depravity and ruination. He'd tried to guide her back to the right path, tried to save her before it was too late, but she'd foolishly rejected his counsel.

She continued to paint her face, wear men's trousers, and work at a job that wasn't at all suitable for a decent woman. Leon had seen the way she *handled* nearly naked male patients. Only the men therapists should work with other men; it wasn't right for people of the opposite sex to touch each other in ways that could only provoke immoral thoughts. And as if her behavior wasn't damning enough, just this week he'd heard from one of the clinic's insurance clerks that she and the black man had convinced the doctors to install some new exercise equipment in the PT department. Computerized equipment.

He had considered trying to talk to her again, make her realize the error of her ways. Now that he'd seen how she and the policeman were together, he knew it was too late.

When the time came to reveal the Truth, he thought he might make an example of Faith McRae.

An example, yes, he liked that idea. Maybe those who witnessed her destruction would be moved to set their own feet upon the right path, before it was too late for them.

Chapter Eleven

Rhys dropped her off in the clinic parking lot at twenty-seven minutes past noon. He didn't say "I'll see you tonight," but they both knew he would.

Faith probably would have spent the entire afternoon thinking about him, about the things they'd both said at lunch, if Tommy Carver hadn't come in for a therapy session at 1:15. Tommy's shoulder and ankle were almost completely healed, his strength and mobility nearing pre-injury levels. He wouldn't need physiotherapy sessions much longer.

"How did the MRI turn out?" Faith remembered to ask as they finished. Tommy was his old ebullient self today, talking her ear off about his roller hockey team and the new in-line skates his dad had bought him.

"A-OK," he said with a grin. "The headaches stopped, too. It was weird. I'd been having at least one killer headache every day, sometimes two or three, then one morning I woke up and they were gone. I haven't had one in more than a week. The doc thinks it might've been a temporary reaction to something I'd come in contact with."

"That's good news," Faith said. "And are you sleeping better now that the headaches have stopped?"

"Oh, yeah, much better. Well, except for the dreams."

Her heart lurched in reaction. "Dreams?"

Tommy nodded. "Majorly bizarre ones. I'd tell you about 'em, but you'd think I'm crazy."

"No, I wouldn't," she assured him. "As a matter of fact, I've been having some pretty bizarre dreams myself."

"You have? What about?"

Her hesitation was so brief he probably didn't notice it. "The bomber."

Tommy's eyes opened wide in astonishment. "No lie?"

"No lie. I saw him planting the second and third bombs, and—"

"And then the cash machine where the last one went off," he interrupted. His voice cracked with excitement.

"You, too?" Faith asked. Her head was spinning.

"Exactly the same thing! Oh, man, this is weirder than weird. Did you see the flowers?"

"Daisies," she confirmed. "And the metal plates with instructions in Braille."

"Braille? Oh, right—those shiny metal things with the bumps! That was Braille? Wait, that doesn't make any sense. Blind people don't drive cars."

"But they can walk up to an automatic teller machine," she pointed out. "Have you seen his face?"

"Hunh-uh. You?"

She shook her head. "The first few times it was too dark, and the last time he wasn't there."

Tommy nodded enthusiastically. "The bomb was, though. They didn't say so on the news, but I'd bet anything that was the explosion that set the photography store on fire last night."

Faith resisted the impulse to confirm his theory. On the one hand, it was tremendously exciting to know that someone else had been having Rat Man dreams. Yet at the same time, she knew the burden those dreams brought with them. The less Tommy knew, the better . . . for him.

"Have you told anybody else about these dreams?" she asked.

Tommy's snort implied he thought she was nuts for asking. "No way! They'd either haul me off to one of those psychiatric hospitals or figure I was making it all up, to get attention or something. Besides, I haven't seen the sicko's face, or an address on a building or even a street sign, so what good would it do? I'd just cause a lot of trouble for myself, and maybe my parents, and the cops still wouldn't know anything important."

His pragmatism amazed her. If only she'd been as savvy at his age.

"Anyway," he added as he tugged on his high top sneakers, "I haven't had a dream since Monday night. Maybe I won't have any more. They could've just stopped, like the headaches."

"But you hope they haven't," Faith guessed.

"Well . . . it is kind of exciting. Except if I'm gonna dream about the guy, I wish just once I'd get a good look at his face, or at least be able to tell where he's planting the bombs."

An icy chill spiraled up Faith's spine. "No, Tommy, get that thought right out of your head. If you're going to wish for anything, wish that you won't have any more of those dreams."

He made a face. "C'mon, don't tell me you wouldn't like to see his face. If we could identify him for the cops, we'd be heroes—prob'ly get our pictures in the paper, maybe even get to be on Oprah with all the other weirdos."

"Is that how you want people to think of you? As just another weirdo?"

"That's how most people think of me already," Tommy said with a shrug and a grin.

Faith would have tried to reason with him—actually, what she wanted to do was give him a good hard shake—but he grabbed his skate bag and headed for the door.

"Gotta motor," he tossed over his shoulder as he left. "Mom's taking me to get some new Fat Boy wheels."

Her next appointment wasn't for forty-five minutes, so after Tommy left, Faith went to the break room and spent some time catching up on paperwork. The last part of their conversation continued to trouble her, but she told herself that so long as Tommy kept the dreams to himself, he'd be all right. She fervently hoped he wouldn't have another one; or that, if he did, he still wouldn't be able to see Rat Man's face. She suspected that if he thought he could identify the bomber, young Mr. Carver would head straight to the police. Or, just as likely, to the nearest newspaper office or television station.

Faith closed the last patient folder and added it to the three others she'd brought up to date. As she started to stand up, intending to take the records to Missy so she could transcribe and file them, she felt as if the air pressure in the room had suddenly changed. It was the same sensation she'd experienced the one and only time she'd been on an airplane, when the plane took off and again when it started to descend for landing. Yes, the uncomfortable pressure in her ears was exactly the same . . . except that now it was followed almost immediately by a droning, low-pitched hum.

It was the hum that lifted the hair at Faith's nape and made her collapse back onto the molded plastic chair. It wasn't just a noise that she *heard;* she *felt* it with her whole body—a soft, steady vibration, like hundreds of bees trapped in a glass jar. The Manila file folders slipped from her hand and went sliding across the table.

"No," she whispered. "Please, no . . ."

But she knew, even as the prayer passed her lips, that it was too late. She looked down at her hands for confirmation. They were pale, the color bleached from her skin like a photograph that's been left for days or months on a table next to a sunny window. Her hands continued to fade as she watched, and then her fingers started to melt, dissolving like icicles under a blowtorch. The melting continued until there was nothing at the end of her wrists.

Not bones or muscles or bloody stumps where her hands had been. Nothing.

Stop it!

The command reverberated through her mind, though she didn't say it aloud. She couldn't have if she'd tried; her body was already beyond her control. Her conscious mind was keenly alert, though, registering her surroundings with heightened awareness.

The walls and ceiling seemed to have retreated, so that the break room appeared to be three or four times its actual size. The monotonous whine of the small refrigerator competed with the vibrating hum inside her. The smell of coffee was so strong it stung her nose, and the fluorescent lights overhead irradiated everything in the room with a brilliant white glare that was almost blinding.

Faith was aware of all these things, but she didn't let herself focus on any of them. It was the attempt to concentrate on physical objects that triggered the perception of melting. She didn't know why this was so, but it always had been. If she tried to *look* at any part of her body during a waking dream, it always dissolved right in front of her eyes.

Waking dreams. That was the name she'd given the phenomenon as a child. The parapsychologists called it astral projection. They'd told her it almost never happened spontaneously, that most people had to undergo years of training and practice to master the ability, and that many who tried never did achieve success. Making it sound as if Faith was somehow blessed because it happened to her all the time, without the slightest effort. She hadn't felt blessed. It was a frightening, completely out-of-control experience.

For a moment an old, familiar panic seized her. Why was this happening? Why *now?*

But then she abruptly descended into the trance state, leaving the fear and dread behind in the physical world.

She knew she'd entered a deep trance because she felt so cold—not the kind of external chill that makes you shiver and break out in goosebumps, but a bleak, numbing cold that originated deep inside—and also because she could feel herself, her consciousness, floating free of her body.

Everything was suddenly distorted and unreal. The walls and furniture assumed warped, twisted shapes, as if they had partially melted and then solidified. The top of the table reminded her of a cheap plastic dish she'd once put in the microwave by mistake—edges drooping toward the floor, center bubbled and translucent so that she could make out the blurred shapes of her white shoes beneath it. They were ridiculously long, clown shoes, while the file folders had shrunk to playing card size.

She glanced at the clock above the door. The second hand had all but stopped. Even her thoughts had become slow and sluggish, as if she'd been given a powerful anesthetic.

Trippin'.

That's what one of the parapsychologists had said when she described what it was like to him. He'd remarked that, back in the sixties, thousands of hippies and hippy wannabes had fried their brains with hallucinogenic drugs trying to achieve the same transcendental experience.

The memory made Faith smile, but it was a small, melancholy smile. Despite the uncomfortable cold and a slight disorientation that she'd never gotten used to, a feeling of calm acceptance settled over her, because she knew she could return to her body at any time. It wasn't the waking dreams, per se, that alarmed her but the sudden exit, often without any warning, into the astral plane.

Why now? she wondered again. What had caused this? When she was young, it had usually happened just before or after some traumatic event. She'd had a lot of waking dreams while they were testing her "gifts," and especially when they were pressuring her to start fires. Maybe what happened last night had triggered this one. Not just Rat Man's handiwork, but what *she* had done. She'd promised herself that she would never again summon that power. It was too dangerous, too unpredictable.

Yes, that was probably what had triggered this waking dream. Everything had happened so fast last night, there wasn't time to think about whether she should use the power, or what the consequences might be if she did. And she hadn't had a chance since to examine her feelings about it. Maybe this was just her subconscious mind's way of getting her attention . . . *making* her think about it.

That must be it, because nothing was *happening*. Always before, something startling or upsetting happened during a waking dream. Nothing at all was happening now. She was just hanging out in the break room, all by herself, watching the walls curl and the furniture melt.

She'd better get back into her body, before Dirk or Rollie came in and found her sitting there staring into space like a zombie. She concentrated on returning and felt herself start to sink like a helium-filled balloon that had lost most of its helium.

Just as she felt the all-over tingle—sort of like a low-voltage electric shock—that preceded the return of physical control, another feeling blindsided her.

An overwhelming sense of menace.

A dark, malevolent presence that hovered just out of sight.

A presence that was sending a strong current of hostility toward her.

The sensation was so overwhelming, so *real*, that Faith reacted by thrusting herself back into her physical body, with such force that for several seconds she skated close to the edge of unconsciousness. She fought frantically to pull herself away from the dark void. If she passed out, there was a good chance her psychic self would drift free of her body again. And if that happened, she knew with a crystalline clarity that whatever was out there, waiting, would spring.

Several minutes passed before she regained enough composure to collect the folders and leave the break room. She was tense and jumpy the rest of the afternoon, constantly on guard against the onset of another waking dream. Thankfully, it didn't happen; but by the time she left the clinic she felt like one large, exposed ganglion.

When Rhys appeared at her front door at a quarter to six, bearing two rib-eye steaks, a bottle of wine, a loaf of Italian bread and the makings for a salad, she still hadn't decided whether to tell him about the waking dream. He gave her a lingering kiss at the door, then stepped back to study her with a focused intensity that made her even more edgy. Faith knew right away that he'd picked up something—some telepathic signal that triggered his detective's instincts. Evidently he decided not to question her, though, for which she was grateful.

She should have known that his patience wasn't limitless. He waited till they finished washing and putting away the dishes, then took her hand and led her into the living room. Faith was hoping they'd walk straight through and on down the hall to her bedroom, but he released her when they reached the couch, uttered a quiet but firm, "Sit," then went to the stereo and put on a CD.

Leonard Cohen's gravelly voice rumbled from the speakers. Not exactly her idea of music to make love by. She tried to discern Rhys's mood—but not his thoughts; she was careful to avoid invading his mind—as he came to sit beside her. All she could detect was concern. For her, no doubt, because of the distress he'd sensed.

"All right," he murmured, slipping an arm around her shoulders. "Tell me what happened this afternoon. And don't say nothing happened, because I know damn well something did."

It was his tone, rather than what he said, that decided her. It wasn't the cop, demanding; it was her lover, asking. So she told him.

He took it better, more calmly, than she'd expected. Of course, she should know by now that Rhys Donovan was anything but predictable.

"Was it a *person* you sensed?"

"Yes. I'm sure it was, but I didn't see a physical image.

There was just a powerful feeling of darkness, and menace."

Rhys's forehead creased in a thoughtful frown and he asked the question that had already occurred to her. "You think it might have been Rat Man?"

"It's possible, I guess. If he's telepathic, he could've picked up my memories of the dreams. Lord knows I've thought about them a lot the past three weeks—while I stood in line at the grocery store or the bank, when I dropped off clothes at the dry cleaners, at work. . . . But let's be honest, it's not very likely that I've crossed paths with another telepath. And even if I have, and he just happened to be Rat Man, how could he know it was *my* thoughts he'd intercepted?"

"Maybe he doesn't," Rhys murmured. "Maybe the animosity you felt this afternoon was directed at somebody he can't identify, but senses is a threat."

Faith shook her head, unconsciously rubbing her hands over her arms as she remembered the fierce hostility she'd felt in the break room. Rhys drew her a little closer in response.

"No." Her voice was low and husky. "Whoever it was, he knew me." She turned her head to look at him. "He knows who I am, and he *wants* me . . . wants to hurt me."

Rhys didn't ask if she was sure. She knew he could feel her certainty, and her fear. He wrapped his other arm around her and pulled her onto his lap. He didn't speak for a full minute. When he did, what he said stunned her.

"Whoever it is—Rat Man or some other psycho—if he comes after you, do whatever you have to to protect yourself."

Faith pushed against his chest, leaning back so she could look into his eyes. She saw that he was utterly serious. Nausea swirled in her stomach.

"You don't know what you're saying."

"Yes I do," he replied grimly. "If the only way you can keep the bastard from hurting you is to turn him into a cinder, that's what you do."

Faith felt as if he'd punched her in the stomach. She shoved out of his embrace and scrambled off his lap. He impulsively reached for her, but she evaded his hand. "No, don't!"

She wrapped her arms around her midriff, hugging herself, and backed away until she'd put several feet between them. Her head started to pound. Her skin felt prickly all over, as if she'd run through a field of cornstalks. She recognized both sensations, from long ago. They frightened her even more than the presence she'd felt that afternoon.

Rhys slowly got to his feet, but he didn't come after her. "Would you rather let him hurt you, maybe kill you?" he said softly.

"If it comes to that . . . yes, I would."

"That's crazy, Faith. You have the ability to stop anybody who tries to hurt you, dead in his tracks, and you'd be acting in self-defense."

She shook her head vehemently, her eyes squeezed shut. "Stop it! You don't know what you're talking about. You don't have any idea—"

She opened her eyes to give him a hard, angry look. "I could make your blood boil in your veins, just by picturing it in my mind and concentrating very hard. I could set your clothes on fire . . . or your hair. Break your bones, maybe even make your heart explode."

Rhys was obviously taken aback, but a reflexive narrowing of his eyes was his only outward reaction. His equanimity made her want to slap him.

"You could do all that?"

"Without breaking a sweat," Faith assured him. She inhaled a deep, cleansing breath and raked both hands through her hair. The prickly feeling had subsided, but her head felt like a crew of little men were bashing at the inside of her skull with tiny sledgehammers.

He said her name, then paused. She felt his reluctance like a physical touch. "Last night, at the fire. Did you . . . do something?"

Faith averted her eyes before she answered. "Yes. I knew there was going to be an explosion, and I sent a bolt of psychic energy to stop it. Don't ask me how I knew, or how I did what I did, because I can't tell you. I just did."

He didn't respond right away. She gathered her courage and looked at him. "How did you know? Did you sense that I was feeling guilty?"

"No." The question clearly surprised him. "The ATF forensic team found fragments of a container—one of those big, heavy plastic barrels. According to the owner of the store, it contained an extremely incendiary chemical compound. A few jagged pieces are all that's left of the barrel, and they haven't found even a trace of chemical residue. The fire marshal says it's possible an explosion of that size might have snuffed out the fire, but it probably would have killed several firefighters and blown out windows four or five blocks away."

"And there should be some chemical residue," Faith murmured.

"There should be, yes. But it's as if whatever was in the barrel just vanished—dematerialized or something."

Faith shook her head, her shoulders sagging in exhaustion. "Maybe that's what happened. I told you, I don't understand how I did it, or how the power works. I never have. Don't you see—that's why it's so dangerous. I can never be sure I'll be able to control it once it's out."

Rhys came to her and placed his hands on her shoulders. His touch was light but intimate, and he was standing very close, only a breath away. She resisted the desire to collapse against him.

"It got out of control once, didn't it?" he said softly. Faith stiffened in involuntary reaction. His hands began a slow, gentle massage. "You told me you'd almost killed a man, one of the parapsychologists who were studying you," he reminded her. His voice had the same tranquilizing effect as the rhythmic movement of his lean, strong fingers. "What happened?"

She didn't want to talk about it—not now, not to him—

yet she found herself doing exactly that. First she explained the experiment. They'd arranged thin strips of kindling into a tipi shape on a metal tray, which was placed on a table in the center of the room. They brought her in and sat her on a chair against one wall, with her back to the table. She'd thought at the time, she told him, that they'd made her face the wall because they suspected she was sending rays out of her eyes to set the wood on fire. That's how stupid she'd been.

"Not stupid," Rhys said gruffly. "Young, and innocent."

Faith closed her eyes and rested her head on his chest. When had he put his arms around her? When had hers found their way around his waist?

"They showed me the wood first, so I'd know what I was supposed to set on fire. Then they put me on the chair and told me not to look at it again, to just concentrate on making it burn." She paused, bit her lip.

"It took a long time. I concentrated as hard as I could, but I couldn't tell if it was working. I didn't smell smoke, and the only thing anybody said to me was 'Keep trying, don't quit until we tell you.' I started to worry that I wasn't going to be able to do it, and they'd be angry. So I saw the sticks in my mind, then reached down for the power and *pushed* . . . as hard as I could. Since my back was to the table, I didn't know that one of them had bent over to check the thermometer beside the tray."

"Oh, Jesus," Rhys muttered.

"I pushed too hard, and he was too close to the wood. When I heard him scream, I turned around. One of the others grabbed the fire extinguisher and started spraying him. He wasn't badly burned, but most of his hair was gone and there were holes in his clothes. The wood got so hot, so fast, that it just exploded." She drew a shuddering breath. "I'll never forget the sound of his scream, the smell of burned hair . . . or how I felt, knowing I'd done that to him."

Rhys's embrace tightened until it was almost painful. "It wasn't your fault." Faith both heard his anger and felt it, a fierce crimson current streaming from his mind into hers. "You were a *child,* for God's sake! They used you, manipulated you as if you were some lab animal. Where the hell were your parents? Why did they let those bastards experiment on you like that?"

"My parents?" She tried to hold back the bitter tears—foolish and futile to cry; it never changed anything and only made her angry at her own weakness—but they leaked out and dampened the front of his shirt. She did manage to keep her voice steady, though, reciting the facts as if she were talking about someone else.

"My father left when I was a baby. After that it was just my mother and me. She was—She had very strong religious beliefs. When I first started to exhibit these unusual abilities, she decided I was possessed by the Devil."

Rhys didn't speak, but his anger increased tenfold.

"She took me to a country preacher, convinced him to perform an exorcism. Some of our neighbors found out and filed a complaint with the local child welfare office. At some point somebody talked to a reporter, and . . . well, you can imagine the kind of publicity the story generated—'Mom Says Daughter Possessed By Demons.'

"That's how the parapsychologists found out about me. Two of them were a married couple. They petitioned the court to have my mother declared unfit, then convinced the judge that I needed intensive long-term counseling as a result of the trauma I'd suffered." She laughed harshly. "If the judge had any idea what kind of trauma he was setting me up for, I doubt he'd have made them my legal guardians."

"How long were you with them?"

"I left on my eighteenth birthday. I'd received an academic scholarship to the University of Louisville. I couldn't wait to get out, my suitcases were packed weeks ahead of time. By then my powers had diminished considerably, so they didn't try to convince me to stay. Besides, they'd found two other, even more 'gifted' girls they were eager to start testing."

"What about your mother? Did you ever see her, after you went to live with them?"

Faith shook her head. "They offered to arrange visits, but she refused."

His condemnation of her mother seared her mind. She lifted her head, overcome by a surprising desire to purge him of the hurtful, destructive emotion. "She didn't hate me, Rhys. She was afraid of me. She loved me, but the love wasn't strong enough to overcome the fear."

He brought one hand around to gently wipe the moisture from her cheek. "It should have been. She should have known you'd never do anything to hurt her."

He slid his hand into her hair and bent to kiss her. It was more than a kiss, though. It was a promise . . . a solemn covenant. As his lips moved tenderly upon hers, the realization broke through like the sun bursting from behind a thundercloud.

He hadn't been afraid. Never, not once, had he felt fear for his own safety.

Not even when she'd stared straight into his eyes and said things that should have struck terror into his heart—*I could make your blood boil in your veins . . . set your clothes on fire . . . break your bones. . . .*

Not even when she told him about the parapsychologist, described the man's scream.

"Hush," Rhys murmured gruffly as he drew her closer.

Faith smiled through a fresh welling of tears and reached up to wrap her arms around his neck. She hadn't said a word.

Chapter Twelve

Rhys didn't stay the night, but he might as well have; it was almost three o'clock when he left. Friday morning Faith smacked the snooze button on her alarm one time too many and had to rush like crazy to make it to work by eight. After a five-minute shower she dashed back to her bedroom and started collecting clothes with one hand while she raked a comb through her still damp hair. As she hustled between closet and dresser, her left foot came down on something that went skidding across the carpet. Slacks, blouse, and comb flew in three different directions as she windmilled her arms to regain her balance.

"What the hell!"

After gathering the items she'd dropped, she picked up the steno book she'd been using to record her precognitive dreams. The last time she remembered seeing it was Wednesday night, after the fire. Rhys had been sitting on the bed reading it. Faith tossed the notebook onto the bed along with her clothes before turning away to fetch clean underwear. When she'd finished dressing, she impulsively stuck the steno pad in her purse, thinking she would go over her notes at work, during one of her breaks.

Traffic was a bitch and the waiting room was already half filled when she arrived for work. The morning went downhill from there. Mr. Baylor hadn't been doing his range of motion exercises at home and consequently both his elbow and shoulder had started to lock up. He grumbled and moaned during his entire half-hour session. After the first ten minutes, Faith tuned out his complaints and put more weight behind her manipulations. *You big crybaby,* she wanted to say. *Next time you decide to go 'blading, maybe you'll wear some protective gear.*

Her next two patients weren't in any better mood than Mr. Baylor. Must be something going around; or maybe everybody else in Louisville had skipped breakfast today, too. By ten, Faith was grumpy and famished. Fortunately she'd stashed a couple of bagels in the break room fridge. Except when she opened the door, she discovered that her bagels had been replaced by half of a gnawed-on, badly dehydrated tuna salad sandwich.

"Dammit, Dirk!" she muttered, tossing the sandwich into the wastebasket. She should have known better than to leave food where he could find it. Even a "Hands off!" note usually didn't deter him. He seemed to think anything left in the break room was community property.

"Ow!"

The startled exclamation made her turn toward the door, where Dirk stood frowning down at the back of his right hand.

"You took my bagels," Faith accused. A second later she noticed his pained expression. "What's wrong, slam the supplies locker door on your hand again?"

"No," Dirk said peevishly. He cautiously flexed his fingers. "Damn, that's weird. It felt like somebody smacked my hand."

"Somebody should," Faith retorted. "And somebody will, if she ever catches you stealing food she paid for."

"All right, already, I'm sorry! I was hungry."

"Then why didn't you finish your own sandwich?"

Dirk ignored the question, waggling his right hand as

he strolled past her to help himself to one of Rollie's Diet Pepsis from the fridge. "Besides, I figured if you wanted the bagels, you'd have taken 'em home."

Faith heaved a resigned sigh and told herself it was no use trying to reform him. He had always been and would always be a world class jerk. "Let's see your hand."

Dirk shifted the Pepsi to his left hand and presented the right for inspection. "Jeez, now it's red. Maybe it's some kind of contact dermatitis."

"Looks more like somebody smacked it," Faith murmured.

A chill slithered up her spine and spread icy tentacles across her scalp. It was only a coincidence that she'd been thinking about the "Hands off!" sign Dirk had ignored on her carton of strawberry yogurt last month . . . wasn't it?

"You must have whacked it against the wall or the doorframe."

"Sure," he said. "I banged it hard enough to leave a red mark, but somehow I didn't notice. I tell you, I didn't do anything to it. I was walking down the hall, and just before I got to the door I felt this sharp, stinging pain—like a slap. Weird."

Weird, indeed, Faith thought. "Well, the redness is already fading, so it probably isn't anything to worry about."

"Did I say I was worried?"

She dropped his hand. "Of course not. How silly of me." Macho Man Malloy, admit he was worried? That would be the day.

Faith rummaged through the cabinets and found some stale crackers and an almost empty jar of peanut butter, and managed to wolf down four mini-sandwiches before her next patient arrived. She tried not to think about the incident with Dirk, but it kept creeping back into her mind to nag at her. She told herself she couldn't be responsible for that "sharp, stinging pain" he'd felt. She had never intentionally hurt another person; and anyway, she would have to consciously *will* something like that. At least, she thought she would. That was how PK had always worked in the past.

But what if it didn't work that way anymore? What if her control had deteriorated over the years, or the power had grown stronger—or, God forbid, what if both those things had happened?

The possibility was too disturbing to contemplate, but much as she'd have liked to pooh-pooh it away, she couldn't. All the powers she had conned herself into believing she'd lost or outgrown had suddenly been revived during the past three weeks—precognitive dreams, telepathy, astral projection. . . . Even the psychokinesis. The night before last, at the fire, she'd proven beyond any doubt that she still had the ability to affect physical objects with her mind.

And now the business with Dirk's hand . . .

She'd half expected Rhys to show up to take her to lunch, and was relieved when he didn't. She was too upset and, if she was honest, scared, and she wouldn't have been able to hide it. She needed time to think things through, try to come up with some answers or explanations.

Dirk went out for a fast food lunch, so at least she didn't have to confront him again. She was finishing a hard boiled egg she'd grabbed on her way out of the house when Rollie entered the break room. He went to turn on the radio, then took a few seconds to tune in an oldies station. Faith hastily closed the steno pad and slid it under the newspaper someone had left on the table. Apparently Rollie had forgotten their conversation about her Rat Man dreams. At least he hadn't mentioned the subject or asked if she was still having them, and she didn't want to jog his memory.

When he was seated across the table with a ham and Swiss sandwich and a bag of pretzels, she asked about the patient he'd just seen, a soccer player recovering from surgery to repair a torn Achilles tendon. They spent the remainder of Faith's lunch break discussing patients and their various ailments.

The radio station's bottom-of-the-hour local newscast began as she tossed a handful of eggshell and an empty milk carton into the wastebasket on her way out of the break room. A reference to Gaines Memorial Hospital caught her attention, and she loitered while the young news reader announced that the formal dedication ceremony would take place the following Tuesday.

"Oh, great, a weekday," Faith complained. "I hope this shindig won't get underway till after we've headed home."

"No such luck," Rollie said. "They're having an all-day open house, followed by a bunch of speeches by public officials and benefactors starting around three, and then the board's hosting a cocktail party and black tie dinner in the hospital auditorium for all the bigshots."

"Well, we might as well plan on bringing our jammies to work next Tuesday. We'll never get out of the parking lot."

Rollie nodded. "I'm seriously thinking about taking the bus. If the rumors flying around the hospital are true, we might not be allowed to park at the clinic, anyway."

"Allowed?" Faith echoed indignantly. "We work here! We're more entitled to a parking space than some society matron or sleazy politician, for Pete's sake."

"Guess that depends on the politician." He started to say more, paused, slid a quick look over his shoulder to make sure no one was eavesdropping. "According to the grapevine, there's a chance some of the security for the dedication will be provided by the Secret Service."

"What! You're kidding."

Rollie shook his head and took a bite of his sandwich.

"Who? The President? The Vice President?"

"Nobody knows," he said around a mouthful of ham and Swiss cheese. "Or at least nobody's admitting they know. But the hospital administrator received several calls from the Secret Service this week, and yesterday morning four guys in suits and starched white shirts were checking out the auditorium."

"Wow," Faith murmured. "If it's true, I wonder why

the hospital hasn't made an announcement. You'd think they'd want to capitalize on a coup like that."

"It's just a guess, but I suspect the mystery guest, whoever he is, is waiting to see if they catch the bomber before he commits to visiting our fair city. Or it could be that he wants to come, but the Secret Service doesn't think it would be such a good idea." He suddenly sat up straight. "Hey, I bet your detective could find out who the mystery guest is!"

Faith liked the sound of that "your detective," but she shook her head dubiously. "I doubt it. I don't think he knows anybody in the Secret Service." The ATF, maybe, but not the Secret Service.

"You could ask, couldn't you?"

"Okay, I will . . . if I remember." She headed for the door, afraid that if this conversation continued, it would jog his memory about the dreams.

"So you've been seeing him, huh?" Rollie asked before she could get away.

"Mm-hmm." She made a big deal of checking her watch. "Oh, jeez, look at the time."

He flashed a good-natured grin. "All right, I can take a hint. By the way, have you had any more of those dreams?"

"Not for a while," Faith hedged. Since Monday night, to be specific.

"I bet it was a relief when they stopped, huh? Having my nightmares come true would scare the hell out of me."

"They were pretty upsetting," Faith admitted. Before he could say anything else, she glanced at her watch again and muttered, "Gotta run, Rollie. I'm already five minutes late for Mrs. Hooper's appointment."

There'd been good news and bad news waiting when Rhys arrived in the squad room—ten minutes late—Friday morning. The good news was that agents Whitley and Hearst were no longer in charge of the bomber investigation. The bad news was that they'd been replaced by a more senior ATF agent and a special agent from the FBI, who were now coordinating the work of close to a dozen federal agents, including four from the Secret Service.

"The Secret Service," Rhys said with a frown. "Why the hell would they be involved in this investigation?"

"Obviously they know something we don't," Herb Aikers replied under his breath.

He and Mort Singer had gravitated to Rhys's desk as soon as Buford Jackson retreated to his office. It was where the three of them congregated for private powwows, since it was the desk farthest from the lieutenant's office door. They'd automatically closed ranks while they waited for the feds to arrive for a departmental briefing.

"And obviously they ain't gonna share whatever it is they know," Mort added sourly.

Rhys rocked back in his swivel chair and stared at the yellowed ceiling tiles. God, he was beat. Too many late nights, too much on his mind—including the nagging worry that he'd fallen head over heels in love with a woman who could literally read his mind—and now he was going to have to deal with a bunch of cowboys from Washington.

"Maybe there's a counterfeiting tie-in, or some kind of credit card fraud," Herb suggested. "Either of those would fall under the Secret Service's jurisdiction. The bomber's hit three ATMs now, and lot of people use their credit cards at cash machines."

"But if they'd established a connection to any kind of bank card theft or forgery, the Secret Service would be in charge," Rhys pointed out. "Lieutenant Jackson said the ATF guy from D.C.–whatsizname—"

"Gonzales," Mort supplied. "Donald Gonzales."

"Right. According to the lieutenant, Gonzales and Eberhardt from the FBI are running the show, and the Secret Service is only 'monitoring' the investigation."

"Which is still more than we've been doing," Mort grumbled.

"That's about to change," Herb said. "Otherwise they wouldn't be coming in to brief us."

"Don't you just love playing catch-up?" Rhys said to the ceiling.

"Almost as much as I love playing second fiddle," Mort replied. "You sick or something? You look like shit."

Rhys sat up and grimaced. "Nothing a couple of gallons of coffee wouldn't cure."

A half-dozen sober-faced bureaucrat types appeared at the squad room door and filed solemnly to Lieutenant Jackson's office.

"Better grab that coffee while you can, Rhys," Herb murmured. "Looks like the *federales* have arrived."

The light inside him—the light of Truth—had grown so strong that he was surprised it didn't leak out through his mouth and ears and eyes.

Leon suppressed a giggle at the thought. Wouldn't that be something? The pathetic, lost souls who surrounded him would be dumbstruck at the sight. The doctors at that new hospital across the street would probably fight each other for the chance to examine him, in their zeal to discover the cause of such an astonishing phenomenon.

Rage swelled inside him, casting a red veil over the light. Fools, all of them! Dangerous fools, so dependent on their precious technology that they'd forgotten how to heal without it.

Well, they would soon realize their mistake. Soon, *very* soon, they would all experience the blinding light of Truth. Of course a lot of them wouldn't live long enough to put the lesson they were about to receive to use. But their deaths would serve Truth's purpose . . . as would his.

"I don't know about you guys, but I'm damned honored."

Mort Singer's sarcasm provoked cynical smiles from a couple of his fellow detectives, but earned him a curt rebuke from Lieutenant Buford Jackson.

"Lose the attitude, Mort."

"Have a heart, Lieutenant," Herb Aikers said. "That's like asking a pig to lose its squeal."

"Besides," Rhys drawled, "Mort's attitude is part of his charm."

The lieutenant swept the room with an astute glance, then perched on a corner of the nearest desk. "All right, let's get it out in the open. We've all felt a little resentful the past couple of weeks. That's understandable. This is our turf—where we live and work and our kids go to school—and Agents Whitley and Hearst weren't exactly diplomatic about the way they took over the investigation. But all that's history. We're part of the same team now, and I expect every one of you to conduct yourselves like the professionals you are. Understood?"

A pointed look at Mort Singer accompanied the question. Mort merely nodded. Several others murmured assent.

"Okay, then. You'll report to me, and I'll act as department liaison with Gonzales and Eberhardt. Just do your jobs the way you've been trained. Be thorough, check out every possible lead. Rhys, I want you to follow up on the statements we got from the screwball brigade."

Rhys rolled his eyes and groaned.

"We can't afford to overlook anything," Jackson said sternly. "So far this guy hasn't hurt anybody. Let's get him before he does."

When the lieutenant had retreated to his office, Herb asked quietly, "Did anybody else notice that they never got around to telling us why the Secret Service is here?"

"Prob'ly because they're just monitoring the investigation, like the lieutenant said before," Mort replied.

"Maybe they're afraid this nut might be warming up for an attack on the White House or the Capitol building," Herb murmured.

"Could be. But what do we care why they're here? We don't have to deal with any of 'em, thank God."

"Amen to that."

Rhys listened to the exchange without commenting. He agreed with Herb and Mort, though: he was glad he would be reporting solely to Buford Jackson. When he got to his desk, he found the stack of Manila folders he'd turned over to George Whitley two weeks ago. Stifling another groan, he decided to start a fresh pot of coffee before he tackled them.

Faith hadn't talked to Rhys all day, so she assumed she'd be on her own for dinner. After checking the contents of the fridge, she got back in her car for a quick trip to a nearby supermarket. She was in the kitchen, putting away the things she'd bought, when he called.

"Have you eaten?" was the first thing out of his mouth. He sounded exhausted. She was assailed by a sudden, overwhelming desire to touch him.

"I was just about to fix a sandwich," she said. "I've got deli cole slaw and potato salad, enough for two."

"I'm on my way."

She had two plates ready by the time he rang the doorbell. His lingering kiss was like a long drink from an icy spring after a trek through the desert.

"God, I needed that," he said, then smiled and draped an arm over her shoulders as they walked to the kitchen.

"Bad day?"

"Long, and frustrating. The FBI and ATF have decided to 'make better use of local law enforcement resources.' Which is apparently fedspeak for: give all the shit work to the Louisville cops. Guess who drew the job of reviewing the screwball brigade statements?"

"Poor baby," Faith cooed, but she couldn't help grinning a little.

"It's not funny."

"Of course not. Sit down. You'll feel better when you've had something to eat."

"Some of those people are really wacko. I'm talking seriously deranged."

"Mmm. You want ice tea or a soft drink?"

"Tea, please. Even worse, most of them seem to think I'm their best buddy."

"No doubt because you have such an open mind," Faith remarked as she set a tall glass of tea in front of him.

He scowled at her for half a second before his mouth tilted in a sheepish smile. "Smartass. So how was your day?"

"Same as yours, long and frustrating." She hesitated, then added quietly, "Something happened."

Rhys's hand froze in midair, a forkful of cole slaw suspended above his plate. "Another episode of astral projection?"

"No. Psychokinesis. At least, I thought—" She broke off and shook her head. "It's possible it was only a coincidence. I could be worrying for no reason."

She was trying to convince herself, more than him, which of course he understood at once. He laid the fork on his plate and reached across the table to take her hand.

"Relax. Just tell me."

Reassurance flowed from his fingers to hers. Faith nodded, took a deep breath, and described everything that happened after she discovered the bagels she'd left in the break room refrigerator were missing.

"Dirk swore he hadn't done anything to his hand, that just before he came into the room it felt as if somebody had smacked him. And the red patch on the back of his hand disappeared in minutes, as if it *was* a mark from a slap."

"You're sure nothing like this has ever happened before?" Rhys asked.

"Well, no," she admitted. "I can't be absolutely sure. But if it has happened before, I didn't know about it."

"*Could* it happen?"

"That's the sixty-four-dollar question, isn't it?" She removed her hand from his light clasp and reached up to rub the tendons at the back of her neck. "I think the precognitive dreams triggered something, set something loose. All the other paranormal abilities have resurfaced since they started."

"And that scares you." He didn't make it a question.

"It scares the hell out of me," she confirmed with a brittle laugh. "Because I'm not controlling any of it. It's just *happening*. I don't know what to expect from one minute to the next—whether I'm going to suddenly jump out of my body, or into somebody else's mind. . . . If I did hurt Dirk's hand, it wasn't intentional."

"I know that," Rhys murmured. "That's the worst part, isn't it—the fear that you might harm someone just by thinking negative thoughts about him."

Faith nodded miserably.

"All right, let's find out."

Her head jerked up in surprise. "What?"

"Let's find out if negative thoughts alone are enough to produce a physical effect. It's the only way to be sure." He looked around, taking inventory of the kitchen.

"I don't think that's such a good idea," she said, but he pretended he hadn't heard her.

"Got it!" He jumped up and went to the cabinet above the stove. When he returned, he was carrying the small jar of petrified instant coffee. He set the jar beside her plate. "You hate coffee, right?"

Faith eyed the jar as if it were a hunk of liver. "Yes."

"Think about how it tastes. That's all. Don't try to *do* anything, don't even look at the jar, just remember how bad coffee tastes."

She gave him a dubious look, but his resolute gaze didn't waver.

"We both need to know," he said softly.

Faith suppressed the sudden fear that made her throat ache. He was right: they needed to know. "All right."

She looked straight into his eyes and concentrated on remembering the strong, burnt, acrid taste. She couldn't. Several minutes passed before she realized it was because she couldn't focus on anything but Rhys's eyes.

"The coffee, Faith," he said softly.

The reminder that he could read her thoughts and emotions startled her for a moment. She nodded and lowered her gaze to the placket of his dark green polo shirt. Specifically the bottom button, the only one that was fastened. After almost a full minute she shook her head.

"It isn't working. I can't remember how it tastes."

Rhys reached for the jar and instructed, "Close your eyes," and when she had, "Now take a deep breath."

She impulsively turned her head to escape the stale, musty smell that assaulted her, but it followed, moving with her. She realized he was holding the jar under her nose. The tactic worked. The smell stimulated her memory of the taste—nasty, scorched, bitter, no matter how much sugar and milk she added. How could people stand to drink the stuff? The remembered taste, and her aversion to it, were strong enough to provoke an involuntary shudder.

"Jesus!"

Rhys's exclamation was followed by a loud *clunk* that knocked the sense memory right out of her head. Her eyes flew open in reaction.

"What?"

He was staring at the jar, which he'd dropped onto her plate. It had fallen to one side and was resting against a mound of potato salad. Faith reached out to remove it.

"Don't!" His hand shot out, seizing her wrist. "Don't touch it!"

He didn't have to repeat the warning. The label on the jar was blackened and the glass had cracked from bottom to top. Tiny ribbons of smoke twirled from the crack.

Chapter Thirteen

Rhys slid the blade of a knife into the jar and lifted it off her plate, gingerly touching the tip of his index finger to the glass.

"I don't think it's hot enough to burn the table, but just in case, . . ."

Faith stared at the jar as he layered several paper napkins to set it on. Terror squeezed her heart and dried her mouth. "I was thinking that coffee tastes burnt," she whispered. "Scorched. Oh, God. I did hurt Dirk's hand."

Rhys didn't argue the possibility. "Maybe. But if you did, it wasn't deliberate."

"Is that supposed to make it all right?"

"No, of course not. But now that you know it can happen—"

"What?" Too agitated to sit still, Faith sprang out of her chair and started pacing. "Am I supposed to censor every thought that pops into my head, never think anything bad about another person? I can't do that! Nobody could! What happens if some jerk cuts me off in traffic? Would his car explode . . . or maybe his heart?"

Rhys got up and came to her, taking her firmly by the shoulders. "Stop it. Calm down."

Faith shrugged out of his grasp. "You have to leave. Get as far away from me as you can."

"The hell I will."

She backed away from him until she came up against the counter at the far end of the kitchen. "I mean it, Rhys. Always before, the more upset or scared I got, the less control I had." A choked laugh escaped her, edged with hysteria. "And right now I have to tell you, I'm scared out of my mind."

He stood his ground, neither advancing nor retreating, his steadfastness and self-control a counterweight to her panic. Reassurance flowed from him, swirling over and around her until she was cocooned in comforting warmth.

"You were a child, then. An emotionally vulnerable girl, alone, and at the mercy of people who were determined to push you to your limits, no matter what kind of damage it might cause."

He took a slow, measured step forward, and then another, holding her gaze, his crushed velvet voice adding layers to the cocoon.

"You're a woman now, Faith." He didn't stop advancing until less than a foot of space separated them. He looked deep into her eyes, letting her feel his confidence, sharing it with her. "A strong, courageous woman who can handle anything life throws at her. And one other thing . . ."

She released a shuddering breath and felt the last of her fear drain away. "I'm not alone."

"Damn straight," he murmured as he reached for her.

Leon found the notebook when he was cleaning the break room. There was no name on it or in it and the handwriting was unfamiliar, which meant it didn't belong to Missy Clarence, the PT department's receptionist. He'd seen lots of notes and telephone messages Missy had written. She made her letters fat and almost perfectly vertical, with lots of curlicues and cutesy-poo little circles above the *i*'s. The person the notebook belonged to had a strong, spare hand. In some words the letters were so right-slanted they almost laid flat on the lines; other words contained some cursive characters and some that were printed. Many of Mother's prescriptions had been dashed off like that, as if the doctor had stopped in the middle of open heart surgery to fill out the form.

Maybe the notebook belonged to one of the doctors. He knew that plenty of people besides the therapists used the break room from time to time: patients—or their families, while the patients were having physical therapy—billing clerks and nurses and secretaries from upstairs. The doctors had their own lounge, though, a lot bigger than this room, furnished with expensive sofas and chairs and a big-screen color television. Besides, he couldn't imagine any of them slumming down here in the basement, sitting at the table and scribbling in a cheap stenographer's notebook.

For a few minutes he thought the notebook must belong to that policeman, Donovan. But then he realized that no self-respecting detective would leave his notes lying around like that, where anybody could find them. Anyway, he didn't think Donovan had been to the clinic since yesterday, and the notebook hadn't been on the table when he cleaned the break room the night before.

It was important to find out who it belonged to. In fact it was more than important, it was *necessary*. Because whoever had written these things had been watching him, knew what he'd been doing.

A cold finger of fear trailed up his back. But *how?* He'd been so careful, waiting till he was absolutely sure there was no one around before he rigged each of the bombs. How could *anybody* know the things in the notebook? There were details about the bombs, the wiring, the trigger mechanisms—components that had been destroyed by the blasts—these were things nobody else could possibly know, unless he'd actually been there, watching. Or unless . . .

The fear spread icy tendrils across Leon's scalp. What if it wasn't just anybody, but someone who was in league with the Devil? One of those Satan worshippers might be able to cast some kind of spell that let him see through walls, or maybe had a crystal ball or a Ouija board or some other tool of Evil and was using it to spy on him.

That must be it. The Dark Lord didn't want the Truth revealed, and he'd sent one of his acolytes to prevent Leon from completing his mission.

Could this servant of Satan see him now? Hear him, read his thoughts? The Dark Lord was powerful, he knew. Powerful enough to seduce good people, so that they abandoned the path of righteousness to worship at the altar of Science. Science was a false god, a traitor and deceiver that pandered to man's vanity, encouraging him to believe he no longer needed the one true God.

He had always known this, but three months ago the doctor whose *science* had just killed his twin brother confirmed his knowledge, when he looked Leon in the eye and said that God was irrelevant. He'd wanted to kill the blind, arrogant bastard then and there. He would have, if Mother hadn't been clinging to his arm, sobbing uncontrollably. He'd have broken the man's neck with his bare hands and watched as the light flickered out in his eyes, and at the end, when the doctor drew his last gasping breath, he would have asked, "Do you still think God is irrelevant?"

He was glad now that he hadn't killed the doctor. He would have been forgiven, he had no doubt at all about that, but the plan that was revealed to him soon after Lenny died was so much better. He had been chosen to serve as the Messenger, the one who delivered the Truth to the world. He would reveal Science for the false god it was, make them all realize, when it was too late, the terrible consequences of their slavish devotion to it.

He glared at the notebook in his hand. Everything had been proceeding exactly as he'd planned, and now, when ıe was so close to completing his mission, this unknown ›erson was threatening its success.

A terrible rage rose in him, an overwhelming desire to ıtterly destroy this meddling servant of Evil, whoever he vas, cause him the kind of agonies reserved for the most lamned and irredeemable souls.

He had to discover who the notebook belonged to, and ıe had to do it soon. Time was running out—only four nore days until he made the final Revelation.

The fingers of Rhys's left hand stroked Faith's bare arm n a lazy, almost absent-minded, caress. She was snuggled ıgainst him in a corner of the living room sofa, her head ›n his shoulder, both arms wrapped around his waist. It ıad been several minutes since she'd moved or spoken. He thought she must have fallen asleep, until she stirred ınd he heard her pensive sigh.

"Penny for your thoughts," he murmured.

She lifted her head and kissed the corner of his mouth. 'I was thinking how thankful I am that you came into my ife when you did. I'd probably be in a room with rubber valls by now if you weren't here to keep me anchored."

"Anchored." He tilted his head, considering. "I like that. Makes me sound dependable . . . stable."

Faith pulled away and raised a bent knee onto the sofa cushion, putting a buffer zone between them so she could study him. Her concern and regret caressed him.

"You are," she said huskily. "But you haven't felt very stable the past couple of days, have you?"

"Reading my mind again?"

"No. Not now. But I've known when you were confused. And, once or twice, a little afraid."

He reached out to brush his fingers across her face. "Understandable reactions, I think, considering everything that's happened. But I'm okay."

She pressed her cheek against his hand. "I know. You

never let the fear take control. You just *reject* it. You'll have to teach me how to do that. All my life, I've—"

She broke off abruptly in the middle of the sentence her expression transforming from soft and loving to alarmed. Rhys impulsively moved his hand to her arm. Her breathing had quickened, but not with passion, and her pupils were dilated. Fear exploded inside him.

"Faith?"

"Nooo," she moaned. Her eyelids fluttered rapidly; her entire body stiffened as if she'd stepped on an exposed electric cable. "It's happening . . . again."

That was all she got out before she seemed to slip into some kind of trance. She stared straight ahead, her eyes glazed and unfocused, her expression blank. Rhys tried jostling her shoulder, calling her name. For a second or two he considered slapping her, but then he realized that bringing her back too abruptly might be dangerous, so he slid his arms around her and pulled her against him. She didn't resist, but it was like guiding an accident victim who was suffering emotional shock . . . or moving a life-sized doll. She leaned against him, but she wasn't *there.*

It's happening again. What did that mean? Was she experiencing another episode of astral projection—what she called waking dreams? Rhys felt panic rising in his throat and forced it back down. This was more unnerving than any of the psychic abilities he'd already seen manifested, including what she'd done to the jar of instant coffee. How could she *leave her body* without dying, for Christ's sake? Yet he knew with a rock solid certainty that she had. He might have been holding a mannequin; the physical form was there, solid and real, but it wasn't occupied by a human consciousness. And, he realized with a combination of fear and awe, her body temperature was falling. Dear God, she was *cold.*

And then, as if he wasn't already spooked enough, he started hallucinating.

First the living room walls began to move, stretching and receding until they appeared to bow outward. A framed print above the television—of an old lobster fisherman and a young girl, rowing their wooden boat out to sea—started to melt and run down the wall. Which was alarming enough, but as he watched the picture dissolve into greasy streaks of color he realized the TV had shrunk to the size of a toaster.

He squeezed his eyes closed to shut out the images. It didn't work; they were still there, just as vivid, just as shocking.

Oh Jesus, they were coming from Faith. This was what *she* was seeing!

It's all right.

The gentle assurance whispered through his mind. Rhys opened his eyes, careful to avoid letting his gaze linger on anything, and turned to her. She hadn't moved; her vacant expression hadn't altered; her skin still felt icy. But, oddly enough, she also wasn't affected by the distortion that was warping and twisting everything else in the room.

"Faith?"

Don't be afraid. Nothing here can hurt us.

Physically, he thought. She must mean nothing could hurt them physically. But what about frying their brains? Or his, at least. She might be used to this, but the images flooding his mind were too damn grotesque. He'd never used LSD, but what he was experiencing—even if it was vicariously—fitted horror stories he'd heard about bad acid trips.

Then another thought hit him. If Faith had sensed his alarm and could send thoughts to him, maybe she wasn't completely out of it.

"Can you hear me?" he asked. "Can you come back?"

Yes. Whenever I want.

"Then for God's sake, come back!"

He waited. Nothing. She didn't reply, or move, or give any sign that she'd heard. And the freakish psychedelic movie kept playing inside his head. How much time had passed since she went into the trance, and out of her body?

It seemed like hours. He was afraid to look at his watch. God knew what it had turned into.

"Faith. If you can hear me, come back. Now! This is too damn weird. And you're as cold as ice. Christ, you feel like a corpse."

I'm all right. I'm waiting.

"Waiting?" he echoed incredulously.

To see if he comes again.

He? Who, he? Rhys didn't ask aloud, and if she heard the question telepathically, she didn't have time to respond. He felt it at the same instant she did—an intangible, invisible, but undeniably *real* presence.

The sensation wasn't altogether alien to him. Over the years his instincts had evolved to the point that he could usually anticipate danger, detect an imminent threat. It was an ability most cops developed and some people possessed from birth—the tingling scalp, the accelerated heart rate, the sudden rush of adrenaline, all were warning signals that had no doubt been inherited from some primordial ancestor of man.

What he was feeling now—or, more accurately, what Faith was feeling and passing on to him—was something like that, only magnified a thousand times. This wasn't some vague, indistinct premonition; this was damn real. And damn terrifying.

Blind, unreasoning hatred. Blood red rage. Scathing contempt. And not just the emotions, but a powerful intention to act on them. To hurt . . . violate . . . destroy.

And then suddenly the savage, pulsing torrent of malevolence was gone. It just stopped, as if a psychic faucet had been shut off. Rhys jerked backward in reaction and blinked a couple of times, struggling to regain his equilibrium. He felt Faith's body twitch spasmodically. A whimpering moan slipped past her lips.

He gradually became aware that not only was the menacing presence gone, the room had returned to normal. But something was wrong. He wasn't receiving any messages or impressions from Faith. Not fear, not relief . . . nothing.

He tried to probe her mind, something he'd never done before. Still nothing. Maybe he wasn't doing it right. This telepathy business was still a mystery; he had no idea how it worked, only that they could each tune into the other's psychic frequency. Obviously not all the time, though, because at the moment his receiver wasn't working. Or maybe it was her transmitter. That thought worried him. In fact, it scared the bejesus out of him.

"Faith?" Her eyes were closed now, and she'd gone as limp as an old rag doll. He grasped her arms and gave her a shake. "Sweetheart, wake up. Come on, I know you're in there, Faith. Wake up, please!"

Terrible thoughts swarmed through his mind. Could the presence they'd sensed somehow have reached out and touched her—hurt her? Was she asleep? Unconscious? Still in the trance . . . only sunk so deep that she couldn't find her way out?

Frantic to reach her, to bring her back, he did the only thing he could think of. He wrapped his arms around her tight, closed his eyes, and silently shouted her name. Screamed it, in fact, trying with everything he had to project the cry into her mind.

The effort sent a bolt of such murderous pain through his head that he thought he'd given himself a cerebral hemorrhage. Several minutes passed before he realized that he was still alive, though at first he wished he wasn't. His head felt like somebody had clobbered him with a six pound sledgehammer. He must have passed out and fallen over; he was on his back, one arm hanging off the sofa, the backs of his fingers resting on the floor. He pried his eyes open and the soft light from a table lamp directly overhead sent hundreds of white hot needles straight through his eyeballs and into his brain. He groaned and lifted his arm to cover his face.

Sounds. Soft footfalls that crashed inside his head like a cannonade. Then gentle hands, moving his arm to lay a cold, damp cloth across his forehead and eyes. The floodlight above his head was replaced by merciful darkness.

Faith.

The pain will stop, but it may take an hour or so. Her voice was like the barest breath of sound in his mind. *Lie perfectly still. If you move or talk, you'll just make it worse.*

He believed her, but despite the warning he groped for her hand and squeezed it hard. She returned the pressure and a second later he felt her lips brush his knuckles.

He had no idea how much time passed, but eventually the excruciating agony subsided to a barely tolerable throbbing. He reached up and gingerly removed the cloth—the fourth one she'd brought him.

"Better?" She spoke aloud, but as softly as if they were in church.

Rhys started to nod, then thought better of it. "Yeah," he muttered. "Now I only feel miserable instead of half dead."

"A hot shower would help, if you think you can make it to the bathroom."

He wasn't a hundred percent sure he could, but pride demanded that he try. Faith stood by, ready to lend a supporting arm if one was needed. When he was on his feet and she was satisfied that he wasn't going to keel over, she went ahead to turn on the water. Rhys made his way down the hall like an arthritic ninety-year-old, one hand on the wall, taking small, shuffling steps to keep the jarring to a minimum. By the time he made it to the bathroom, clouds of steam were billowing out the door. Faith stood next to the tub. She wasn't wearing a stitch.

Without a word, she came to him and started undressing him. He didn't object, but neither did he give her much help. When he was down to his birthday suit, she pulled the shower curtain back and stepped into the tub, then held out her hand. Rhys took it gratefully. He was feeling a little light-headed, and not just because of the psychic equivalent of a migraine.

"Stand right under the spray," she directed. "Let it hit the top of your head and breathe deeply through your nose . . . inhale lots of steam."

After a couple of minutes, she turned him so that the water was pelting the back of his head and neck. By now his head felt immeasurably better, and the glide of her hands across his wet skin had a predictable effect.

Faith smiled and stepped in close, pressing against him from shoulders to knees. "My, that was a fast recovery."

"I have an exceptionally talented nurse," he replied as he lowered his head to kiss her.

Before things got out of control they tacitly agreed that making love in the shower was too awkward, not to mention dangerous, and adjourned to Faith's bed. Rhys was a little tentative at first, as if he'd suffered bruised ribs instead of a psychic headache, but pleasure quickly superseded the fear of pain. Later, when they were twined together under the sheet, he brought up the extraordinary experience they'd shared in the living room.

"So that's what astral projection is like. Funny, I would've assumed you'd travel . . . you know, float through the wall or ceiling or something. I mean, what's the point of leaving your body if you stay in the same place?"

"You don't stay in the same place. I left the physical dimension—what most people would call the 'real world'—and entered the astral dimension."

"But you were seeing your own living room. Everything was the same, but . . . weird. Psychedelic weird, like you were on some hallucinogenic drug."

Faith nodded. "Familiar, but changed. Astral matter is sort of like photographic film. You develop an image by exposing film to light. Thought does the same thing to astral matter. My thoughts, my consciousness, created the image of the living room because that's where I was when it happened. But you have to concentrate really hard to make astral images hold their shape, because they're not made of physical matter. They don't have physical properties—mass, weight, form."

"They're not real, then."

She shrugged. "Who's to say what's 'real' and what isn't? It seemed real to you at the time, didn't it?"

Rhys stubbornly declined to answer that. "So why didn't you go anywhere?"

"I just told you, I did. I went into another plane of existence. I think you're confusing astral projection with an out-of-body experience."

"They're not the same?"

"No, they're very different. There's no trance state preceding an out-of-body experience. At least, not for me. I understand some people have to enter a trance to do it, but I just relax and concentrate on floating up out of my body. Then suddenly I'm looking down. I can see myself, but I'm *outside* myself."

"Sounds like a near-death experience," Rhys murmured, impulsively tightening his embrace.

"Yes, exactly, except I never had to be at death's door to do it. When I'm out-of-body, I can only see objects that are nearby—within the range of my normal vision. But I can travel." She tilted her head to grin up at him. "Not through walls or ceilings, though. It's like flying, but without wings or a physical body."

"Like in your Rat Man dreams," Rhys said.

Faith nodded and nestled closer. "Yes. I'm traveling out-of-body in the dreams. I haven't done it while I'm awake for years. I don't even know if I still can."

"And you don't want to know," he said intuitively.

"No."

He gave her a hug and let the subject drop. "What about the presence you felt tonight? Was it the same as yesterday?"

Her shoulders rose and fell as she heaved a restive sigh. "Not exactly. The emotions were the same, but this time I didn't have the sense that he knew me. His animosity wasn't *personal,* if that makes any sense."

"I know what you're saying. Whoever the guy is, he's carrying around a king-size hate for somebody, but I didn't have the feeling it was directed at you, specifically."

He thought about that for a minute.

"So does that mean it *wasn't* the same person you sensed esterday?"

"I don't know," Faith said glumly. "The intensity was ertainly the same. And I can't think of *one* person who vould have a reason to feel that kind of loathing for me, nuch less two people."

Rhys couldn't imagine her doing anything that would rovoke such hatred, either. The trouble was, they couldn't pply objective reasoning or any brand of logic to deduce ier nemesis's identity. The out-of-control emotions they'd oth felt tonight suggested severe mental derangement, if ıot full-blown psychosis. This person, whoever he was, night not *have* a sound, rational *reason* for his hostility. Vhich, of course, would make him all the more dangerous. Rhys didn't voice that opinion, though. He was fairly sure 'aith had figured it out for herself.

How in God's name was he going to protect her from n unknown and unknowable madman?

It began like any ordinary dream, which is to say she lidn't realize it was a dream. She was in a spacious, comfortbly furnished room—some kind of lounge, or maybe a obby or large waiting room. The place seemed vaguely amiliar, or maybe it was the way it was furnished: sofas, hairs, carpeting, wallpaper all had that neutral, nondecript, public-holding-pen look that's supposed to soothe nd comfort the masses. Lots of potted plants too green nd lush to be real. Soft, mind-numbing piped-in "easy istening" music.

There were other people in the room. Lots of them, in act. Faith was aware of them, though she couldn't see hem. She could hear their muffled, unintelligible voices nd the whish and rustle of their clothing as they moved; mell their perfume and deodorant, shampoo and ftershave. She could even feel their energy, the life force manating from and surrounding them. But she couldn't *see* anyone. It was the strangest thing, knowing they were there but for some reason not visible.

She got up from the chair where she'd been sitting and started to wander around the room, peering behind foliage and furniture as if she expected to find some of the people hiding. Of course she didn't really expect any such thing, and she felt foolish creeping up on sofas and fake ficus trees, but her curiosity overcame the embarrassment. If someone suddenly materialized and asked what on earth she was doing, she would claim she'd lost a contact lens or an earring or something.

When she'd finished a fruitless serpentine exploration of the room, she found herself standing at the wide, open entrance, facing out. Two soft-drink machines were tucked into an alcove directly across the hall. The quiet hum of their refrigeration units joined the symphony of phantom sounds. Suddenly realizing she was thirsty, she dug into the pocket of her sweatpants and came up with sixty-five cents in change, exactly enough for a can of soda.

She crossed the wide hall, the squeak of her rubber soles against the waxed vinyl floor sounding unnaturally loud, and bought a Coke. The pop and fizz when she opened the can, like the squeak of her shoes, was much louder and more distinct than the other, muted sounds.

"Weird," she said as she raised the can for a drink.

To the right of the alcove and slightly to one side of a set of wide plate glass doors was a long, L-shaped, waist high counter that held four computer terminals. Some kind of reception desk? She went to lean over the counter to see what was behind it. A narrow ledge that held several multi-line phones backed both sections of the L. A tall stool was precisely placed at each terminal and there were a couple of laser printers, but no desks or chairs. Faith backed away and turned toward the plate glass doors. Assuming they led outside, it must be night. All she saw was herself and the long counter, reflected in the glass.

What was this place? Where were the employees who should be manning the phones and computers? Who were the people she could hear and smell and feel, but couldn't see? Were they all ghosts?

Not yet, but soon.

The answer came out of nowhere, slamming into her mind with a force that sent her staggering back toward the drink machines. That's when she realized it wasn't an ordinary dream . . . and that the voice in her mind belonged to the dark presence she'd sensed twice, now.

Chapter Fourteen

Faith woke in a cold sweat. Her heart was doing its level best to hammer its way through her rib cage. Rhys lay on his stomach beside her, sleeping as peacefully as a newborn, obviously untouched by her dream.

She reached out to wake him, then stopped herself. What was it he'd said just a few hours ago—"You're a woman now. A strong, courageous woman who can handle anything life throws at her."

Strong, courageous women didn't wake their lovers in the middle of the night and beg to be held and comforted, just because they'd had a nightmare.

On the other hand, how many women—strong and courageous or not—had nightmares that were in fact precognitive dreams about a psycho bomber?

Besides, at the moment she didn't feel especially strong or courageous. What she felt was mortal terror. And what was the point of having a strong, courageous *man* lying next to you if you couldn't call upon *his* strength and courage?

She couldn't do it, though. What would she say—I had a dream about a lot of people this anonymous menacing ntity plans to kill, but I couldn't see any of them so I lon't know *who* they were or even *where* they were?

He'd probably pat her on the head and tell her to go ack to sleep. Or grab his clothes and set a new land speed ecord getting out of the house . . . and maybe out of her ife, while he was at it. Not that she would blame him. At he moment, *she* would like to get out of her life, or at east exchange it for the nice, monotonously predictable ife she'd had four weeks ago. Before the damned Rat Man lreams started.

She edged closer to Rhys until his arm was lightly pressng against her breasts, careful not to wake him but seeking he comfort of physical contact.

Had this dream been another installment in the Rat Ian saga? Was it his voice she'd heard—and, therefore, is presence she'd felt during the waking dreams? If this *vas* a precognitive dream, it was different from the others n several ways. She hadn't seen any evidence of a bomb, or one thing. Of course that didn't necessarily mean there adn't been a bomb. It could have been concealed behind he counter, under a chair or sofa, even buried under one of the fake plants.

And what about the people she'd sensed, but not seen? 'hat was the most disturbing part of the dream. They *were here,* she knew it! They existed; they were real. And yet hey weren't *physically* there, occupying real time and space. Vhat the hell did it mean?

Always before, Rat Man had been the only person in the lreams. Faith had never given that detail much thought, ut now she did. He worked alone. He planted his bombs vhen there was no one else around, and they exploded n the middle of the night. Was that simply because he vanted to reduce the risk of discovery, or had he been rying to make sure nobody got hurt?

And if he had been taking care to ensure that no one vas injured by his bombs, did this new dream mean his genda had changed? That now he *wanted* to hurt people—

and not one or two specific individuals, but a large number of people he probably didn't even know?

She remembered standing in front of the counter and wondering: *Were they all ghosts?*

And the chilling reply: *Not yet, but soon.*

Yes. That was it. She knew it in a primitive, completely instinctive part of her mind. Whatever twisted compulsion had been driving him was out of control; he'd crossed the boundary into madness. No longer satisfied with destroying empty offices and warehouses and cash machines, the monster inside him now demanded human sacrifices.

A dark, suffocating dread pressed down on her. Dear God, he *was* going to kill all those people. And unless she had another dream, managed somehow to determine where they were, there wasn't a thing she could do to stop him.

Stark terror and a crushing sense of helplessness made her press even closer to Rhys. Some of her mental anguish must have penetrated his sound sleep. He draped an arm over her waist and mumbled a husky endearment, but he didn't wake. Faith bit her lip to keep herself from whimpering, or crying out to him. She'd never felt more alone in her life.

She decided to tell him about the dream Saturday morning, over breakfast. But before she could, Rhys announced that he had to go in to work. He was apologetic; he'd looked forward to spending the day with her, but he had to make a start on reviewing the files the ATF had returned.

Faith could tell he was distracted, his mind already on the work awaiting him. Besides, she'd given him enough nasty surprises in the past twenty-four hours. Guilt and remorse tugged at her. He had so much to deal with already—the FBI and ATF, his "screwball brigade," a serial bomber, not to mention a girlfriend who spent half her time in the Twilight Zone . . . and had now started dragging him in with her. An account of her latest bizarre dream could wait.

After Rhys left, she took out her bucket of cleaning supplies and plunged into scrubbing the kitchen and bathroom until every surface gleamed. Physical activity was what she needed, and lots of it. Use those muscles; work up a sweat. Stay busy . . . too busy to think. Mustn't give the panic lurking there at the edge of her consciousness an opening.

The past three weeks had taken a heavy toll on her nerves and all but demolished her self-confidence. She felt brittle, ready to shatter into a million pieces. When she'd told Rhys last night that, if not for him, she would probably be in a rubber room by now, she suspected he hadn't guessed how brutally honest she was being. He'd been a godsend, her salvation, but even he couldn't save her from herself. She was being pulled apart, her longing for a normal, peaceful life in direct opposition with her resurrected psychic abilities. As she lay in the dark this morning, unable to get back to sleep, she'd wept silent, bitter tears—for herself, for the life she'd struggled so hard to build and now felt slipping away.

When she finished with the kitchen and bath, she dragged out the vacuum cleaner and started on the living room. How much more could she take? How long before the strain became unbearable? She knew the signs: the mounting anxiety; the hovering dread; an increasing awareness that she was walking the razor edge of control. She'd felt this way before, during the twelve long months between her seventeenth and eighteenth birthdays. The difference was that then, she'd known a reprieve was in sight—soon she would be free, off to college and a new life in a new place, where no one knew anything about her.

Now, though, there was nothing to look forward to but more of the same; or worse, a regression to the kind of existence she'd fled. How much longer could she continue to function, when it was impossible to know from one minute to the next if she might be suddenly zapped out of her body? The nighttime dreams were hard enough to deal with, but eventually she would have one of the waking dreams when there were other people around. Then what? How understanding would the doctors be—or Rollie, for that matter—when she started taking minivacations to the astral plane in the middle of a therapy session? Would her job be protected under the Americans With Disabilities Act? she wondered with a touch of hysteria.

God, she was already losing it. She switched off the vacuum and collapsed onto the sofa, dropping her head into her hands. "Stop it!" she muttered fiercely. "Just stop it!" At this rate, she wouldn't have to worry about ending up in the unemployment line; she was going to drive herself 'round the bend long before that possibility materialized.

Obviously physical activity wasn't what she needed; the exertion had only fueled her anxiety. Kicking off her shoes, Faith stretched out on the sofa, closed her eyes, and ordered herself to relax. It wasn't easy. Her psyche, like her muscles, was cramped with tension.

All right, concentrate. Face first: tongue off the roof of your mouth; cheeks loose; jaw slack. Now down to the feet: toes, arches, ankles, calves. Fingers and hands. Finally she was relaxed enough to sink into the cool, still place deep inside that always soothed and restored her. Her calm center. Nothing and no one could touch her here. Not Rat Man, not a waking dream . . . this was her refuge, an impenetrable fortress hidden deep within her own mind.

It had been so long, she'd forgotten the power she had to renew and heal herself. She had discovered her calm center years ago, but she seldom sought refuge there anymore. Partly because it was no longer necessary—or hadn't been, before the Rat Man dreams started—and partly because she recognized the danger in retreating within herself. None of the pressures or concerns of the outside world existed here. There were no decisions or choices to be made, no confrontations, no appalling headlines to remind her that the world was a troubled and troubling place. Here, there was only total peace and harmony.

And therein lay the danger. At one point, just before she graduated from college, she was so consumed by anxiety that she withdrew for hours on end. She'd been racked by doubt and uncertainty—would she be able to find a job, a place to live, to manage the dozens of details that make up everyday life?

When she realized, almost too late, that she was using her private little retreats as an escape rather than as a means of renewal, and that she was escaping more and more often and for longer periods, she stopped. That had been the most arduous, and in some ways the most frightening, period of her life. She'd gained an appreciation for the agony a drug addict trying to quit cold turkey must endure. The knowledge that, for a while, she had been tempted to withdraw completely and permanently was terrifying.

Since then she had only retreated to the safety and security of her calm center twice. Once during the week she started work, and again on the day she took the polygraph test. Rhys's stubborn refusal to accept the truth had been so frustrating that for a fleeting moment she almost lost control. She'd been so shaken by the intensity of her own anger that she instinctively sought the solace which could only be found within.

But now she knew the dangers of staying too long, so she didn't surrender to the temptation to sink deeper, lose herself completely. Escape was the coward's way of dealing with adversity. And whatever else she might be, she wasn't a coward!

When both her mind and body were relaxed and rested, she inhaled a deep, cleansing breath and returned to face her fears and confront her demons. Other people—first the team of parapsychologists, and now Rat Man—had controlled her life for too long, but only because she'd let them. No more. Her life was *hers,* damn it! From now on, no one else would be *allowed* to manipulate or use her.

She wasn't sure exactly how to go about achieving that kind of liberation, or where she should start. She'd just have to figure it out as she went, trust her own judgment and instincts. A soft smile curved her lips. Which, of course, was what Rhys had urged her to do.

Something else he'd said came back to her—something to the effect that the rules he'd always taken for granted no longer applied. Well, maybe it was time to start making up some new rules. The only thing she knew with absolute certainty was that any action, even if it was reckless or foolish, would be better than sitting around and waiting to see what happened next.

The first thing she should do was write down everything she could remember about last night's dream. She should have done that right away. She got up and went in search of the steno book she'd been using to keep a record of the Rat Man dreams, and didn't realize until she'd turned the house upside down that she must have left it at work.

Rhys added another folder to the stack he'd already read. The additional weight was enough to send the entire stack cascading to the floor just as Lieutenant Jackson approached his desk.

"Goddamnit!" he snarled, shoving out of his chair to retrieve the avalanche of papers.

Buford Jackson dropped a two-page computer printout in Rhys's in-basket and got down on his knees to help. "Are these the statements you've gone over twice already and the ATF has seen, or the ones you haven't got around to reviewing?"

"The ones I've gone over twice," Rhys said irritably. "Which, if you want my considered opinion, is one time too many."

He couldn't tell whether the lieutenant's deep grunt indicated agreement or disapproval. Jackson started using his big, powerful hands to sweep the papers into an untidy pile. "In that case, just throw 'em all in a file box for somebody to sort out later."

Rhys nodded gratefully and went after a form that had landed under Herb Aikers's chair. When he returned to add it to the heap, the lieutenant was standing beside his desk, holding the printout sheet he'd deposited in the in-basket.

"This just came in. It's the results of the database search you had Mort request last week. You think the bomber might have some kind of phobia or fixation or something about computers, is that right?"

Rhys gathered an armload of papers, then had to put them on his chair because there was no room left on the desk. "It makes sense. Look at his targets—a software company, a warehouse where UPC equipment was stored, and the ATMs, which are basically computer terminals that record bank transactions."

Jackson pursed his lips and cocked his head to one side. "All right, maybe you're on to something. God knows we haven't come up with any other connection between his targets." He tossed the printout back in the in-basket. "Follow up on it when you finish reviewing those statements."

"I think the computerization lead should take precedence," Rhys said, but Jackson shook his head.

"It isn't a lead, it's a theory."

"It's a *connection*. The only one we've got, you just admitted as much." Rhys waved a hand at the stack of folders he still had to wade through. "This garbage—"

"Comes first," the lieutenant interrupted. His tone left no room for argument.

When Jackson had returned to his office, Rhys hunted down an empty file box and dumped the statements he'd finished rereading into it, then added another half dozen to the stack before he gave in and reached for the printout.

The heading read Search Criteria: Vandalism OR Malicious Vandalism AND Computer. Beneath the heading was a short list of cases that had been investigated by the

Louisville PD. Six cases, six names. The current address of three of the six was the county jail. Of the remaining three, the first was a thirty-year-old man who'd gone nuts in an electronics store and heaved a Pentium computer through the window because the store manager refused to throw in the additional four megs of RAM the system needed to run a particular CD-ROM program. No doubt one of those street ninja, rip-out-your-opponent's-spine games.

Rhys took a pen from the mug on his desk and scratched that name off the list, which left two possible suspects. One of them was a sixty-year-old woman who'd carried a jelly jar filled with goat blood into a doctor's office and dumped it on his receptionist's computer while screeching Bible verses at the top of her lungs. Jesus. Her name—Leona Timmons—wasn't familiar, which, when he thought about it, was strange. Loony Leona sounded like a charter member of the screwball brigade.

Scratch Leona, too. The bomber didn't have to be a man, but Rhys couldn't imagine a batty, gray-haired little old Sunday School teacher lugging thirty pounds of explosives around town without being noticed. Well, maybe if she used a shopping cart . . . He grinned and moved on to the last name.

Patrick Dean, age twenty-five. Apprehended red-handed—after he set off the silent alarm he obviously hadn't known about—smashing various pieces of equipment in the back room of the computer store he'd been fired from the previous week. Well, well. It seemed young Mr. Dean was a licensed computer technician with a taste for larceny. He'd been fired because his employer caught him stealing and reselling the store's inventory. The former boss was either a prince among men or a fool: he'd declined to press charges, instead working out a deal for Dean to pay off the costs of his theft and vandalism.

"Bingo," Rhys murmured. He circled Patrick Dean's name and address, folded the printout, and stuck it in the pocket of his jeans before returning to the odious job of reviewing statements.

Fifteen minutes after Leon hung up, he was still in a state of euphoric bliss. When he'd answered the phone and realized it was his boss calling, his first, instinctive reaction had been apprehension. Mr. Jenks almost never phoned employees at home; when he did, it usually meant they were in trouble. But Mr. Jenks quickly let him know that wasn't the case this time. He was calling, he said right away, to inform Leon that his schedule for next week had been changed. The head of Gaines Memorial's housekeeping department had requested several reliable people for Monday and Tuesday, to help her staff get the hospital shipshape for the official dedication. She'd specifically asked for people who had previous experience at medical facilities, so her crews wouldn't have to waste time teaching them which cleaning procedures to use in which areas.

It was a sign. It had to be. He'd already scouted out the hospital and determined the best place to plant the bomb, but he needed to make at least two more trips to set everything up. He'd been worried about that. Every time he went there, the risk increased that he'd run into somebody who would remember him from the night Lenny died. Or, even if that didn't happen, one of their private cops or a nosy clerk might start to wonder why he kept coming to the hospital, when it was obvious there was nothing wrong with him. He didn't like to draw attention to himself. If he was stopped and questioned, it could ruin everything, force him to delay his plans for who knew how long.

But now Mr. Jenks had solved all his problems. He would be *working* at the hospital on Monday and Tuesday. He'd have a legitimate reason for being there, and if anybody mentioned seeing him before, he could say that he'd filled in a couple of times when somebody in the housekeeping department was sick. He'd been wearing his work clothes every time he went to the hospital, so he didn't think anyone would question the story.

It was perfect! He couldn't have come up with a better solution if he'd had months to think about it. It *must* be a sign.

His exuberance faded when his gaze lit on the steno book on the table beside his bed. There was still the possibility that he might fail to complete his mission, if whoever the notebook belonged to found out about his plans for the final Revelation. If it was somebody who worked at the clinic—and he had to assume it was—they might wonder why he wasn't there Monday or Tuesday and start snooping around.

Leon wished he knew what kind of powers this person had. For instance, could he really see what someone was doing even if he wasn't *there?* He told himself it didn't matter; he had special powers, too, and his powers were probably stronger. He was, after all, the Messenger of Truth. If someone tried to stop him, he would eliminate that person along with Faith McRae. He had almost finalized his plans for her. He still had to make one small but important decision, but there was no rush. It could wait another day or two.

Which reminded him, he should spend some more time practicing before Mother called him to the supper table. He picked up the steno book and turned to a blank page, then opened the drawer of the night table to take out a ballpoint pen and a handful of message slips he'd collected from the wastepaper basket under Missy Clarence's desk.

Duplicating Missy's looping, aggressively feminine handwriting was more difficult than he'd thought it would be when the idea first occurred to him. After twenty minutes his fingers were painfully cramped, but the last few lines he'd written could almost pass a close inspection. A little more practice and even Missy wouldn't be able to tell one of her own messages from one he'd written. He took a minute to massage the fingers of his right hand, then spent a few more minutes repeatedly writing two names in Missy

Clarence's hand. The names were Detective Donovan and Tommy Carver.

Faith couldn't decide whether she should be worried or annoyed. She *knew* she'd left the notebook in the break room, but now it wasn't there. Not on the table, or the counter, or in the base cabinet or either of the two overhead cabinets. She even looked inside the fridge, feeling like an idiot, before checking Missy's desk in case whoever found it had assumed it belonged to the receptionist. It was gone. Vanished. Kaput.

Okay, so whoever found it had either taken it—it was mostly blank; she'd only used a few pages—or thrown it away. She found herself hoping it was the latter, even though that would mean all her notes about the Rat Man dreams were lost. She didn't like the idea of someone else reading those notes. In fact, just considering the possibility made her feel a little queasy.

She tried to put the thought out of her mind as she locked the PT department doors behind her, telling herself that even if someone *had* read her notes, it was no big deal. Her name wasn't on the steno book and there was nothing to connect it to her.

Well, except for her fingerprints.

Oh, Lord. What if whoever found it read her notes, then leapt head-first to the conclusion that they were the scribblings of the serial bomber?

Right on the heels of that appalling thought came another: Rhys's fingerprints were on the notebook, too.

On the way home she stopped to pick up a few groceries, but she was so distracted that she forgot to get bagels and tea and had to return to the store. Twice. Both times she'd already started her car and was on the way out of the parking lot when her memory lapse caught up with her. By the time she carried the groceries into her kitchen, she had a stomachache from worrying. She brewed a pot of green tea, then sat down at the table with the new steno book she'd remembered to buy when she went back for the bagels.

She'd had three cups of tea and filled two pages when the phone rang. It was Rhys, calling to say he'd turned up a promising lead and was going to check it out, but would she like to go grab a bite to eat about six? Faith said no, she'd rather stay home and cook. She wanted to tell him—in private—about the dream and the missing notebook. Well, to be honest, she didn't *want* to tell him about the notebook, but she thought she should prepare him in case a platoon of his colleagues showed up to arrest one or both of them.

Fortunately chicken breasts had been on sale. She found some snow peas in the freezer and a small bag of slivered almonds hiding behind a box of cornstarch. With a few additions—sweet and sour sauce, ground ginger, chicken bouillon, maybe a dash of soy sauce—she had the makings for an impromptu Oriental Chicken Something-or-other to serve over noodles. Since it was only four o'clock, she assembled everything next to the stove and went back to writing down everything she could remember about last night's dream.

Rhys was in a foul mood when he left Patrick Dean's apartment. The young man had readily admitted his act of vandalism. In fact, he'd bragged about the amount of damage he'd managed to do before the patrolmen who responded to the silent alarm arrived. His surly insolence was so in-your-face that Rhys's first, spontaneous reaction had been anger.

But then it occurred to him that Dean might be displaying symptoms of a mental or emotional illness. Some disorders, or so he'd read, turned normally courteous, respectful people into hostile jackasses. Hostile enough, maybe, to blow up a couple of buildings and a bunch of automatic teller machines?

He'd just started to get excited about the possibility when

young Patrick clued him in about the reason his former employer hadn't pressed charges. The man who owned the computer store, the man who had fired him for stealing, was his stepfather. Patrick's grievances against him were numerous. Delighted to have an audience, he'd recited several of them, until Rhys rudely cut him off. That happened as soon as he'd heard enough to conclude that the man had spent the past ten years or so bailing his stepson out of one jam after another, and that the two of them would probably spend the next twenty years locked in the same cycle.

"Spoiled asshole," Rhys snarled as he yanked open the door of his car. Dean's stepfather should've let the prosecutor throw the book at him. A couple of years in prison were just what the little twerp needed.

So far the entire day—which, until yesterday, he'd looked forward to spending in various pleasurable pursuits with Faith—had been a colossal waste of time. And now the trip to Dean's had deprived him of his only solid suspect. His entire "possibles" list now consisted of a Bible-quoting sixty-year-old crazy woman.

And, dammit, he still had a mountain of statements to wade through on Monday.

He stopped at a liquor store on the way to Faith's and bought a fifth of Scotch.

Chapter Fifteen

The Chicken Whatever turned out surprisingly well, though Faith suspected Rhys might as well have been eating shredded cardboard. He wasn't exactly in an ebullient mood. In fact, he was downright unsociable, which was going to make it even harder to bring up the things she wanted to talk to him about.

Her first clue that he'd had a rotten day came when she opened the front door and saw the liquor-bottle-sized brown bag in his hand. He gave her an indifferent, Hi-how-are-you? kiss and then made straight for the kitchen, where he removed a bottle of Scotch from the bag and a tumbler from the cabinet, poured himself two fingers of the whiskey and threw it back as if it were water.

Faith was tempted to peek inside his mind to find out what was bugging him, but she didn't. Partly because she knew how he felt about deliberate probing—that it was a gross invasion of privacy, which of course it was—but also because she was a little afraid to find out what had put him in such a mood. She had enough knotty problems of her own to deal with at the moment, without taking on any of his. Still, when they were seated at the table, his grim expression and the tension visible in the rigid set of his shoulders and jaw tugged at her until she had to ask, "Bad day?"

He grimaced. "The pits. I'm half blind from reviewing enough absolutely worthless statements to fill the damned Astrodome. Those were the ones I could read. I'll need some kind of idiot savant interpreter for the rest."

He shoved a forkful of food into his mouth and continued speaking around it.

"Apparently teachers are so busy breaking up fights and dodging bullets nowadays, they don't have time to teach people how to write, much less spell."

Obviously he needed to vent. Faith made a sympathetic noise. She didn't think he even noticed.

"Then this afternoon, just when I started to think the end was in sight, I got buried under another mountain of file folders. It wasn't enough I got saddled with our homegrown screwballs. Now I have to deal with a bunch of imports."

"Imports?"

"Statements the FBI has collected from surrounding counties, plus the most bizarre anonymous tips that have been phoned in since the bombings started. The feds, in their infinite wisdom, have decided to have somebody who's familiar with the local 'eccentrics' weed out the ones that aren't worth wasting their precious time on."

Faith thought that sounded like a sound strategy, but she prudently refrained from saying so.

"Still, despite the combined efforts of my own department and the Federal Bureau of Incompetents to waste my time, for a while it looked like I'd turned up an honest-to-God suspect."

Faith had drifted into half-listening mode, marking time until he finished blowing off steam, but those last few words caught her attention. She stopped eating and leaned forward. "A Rat Man suspect?"

"I thought so, for a few hours. It was one of six names the mainframe spit out after I requested the database search last week," he explained, then paused and frowned. "I told you about that, didn't I?"

She shook her head no. "I don't think so."

"Well, I have this theory, that Rat Man is a cyberphobe."

Faith had never heard the word before, but it wasn't hard to deduce its meaning. "You think he fears computers or computer technology."

"More to the point, that he has a major grudge against computers . . . or maybe against people who make and or use them."

She nodded thoughtfully. "That makes sense. A lot of people are still intimidated by computers. And there are probably quite a few who've lost their jobs because of computerization in the workplace."

"Exactly. And all his targets have had something to do with computer technology. So I requested a database search for the names of people who have been charged in vandalism cases that involved—"

"Computers," Faith finished for him. "And your search produced six names?"

"One of which looked promising . . . until I went to interview him." He told her about his visit with Patrick Dean, which explained why he was so bummed. The interview had been the last in a daylong series of frustrations and disappointments.

"You're sure none of the other five could be Rat Man?" she asked.

Rhys heaved a dejected sigh, planted an elbow on the table and rested his chin on his hand. Apparently his bad mood hadn't affected his appetite; he'd managed to polish off every last noodle, chunk of chicken and snow pea on his plate.

"Any one of the first three would have been a dream suspect, but I eliminated them because all three were in jail when at least one of the bombings took place."

"I can see how that would make it hard to get a warrant," Faith said wryly.

"The fourth name was a guy who flipped out when a

computer salesman refused to give him enough free memory so he could play his favorite game. His problem isn't that he hates computers, it's that he's addicted to them. And the sixth person on the list is a sixty-year-old woman."

She had to admit neither of those last two sounded like a serial bomber.

"But what on earth did a sixty-year-old woman do to be charged with vandalism?"

By the time he finished telling her about the incident with the goat's blood, he was grinning. Reluctantly, she could tell, but it was a definite improvement over the glum expression he'd worn since he arrived.

"Maybe she was protesting the high cost of medical care," Rhys speculated.

"Or being made to fill out a ton of forms and then sit in the doctor's waiting room for two hours," Faith suggested.

He shook his head in puzzlement. "Makes you wonder, doesn't it? Why *would* an elderly woman—or anybody, for that matter—do something like that?"

Faith shrugged and collected their plates and flatware. "She was probably just fed up with the system. Maybe her insurance company refused to pay for a blood test the doctor ordered, or his receptionist screwed up the appointment schedule. There's a lot of antagonism toward the health care system in general and doctors in particular. I see it every day. I assume this doctor was a specialist."

"A surgeon, I think."

"Well, there you go," she said dryly.

She turned toward the sink as she spoke, so didn't see Rhys get up from the table. She jumped in surprise when his arms slid around her from behind.

"I take it that means surgeons are especially reviled," he murmured against the side of her neck.

"They have a reputation, often deserved, for being arrogant megalomaniacs. Does this belated display of affection indicate that you're in a better mood, I hope?"

"Mmmm, good food and the company of a beautiful, intelligent woman always put me in a good mood."

She leaned back into his embrace and laid her hands on top of his. "No doubt the Scotch helped, too."

He caught her earlobe between his teeth and tugged, sending shivers of sexual awareness rippling through her body. Faith did her best to ignore them, but her best wasn't good enough.

"I'm sorry," Rhys said in her ear. "I shouldn't have taken my rotten day out on you."

She struggled to resist the effect of that sinfully seductive voice, his hot, moist breath . . . the hand that had crept up to fondle her right breast. Reminding herself that there were things she wanted to talk to him about, she pulled out of his arms while she still could.

"I'll forgive you if you'll share some of that Scotch."

He gave her a surprised, slightly puzzled look, but all he said was, "I hope you handle Scotch better than you handle wine."

So did Faith. She needed a clear head for the conversation they were about to have. But she also needed a little extra courage. After her first sip of watered-down Scotch—the way he insisted she drink it—she knew there was no chance she would overimbibe.

"God, this is *awful!* You can't tell me you actually *like* it."

"It's an acquired taste," Rhys allowed, his amused grin disappearing as he looked into her eyes across the kitchen table. "Whatever it is you've got to tell me, it must be pretty bad."

Faith sighed and forced down another tiny sip. "No actually, I think it's good."

"So tell me."

"I had another dream last night."

She said it matter-of-factly, trying to blunt the impact but he snapped upright as if she'd taken a swipe at him with a steak knife.

"What! Why didn't you tell me? Hell, I was right there *next* to you, for God's sake! Why didn't you wake me?"

She shrugged, staring into her glass rather than mee

his indignant gaze. "I started to, but then, . . . Now don't go all macho, I know it was foolish of me—*now* I know—but suddenly it seemed like a cowardly, stereotypically female thing to do—wake the big, strong man just because you had a bad dream. So I didn't."

She looked at him then, bracing herself for the explosion she half expected. A muscle twitched in his jaw. His shirt pulled taut across his chest as he inhaled deeply, but then he released his breath in an exasperated whoosh, poured a couple of ounces of Scotch into his glass and downed half of it.

"That's just plain stupid."

"I know," she muttered.

"It isn't as if you had a nightmare about vampires, or aliens that suck out people's brains, for God's sake."

Faith bit her lip to keep from smiling; partly in relief that he wasn't going to explode, but also because his gruff tone told her he wouldn't have minded being awakened because she'd had a nightmare about brain-sucking aliens.

"I'm as involved in this as you are, dammit. Your dreams affect both of us. They're *important* to both of us."

"Yes, I realize that."

"It has nothing to do with any idiotic male-female stereotypes."

She nodded. "I'm sorry. Next time I promise to wake you. Even if I have to call you on the phone."

"You won't," he said flatly. "Just reach over and give me a shake." He took another drink of Scotch, then gave her a sharp, penetrating look. "You sound pretty sure there'll be a next time."

Faith folded her hands on the table to keep from picking up her own glass. "I am sure. I know now that the dreams won't stop until you catch him or he blows himself up with one of his bombs. But we can't afford to wait for either of those possibilities. I'm only getting bits and pieces about him from dreams. It's not enough, and it's taking too long." She paused to wet her lips, then said it all in a rush, so he couldn't interrupt.

"I've decided to try to use out-of-body experiences to find him. If that doesn't work, I'll see if I can locate and identify him from the astral plane."

She was encouraged when Rhys didn't immediately start arguing, but she felt his instinctive resistance.

"It's the only option we have," she said.

"No, it's not. The FBI and ATF are on the case, and—"

"They're not getting anywhere! Rhys, time is running out. He's planning to kill people. A lot of people."

"Is that what you saw?" he said sharply. "Last night, in the dream?"

"Yes. I was in the next place he intends to bomb. I couldn't tell where it was, but there was something familiar about it. I think I've been there." She hesitated, shook her head in frustration. "Though it's possible I've only seen a picture of it, or been someplace similar."

"And you saw people?"

Faith lifted a hand to rub at her forehead. How was she going to explain, much less convince him? "No. I couldn't see them, but I could hear them and *feel* them . . . their presence, their psychic energy. It was a fairly large number of people—men, women, adults, children."

"Children." Rhys repeated the word in a voice heavy with dread. "You're sure about this? Was he there?"

"Yes, I'm sure," she murmured. "And he was there. I didn't see him either, but—"

"Then how can you be a hundred percent sure it was another precognitive dream about Rat Man?"

She closed her eyes for a moment, striving to stay calm and focused. She had to convince him. What she was going to ask him to do wouldn't work if he had the slightest doubt. He had to believe in her, had to *trust* her.

"Because he spoke to me."

She looked deep into his eyes, letting him see the conviction in hers, at the same time baring her mind and feelings. She told him how she'd wondered if the people she sensed were ghosts, then repeated the answer that had slammed into her mind like a lightning bolt.

" 'Not yet, but soon.' I heard it as clearly as if he'd been tanding right in front of me. It was as if he *wanted* me to now . . . as if he was taunting me."

Rhys started to pick up his glass, saw that it was empty, nd splashed in more Scotch. After he'd gulped down nough to dissolve the lining of his esophagus, he asked, Is that what you think—that he's taunting you?"

His tone was carefully neutral, and Faith was picking up uch a churning confusion of emotions from him that it 'as impossible to determine what *he* thought.

"I don't know. Maybe. If the threatening presence I felt t the clinic and then here *was* Rat Man, this dream could ave been a continuation or escalation or whatever you 'ant to call it. If he's somehow found out that I know bout him, that I've been, in effect, watching him—"

She broke off suddenly, but Rhys interrupted at the same me and so didn't notice.

"No, hold on. Think about what you're saying. This guy real. He exists outside your dreams. If he knew, or even *uspected,* that you have that kind of knowledge, he'd come fter you. In person, Faith, not just in a dream."

"Not if he doesn't know who I am," she murmured.

"If he doesn't know who you are, how could he possibly e taunting you?"

She shook her head in frustration and took another sip f Scotch. It didn't taste any better than the first few sips ad. "What I'm saying is, he could have realized that *some-ody* knows about him, but not who that somebody is."

"How—?" Rhys began, but she didn't let him finish.

"My notebook. The steno pad I've been using to keep record of the dreams. I lost it."

It took a moment for the implications of that to sink in. Vhen they did, he blanched. "Oh, Jesus."

"I took it to work yesterday, to go over my notes. I know had it in the break room at lunchtime. I forgot all about until this morning, when I decided to write down the letails of last night's dream. I couldn't find it anywhere. 'hen I realized I must have left it at work, but when I went to get it, it wasn't there. Don't ask if I looked everywhere I did. It's gone. The good news is, my name isn't on it and there's nothing in the notes that could identify me."

Rhys raked both hands through his hair. He looked stressed to the max, literally at the end of his emotional limits. Faith empathized. It was exactly how she'd felt earlier in the day. The difference was that he didn't have to withdraw to an internal fortress to regroup and recharge. She saw him back away from the edge, subdue his alarm, begin to organize his chaotic thoughts. It wasn't a question of eavesdropping on what was going on inside his head; she actually *saw* him pull himself together. It was amazing. From what inner reservoir did he draw that kind of strength and assurance?

"All right," he said, shoving the bottle and his glass to one side. "Let's start from square one. Who could've found the notebook?"

She made a helpless gesture. "Any number of people—clinic employees, patients, their relatives. Several of the people upstairs take their coffee breaks and lunches in our department. Makes it harder for somebody to cut their break periods short and call them back to work. Short of questioning everybody who was in the building yesterday afternoon, I don't think there's any way to find out who took it."

"And even if we did question everybody, we'd have to give them all polygraph tests to be sure they were telling the truth," he muttered. "You're sure your name isn't on the notebook?"

"Positive."

"How about your handwriting? Who would recognize it?"

Faith considered for a moment. "Only the other two therapists and Missy, our receptionist. She types our reports for the doctors' files. Our handwritten notes stay in our department."

He released a sigh of relief. "So unless he saw you with the notebook, he can't know that it's yours."

"I'm sure he doesn't. As you said a couple of minutes ago, if he knew, he'd come after me. He'd have to, wouldn't he? He couldn't gamble that I wouldn't go to the police, especially since he's planning to plant another bomb."

"But, assuming he has the notebook, it doesn't contain anything about this last dream," Rhys said thoughtfully.

"No. I bought a new steno pad. The notes about last night's dream are in it."

She got up to retrieve the new notebook from the top of the microwave and handed it to him. He sat staring at it, but didn't immediately open it.

"You're beginning to see it, aren't you?" Faith said as she slid back onto her chair. "He doesn't know that *I* know he's planning to blow up another building. There has to be a way to use that. If I can initiate an out-of-body experience, try to get to the same place I visited in last night's dream—"

"I don't like it," Rhys said bluntly. "You said you haven't tried that for years. What if you can't control it, or something happens? Hell, what if once you leave your body, you can't get back?"

She took a deep breath. "I know, there's some risk involved. That's why I want you to be with me when I do it. If you see that I'm in trouble you can call me back, like you did last night."

He started shaking his head before she finished.

"Rhys, I have to at least *try*."

"No. It's a bad idea. Hell, it's a *terrible* idea! I don't know a damned thing about out-of-body experiences, for God's sake. What makes you think I'd have a clue that you were in trouble? You could be orbiting Pluto for all I'd know."

Faith had expected something like this. He wasn't just afraid for her; he was loath to accept the responsibility for keeping her safe.

"You'd know I was in trouble if we were linked telepathically."

He stared at her as if she'd suggested he join her on that jaunt to Pluto. "Oh, no," he muttered.

"It wouldn't be like last night," she hurried to assure him. "Out-of-body travel isn't anything like astral projection. For one thing, everything looks exactly the same—paintings don't melt, furniture doesn't stretch or shrink. Your consciousness just sort of floats up out of your body. The next thing you know, you're looking down on everything."

"Sort of like what's supposed to happen when you die."

"I give you my word, neither of us will die." She gave him a small, coaxing smile. "Or end up on Pluto, either. Nobody knows for sure how far it's possible to travel from your corporal body, but it isn't an unlimited distance. If the place I saw in the dream is very far away, I may not even be able to get there."

He just sat there, scowling at her, for a full minute. Faith scrupulously avoided invading his thoughts lest she should unconsciously apply any mental pressure. This had to be his decision.

"If I refuse to go along with this, you're going to think I'm a real wuss, aren't you?" he said at length.

"Of course not! I'll respect whatever decision you make."

"But you've made up your mind to do it anyway, with or without me."

"Yes."

His mouth thinned, his beautiful blue eyes narrowed; for a moment or two she thought the explosion she'd expected earlier had only been delayed. But then he expelled a long-suffering sigh and reached for the Scotch.

"God deliver me from stubborn women," he said as he tipped an ounce into his glass. "All right, damn it, I'll give it a try. But we have to work out some kind of game plan first. And I want a thorough briefing about what to expect before you take off for parts unknown."

Faith felt both her mind and body droop in relief. "Okay. But you'll be with me, remember."

"On the enemy's turf," he said grimly. "Which makes it even more important that I have some idea what to expect. I suppose now that you've made up your mind, you want to try this tonight."

"There's no reason to wait," she said. "And, anyway, I don't think we can afford to. Whatever he's planning next, it's going to happen soon." She watched him throw back another ounce of whiskey and remarked dryly, "It would probably be better if you weren't half drunk."

"Wrong," Rhys muttered. "For your information, I always get half drunk before I fly."

Leon was worried. Mother hadn't been herself since Lenny's death, but the changes he'd seen in her during the past two weeks were frightening.

She'd always been a strong woman. Widowed twice before she was thirty, she'd raised her twin sons alone—fed and clothed them, kept a roof over their heads, made sure they had the right spiritual and moral values—sometimes working two or three jobs at a time. She'd taught her boys by her example that family always came first. Always. You stood by each other no matter what, because family was all you could count on through good times and bad. Her boys had taken the lesson so much to heart that over the years they and Mother had melded into a single unit; not three individuals who depended upon each other, but one indivisible whole.

Until one day, suddenly and without warning, Lenny was gone, and it quickly became clear to Leon that his brother had been the cement that held them together. Not Mother, but Lenny.

Of course he'd always known Lenny was special. Everybody liked Lenny. He never had trouble making friends. He'd always got good grades and good jobs. He was always happy, and why shouldn't he be? He expected good things to happen to him, and they did.

Leon had never minded any of that. He'd worshipped his brother. And Lenny always looked out for him, never let anyone treat him badly, never let *him* do bad or stupid things. Whenever he had a problem, or was confused about something, all he had to do was talk to Lenny. Lenny always knew exactly what to do, always gave him good advice.

He wished Lenny was there to talk to now. Lenny would know what he should do about Mother. Of course, if Lenny was still here, Mother would be all right. *Everything* would be all right.

If only their regular doctor hadn't been called away on some emergency the night Lenny got sick. If only they hadn't taken him to that brand new hospital, with its million-dollar computers that had taken the place of wise, caring humans, and its dedication to the gods of Science and Technology.

One mistake. Just one, that's all it had taken. A single instruction somebody forgot to give the almighty computer. Because of that one little mistake, the wrong anesthetic was administered. His brother was dead. And Mother . . .

Well, Mother hadn't been right since that night. First there was the incident at the doctor's office—the doctor who had been removing Lenny's burst appendix when he died. She'd tried to explain why she did it—something about the blood of the lamb, or Lenny's blood on the doctor's hands—but she was so upset that Leon hadn't been able to make sense of what she said. She'd been like that a lot lately, especially the past couple of weeks.

And then at supper tonight, she'd asked him whether the doctor had found homes for all the puppies yet. For a split second he almost corrected her, almost told her it had been her other son, Lenny, who was the veterinarian's assistant. Then he realized that she thought he *was* Lenny and he felt as if he'd been grabbed by a giant, icy hand.

Back in his room, he sat on the bed, staring at the framed picture of him and Lenny that Mother had sent them to Olan Mills to have taken last year. A stranger wouldn't have been able to tell which of them was which, but Mother had *never* confused them, not even when they were little and she'd dressed them just alike. She *knew* Lenny was dead; she'd been at the hospital that night, had watched as they lowered his casket into the ground. Was her mind playing tricks on her now because she wished it had been him who died, instead of Lenny? God knew he'd wished it, a hundred times in the past three months.

He would be joining his brother soon, but what was he going to do about Mother?

Chapter Sixteen

Faith wanted to get as comfortable as possible before trying to initiate an out-of-body experience, so they moved to her bedroom. She took off her shoes and stretched ou on the bed, while Rhys settled in her rocking chair. She insisted that he leave the bottle of Scotch in the kitchen

They'd agreed that this first attempt would be a dry run so to speak; assuming Faith could leave her body withou any trouble—which was a pretty big assumption at thi point—she wouldn't attempt to find either Rat Man o the place she'd visited in last night's dream. Knowing i advance that he wasn't going to be telepathically dragge along on a high-speed out-of-body pursuit had eased Rhys' anxiety considerably. Of course the whiskey had helped too.

Establishing the telepathic connection was as effortles as breathing. Faith simply reached out and he was there His thoughts whispered through her mind, as naturally a her own.

You're sure I'll know when it happens.

You'll know, she replied. *Just try to relax. Close your eyes an take deep, slow breaths.*

She wasn't at all certain this was going to work, but she new that the longer she delayed, the greater the risk that ie'd get too tense and distracted. And so, without further do, she crossed her fingers for luck and willed herself to se from her body.

Up . . . up . . . slowly at first, like a blind woman feeling er way through a door and into an unfamiliar room. or just an instant there was a slight resistance, and then uddenly she was free, hovering weightless and formless bove the bed, looking down . . . at herself, and at Rhys.

"Holy Christ," he said in a shaken murmur. His eyes ere closed, his head resting against the tall back of the ocker. He was gripping the chair's arms so hard that his nuckles showed white through his skin.

Do you see what I'm seeing?

He nodded. "Yes."

Don't be afraid.

"I'm not." A small, nervous laugh escaped him. His eyes tayed closed. "I probably should be, but I'm not."

Faith drifted closer to him, and both saw and heard his oft gasp. *Then why are you holding on to the chair like that?*

His hands relaxed their grip—slowly, cautiously. He ughed again. "I don't just see what you're seeing, I *feel* , too. It's . . . God, how can I explain it? It's as if I'm in ero gravity, or pumped full of helium."

Weightless, Faith concurred. *Lighter than air.*

"I know it's an illusion, but it's so damned *real!* I thought 'd float up out of the chair if I let go. What'll happen if open my eyes?"

Beats me. I guess there's only one way to find out.

He hesitated a moment. As soon as his eyes were open, e muttered, "Whoa!" and closed them again, but only or a second or two. He rocked the chair forward so that e was sitting upright and blinked rapidly, as if to clear is vision. Then he tilted his head a little, first one way nd then another. The small, delicate movements eminded Faith of a bird.

What? she asked. *What's happening?*

"This is *really* bizarre. I'm seeing through my eyes *and* yours . . . at the same time. What I'm getting from you is very faint—like when one television channel bleeds through to another. What do you call that?"

A ghost image?

"That's it, a ghost image." He leaned forward and stared at the bed. Or rather, she suddenly realized, at her, lying on the bed. "If I concentrate on what *I'm* seeing, the image I'm getting from you fades until it disappears completely."

Can you pull it back?

"Just a sec. Yeah, no problem." He suddenly looked up toward the ceiling. "Oh, *wow.*"

This time Faith didn't ask for an explanation. He was looking straight at her, except there was no physical form hovering above him. Instead, he saw the ghost image of his own upturned, awestruck face. He lowered his gaze and shook his head in wonder.

"Incredible! How long can you keep this up?"

I have no idea. I wasn't even sure I could still do it, but guess it's like riding a bike—once you learn, you never forget.

"I'd say this is a helluva lot harder than riding a bike," Rhys said wryly. "You said you could travel. How far—to the living room?"

Faith knew that short a distance wouldn't be any problem, so she answered by sailing through the open bedroom door and into the hall.

"Slow down, for pity's sake!" Rhys called out behind her. "You're making me dizzy."

Sorry, she replied. *Close your eyes, sit back, and relax. Don fight it. Describe what you're seeing.* She was pleased and relieved that he was reacting so well to what had to be an unnerving experience, to say the least. But this was supposed to be a test, after all; not only of her ability to travel out-of-body, but of whether they could maintain the link and across how great a distance.

As she zoomed around the corner at the end of the hall where the small entry opened into the living room, she felt a momentary flutter in her stomach. The kind c cared-but-excited little tickle you get on a roller coaster. he'd never had such a reaction before. It had to have ome from Rhys, which meant the transfer of sensation as working both ways. She coasted to a stop in front of he sofa.

Sorry about that turn. You okay?

She heard his dry response with her mind, rather than er ears. *If you'd been out on the street, I'd have given you a icket for reckless driving.*

You'd have to catch me first. Tell me what you see.

You're in the living room, in front of and facing the couch. verything looks exactly like it's supposed to . . . normal, I mean.

I told you it would. She slowly rose toward the ceiling, otating in a 360-degree circle as she ascended.

Showoff, Rhys remarked. *Can you do a backflip?*

She ignored the question. *What did you see, just then?*

You floated up in the air. Or I guess I should say we *floated p in the air, because that's how it felt. And turned around in circle. Now it looks like we're sitting upside-down on the ceiling.*

Are you still seeing everything clearly?

As clearly as if I was plastered to the ceiling with you. Thank od I'm not afraid of heights.

Are your eyes still closed?

Yes.

Open them, see how much difference it makes, Faith instructed. he waited a couple of seconds, then began to circle the oom, still at ceiling level.

Rhys? Talk to me.

You're moving around the room, along the walls, still close to he ceiling. You just passed a cobweb, there in the corner.

I forgot to mention, it's okay to ignore stuff like dust and obwebs.

His soft, sexy laugh reverberated through her mind. *I'm etting a ghost image, like before, but now I have to concentrate arder to keep it in focus. Is that because you're farther away?*

Probably. I'm going into the kitchen. Keep talking to me.

It quickly became obvious that increased distance did eaken their telepathic link. By the time Faith reached

the kitchen table, Rhys had to close his eyes—blocking hi
own visual input—in order to clearly discern the imag
she was sending. That was discouraging; it meant she woul
have to stay close to him, or he wouldn't be able to monito
her out-of-body experiences. Their telepathic link was stil
very new, though. Maybe with practice, they coul
strengthen it.

On the other hand, the second part of the test was ver
encouraging. She'd traveled forty or fifty feet from he
body and wasn't experiencing any negative effects—n
faintness or disorientation, no depletion of her psychi
energy. She felt as though she could keep going indefi
nitely . . . out the front door, down the street, across town
Maybe for miles. Was that possible? Logically, she though
there must be a limit. At the moment, though, she fel
vigorous, strong, inexhaustible.

Get that idea right out of your head, Rhys said clearly
reminding her that he was still tapped into her thoughts
In case it's slipped your mind, there's a psycho out there who isn
exactly your number one fan. Besides, I'm getting lonely. Wh
don't we call it quits for tonight.

For a moment Faith was tempted to argue. Except fo
the Rat Man dreams—and even in a lucid dream state th
experience was like a dim, distant memory compared t
the real thing—she hadn't traveled out-of-body for years
She had just begun to rediscover the freedom and exhilara
tion, the sheer joy. She didn't want to go back just yet
But that *I'm getting lonely* plucked at her emotions an
persuaded her to join Rhys physically as well as mentally

All right. She suspected he picked up her reluctance, bu
she didn't feel a smidgen of guilt. Now that he'd share
the experience, he would understand that it was sometime
difficult to return.

As she reentered the bedroom, he said, "I'm curiou
about something. Why did you only communicate telepath
ically once you left your body?"

Because when I'm not in my body, I can't control it, Fait
answered. She drifted over her own inert form on th

ped and hovered, preparing herself. While reuniting her psyche and physical body wasn't difficult, it could be emotionally jarring if she didn't pause a moment or so to anticipate the adjustment.

"You mean you can't *move?*" Rhys demanded.

Not until I'm back, she replied absently. *And even then, to be honest, I'm a little uncoordinated for the first couple of minutes.*

He said something else, but she was no longer listening. All her attention was focused on bringing her body and consciousness together without disturbing the harmony between them. She visualized her arms lifting off the bed, reaching out in welcome, and willed herself to return to her corporeal home. The joining was as easy as the separation had been; much less stressful than she remembered from past experiences.

Unfortunately she returned to find Rhys standing over her, fists planted on his hips and a dark scowl on his handsome face.

"Are you listening to me? You didn't say anything about that before—not a word!"

Faith blinked up at him in confusion. "I didn't say a word about what?"

"About not being able to move! No way am I going to let you leave your body, for God's sake, to go chasing after some psychopath. If he spotted you and went after you, you'd be helpless."

Faith sat up, too fast, then had to close her eyes until a wave of dizziness passed. "But you'll be there to protect me," she mumbled. "You're going to be my bodyguard. Literally."

He sat on the bed beside her. "What's wrong?"

"Nothing. I forgot that I shouldn't make any sudden moves for a minute or so, that's all."

"I see. I assume that would include run-for-your-life-because-some-maniac-with-a-bomb-is-trying-to-kill-you sudden moves?"

He was furious. Even if she hadn't felt his anger like a series of progressively harder shoves, she'd have heard it

in his voice. She strove to keep her own temper in check
telling herself he was only reacting this way because he
was unnerved by what he'd just experienced, and obviously
also because he was worried . . . for her.

"You're upset," she said, her tone as moderate as she
could manage. "When you've calmed down—"

"Damn right, I'm upset! How can you even *consider* put
ting yourself in that kind of danger? Do you have some
kind of death wish, for God's sake?"

"Of course not, don't be ridiculous." Faith scooted of
the bed and slipped her shoes back on. "I'm not going to
discuss this until you can be rational."

She expected him to follow her when she left the bed
room, and he did. His angry indignation pressed agains
her back, almost propelling her down the hall and through
the living room. Lord, if he ever learned to control hi
own latent psychic abilities, the criminal element wouldn'
stand a chance.

"I'm perfectly rational," he snarled as she entered the
kitchen and started preparing to brew some green tea
"Am I ranting or raving? Am I foaming at the mouth
What are you doing?"

"Making a pot of green tea. It calms your nerves an
settles your stomach."

"I'm *calm,* dammit!"

"It isn't for you."

"Oh," he said after a beat of silence.

Faith felt him back away, not physically but mentally
When he had his own emotions under control, he reache
out and tentatively probed hers. But he didn't stop there
He actually penetrated her thoughts. She *felt* him—dig
ging, analyzing. How long had he been able to do that
She spun around and glared at him.

"Don't," she said sharply. "Stay out of my head."

The outburst surprised them both. They stared at eac
other in self-conscious silence for several agonizing se
onds, then blurted, "I'm sorry," at the same time. Whic
eased the tension but didn't completely dispel it.

"I shouldn't have snapped at you like that," Faith murmured.

"No, you were right. I shouldn't have—" Rhys broke off, shook his head. He was obviously disconcerted. "But I didn't even know I *could,* until I did it."

Faith wondered which of them was more rattled by the admission. He was the only person she'd ever known who possessed the ability to read her thoughts. And now, apparently, he could do it whenever he wanted. Upsetting as that knowledge was to her, it was probably even more disturbing to Rhys.

"I think I'd better make enough green tea for both of us," she murmured as she turned away to get the teapot.

Neither of them said anything until they were seated across from one another at the table. Faith was careful not to intrude into his thoughts, and she knew he was respecting her privacy just as scrupulously.

"What's happening here?" she said softly.

Rhys sat hunched over his cup of tea, both hands curved around it as if he needed to absorb the warmth. "I don't know. But whatever it is, I don't like it."

"It's been a long, hard day, for both of us. Maybe we're just stressed out."

He looked up, straight into her eyes. "That's part of it, but there's something else. You feel it too, don't you—some . . . obstacle, that wasn't there before?"

"Yes," she admitted with a sigh.

"Everything's happened so damned fast. I feel like I'm living on the world's most active fault line, and I keep getting knocked on my ass every five minutes."

"Interesting analogy," Faith said wryly. "I'm sorry. I know I'm responsible for most of the shocks you've had in the past couple of weeks."

"Don't turn into a martyr on me, for God's sake," he muttered.

She drew back in surprise and offense. "I'm not!"

"Good. Because none of this is your fault."

"I know that."

"I'm not assigning blame."

"How generous of you."

"Although if I were inclined to criticize, I'd point out that this harebrained idea of chasing Rat Man through the astral plane is just plain nuts, not to mention suicidally reckless."

"I told you before, I don't have a death wish," Faith said coolly. "I wonder . . . could it be that this *obstacle* that's suddenly appeared between us is your aversion to letting me make any decisions or initiate any action on my own?"

His head jerked back as if she'd stuck a dead rat under his nose. "What!"

"You've resisted the idea ever since I brought it up."

"Of course I have, for God's sake! I'd resist the idea of you dousing yourself with gasoline and lighting a match too."

Faith smiled thinly. "You're forgetting, I wouldn't need either the gas or the match."

Rhys's expression instantly changed from combative to contrite. "Oh, Jesus. I'm sorry. I didn't think—"

"Forget it," she dismissed.

"No." One of his hands suddenly shot out, grabbing her wrist before she could evade him. "Don't, Faith. Don't shut me out. This is important. We need to talk about it, work it out."

The desire to retreat, just withdraw to her quiet, safe place and avoid the confrontation he sought, was strong. His impulsive reference to fire had felt like a knife thrust to the heart, even though she knew it wasn't intended to hurt. How ironic, that her long-overdue decision to be more assertive, to finally take control of her life, had led to this. She'd handled it wrong, hadn't explained well enough, hadn't managed to convince him; worse, somewhere along the way she had alienated the one person she needed as an ally.

She knew he was right. They had to work out their differences, now, before the rift grew too wide to repair. But at the moment she felt very vulnerable. He was such a strong, forceful personality, always so sure of himself. If she wasn't just as strong, he might convince her to abandon her "harebrained idea." She nodded warily, but at the same time tugged her arm out of his grasp.

"All right," she murmured. "Let's talk. You first."

Relief flickered in his eyes, but there was a spark of surprise, as well. "All right. There's probably more than a grain of truth in what you said a minute ago—that I'm reluctant to relinquish control. Until tonight, you've been willing to let me call the shots, decide what we should do."

"I knew it," Faith muttered. "It's some idiotic male ego thing."

"Partly, yeah, I imagine so. But there's more to it than that. I'm a cop, for Pete's sake! Investigating crimes and catching bad guys is what I get paid to do. And, ego be damned, I'm very good at it."

"I've never doubted that," she assured him. "So you're feeling some kind of professional resentment, too, on top of the chest-beating macho garbage? That's . . . silly." She almost said "stupid" but caught herself at the last second. "You rely on witnesses to help you solve crimes all the time, don't you?"

Rhys made a sound halfway between a sardonic laugh and a groan. "Damn, when you decide to go on the offensive, you don't pull any punches."

"Well, don't you?" she persisted.

"Of course I do. But I usually deal with people who witnessed a crime *when* it happened, not *before*. I take their statements and then work backwards, checking and double-checking to verify the information they provide. I have to keep careful, detailed notes, write and then periodically update reports, fill out a mountain of forms. Everything's documented. *Everything*—every interview, every anonymous tip, every scrap of physical evidence. Without that documentation, we'd never convince a prosecutor to bring charges. Good police work gets criminals caught, but it's good record-keeping that gets them convicted."

"And you have no record of the information you've gotten from me," Faith murmured.

"Nothing I could hand over to my lieutenant. Not unless I want to seriously jeopardize my career prospects and be escorted straight to the department shrink's office."

He ran a hand through his hair in exasperation. "I've taken everything on trust because I believe in you, and in your psychic abilities. I'll never understand them if I live to be a hundred," he added wryly, "but I for damned sure know they're real."

"That doesn't help, though, does it?" Faith said. "You can hardly go into court and say, 'I give you my solemn word, Your Honor, this woman really did see the defendant planting those bombs in her dreams.'"

"No," he agreed. "That isn't even a remote possibility. Do you see the hopeless predicament I've got myself into? I can't use your dreams as evidence, and even if I could, you've never seen his face, so you can't identify him. Now it looks like he's discovered that you're onto him, which puts you in danger even if he hasn't figured out who you are. Because he could, at any time. And since you know so much about him, he probably assumes that you *already* know who *he* is. If you were an ordinary, run-of-the-mill material witness, I could get you 'round the clock police protection. But since I'd probably be shipped off to a psych ward if I put this fantastic tale into a report, that isn't an option."

"You really believe I'm in danger?" Faith said skeptically.

"Yes, I do. I realize you're not convinced, but I've had a little more experience dealing with criminals, so on this subject my opinion is the one that counts."

"Oh, really?"

"Yes. Really. Now shut up and let me finish. You'll get your turn. Not only is it my duty to protect you, I *want* to protect you. No, that doesn't cover it—I *need* to protect you. It goes way beyond being a cop-witness thing. It's a man-woman thing. An *us* thing! You can write it off as supercharged hormones or societal conditioning or any damned thing you want, I really don't give a rat's ass. That's the way it is."

Faith stared at him in dumbfounded silence. She'd done a pretty good job of maintaining her resolve not to cave in, until that last vehement speech. How could she argue that she was perfectly capable of taking care of herself, now? Well, she could honestly say she didn't think she *needed* his protection, but she would be telling a black-hearted lie if she claimed she didn't want it. And of course he would know she was lying.

"Finished?" she asked huskily.

"For now." He picked up his cup and gulped down the remainder of his green tea. "All right, go ahead, light into me. Tell me what a despicable chauvinist I am."

Faith sipped at her own tea, hiding behind the cup. "Yes . . . well . . . That remark about chest-beating macho garbage may have been a slight overreaction on my part."

Rhys gave her a narrow-eyed look that made her tense up for a moment, but then his mouth stretched into a slow, heart-stopping smile that displayed his dimples to maximum effect.

"The tea must be working," he drawled.

She laughed. But then she sobered, set down her cup and reached across the table to clasp his hand. His smile vanished. The sudden intensity of his gaze was unnerving. Faith inhaled a deep, fortifying breath and started talking before she could lose her nerve.

"After that dream I had last night, I was an emotional wreck. I've spent the past eight years trying to create a normal life for myself . . . trying to put the past behind me, forget it ever happened, pretend I've always been just like everybody else. And then suddenly my psychic powers were back and it looked like the whole nightmare was starting all over again. For a minute this afternoon I actually thought I was having some kind of nervous breakdown."

Rhys squeezed her hand, hard. "Damn it, I wish you'd called me."

She shook her head. "I had to work through it myself.

And I did. I decided it's past time I stop thinking of my abilities as some kind of curse and myself as a victim. I'm not just like everybody else. I probably never will be. But that doesn't make me either inferior or superior, just different."

"Delightfully, wonderfully different," he murmured, lifting her hand to plant a kiss on the back.

"Thank you," Faith murmured. "But you may be just a tad prejudiced."

"Much more than a tad." For a moment he seemed about to say more, but instead he settled for kissing her hand again. "I assume this determination to try to find and identify Rat Man grew out of your crisis this afternoon."

"That's right. For better or worse, I have abilities other people don't have. I've wasted a good part of my life wishing I didn't have them, but that's water under the bridge. From now on, there'll be no more hand-wringing or agonizing over the very things that make me who I am."

"Good for you," Rhys said.

"I hope you mean that. Because I've decided I must have been given these abilities for a reason. Instead of trying to deny them, or hoping they'll go away, I'm going to start using them. Hopefully in positive, constructive ways. And right now, the most positive, constructive thing I can think of is to find Rat Man before he kills somebody."

Rhys didn't respond for some time. He lowered his gaze to their clasped hands, absently rubbing his thumb across her knuckles. The silence stretched out until it started to worry her, but she was determined not to probe his thoughts or emotions.

"I still don't like it," he said at length. He spoke softly, his tone carefully controlled. "It's dangerous. You could get hurt, and I don't just mean physically. We don't have any idea what kind of psychological damage you'd be risking." He lifted his head, speared her with a look that took her breath away.

"I don't want to lose you."

Faith wrapped both her hands around his. "I don't want to lose you, either."

"I can't talk you out of this?"

She gave him a small, bittersweet smile. "As a matter of fact, I'm afraid you could. I'm asking you not to try. A couple of days ago you encouraged me to trust my instincts, remember?"

He nodded. "At the Burger King. But I was talking about us, not some perverse compulsion to hunt down a dangerous criminal. Besides, *my* instincts are telling me this is a stupendously bad idea."

Faith sighed in frustration. His determined resistance was like a brick wall. Should she just give up, admit defeat? She didn't think she'd be able to do this without him; she needed not only his cooperation, but his emotional support. Nothing she'd said had convinced him, and she was fresh out of reasoned and reasonable arguments. In desperation, she resorted to a last-ditch, purely emotional appeal.

"Please, Rhys . . . trust me. Just trust me to decide what's right."

She only realized that she'd repeated his words, almost verbatim, after she spoke them. She knew at once that he was remembering, too.

"Damn it," he said after a short, taut silence. "That's an underhanded tactic."

Faith gave an apologetic shrug. The tension that had gripped her was already loosening its hold. "Desperate situations call for desperate measures." She squeezed his hand. "Don't be mad. I need you. Help me, please."

"And that's even worse," he said gruffly. "Next you'll be batting your eyelashes and simpering."

"Simpering? Please. No self-respecting feminist would ever simper."

"You know damn well I trust you. Hell, I let you take me on a tour of the ceiling, didn't I?"

She thought he'd come around, but she wanted a definite commitment. "So you won't waste any more time trying to talk me out of this? And you'll come along when I try to find him?"

"You think I'd let you chase a mad bomber through the ether alone? I'm your bodyguard, remember?"

Faith impulsively jumped up and stretched across the table to kiss him, catching him by surprise. She pulled back just as his mouth began to return the pressure of hers and his hands came off the table to reach for her.

"We should go over the notes I made about the dream I had last night," she said, dropping back into her chair and flipping open the new steno pad. "Maybe you'll recognize something about the place."

Rhys muttered something unintelligible under his breath. She ducked her head, smiled, and didn't ask him to repeat it.

Chapter Seventeen

They reviewed her notes for half an hour, then Faith let Rhys think he coaxed her into the bedroom. In truth, she didn't need coaxing. She wasn't so eager to find a mad serial bomber that she had abandoned her principal obsession. Namely, Rhys Donovan.

On the way through the living room, Rhys detoured to the stereo to start a Righteous Brothers CD. They made love with slow, sensual precision while "Unchained Melody" wafted down the hall. They shared and savored every sensation, each of them understanding exactly what pleasured the other most, without a word being spoken. When Rhys shifted to lie beside her and gently eased her onto his chest, for the first time in her life Faith wept tears of happiness.

Unfortunately, Sunday morning began with a minor tiff. It had been a stressful week. He wanted to stay in and relax—have a huge, late breakfast, make love, linger over the sports section, make love, maybe go see a movie in the afternoon, come back home and make love. Et cetera. Faith was determined not to fritter the day away on self-indulgence.

"This is the only entire day we've had together," she pointed out.

"Exactly. I'd prefer not to spend it zooming around the city on your astral charter service."

"We could get a lot accomplished, maybe even find the place I saw in the dream."

She waited, giving him one last chance to acquiesce. He stood with his back to the kitchen sink, lean hips resting against the edge of the countertop, arms folded, jaw set in stubborn resistance. He hadn't shaved. Faith had offered a disposable razor, but he refused. It was Sunday, his attitude said; he didn't have to shave if he didn't feel like it. His dark beard stubble, uncombed hair, bare feet, and the wrinkled white T-shirt hanging loose over navy dress trousers should have made him look like a vagrant, or worse. Instead, she found herself wondering if she'd lost her mind because she wasn't leaping at the chance to spend the day in bed with him.

"No?" she said after he let two minutes pass in silence.

"No."

"All right. I guess I'll see you later."

She was halfway across the living room when he caught up with her.

"You're going anyway," he said flatly, making it sound like an accusation.

"I told you, Rhys, I don't think we can afford to waste any time." She stopped at the bedroom door and faced him. "It isn't that I don't want to be with you. You know I do. But we have the rest of our lives to be together. Those people in the dream, whoever and wherever they are, don't have much time left. I have to know that at least I tried to save them, that I did everything I could to stop this maniac. I'd be a lot more comfortable if you came with me, but I have to *try*, with or without you."

He stretched out an arm and planted his hand on the doorjamb, then leaned forward until their noses were an inch apart. "You know what's the most aggravating thing about you?"

"No. What?"

"That you always end up being right. We'll have to go to my place first, so I can shave and get some clean clothes."

"You don't have to shave," Faith said with a grateful smile.

At first they worked their way through the neighborhood surrounding her house, on the assumption—which, she readily admitted, was based on nothing more than intuition—that since the place from the dream had seemed familiar, it might be close by. She hoped that if they passed near the building, she might pick up some kind of psychic signal.

"This isn't going to work," Rhys observed when they'd been cruising for almost an hour. "Louisville is a big city. It would take us weeks to cover it, maybe months if we try to hit all the suburbs. And there's no guarantee you'd recognize this place if we stopped right in front of it."

"I know," Faith said with a sigh. "It's just that I'm *sure* I've either been there or seen it—maybe in a television commercial, or a newspaper photo. I thought it might be some place I pass every day on the way to work and just don't usually notice."

He turned a corner and reached over to give her hand a squeeze. "Don't get discouraged. Let's try to narrow the possibilities a little. Describe it again."

She let her head fall back against the seat's headrest and closed her eyes, summoning the images from the dream.

"In the beginning, I was in this big public room, maybe thirty or forty feet square. It looked like a lobby, or some kind of waiting room."

"Like at a doctor's office?"

"Yes, but I think it would have to be a group practice. This room was *big*. The walls were painted sort of off-white. No, wait. It was beige, not off-white, and it wasn't paint. The walls were covered with one of those vinyl-coated papers that look like fabric. Burlap or unbleached muslin, something nubby."

"Nubby?" Rhys repeated in amusement.

"That means it has little bumps in it, smartass. A lot of businesses use that kind of wall-covering because when it gets dirty, you just wash it off. Let's see, what else? Ugly, practical gray carpet. Several shades of gray, sort of like a tweed. Looped, not cut pile. A bunch of matching armchairs and loveseats upholstered in blues and grays. Heavy-duty upholstery fabric. Oh, and a few maroon chairs thrown in. Low maple tables with glass tops, about a half dozen fake potted trees, fake hanging plants."

"Anything on the tables?"

"Lemme think. Yes, magazines. Not many, though. The ones I saw were dog-eared."

"It's sounding more and more like a doctor's waiting room to me," Rhys said. "Did it have that piped-in elevator music that makes you want to rip the speakers off the walls after five minutes?"

She laughed, but didn't sit up or open her eyes. "Yes!"

"No wonder it seemed familiar. Except for the size of the room and the color of the chairs, it could be the waiting room at my g.p.'s office, or my dentist's, for that matter. Or a lawyer's waiting room, or a hotel lobby—"

"All right, all right, I know," Faith interrupted. "But how many lawyers would have a couple of soft-drink machines just outside the waiting room?"

"Or how many dentists?" he added. "Hadn't thought of that. A hotel or motel would, though, or some other consumer-oriented business—an insurance agency, an auto dealership?"

Faith sat up and shook her head. "No. There would have been offices nearby. I didn't see any, just that big L-shaped thing that looked like a reception desk."

"Or a registration desk?"

"Like in a hotel? I don't think so. This one was too plain, almost sterile-looking."

"Sterile-looking? Why do you say that?"

"I guess because it was white. Omigosh! I didn't remember that till now—it was covered with shiny white Formica. It was so bright it almost hurt my eyes."

"That's good," Rhys murmured. "Keep going. The more you go over it, the more you'll remember. Lean back and close your eyes again, try to put yourself back in that corridor outside the waiting room."

She did as he said, drifting back. "The floor was tile or vinyl. My shoes squeaked when I walked to the Coke machine."

She recited what she remembered about the computer terminals, the phones, the laser printers. "No desks behind the counter. And only three or four stools, I guess for whoever uses the computers."

"Back up a minute. You bought a Coke from the machine. That means you had money with you. Were you carrying a purse? What were you wearing?"

A thread of excitement had entered his voice. Faith turned her head to peer at him through slitted eyes.

"What was I wearing? What does that have to do with anything?"

"Keep your eyes closed," he ordered.

She frowned, but shut them. "Are you going to tell me what you're thinking, or do I have to snoop around inside your head?"

"You said your shoes squeaked," he said cryptically.

"Yes. So?" She felt the car brake to a stop and started to sit up again. "Where are we?"

She heard the click of Rhys's seatbelt being released, and a second later he clamped one hand over her eyes, pressing her shoulder back against the seat with the other.

"Shh. Be still. Don't talk, don't think, just feel."

"What—?" she began, but whatever would have followed the impatient query was cut off by a choked gasp.

"What's happening?" Rhys said sharply.

"Oh, God. I think—"

She was suddenly submerged in a flood of feeling. Not visual images now, but raw, seething emotion—the same malevolent emotions she'd sensed during the two waking dreams. She reached up and grabbed his wrist, yanking his hand from her eyes.

"This is it! This is the place! Where—?"

He moved so that she could look through the windshield. She leaned forward, then immediately recoiled in shock. Familiar? Dear Lord yes, this building was familiar. She came to work here five days a week.

"You said your shoes squeaked when you walked across the hall," Rhys explained as they returned to the car a few minutes later. "And it suddenly hit me that maybe they were those rubber-soled nurse shoes you wear to work."

"I'm impressed," Faith replied. "But I won't be absolutely sure until we can take a look at the main waiting room on the ground floor."

She only had keys to the PT department and an exterior door at the side of the building that opened directly into the stairwell. They'd tried peering in through the main entrance, but the glass in the wide electrically controlled doors was treated with some coating that reflected the sunlight and made it impossible to see inside.

"You weren't convinced by what happened when we pulled into the parking lot?" Rhys asked.

Faith shivered at the memory. "I admit that was pretty damned convincing, but whatever it was, it's gone now. And neither of us has ever actually been *in* the waiting room. You admit you don't remember seeing a big, white, L-shaped counter. I know I don't remember seeing it. Of course the only time I've even been up there was the day I applied for a job, and that was almost four years ago. They could've remodeled the reception area a half-dozen times by now."

"All right, you can check out the waiting room tomorrow," he said as he pulled onto the street. "Meanwhile, I think it would be a waste of time to keep driving around aimlessly."

"So do I. Stop at the next corner and drop me off."

He shot a startled look at her. "What?"

"We can spend some time strengthening the telepathic link. It's too weak. We need to be able to communicate over a greater distance, especially if you're going to monitor my out-of-body experiences."

Rhys opened his mouth, she suspected to argue, but then apparently decided to be a good sport if it killed him. He wouldn't drop her at the corner, though, because he didn't like the look of a group of young men gathered outside a video arcade across the street. Instead he drove back to her house.

Since Faith knew he was only going along to please her, she said he could stay there and she would take a stroll around the neighborhood. She suggested that rather than trying to maintain a constant link, they should attempt to connect with each other every two or three minutes. Rhys agreed, but with a noticeable lack of enthusiasm. She decided to reward him later for being so patient and accommodating.

She walked to the end of the block and stopped. *Rhys? Can you hear me?*

Loud and clear, came his reply.

You should have come out, too. It's a beautiful day for a walk.

I'll take your word for it.

Obviously there were limits to how far he would go to be accommodating. *Next time you contact me. Two minutes.*

Yes, ma'am.

She was a little put out by his apathy, but it *was* a gorgeous day to be outdoors. She closed her eyes for a moment to inhale the fragrance of a lilac bush that spilled over the picket fence of the house on the corner, then set off again at a leisurely stroll. About four blocks away there was a small neighborhood park that would probably be crawling with children. She crossed the street and headed in that direction.

They didn't have any trouble communicating telepathically until she was two streets away, almost three blocks from the house, when Rhys's thoughts suddenly became faint and distorted—sort of blurred, as if the two of them were separated by a thick fog. Faith was a little disappointed that they had apparently reached the distance limit, but at the same time thrilled that the link had been reliable up to that point. She'd never been able to read the thoughts of someone so far away. Of course, she reflected with a small smile, she'd never really tried.

She was close enough to the park to see several children clambering over playground equipment, and to hear their laughter and an occasional squeal of delight as a small body went hurtling down the slide. Since she was already so close, she decided to spend a few minutes sitting on a bench and watching their antics before she headed home.

She had just settled down on the only bench in the park that wasn't covered with bird poop, when she noticed the humming. She glanced around, hoping the birds hadn't given the bench a wide birth because there was a wasp nest plastered to it. No wasps. No bees, either. Then she realized that the humming was growing louder, and that it was originating inside her.

Oh, no. Not here, not now. The numbing cold inexorably enveloped her. She looked at her hands. Her fingers were already melting. *Fight it. Don't let it take you.* But it was too late. As she descended deeper into the trance, she realized there might have been time, if she'd recognized the humming for what it was right away, and not wasted precious seconds looking for a nonexistent wasp nest.

She'd never had a waking dream out of doors. Once her discomfort at the loss of control and the momentary disorientation had passed, it was an extraordinary experience. Trees, flowers, grass, all looked like images from a drunken, color-blind surrealist's nightmare. And the playground equipment! The jungle gym and swings resembled instruments of torture from some medieval dungeon. She was careful not to look at any of the children.

God, the children! She had to get back into her body, before one of them mistook the zombie lady on the bench for a junkie and ran off to summon Officer Friendly.

But before she could reunite her mind and body, she felt him. The dark presence. Hovering, menacing, his malevolence so strong now that she could smell it. It smelled like disease and decay . . . like tissue ravaged by a staph infection, or worse.

Who *was* he? Was he following her? Could he sense her presence, the way she could sense his? Or was it only that his terrible enmity had attracted her attention, called out to her in some way?

Before, she had been so overwhelmed by fear that she fled rather than risk letting him come closer. She was afraid now, but this time she wouldn't run. From somewhere she found the courage to reach out to him with her mind, deliberately seeking to make a connection. If she could touch his consciousness, just for an instant . . . long enough to capture a name, a face . . . an image, or a random thought . . .

It happened so suddenly that the shock almost sent her reeling into unconsciousness. She was *there,* inside his mind, but what she found was so unexpected that for a moment her own mind refused to accept it. Images, yes; astonishing full-color images that repeated endlessly, like a videotape loop. A man and a woman came out of a building, made their way across a lot half filled with parked cars, and got into a black Chevy Lumina. The man was Rhys. She was the woman. And the building was the clinic where she worked.

Stunned senseless by shock and horror, afraid to even consider what the pictures meant, Faith broke the connection and pulled away. As soon as she did, he was gone. Vanished, as if he'd never been there. She knew he had been, though, and that he would return. She couldn't get back into her body, and the physical world, fast enough. The first thing she saw when her eyes focused was Rhys, on his knees in the grass in front of her. The second thing she registered was a semicircle of small, round faces, all staring at her curiously.

"See, told ya she wasn't dead," a little boy remarked. He sounded disappointed.

"Bet I know what's wrong with her," another said sagely. "She's got ep . . . ep . . . somethin' wrong with the wires in her brain. My cousin's got it, and sometimes he sits and stares just like that."

A little girl with ribbon-bedecked braids chimed in with, "Maybe she was just taking a nap."

"With her eyes open?"

"Horses sleep with their eyes open."

"No they don't."

"Do, too."

"Do not. They sleep standing up, but they close their eyes. Anyways, she's not a horse."

"Well I think somebody should call a ambliance. Damon said she's got wires in her head. That could be dangerous."

"She's okay, guys," Rhys said to the children. "I'll take her home now."

"Is she your wife?"

"No."

Damon, the one who had a cousin with epilepsy, stepped forward. "You better not go with him, lady. Bad men come to the park sometimes and tell lies to get you to go with them."

This incredible scene, coming on the heels of the waking dream, was too much. Faith put a hand over her mouth to hold back hysterical laughter. Rhys gave her a sharp look and got to his feet.

"Come on, let's get you home."

But when he bent over and clasped her arm, her self-appointed pint-sized protector shrieked, "Child molester! Child molester!" and kicked his leg.

The gamin in pigtails started yelling, "Somebody call the cops!" A second later another girl and a boy took up the cry.

Rhys let go of Faith's arm to fend off Damon, who was drawing back his foot for another kick.

"Don't even think about it," he said sternly, then turned to the trio who were screaming for the police. "And you three, stop carrying on like that. Everybody just settle down. For your information, I *am* a cop."

He fished the bifold wallet that held his detective's badge

out of his pocket and flipped it open. The children fell silent at once, their alarmed gazes swinging in unison from Rhys to Damon.

"You gonna arrest me?" the boy asked.

Rhys gave him a crooked grin. "No. If it's all right with you, I'm just going to take the lady home and fix her a cup of tea. I think we've both had enough excitement for one day."

He turned back to Faith and held out his hand, letting the children see that she would go with him willingly. She pried her hand away from her mouth and put it in his, and let him pull her to her feet. His eyes darkened with anxiety when he felt her chilled skin and the way she was trembling.

"Thank you for wanting to protect me, Damon," she murmured. It was a struggle to keep her voice steady, but she didn't want to leave them with any doubt that they'd reacted correctly to a perceived threat. "You're very brave. I'm sorry if I worried you guys. Sometimes I sort of start . . . daydreaming, and I don't pay attention to what's going on."

"We weren't worried," one of the boys told her. "We thought you were dead."

"Did not."

"Did, too."

"*I* never thought she was dead."

"Damon said the wires in her head was broke, that's the only reason I thought she was dead."

Rhys wrapped an arm around her waist and guided her out of the park while they were busy wrangling.

"I'd carry you," he said when they reached the street. "But if they saw me pick you up, it might set them off again."

"I'm all right," she murmured. A second later her throat convulsed on a brittle laugh that sounded more like a sob. "Well, maybe not, but I can walk. What were you doing at the park?"

"When I didn't pick up anything else from you after

that last contact, and you didn't come home, I got worried and came out to find you."

She leaned into him, letting him take most of her weight. "I'm glad you did. It happened again. I had another waking dream."

"I know," Rhys said grimly.

She tipped her head back to look at him. "Did you see—?"

"The two of us, leaving the clinic, getting into my car. You know what it means—he was there, watching us."

Faith shuddered violently. Yes, she'd known, but hearing him say it somehow made it more real, more terrifying. Rhys swore under his breath, then stopped in the middle of the sidewalk and swept her up in his arms. If the children back at the park were watching, they didn't set up an outcry.

He carried her the rest of the way to her house, and didn't put her down until they reached the sofa in the living room. Then he ordered her to stay put and disappeared into the kitchen. True to his word, he returned ten minutes later with a cup of green tea. By then Faith's hands were steady enough to hold the cup without splashing tea all over the front of her shirt. Rhys sank down beside her and started massaging her neck and shoulders.

"Better?"

She nodded. "Except for feeling incredibly foolish and embarrassed. I don't know why I overreacted like that."

"You didn't overreact," he said flatly. "There's a crazy man out there who's been watching you, for God knows how long. He's probably obsessed with you. He may have been stalking you, possibly for months."

Faith finished the tea and set the cup on the end table. "Are you trying to scare me half to death?"

"No. Just enough to get your attention." His fingers kept massaging, his touch firm but gentle. There wasn't a trace of softness in his expression or his voice, though. He was deadly serious.

"You've got it," she whispered.

"Good. There's no way to know for sure if this guy is Rat Man or some other psycho. Makes no difference. Whoever he is, you have to know now that he's a very real threat to you."

Faith nodded mutely, afraid to even try to speak.

"From now on, if you're not here, with all the doors and windows locked, or at work, you're with me. Every minute. Understand?"

She nodded again and managed a tremulous, "Yes."

"He could be anybody—someone you work with, a patient, a neighbor, the paperboy. He could be someone you think you know, someone you trust. Until we find out who he is, you will *never* be alone with *anybody* but me." His hands stopped kneading, shifted to hold her head while he drove the message home with fierce intensity. "Never! Not for five minutes. Got it?"

She knew his intent was to shake her up, force her to acknowledge the danger, so she wouldn't do anything foolish. The tactic backfired, though. The emotion in those last few sentences kindled a warmth inside her that obliterated the cold clutch of fear.

"Got it."

"Good. One more thing, and it isn't open for discussion. I'm moving in with you till this is over."

Chapter Eighteen

Rhys didn't want to be at work. No, that wasn't strictly true. He wanted to be working, he just didn't want to be stuck at his desk, facing another towering stack of forms.

Reviewing the last of the screwball brigade statements was taking longer than it should have, because part of his mind was still obsessed by what had happened to Faith at the park yesterday. He had been—still was, to be honest—shaken by the intensity of his reaction. If the sick bastard who'd been watching her had been there in the flesh, he might be dead now.

He sighed and reached for another manila folder. He was nearing the bottom of the stack of locals. Next he'd have to tackle the imports, a task he especially dreaded. The instant he read the name at the top of the statement in front of him, though, his despondent mood improved considerably.

Leon Perry. Damn, he'd forgotten all about ol' Leon. He quickly skimmed the tidy lines of his own printing to refresh his memory, checked to make sure the man's signature was where it should be at the bottom of the form, then looked for any notations ATF agents Whitley or Hearst might have made. There were none. They must've dismissed Leon's statement, just as Rhys had expected they would.

He circled the phone number at the top of the form and reached for his telephone. There was no answer. Not surprising; Leon was probably at work. Rhys hesitated a moment before opening his desk drawer for the phone book. He was facing a couple weeks' work, as it was. Was this statement really worth following up on? He'd already checked the convicted felons database for a man who matched the description Leon provided, and turned up zilch.

"Hell," he muttered, yanking open the drawer. "Wasting time is part of the job description. What's another fifteen minutes?"

The secretary who answered the phone at Jenks Janitorial Services—now why hadn't he been able to remember that name?—put him through to the proprietor, who wasn't terribly cooperative until Rhys explained that his employee might be able to identify the serial bomber who was terrorizing the entire city. The prospect of fame and hero status, even if it was second-hand, moved Mr. Jenks to provide the information that Leon Perry was on special assignment today. Rhys raised an eyebrow at that. What would qualify as a "special assignment" for a rent-a-janitor service, he wondered. Shoveling out stalls at Churchill Downs, maybe? Mr. Jenks took his name and number and promised to personally make sure Leon Perry got the message to return his call.

Rhys hung up and checked his watch. Two hours until Faith's lunch break began. He should be able to get through the rest of the screwball brigade statements by then . . . if he could keep his thoughts from drifting back to how scared and vulnerable she'd looked when they left the park yesterday, and what seeing her like that had done to him. Instead of adding Leon Perry's statement to those in the cardboard file box at his feet, he tossed it into his in-basket, then reached for another folder.

* * *

Faith was cleaning a massage table when Missy Clarence came in to hand her a memo from the clinic director.

"Isn't it great?" Missy gushed as Faith read the two short paragraphs. "We all get off early tomorrow."

"So I see," Faith murmured. The memo was a notice that all appointments after 2:00 P.M. on Tuesday had already been or would be rescheduled and the staff of all departments would be free to leave at 2:15. Employees would, however, be paid for the entire day. She assumed the decision to close early had been made because of the traffic snarl the hospital dedication ceremonies were expected to create. Then she got to the second paragraph which encouraged all employees to attend the ceremonies.

"Whoa!" she exclaimed. "Hold the phone. The First Lady is going to be there? The *President's wife?*"

"You mean you hadn't heard?" Missy said in surprise. "It was all over the radio and TV, all weekend. Where were you, in a cave or something?"

"I was pretty busy this weekend," Faith said with a droll smile. "How about that, Rollie's grapevine gossip was right for a change. He told me on Friday that the Secret Service would be providing security for the hospital dedication."

"How come they're just now getting around to the official dedication, when they've been open for months?" Missy asked.

Faith shrugged and handed the memo back to her. "I guess they wanted to wait till the painters and carpet installers were gone and all the trees and flowers had been planted, so the place would look 'finished.' Besides, I think some of the units have only been accepting patients for the past week or so."

"If you ask me, it's a wonder they're accepting patients at all, considering the problems they had with that fancy central computer system when they first opened," Missy confided. She had instinctively lowered her voice, in case a patient was passing by."A friend of mine works in the risk management office, and she says several patients almost died because the computer screwed up the orders for their lab work or meds or something. One guy did die, during emergency surgery. The board is still sweating it out, waiting to see if his family will file a huge malpractice suit."

"They ought to," Faith said flatly. "If he died because a computer prescribed the wrong medication and nobody caught the mistake. That's the kind of thing that makes some people paranoid about computers."

She was thinking of Rat Man, but it occurred to her as she made the comment that it could also apply to Leon Perry. During one of his sermons, he'd told her that computers were a tool of the Devil. For Leon, everything ultimately came down to religion and the age-old struggle of good versus evil.

"So, do you think you'll go over to see the First Lady?" Missy asked.

"I doubt it. I'll probably leave as soon as the last patient's gone, try to beat the worst of the traffic. I can always catch her speech on the news tomorrow night, or read about it in the newspaper."

Missy looked disappointed. "I'm going. I've always really admired her, and this might the only chance I get to see her in person."

After Missy left to make sure Rollie and Dirk had seen the memo, Faith thought about the patient who had allegedly died because of a computer screwup. If it was true, anyone who'd been close to the man would have good reason for a grudge against computers. She would have to remember to tell Rhys what Missy had said when he picked her up for lunch.

In the meantime, though, she had four patients scheduled, back to back. All three of the therapists had been so busy that they'd had to skip their midmorning breaks, and it looked like she wasn't going to have a chance to go upstairs and check out the main waiting room until lunchtime.

She didn't feel any special urgency about that, though, because she was fairly sure the waiting room upstairs wouldn't turn out to be the one in her dream. If it was, she should have picked up some negative impressions or signals, just from working in the same building every day. So far, the only negative psychic experience she'd had here was the waking dream in the break room last week.

She went to call the next patient, and noticed that Tommy Carver had an afternoon appointment. Had Tommy dreamed about the invisible people, too? Should she ask him—assuming she was the therapist who saw him and got the chance—or wait to see if he mentioned it?

Rhys arrived at the clinic ten minutes early and stopped in at the director's office, where he requested and was given a list of employees' names. He was relieved when the director didn't insist on a court order before handing them over. After Rhys bluntly informed him there was a possibility that someone connected with the clinic might also have a connection to the serial bomber, he punched in a couple of commands on his terminal keyboard, and seconds later his laser printer regurgitated the list. Names only, no addresses, phone numbers, or personal information.

"That's all I can give you without the employees' written authorizations," he said. "I hope it helps catch the bomber before he decides to blow up a doctor's office or a hospital."

Rhys gave him a startled look. "Why do you say that?"

The director—a trim, middle-aged man named Horace Richmond—leaned back in his leather executive's chair and gazed at him with shrewd, intelligent eyes. "Because I assume that in addition to having a phobia about computers, he's striking out at the medical profession. The first place he hit was a software company that specializes in making applications for doctor's offices. That was his opening salvo, his declaration of war, if you will.

"I could be wrong, but I believe this individual has a powerful animosity toward doctors, probably based on a personal grievance. There could also be some kind of tangled association at work here. Nowadays, most doctors make extensive use of computers. He may blow up a variety of computer equipment to protest our increasing reliance on them, but eventually I think he'll get back to the medical aspect. Frankly, I've been worried about our security ever since the first bombing. I've upgraded our alarm system and hired a private guard to patrol the place at night."

Rhys shook his head in amazement. He felt like kicking himself. "Have you ever been a cop?"

Richmond laughed. "Close, but no cigar. I have a master's degree in clinical psychology."

"Can I use your phone?"

"Sure. Punch nine to get an outside line."

"I want you to repeat what you just told me to my lieutenant," Rhys said as he dialed. "I'm going to ask him to pass it on to the agent from the Bureau of Alcohol, Tobacco and Firearms who's in charge of the investigation. He may want to talk to you."

When he left the director's office, he started down the central hallway toward the elevator. The stairwell door beside it opened just as he punched the down button, and Faith emerged. He felt a smile take possession of his face as soon as he saw her.

"I was just on my way down," he said. "I got the list of clinic employees."

"Good. I came up to have a look at the main waiting room. We've been so busy all morning, I haven't had a chance till now."

They checked out the waiting room—or Patient Lounge, as a brass plate on the wall beside the door designated it—together. It was almost big enough, but the carpet and upholstery material were maroon and gray instead of blue and gray, and the wall-covering was gray with tiny maroon dots. Also, about half the plants were the genuine article, rather than fakes.

"The clinic could have used the same decorator though," Faith murmured as they turned toward the recep tion desk. "The furniture is the same style, just differen colors."

"You're not surprised this isn't the place," Rhy observed.

"No. If this was the place I saw in the dream, I'm prett sure I would have picked up some negative vibes befor now."

The patient registration desk *was* a long counter, but single section, with no L at the end. It was covered i dandelion yellow Formica, not white, and topped by a hug sheet of Plexiglas or Lexan or some other clear polyme that separated the clerks behind it from the public an added a layer of sound insulation.

"Back to square one, I guess," Rhys muttered as the left the building. When they were seated in a booth at nearby sandwich shop, he leaned his arms on the tabl and looked at Faith with a puzzled frown.

"There's something I don't understand. If the clini waiting room wasn't the one in your dream, what the hel happened yesterday, when I pulled into the parking lot?"

"I don't know," she said with a dispirited sigh. "I fel the same presence I sense in the waking dreams. It wa the same, I know it was! I couldn't mistake that feelin for anything else. And we know he was at the clinic las Thursday. He saw us leaving to go to lunch."

Rhys reached into his sport coat and pulled out th list Horace Richmond had provided. "Let's go over thes names. Tell me if anybody on the list might have a reaso to resent you, or want to get back at you for something. An reason at all," he stressed. "This guy's obviously mentall unbalanced. He might be obsessing about something trivia that happened months ago and you've already forgotte about."

None of the names on the list triggered any memorie or flashes of insight. They ate in silence for a while absorbed in their own thoughts.

"I almost forgot," Faith said as she reached for a plastic cup of chocolate pudding. "Missy Clarence told me something this morning that I thought you should know."

She repeated what Missy had said about Gaines Memorial's state-of-the-art computer system having been responsible for several close calls and one patient death.

"When she told me that, I thought about your cyberphobe theory. If the patient who died was a friend of Rat Man's, or maybe even a relative—"

"He'd have a hell of a reason for hating computers," Rhys finished. "Damn, that's uncanny. Horace Richmond thinks the bomber has a grievance not only against computers, but doctors who use computers. He's so convinced there's a medical tie-in that he's increased security at the clinic."

"He told you that?" Rhys nodded, his mouth full of tuna salad. "It is weird that we'd both hear these things at the same time, don't you think?"

He wiped his mouth with a paper napkin. "Fate?"

"Fate, luck, call it whatever you want, I don't think we should just write it off as coincidence. Especially since the new hospital across the street is so heavily committed to computerization. Oh! Do you think—"

"What?"

"The hospital! It's right across the street from the clinic. He could have been watching the parking lot from there last week."

"And he might have been there yesterday, when we went to the clinic. That would explain why you felt his presence."

Faith shook her head skeptically. "I'm not sure he has to be nearby for that to happen. It's possible he's only thinking about me, and his feelings are so strong I pick them up. Or it could be that he's *been* where I am when it happens, and left some of his hostility behind."

"Not unless you've had him over for dinner," Rhys reminded her.

She smiled sheepishly. "Good point. I never claimed to be an expert on psychic phenomena. Maybe it can happen either way—if he's been there, or he's thinking about me. Whatever, I think you should alert the ATF people that the hospital is a potential target."

"I already have." He checked his watch. "Time to head back. I expect Agent Gonzales will let the Secret Service decide whether to increase security for the First Lady's visit tomorrow."

"You knew about that?" she said as they walked to the entrance.

He held the door for her. "Not till yesterday. It was on the front page of the Metro section. You mean you didn't know?"

"I found out this morning." She gave him a wry smile. "I never got around to reading the Sunday paper, remember?"

On the way back to the clinic, Rhys told her that several Secret Service agents had been in town since the previous week. "But if this visit was in the works all along, nobody's been talking about it. We were told they were here to monitor the bomber investigation."

"Do you think they'll call off her visit, once they know about the computer screwups at the hospital and Mr. Richmond's theory?" Faith asked.

"Probably not, it would be a PR disaster for both the hospital and the President, but they should. Providing security for the dedication would be a nightmare under ideal conditions."

"Won't they check everything anyone brings into the hospital?"

"You bet. At least, anything that'll be anywhere near the First Lady. They'll have metal detectors, maybe even a portable x-ray machine. They'll hand search women's purses, briefcases, lunch boxes, anything like that. They've probably already gone over the building from top to bottom, and they'll thoroughly inspect anything new that comes in. The trouble is, you can't open sterile medical supplies or equipment and paw through it."

"Maybe they'll bring in dogs. Aren't some police dogs trained to sniff out explosives?"

"Yes. And they might use one or two outside, but the hospital administration probably wouldn't want animals in treatment areas. Besides, there are so many strong smells in a hospital that a bomb-sniffing dog might not be able to find a package of plastic explosive right under his nose."

"You're right," Faith said. "It does sound like a security nightmare."

When he dropped her off at the clinic, he said he would check all the names on the list of clinic employees against the police department database to see if any of them had an arrest record, but it might take several days. In the meantime, he reminded her that she wasn't to be alone with anybody.

"Except the patients," Faith amended gently.

Rhys relented with a wry smile. "Well, all right. But get 'em in and then get 'em out. If anybody tries to keep you around after a session's over, tell him you have a highly contagious disease and then get to a phone and call me."

She laughed and leaned across the seat to kiss him good-bye. As soon as she left the car, his smile evaporated. He didn't pull away from the building until she was safely inside.

Tommy Carver greeted Faith with a grin when she entered the PT waiting room.

"I told Missy I wanted to work with you today, since it's my last session."

"Great! I was afraid I'd miss seeing you. Just let me stash my purse and collect your file, and we'll get started."

She didn't have to decide whether to ask if he'd had any more dreams about the bomber; less than five minutes into the session, Tommy asked her. Faith wrestled with her conscience for all of ten seconds.

"No. No more dreams about some creep planting bombs, thank goodness."

"Me, either," he said. "Maybe if we've stopped drean
ing about him, it means he's stopped, too."

Relief washed through her. "I hope so," she murmurec
"How's the roller hockey going?"

"Great, but I've only been practicing with the team, s
far. I go up to see Dr. Nance after I leave here. If sh
gives me the all clear, I'll play in my first game tomorro
afternoon."

"Just be sure to wear your helmet and pads," Fait
warned. "I'm going to miss seeing you, but I don't war
you coming back as a patient next month."

"Not to worry. I don't want that, either. I'm gonna mis
all of you guys, too. Maybe you could come and watch on
of my games."

"I'd love to," she said sincerely. "Do you have a schedul
I could photocopy?"

"Not with me, but I could copy the days and times fror
my schedule at home and bring it in. Then you coul
make copies for Rollie and Dirk. Maybe Leon would lik
one, too."

Faith was in the middle of making a notation on th
chart for this session. She stopped writing and looked a
him in surprise. "Leon?"

"Yeah. I think his last name is Perry. You know—th
janitor. We're sort of friends, but I don't know where h
lives, or his phone number. Would you give him a cop
of the game schedule, when I bring it in?"

"Sure, I'll see that he gets a copy," Faith hedged. Sh
could always leave it with Missy to pass on to Leon. "Ho
on earth did you and Leon become friends?"

Tommy grinned. "Well, he wasn't very friendly at firs
One day, when I was leaving, he stopped me and starte
preaching at me about this." He held up a silver ank
hanging from a chain around his neck. "He said it wa
an upside-down cross, and I was being disrespectful an
sacrilegious. I told him he was wrong, that it's an ancier
Egyptian symbol of life, from way before Jesus was borr
Then I told him I go to Sunday School every week an

sing in the youth choir, and anyway my parents would have a stroke if they caught me wearing something that has anything to do with Satanism or witchcraft or that kind of junk. Not that I ever would, but you know how parents are."

"And he left you alone after that?" Faith asked. "Didn't preach anymore, I mean?"

"Oh, once he found out I go to church, he was cool. I'd always say hi to him, just to be polite, you know? Then he started taking a break to keep me company if I had to wait for my mom or dad to pick me up. We usually sit outside and just talk. I feel sorry for him. Did you know he had a twin brother?"

"No, I didn't," Faith murmured. She was having trouble accepting the idea of Leon Perry and Tommy Carver as bosom buddies.

"He got sick and died just a few months ago. Now the only family Leon has is his mother. From what he says about her, I get the idea she's a little nutty on the subject of religion. That's prob'ly where he gets it. But he's not a bad guy, just a little mixed up, and lonely."

"A little mixed up" didn't say it by half, as far as Faith was concerned. Still, she was touched by Tommy's sympathy for Leon. He was a really terrific kid.

"Are we done?" he asked when she slipped the chart into his file. " 'Cause I'm supposed to be up in Dr. Nance's office in five minutes."

"All done," she confirmed. "You can tell Dr. Nance we're all finished with you down here."

Tommy hopped down from the table and gave her a huge bear hug, then ran out before she could embarrass him by making a big deal of it.

Faith was smiling when she dropped his file in Missy's in-basket, but she was also a little misty-eyed. Had she ever been that young, that innocent? That trusting? Maybe she owed Leon Perry an apology. Tommy was a very perceptive kid. If he had seen a kind, caring side of Leon, it must be there. Maybe she just hadn't made the effort to look for it.

Leon had pushed her hot buttons, no doubt about it. But just as she hadn't known about his brother's death or his zealot mother, he had no way of knowing that she was hypersensitive about the subject of religion. She would have to sit down and reexamine her own behavior and attitude, maybe even think of a way to make amends. But later. For now, she had to get through the rest of the afternoon and then go with Rhys to collect some clothes from his apartment. She was looking forward to that—not just helping him pack up his stuff, but making room for his things alongside hers.

Leon could hardly believe everything was finally ready. Getting the separate components into the hospital hadn't been as hard as he'd feared. The guard and the plain-clothes policeman had actually handled the explosive charge and the primer when they made him open his lunch box and inspected the contents. Except for a small blasting cap and a couple of short pieces of wire, the bomb wouldn't contain any metal, so he hadn't been worried about the little x-ray machine. But he hadn't expected the by-hand search, and he'd had a few anxious moments before the policeman closed and latched his lunch box and waved him past.

Now there was only one thing left to do, and his preparations would be complete. He felt feverish with anticipation and excitement. The effort of presenting a calm face to the world was almost more of a strain than he could bear. The final Revelation was at hand!

He knew he still had to be careful, though. The forces of darkness were aligned against him, watching and hoping he would slip up, make some stupid mistake. He couldn't afford to let down his guard for a minute.

He slipped a hand into the pocket of his trousers and felt the telephone message slip, just to reassure himself it was still there. There was only one part of his plan left to carry out, and in a way it was going to give him even more satisfaction than completing his mission to deliver the Truth.

The policeman, Donovan, had been there again today. Leon had seen him bring Faith McRae back to the clinic at the end of her lunch hour. He'd also seen her lean over and kiss him before she got out of the car. Right on the mouth, in broad daylight, and in public. The slut. He'd stopped being disappointed in her. Now all he felt was righteous anger. She deserved what was going to happen to her.

Chapter Nineteen

Shortly after Rhys returned to his desk, Buford Jackson called him into his office. Gonzales, the senior ATF agent, and Special Agent Eberhardt from the FBI were already there. Donald Gonzales didn't waste time with pleasantries.

"Lieutenant Jackson tells us you came up with the theory that the bomber has a thing against computers before you spoke to this man Richmond."

"That's right," Rhys said. He glanced at the lieutenant for a cue, but Buford Jackson's stoic expression was no help.

"Our people formulated the same hypothesis," Eberhardt remarked dryly. "It just took them a little longer. We'd like to know what action you've already taken so we don't waste time duplicating your work."

Rhys bit back the urge to point out that if agents Whitley and Hearst had been inclined to work with the local police department, they would have known about his theory, and the database search, a week and a half ago. There was no point stating the obvious.

"When the computer connection first occurred to me, I ran a cross-referenced database search to see if I could find anybody who'd been charged with vandalism involving computers."

"And did you?" Gonzales asked.

"The search produced six names, but none of them panned out." He gave them a quick summary, including his interview with Patrick Dean, and hoped Lieutenant Jackson would overlook the fact that he'd disregarded specific instructions to set the computer report aside until he'd finished reviewing statements.

"I only went back six months, though, and only checked city and county records."

Buford Jackson astonished him with the observation, "At least you started the ball rolling."

"Right," Gonzales agreed. "And since you did, I think you should continue with this. We'll see that you have access to whatever systems resources you need."

Rhys nodded. "All right. I'll get right on it." Anything to get out from under the rest of the damned statements. "On the subject of computers, I heard something else today that could be relevant—a rumor about the hospital the First Lady will be visiting tomorrow."

He repeated the story about computer errors having resulted in several close calls and one patient death. Eberhardt said he would ask the Secret Service to check it out, since their agents were already at the hospital.

Rhys returned to his desk, then sat there for a minute or so organizing his thoughts. He should begin by ordering another computer search, this time going back at least a year. If that didn't turn anything up, he would go beyond the Louisville area, maybe use the FBI's mainframe to run a nationwide search. How many cases of computer vandalism were investigated nationally every year? Dozens? Hundreds? How much manpower were Gonzales and Eberhardt willing to commit—enough to question every man, woman and child whose name the computer kicked out? Probably not that much. But he could narrow the search considerably by adding a parameter for doctors' offices or hospitals.

Doctors' offices.

"Shit," he muttered under his breath. The elderly woman who'd thrown blood on the computer in a doctor's office. What was her name?

He spent another minute shuffling through the folders that covered his desk before he located the two-page printout in his in-basket, under Leon Perry's statement.

Leona Timmons, age sixty. Rhys picked up the telephone receiver and dialed the number of the precinct house that had received the call. The patrolman who'd been dispatched was on vacation, but his sergeant remembered the case.

"That was a sad story," he told Rhys. "Her son died on the operating table and she blamed the doctor. I suspect she was a little batty to begin with, but his death pushed her over the edge for sure."

"Where'd she get the goat blood?" Rhys asked.

"As I recall, the son had worked for a vet. I think she stole it from his office."

"Wait a minute. Veterinarians keep animal blood in their offices?"

"Well, sure, if they do much surgery. You know, for transfusions. They can't very well go to the Red Cross and ask for a pint of goat blood or dog blood. Though sometimes they use live donors. Our vet has this huge, and I mean *huge* black cat. Thing stands almost two feet tall and weighs close to thirty pounds. When the vet gets a cat in that's been hurt bad, or if one loses too much blood during surgery, he just draws some from ol' Midnight."

"You don't say," Rhys murmured. Cat blood donors, yet. "So what happened?"

"When?"

"With the Timmons woman. What was the disposition?"

"Oh. The doctor declined to press charges, said his insurance would cover the damage to the computer. I think he was afraid of the publicity if the case went to court. Wouldn't look good, you know—first the old lady's son dies under his knife, then he's responsible for sending her to jail. He did get a restraining order against her, though. I never heard any more about it, so I guess she stayed away from him."

Rhys tapped the point of a pencil against his desk blotter, his brow furrowed in a frown. No matter how he phrased the next question, he was going to sound like an idiot, but he had to ask.

"Listen, we think this serial bomber may have a personal grudge against the medical profession. Did you see Mrs. Timmons when she was brought in? Can you tell me if she's big enough—"

The sergeant's whoop of laughter blasted his ear before he could finish.

"You think she might be the bomber? Is that what this is all about? Oh, that's rich!"

Rhys dropped the pencil and rubbed at his forehead. "Look, I need a physical description of the woman. Can you give it to me, or not?"

"Sure, I can do that. I'd say she's two or three inches shy of five feet tall, weighs maybe a hundred pounds dripping wet. Did I mention that she's sixty years old? Wears her hair in a little old lady bun. That's *gray* hair. Well, mostly gray, but there's some white mixed in with it. You remember Granny on *The Beverly Hillbillies?* Mrs. Timmons could be Granny's twin."

"Thanks," Rhys muttered. "Now would you transfer me to somebody in records, so I can get the doctor's name."

"Sure thing. Let me know if you decide to charge her for these bombings. That's one arrest I'd buy a ticket to see."

By the time Rhys got off the phone, he'd decided there was no point in taking this any further. He got a blank requisition form for a new database search from a file cabinet and, as he sat down to fill it out, wondered how long it would take for the grapevine to spread the word that the chief suspect in the bombings was a sixty-year-old woman.

* * *

Rhys's clothes and personal items were put away by six They went out for a barbecue, then stopped at a video store on the way back to Faith's and rented a movie. They were in bed by 10:30. Faith was smiling when she drifted off to sleep an hour later.

This time she knew at once that she was dreaming. It was the same dream she'd had Friday night, with one startling difference. Now, she could see the people in the waiting room. She woke with a choked cry as soon as the realization registered. A moment later Rhys was looming above her, propped on an elbow.

"Faith?" he said anxiously. "What is it? Did you have another dream?"

She struggled for air, her heart thudding painfully "No," she gasped. "The same dream . . . but . . ."

"Easy," Rhys soothed. He lay back and pulled her on top of him. One hand stroked her hair; the other rubbed the spot between her shoulder blades. "It's all right. Take deep breaths. Relax."

Faith closed her eyes with a shuddering sigh and absorbed his strength and tender concern, let it seep into her.

"Better?" he murmured after a while.

She nodded. "It was the same place, but this time I could see the people."

"Could you tell who they were, why they were there?"

"No. I could see them, but they weren't entirely *there* They looked like ghosts. Movie ghosts."

"Transparent?"

"Yes, sort of. The walls, plants, furniture, all those things were solid, substantial, but the people weren't. They looked like they were made of . . . mist. Fog, or something."

He thought about that for a minute. "What do you think it means?"

"Exactly what you think it means," she said bitterly "When they're completely formed, they'll die. That's when he'll kill them. Their time is running out, Rhys. We have to find him and stop him."

He wrapped his arms around her and held her tight, but he didn't offer any false reassurances or empty promises. They both knew time was running out for them, too.

Tuesday morning's schedule was even more packed than Monday's had been. Primarily because most of the afternoon patients were calling to ask if they could come in before the clinic closed, rather than reschedule their appointments for another day and disrupt the course of their therapy.

Faith felt awful and suspected she looked even worse. She'd slept fitfully, unable to fall into a deep sleep because she fully expected to have another precognitive dream if she did. The added stress of discovering that she would have to see two to three times as many patients as she'd expected made her uncharacteristically cranky.

She skipped lunch, as did Rollie, and said good-bye to her last patient at 1:50. As soon as the door swung shut behind him, she collapsed onto a chair in the waiting room. Rollie dropped down beside her and loosened his tie.

"God, I hope we never have another morning like that," she said with feeling. "It would have been better to stay open this afternoon, even if it meant we couldn't get out of the parking lot till midnight."

Rollie patted her shoulder. "Well, it's over now."

"Next time, you or Dirk has to take Mr. Tenbarge. He's put on thirty pounds since his surgery, and he refuses to give me any help. If one of you doesn't start working with him, we're gonna have to buy a forklift."

He laughed and heaved himself off the chair. "Okay, from now on I'll take him. Speaking of Dirk, where is he?"

"He sneaked out about twenty minutes ago," Missy answered from her desk. "Which is what I'm about to do. If I don't get across the street right now, I'll miss seeing the First Lady. Her motorcade is supposed to arrive at two o'clock."

"Those motorcades are never on time," Rollie told her. "She probably won't be here for another half hour, at least."

Missy gave him a worried look. "Does that mean I can't leave early?"

"Of course not. Grab your purse and scoot. I'll be right behind you."

"Are you going over, too?" Faith asked him as Missy rushed out.

He made a face. "I'd rather not, but Mr. Richmond expects me to be there."

"One of many crosses the head of the department must bear, I suppose," she teased. "I'll think of you, standing in the sun listening to a bunch of dull speeches, when I'm propping my feet up in front of the TV."

"Sadist," Rollie said as he adjusted his tie. "Just for that, you can lock up."

She was switching off the lights in the last treatment room when she heard sirens. A lot of sirens. Hah, Rollie, you were wrong! The First Lady's motorcade was right on time. On impulse, Faith dashed up the stairs and out the side door to catch a look at the limo as it turned into the hospital's front drive. She felt a little self-conscious—she probably looked like a giddy teenager racing to glimpse her favorite greasy-haired rock star—but what the hell, there was nobody around to see her.

It was past 1:30 before Rhys remembered that Leon Perry had never returned his call. He phoned the janitorial service again and asked to speak to Mr. Jenks.

"I put the message in his mailbox here at the office," Jenks assured him. "I don't think he's picked it up yet, though." He asked Rhys to hold on and yelled at somebody named Alice to look in Leon Perry's box.

"Nope, it's still there," Jenks said a minute later. "Is it

really important that you talk to him right away? 'Cause I doubt he'll get around to calling you for a day or so. He phoned in this morning to tell Alice that his mother had a stroke sometime during the night. He's with her at the hospital."

"No, it's not urgent," Rhys said. "I just wanted to go over the statement he gave me earlier, see if he might have remembered anything else about the man he saw."

"This guy Leon saw, there's a chance he might be the bomber?"

"Let's just say if we can identify him, we'd like to talk to him."

"Well, I guess you could go see Leon at the hospital."

Rhys grimaced. Mr. Jenks obviously wasn't burdened with an excessive amount of sensitivity. "Thanks for the suggestion, but it sounds like he has enough on his mind right now. It can wait."

"Okay, I'll just leave the message in his box, then. If you change your mind, he told Alice his mother's at Gaines Memorial. Her last name's Timmons, though, not Perry."

Rhys sat bolt upright. "Did you say Timmons?"

"That's right. Leona Timmons. Her first name's easy to remember because it's like the female version of his—he's Leon, she's Leona."

As soon as Rhys got off the phone, he dived into his in-basket for the computer printout. Leona Timmons was Leon Perry's mother! It couldn't be mere coincidence, but what the hell did it mean? He checked the surgeon's name he'd scribbled on the printout and got his number from the phone book. His mind raced furiously while he waited for somebody in the doctor's office to answer the phone. Five minutes later he called Mr. Jenks back, and two minutes after that he dashed across the room and charged into Buford Jackson's office without knocking.

"Are Gonzales and Eberhardt here?" he blurted.

"Eberhardt is," the lieutenant replied in an irritable growl. "Down the hall in the assistant chief's office."

"Get him in here. I know who the bomber is."

The lieutenant took in his avid expression and picked up the phone on his desk. A minute later the FBI agent arrived with the assistant chief in tow.

"His name is Leon Perry," Rhys said without preamble. "About three months ago he and his mother took his twin brother to Gaines Memorial with a burst appendix. This was right after the hospital opened. Some kind of computer error resulted in the brother's being given the wrong anesthetic. He had an allergic reaction and died on the operating table."

He told them about Leona's trip to the surgeon's office, and that Leon himself had come in and given a statement, claiming to have seen someone lurking around the warehouse just before it was bombed.

"He was on a fishing expedition," Rhys concluded. "Trying to find out what we knew."

"Or maybe playing a little cat and mouse," Eberhardt remarked. "This guy is definitely somebody we should talk to. Let me have his home and work addresses and I'll send a couple of agents to pick him up."

Rhys shook his head. "You wouldn't find him at either place. His mother had a stroke last night, and he took her to Gaines Memorial. That's where he is now."

"Gaines!" Lieutenant Jackson repeated. "Considering how his brother died, I'd think that's the last place he'd take her."

"Exactly," Rhys said. "Unless there's some crucial reason he has to be there today."

The lieutenant muttered, "Holy shit," snatched up his desk phone, and punched out the three-digit extension for central dispatch, while Eberhardt pulled a cellular phone from his suit coat.

"I'll alert the Secret Service. What time is it?"

Rhys and the assistant chief both checked their watches. "I've got 2:08," the chief said.

Jackson thrust his telephone receiver at Rhys with an order to give the dispatcher a description of Leon Perry. When Rhys finished, he handed the phone back and said,

"I have to go to the hospital. I've seen him, I can identify him by sight."

Eberhardt put a hand over the mouthpiece of his cell phone. "I'll go with you. But let's not get spooked, people. How likely is it that he stopped to put together a bomb before he rushed his mother to the hospital in the middle of the night?"

"He may not have had to," Rhys told them grimly. "It could be there already. His boss says he was assigned to work at the hospital all day yesterday."

There was a beat of stunned silence, and then Eberhardt rapped out, "Let's move," and headed for the door, the cell phone clasped to his ear. Rhys hurried after him.

Eberhardt briefed one of the Secret Service agents on the run, while the two of them dashed to Rhys's car. As he pulled out of the small parking lot, one part of Rhys's mind started plotting which route to take to avoid the worst of the traffic. Another part was wishing he'd had time to call Faith and tell her what was happening. The digital clock on the dash read 2:18. At least, thank God, she was well away from the hospital area by now.

It was fitting, in a way, that Mother was going to die in the hospital that had killed her son. The doctor had told Leon to prepare for the worst. It would be a miracle if she regained consciousness; unless they hooked her up to machines, she wasn't expected to live more than a few hours. The doctor thought she'd had at least one little stroke before this big one. He asked if she'd been forgetful or confused lately. Leon told him that yes, she had been, but he'd thought it was either old age or grief making her that way. It was a relief to know that a stroke was the reason she'd mistaken him for his brother. He had hated thinking Mother wished he'd been the one to die.

He'd signed a form that said they weren't allowed to use any extraordinary measures to keep her alive. Now he was completely free to carry out his mission. He no longer had to worry about what would happen to Mother after he was gone. In fact, he was excited by the knowledge that the three of them would be together again very soon.

Yes, it was fitting that she was going to die here. Even better, the two of them would join Lenny at the same time. It was going to be a wonderful reunion. He could hardly wait. In fact, things had worked out so well that he wasn't terribly upset over having to change one part of his plan.

It was the President's wife's fault that he wasn't going to be able to bring Faith McRae to the hospital. Because she had decided to give a speech at the dedication, extra policemen and Secret Service men were swarming all over the place. There were far too many of them to get an unconscious woman past. His original plan had been to carry Faith McRae in through the emergency entrance—he could always claim she'd fainted or been hit by a car or something—but when he saw how many cops there were, he'd decided that was too risky. If they caught him they would probably take him straight to jail, and he had to be at the hospital when the bomb went off. It was his mission. He was the Messenger of Truth. He had to be there.

He'd thought about it all morning while he sat next to Mother's bed, and finally he'd come up with another plan. He looked at his watch. It was fifteen minutes before two. Time to leave. He got up, leaned over the bed to kiss Mother's cheek, and walked out of the room.

When the limo disappeared from sight, Faith went back down to the PT department to collect her purse and lock up. Even though she'd seen Missy just before the receptionist left, she checked her mailbox out of habit. She was surprised to find a telephone message slip inside, with a terse note in Missy's florid script:

Detective Donovan called. Wait for him. He'll meet you here at 2:30.

Faith's first thought was: odd that Missy hadn't mentioned the message before she left. But then, she'd been in a hurry to get over to the hospital. It probably just slipped her mind.

Her second reaction was a flash of annoyance, at Rhys. Darn it, he knew traffic around the hospital was going to be murder this afternoon. Both sides of the street were already lined with vehicles parked bumper-to-bumper, and just now she'd seen two yellow school buses pulling into the clinic lot. If she didn't leave right away, it would take her forever to get home. She appreciated his desire to protect her, but this was carrying things a bit far.

She picked up the phone on Missy's desk, intending to call and tell him not to bother coming to the clinic because she was already on her way out the door.

There was no dial tone. A second later the lights went out.

A uniformed patrolman at the entrance to the west parking lot waved Rhys into to an area set aside for VIP parking. Rhys and Special Agent Eberhardt both spotted the limo as they got out of Rhys's car.

A blond man and a redheaded woman wearing a dark gray pants suit were waiting for them at the hospital's side entrance. "I'm Agent Westerburg, this is Agent Dodd," the woman said brusquely. "Secret Service, assigned to the First Lady. We've got the Timmons woman's room number. She's up on five. Let's go."

Eberhardt introduced Rhys, and Westerburg quickly filled them in as they followed Agent Dodd to an elevator that was standing ready, door opened. "Her son has been up there with her since she was admitted. Four of our people are on the unit now—two at the elevators and two covering the stairs. We were just waiting for you to get here and make a positive ID."

"What about the First Lady?" Rhys asked. "Isn't that her car outside? You should get her out of here."

He saw the Secret Service agents exchange a look as the

four of them entered the elevator. "She doesn't want to leave," Dodd said tersely.

"What! Well for God's sake *make* her leave."

Dodd and Westerburg gave him blank, stoic stares. Eberhardt cleared his throat softly. "Nobody *makes* the First Lady do anything, Donovan," he said dryly. "She is the First Lady, after all. Besides, if the crowd and that mob of reporters outside saw her Secret Service escorts hustle her back out to the limo minutes after she got here, people could panic. Somebody might get hurt."

Rhys stared at him in disbelief. "Hurt? You're worried that somebody will get *hurt?* If he's planted a bomb somewhere in this hospital, people are going to be *killed.*"

He turned to the Secret Service agents. "Up till now all his bombs have gone off in the middle of the night. He's nowhere around. Either he uses some kind of timer or he detonates them by remote control."

"We know all that, Donovan," Eberhardt said. "But think for a minute. There's no way we could evacuate the entire hospital."

"And we might tip him off if we tried," Dodd put in. "The First Lady is waiting in an office near the main entrance. We can get her out in a flash if the situation goes sour."

Rhys couldn't believe these people. If the situation went *sour?*

The elevator stopped on the fifth floor. As soon as the door slid open, one of two Secret Service agents standing at parade rest in the hall informed Westerburg that no one had come out of Mrs. Timmons's room. She nodded curtly and started down the hall. Dodd kept abreast of her while Rhys and Eberhardt followed. Rhys observed that both Westerburg and Dodd were wearing earphones.

"She's in 528," Westerburg said. "The rest of us will stop this side of the door, Donovan, but you keep going. Stroll past and glance inside. If the man with Mrs. Timmons is Leon Perry, after you've passed the room, turn around and nod. We'll handle it from there."

Yeah, Rhys thought, I'll just bet you will. And more than likely finish Leon's poor old mother off in the process. Assuming she was still alive, and conscious, she'd probably have a fatal heart attack when a bunch of federal agents charged into her hospital room, guns drawn, and dragged her son out.

He didn't say anything, though, just gritted his teeth and kept his opinions to himself. Just before they reached room 528, the other three drew their weapons and plastered themselves against the wall. Rhys kept walking. When he drew level with the door, he turned his head just enough to look inside. Then stopped dead in his tracks. Then pivoted to face the open door.

"Donovan!" Westerburg whispered fiercely.

He turned and told her, not bothering to keep the contempt out of his voice, "He isn't here."

Chapter Twenty

Agent Westerburg rushed forward. Dodd and Eberhardt were right behind her. "What do you mean, he isn't here?"

Rhys didn't bother to repeat the statement. By now she could see for herself that the only person in the room was the elderly, obviously unconscious, female patient lying in the bed.

"God *damn* it!" Eberhardt swore as he holstered his gun.

Having observed the excitement in front of room 528, the two Secret Service agents stationed at the elevator left their posts and trotted down the hall. When they arrived, Westerburg started grilling them, as if they were to blame for Leon Perry's disappearance. Apparently it hadn't occurred to her yet that he must have left before they were dispatched to keep him from leaving. While she ranted two nurses wearing starched white uniforms and ferocious frowns came bustling down the hall, probably to evict the lot of them. Rhys started walking back to the elevator.

Eberhardt caught up with him before he'd gone ten feet. "Where are you going?"

"To try to find Leon Perry," Rhys said in disgust. "Or

iling that, to find somebody who's seen him in the past
venty-four hours and might have some idea where he is."

The elevator door was still open. Rhys stepped inside
ıd punched the button for the first floor. Eberhardt
ayed with him.

"Louisville's a big city," the FBI agent said dryly. "You
lan to go door to door?"

Rhys watched the changing floor numbers above the
evator door. "No, I thought I'd stay right here."

"Here? At the hospital? There are several hundred peo-
le on the grounds. Which of them did you plan to start
ith?"

Rhys finally looked at him. Hard. "The head of the
ospital's housekeeping department. Leon spent yesterday
orking for her."

"Damn," Faith muttered into the blackness.

It was a hell of a time for the power to go out. And since
ıe clinic management had installed one of those fancy-
:hmancy intercom phone systems a few months ago, of
ourse the phones were out, too. If she hadn't run upstairs
› get a look at the First Lady's limo, or taken time to
heck her mailbox and discovered the message slip, she'd
lready be headed home. Now she was going to have to
umble around in the dark until she found her purse,
nd her keys, then stumble around some more till she
ocated the stairwell door, then fumble with the keys until
ıe found the one that would lock the door behind her.
Vhy in heaven's name couldn't they have put the PT
epartment on the ground floor, instead of sticking it in
ıe basement?

She suddenly remembered that Rollie kept a flashlight
round somewhere. But where? His desk? One of the treat-
ıent rooms? The break room? She decided to try his office
rst, simply because it was closest—about ten feet away,
n the other side of the shelves where the patient files

were kept. She knew exactly where the shelves were: rig
behind Missy's desk.

She inched forward, hands held in front of her a litt above waist level, until she felt the end of one of the ta metal shelving units. After that, it was easy to make he way along the rows of file folders to the other end. No the hard part. Where the hell was the door to Rollie office? Had she come down the aisle between the first an second row of shelves, or the aisle between the second an third row?

All right, just take a minute to think. You know this plac as well as you know your own house.

She impulsively closed her eyes. Oddly enough, helped. She saw Missy's desk, including the position of th telephone and computer, and the three shelving uni beyond. All right! She'd come between the second an third rows, which meant Rollie's office was straight ahea

And locked.

Damn it to hell, when had he started locking his offic door? Faith lifted her hand to whack the door in frustr tion, then froze.

What was that? She could have sworn she'd heard som thing—a soft, squishy-squeaky sound, like rubber soles o linoleum. She opened her mouth to call out, to ask someone was there, but caught herself at the last secon

Fear corkscrewed up from the pit of her stomach an lodged in her throat. If someone else *was* here, he or sh was trying not to be heard.

Until we find out who he is, you will never *be alone wi* anybody *but me.*

Oh, dear God.

A few seconds later she heard the sound again, clear this time. And closer. He was in the waiting room, slow making his way toward Missy's desk.

Comprehension blossomed in Faith's mind. The ele tricity hadn't gone out. It had been cut. He was here, on a dozen feet away, coming for her. The dark presenc The *dark* presence! She had always associated him wit arkness. Now she knew why. The waking dreams had been prescient warning.

For a moment she was afraid she would faint from sheer error. She felt a whimper forming in her throat and lamped a hand over her mouth, pressing so hard that er lips were smashed against her teeth. The taste of her wn blood, warm and coppery, jolted her enough to free er from the paralyzing grip of fear.

She had to do something. She couldn't just stand here nd wait for him to find her. Moving with agonizing slowess, she scrunched down to slip off one shoe and white port sock, then the others. She quickly stuffed the socks nto her shoes. Clutching both shoes in her left hand, she dged away from Rollie's office door, back toward the helves, letting her bare toes lead the way.

She hadn't heard anything for a long time—at least a ninute, maybe two. Where was he? Had he reached Missy's lesk? Passed it? Veered off to the right, toward the break oom? Or left, to the treatment rooms?

Was he creeping between the shelves, heading straight or her?

Faith reached the end of one of the shelving units and ressed her body against it, her head turned so that her heek rested on the cool metal. She was shaking so hard he was afraid the shelves would start rattling against the rame.

Think! she ordered herself fiercely. No electricity meant o elevator, so she would have to make it to the stairwell loor. The trouble was, the swinging double doors were etween her and the stairs, and both doors made a distincive clacking noise when they were pushed open. She would ave to go through them, though; there was no other way ut. If only she knew what it was about the doors that aused the noise, she might be able to use PK to silence t.

Her breath caught. She felt as if a stadium full of floodights had suddenly switched on in her mind. PK. Psychoinesis. Did she dare try to use it? She couldn't see

anything. What if she made a mistake, directed the powe
in the wrong direction? What if the darkness affected he
ability to control it?

If he comes after you, do whatever you have to to protect yoursel

No!

Her reaction to the memory of Rhys's words was as vic
lent as it was instinctive. *No,* she would *not!* She mustn'
even think it!

Turn him into a cinder, if that's what you have to do.

Her head began to pound. The prickly, itchy feelin
spread over her skin. She realized that the metal beneat
her cheek, which had been cool a minute ago, was no
toasty warm.

No! Stop it! STOP IT!

She breathed deeply through her mouth, enforcing con
trol, driving the power back into its prison. Just as sh
began to relax, she heard the squish-squeak of rubber sole
again. It was almost directly ahead, a little to her left, n
more than two or three feet away. He was in the aisl
between the shelves.

The director of the housekeeping department hadn'
seen Leon today, though Mr. Jenks had called this mornin
to explain why another employee would be taking his place

"Too bad about his mother," the woman said with
shake of her head. "And God knows I'd have preferre
to have him back today instead of the man Jenks sent me
Perry's replacement would probably do fine in an offic
building, but he knows zip about cleaning a medica
facility."

"And Leon Perry does?" Eberhardt asked.

"Oh, yes. One of his regular jobs is at the orthopedi
group practice across the street."

Rhys felt as if he'd been kicked in the stomach. "Leo
Perry works at the clinic across the street?"

The woman nodded. Both she and Eberhardt were look

g at him strangely. Probably because all the blood had ained from his face.

He didn't say a word to either of them, just wheeled ound and made for the hospital's main entrance at a ad run. He didn't encounter any obstacles until he was itside, but then he ran into a solid wall of humanity. He arted bulldozing his way through the crowd that had thered for the speeches which were about to begin. He eard someone—Eberhardt, he thought—yell his name, it he didn't stop.

Leon Perry worked at the clinic. The clinic where Faith orked. He *knew* her. The hostile presence she'd sensed ad been Leon, all along. Rhys knew it, with a conviction at turned his blood to ice water. Please God, let her have one home when she was supposed to.

He reached the outer fringes of the crowd, where there as less resistance. Charging through, he shouldered peo-le aside without regard to gender or age, sprinted across strip of grass and the wide drive beyond, dodged between arked cars. Finally he reached the street. A young uni-rmed officer who'd been directing traffic started toward im, eyebrows pushed together in a suspicious frown, one and on his nightstick. Rhys stopped and reached inside is jacket for his badge. The patrolman immediately aban-oned the nightstick and drew his revolver.

"Freeze!" he yelled.

If he hadn't been staring down the bore of a .38, Rhys ould have laughed. The kid had obviously watched too any episodes of "Cops" on TV. "Take it easy," he said. I'm—"

"FBI!" a third voice rapped out. Rhys glanced around nd saw Eberhardt squeezing between a car and a minivan, is left arm extended stiffly so the young patrolman could e the badge he held. He jerked his head toward Rhys. And the man you're about to shoot is Detective Rhys onovan, one of yours. He's only reaching for his identifi-ation. Put your weapon away, officer, everything's under ontrol."

The young man paled, then flushed beet red. "Sor sir. I, uh . . . I'm sorry. I didn't know. . . ."

Eberhardt put his badge away and made a dismissi gesture. The patrolman returned to directing traffic, ar Rhys continued across the street. Eberhardt hustled keep up with him.

"You want to tell me where we're going," he said dry

Rhys didn't answer. He'd stopped at the edge of tl clinic parking lot, which was filled with the cars, truck vans and motorcycles of people attending the hospital de cation. He was looking for a turquoise Geo Storm, hopi it wasn't there. When he saw that it was, he flinched as he'd taken a physical blow.

Faith slipped around the right side of the shelving un putting a layer of Manila file folders between them. Sh knew when he passed her on the other side. She *felt* hir he exuded cold, unyielding purpose.

She held her breath till he'd moved past, then bega creeping toward Missy's desk, inch by harrowing inc Once he discovered that she wasn't back there, he wou head this way again. And this time he might come dow the aisle where she was hiding. Still clutching her sho in her left hand, she extended her right arm, trying locate Missy's desk.

She found Missy's chair first, but with her shin rath than her hand. It rolled into the desk with a *clunk* th sounded like a rifle shot in the silence. Behind her, h pursuer grunted softly in satisfaction and started ba between the shelves, forsaking stealth for speed now.

Faith dropped her shoes and reached out blindly, gro ing for something—anything—she could use to slow hi down. Her hands found the back of the chair. She grippe it and spun, flinging it straight at him. She was alrea feeling her way around the desk when she heard hi collide with the chair and stumble into one of the shelvin units.

The shelves! She ducked around the corner, tucking erself into the niche between the wall and the supply abinet, closed her eyes, and assembled an image in her ind—the three, six-foot-tall metal units toppling like ominoes, folders and charts spilling from the shelves, hirling in a furious blizzard of paper.

As soon as the creak of metal told her it was happening, ie bolted into the waiting room . . . and almost immeditely tripped over the corner of a chair. She went sprawling, nding hard on her stomach, the wind knocked out of er. She could hear him back there, fighting his way clear f the toppled shelves, but precious seconds passed before ie caught her breath and managed to get her arms and gs under her.

She pushed off the floor and had taken three steps when e slammed into her from behind, dragging her down ith him. Faith's right hip caught the edge of a low table. he cried out in pain and fear. His rage was a living thing, nking white hot claws into her mind, shredding her anity.

She was dimly aware that her left arm was partially numb. he didn't think it was broken; her elbow had rammed ito his stomach when they fell. He was wheezing, gasping or air. The sound of his labored breathing gave Faith a udden, desperate burst of energy. Knowing it might be er only chance to get away from him, she planted her alms on the floor and heaved with all her strength. The nstant she felt his weight shift to the left, she twisted in that lirection. When he realized what was happening, talons of ury scored her mind.

"No!" he roared as he toppled onto his side and Faith crabbled out from under him. His right hand shot out, inding and seizing her ankle in a crushing grip.

The pain was intense. Her ankle felt as if it was being ulverized by a giant vise. But worse than the physical pain ras the shock of recognition that ripped through her when is fingers closed on her skin. The flesh-to-flesh contact

somehow sent a swarm of thoughts and images into h
mind. Emotions. Faces. Tommy Carver's, and hers.

She knew him! Dear God, it was Leon Perry.

"No!" he bellowed again. "You won't escape judgmer
harlot!"

Faith heard the madness in his voice, felt its horrib
caress in her mind. She drew her right leg up, ignorir
the pain in her hip, and kicked out as hard as she coul
aiming for the source of that dreadful voice. Her he
connected with something and an instant later was i
agony. He didn't let go. Sobbing with desperation, sh
kicked him again, in the same spot. This time his gri
slackened enough for her to wrench her ankle free.

She crawled out of his reach and then staggered to he
feet. She could feel blood leaking from the heel of he
right foot, making a sticky puddle on the floor. Her le
ankle was sore, but she could tell he'd only bruised it. He
left arm was all pins and needles below the elbow. He
right hip throbbed with a deeper pain. But the aches an
pains were minor irritations compared to the fear th
made her quiver like a leaf in the wind. Where was she
In the waiting room, but facing which way?

She heard a thick, gurgling sound, knew it was him an
that she hadn't managed to incapacitate him, only dela
him for a few moments. If she fled in the wrong directio
she could end up trapped in one of the treatment room
And Leon knew the layout of the PT department as we
as she did.

She closed her eyes, pictured the room and the arrange
ment of furniture. Then she imagined the chairs and table
sliding away from the walls, toward her. It wasn't easy; sh
had to concentrate on *pulling*, rather than pushing. Slowly
almost inaudibly at first, soft scraping sounds drifted t
her through the darkness. The square, heavy table she'
hit when she fell made a different sound than the small en
table across the room. The two chairs fastened together a
the arms sounded different than the row of single chair
When she'd isolated and identified all the sounds, sh

ised them to construct a kind of mental map and turned oward where she knew the double doors would be.

"What . . . what is that?" Leon said. He sounded like he iad a mouthful of chocolate syrup. Faith realized she must iave kicked him in the mouth, maybe knocked some teeth oose. That's why her heel was bleeding.

"What's that noise?" Now his voice was edged with fear. Ie was struggling to his feet.

Faith inched toward the double doors. *Afraid, Leon?* she hought. *Good.* Maybe she could make him too afraid to nove. She shoved a chair across the room, right in front of him, and heard his gasp of fright as the legs skittered icross the floor, no doubt leaving black scuff marks on his iice wax job.

Only a couple of feet to the double doors now, and he vas still in the same spot, probably afraid to move again ind attract whatever was moving around in the darkness. Ie was breathing heavily, through his mouth. Faith locked onto a maple magazine rack and sent it tap dancing toward iim on dainty feet.

His terrorized *"Ahh!"* made her smile thinly as she hobbled the final couple of feet to the double doors.

He'd locked them.

Standing at the edge of the clinic parking lot, looking t Faith's car, Rhys was overwhelmed by the feeling that he was there—not somewhere close by, but *there,* with him. Vas she reaching out, trying to connect telepathically? No. he wouldn't have to *try;* she would just do it. Of course, he had no way of knowing he was there.

"Is this the place the housekeeper mentioned?" Eberiardt asked. "Where Perry works?"

"Yes," Rhys murmured.

She was in trouble. It hit him without warning, coming out of God knew where. She was inside the clinic, and she as in danger.

"You think he might have come over here?"

Rhys nodded curtly and started jogging across the par ing lot, toward the side door that led down to the F department. "He's here, but nobody else should be. Th closed early today because of the hospital dedication."

"Hold up a minute." Eberhardt caught him, snagg his arm. Rhys shook him off without stopping or eve slowing. An urgency was building inside him, an awarene that he had to move quickly.

"Damn it, wait up! Let me at least get some backup ov here."

"There's no time," Rhys said. He reached the door. was locked. He swore angrily and looked around f another door, or a window. This was the only way in, least on this side of the building. "Perry's in there, an he's got somebody with him. A woman."

"What! How the hell can you know that?"

Rhys turned and looked him in the eye. "Take my wo for it, I just *know.* We'll have to break in."

Eberhardt was giving him that strange, what-the-hell-i going-on-here look again. "You're *sure* he's in there?"

Rhys had neither the time nor the inclination to co vince him. He closed his eyes and tried to activate h telepathic radar or sonar or whatever the hell it was. Ye *Faith,* really with him now, in his mind, so real that h expected to hear her laugh, feel her hand light on h arm. But something was wrong. He wasn't picking up a visual images. She was surrounded by pitch blackness, if she were on the bottom level of a mine. And Leo was there with her, searching for her, stalking her in th darkness.

"God, no," he said thickly. His eyes snapped open an he shoved Eberhardt aside, running for the clinic's fro entrance.

"I guess that means you're sure," Eberhardt muttere as he followed.

* * *

Faith wanted to scream in frustration. Had he locked very door in the building? Yes, probably. He'd wanted to onfine her, make sure there was no escape.

He was moving again, coming after her. His tread was eavier now, telling her that he was also hurt. She sent wo more chairs flying across the room. She heard one of hem glance off him with a soft thump. Incredibly, despite verything—she knew the chairs were so light they ouldn't possibly cause him any real injury, and that he neant to *kill* her, for God's sake—she felt an instant's flare f guilt.

The emotion ignited a spark of anger . . . at herself. She ad programmed herself to be ashamed of her powers, to eel guilt when she used them. So stupid! They were all he had now, her only means of defense. She wouldn't urt him, not that way—and she knew now that she could ontrol whether she did or not—but she wasn't going to et him hurt her any more, either.

"Stop, Leon," she said quietly.

Hearing his name startled him. His shuffling steps halted hree or four feet away.

"Yes, I know it's you. Don't come any closer. I don't vant to hurt you, but I will, if you try to hurt me."

"Slut." His harsh laugh was as ugly as the word. "You hink your threats frighten me? Your powers are nothing ompared to mine."

Faith's mind reeled in confusion. His powers?

"I bring the Truth to the world," he raved, his voice a oarse shout. "I was *chosen!* God's *will* be done! You and he Evil you serve will be brought down and *destroyed!*"

His voice rose to a shout at the end, and Faith realized hat the reference to his "powers" had been no more than he ranting of a madman. But that "the Evil you serve" ouched a raw nerve. He took two heavy, shuffling steps oward her.

"Stop," she said quietly, and when he took another step, he reached out with her mind and pushed him. Not hard, ust enough to make him stagger back a step. At the same time, she pictured the lock on the doors at her back visualized the deadbolt withdrawing into its housing. Sh reached behind her and gave one door a tentative nudge It moved freely. Too freely. Leon must have oiled th hinges. The familiar, distinctive *clack* was gone but th door swung open so fast that it made a soft whishing sound

He must have heard either the scrape of the deadbol or the whish of the door; or maybe he was just enraged because she'd pushed him back. He charged with a furiou scream, and was on her before she could evade him or d anything to stop him. Faith spun away at the last second stumbling into the other door, which immediately swung away from her. She managed to stay on her feet, but Leon grabbed a handful of her blouse and his momentum dragged her halfway across the lobby.

As her bare feet skidded across the floor, Rhys's franti voice blared inside her mind like a trumpet.

Faith! I'm here!

When he reached the front entrance, Rhys didn't waste time or hesitate. He drew his gun and fired two shots into one of the glass doors. The safety glass crumbled into a million pebbles. He waited for the shower to stop, then ducked inside. Behind him, Eberhardt made a strangled sound that might have expressed either disbelief or speechless anger. He came along, though, drawing his own weapon only after he was inside.

"He's cut the power," Rhys said. "Thrown the master circuit breaker, or something. They're in the physiotherapy area, in the basement. We'll have to take the stairs."

Her fear was stronger now, almost paralyzing. And he wasn't getting just fear, but pain with it. The bastard had hurt her.

The stairwell door was locked. Rhys stepped back and aimed his revolver at the lock.

"Don't!" Eberhardt said. "That's a fire door. You'll just jam the lock. Is there another way into the stairs."

Rhys shook his head. It was almost impossible to control is panic. "The only one I know about is the door we just ied, around the side of the building."

Eberhardt licked his lips. "And the circuit breaker's robably in the basement. All right, try shooting it open. ake a count of three. Don't aim at the keyhole."

"I know," Rhys said, and leveled his gun. "Stand back."

"Christ, you'd better be right about him having some- ody down there," the FBI agent muttered. "You lead, oing down. I don't want to get shot in the back."

Impatient with his yammering, Rhys started counting. One . . . two . . ."

The two shots he fired into the seam where door met ame drowned out the "three." Rhys was aware of some ind of commotion at the front of the building as he houldered the door open, but he didn't stop. He didn't ven know if Eberhardt was behind him, and didn't care. irectly in front of him, on the other side of a small land- ng, was the locked exterior door. As he stepped past it, nto pitch blackness, the stairwell funneled up the muted ut distinct sound of something heavy crashing to the oor.

He clattered down the cement steps, oblivious to the anger of falling, his revolver still in his right hand. When e got to the bottom, he wasn't surprised to find that door as also locked. He swore savagely. He didn't dare try to hoot out the lock in the dark.

And then suddenly the beam of a flashlight was descend- ng the stairs. Eberhardt's voice came from behind it.

"Don't shoot, it's me."

Rhys turned toward him, raising an arm to shield his yes. "Where'd you get the light?"

"From one of Louisville's finest. Looks like half the force esponded to the report of shots being fired. I didn't care or the idea of a bunch of people with guns running around own here in the dark, so I told them to stay upstairs and ecure the building. Let me guess—this door's locked, too."

"Yeah," Rhys muttered. He'd had an idea, but he

couldn't share it with the FBI agent. "Which means he still in there. Why don't you go back up and send somebo for a locksmith."

Eberhardt's grin looked evil in the yellow glare of th flashlight. "I can do better than that. Sit tight."

Rhys watched until the flashlight beam reached the to of the stairs and disappeared, then turned back to th locked door and rested his forehead against it. If he coul connect with Faith, send her a telepathic message, h thought she would be able to use her PK powers to ope the door. One thing made him hold back, though: th knowledge that she was trapped in there with a homicid maniac. He was afraid of what might happen if he di tracted her, pulled her attention away from Leon at crucial moment.

Doubt gnawed at him. Which risk should he take? Co tact Faith, or wait for Eberhardt to come back with som body who could unlock the damned door? Either way— acting or willfully neglecting to act—he might get he killed. And then Leon Perry's demented voice sudden erupted on the other side of the door, impelling hi toward action.

"I was *chosen!* God's *will* be done! You and the Evil yo serve will be brought down and *destroyed!*"

Seconds later Leon bellowed with rage. The soun decided Rhys in a heartbeat. He squeezed his eyes sh and sent out a telepathic shout he prayed would be stron enough to reach her.

Faith! I'm here! If you can hear me, unlock the door and tu on the lights!

Opening his eyes, he put his left hand on the doorkno and held his breath. The instant he felt the slight vibratio of the bolt sliding back, he twisted the knob, wrenche the door open, and lunged into the lobby.

The sudden bright glare of the overhead fluorescen temporarily blinded all three of them. Rhys instinctive brought his gun up, squinting and pivoting from left t right, knowing he had only seconds to locate Leon Perr

There! In front of the elevator! One of Leon's hands clutched a handful of Faith's blouse. The other gripped the handle of a screwdriver, its foot-long blade poised to plunge into her chest.

"Drop it!" Rhys yelled. "Drop it *now,* Perry!"

Faith had turned her head away from the blinding light. When he shouted the command, she looked up, saw the screwdriver. Rhys was watching Leon, not her, but he knew the instant she reached for the power to disarm him. He eased his finger off the trigger of his revolver. The single shot that caught Leon Perry in the center of his chest and knocked him back three feet came from the stairwell door.

Chapter Twenty-one

Rhys returned the revolver to his shoulder holster and went to Faith. She was staring down at Leon in surprise and confusion.

"Are you all right?" he asked as Eberhardt entered the lobby and knelt beside Leon.

"Yes. Why did you shoot him? You knew I—"

Rhys clasped her arm in warning and hurried to cut her off. "I didn't." He nodded at Eberhardt. "Agent Eberhardt saw that he was about to stab you and fired from the stairwell."

Several Louisville police officers filed through the stairwell door. A couple of them continued through the double doors into the PT department.

"Somebody call for an ambulance," Eberhardt barked. "He's still alive."

Faith pulled away from Rhys and went to Leon. She sank to her knees beside him. Rhys followed, taking note of her slight limp and the smears of blood her right foot left on the floor. She'd taken off her shoes so he couldn't track her movements in the dark. Smart.

She leaned over Leon, putting her face close to his.

"Where is it?" she said. "I know there's another bomb, Leon. Where did you hide it?"

His mouth twisted in a rictus that might have been a deranged grin. "You won't . . . find it." A bubble of blood burst on his lips. He gurgled, "Too late . . . but the Truth . . . will set you free." And then the light of madness in his eyes flickered out and his head lolled to one side.

"Christ," Eberhardt muttered. "All right, everybody out! Clear the building, *now!*"

Rhys reached down to lift Faith to her feet. She looked up at him and gave a slight shake of her head.

It's in the hospital. We have to hurry.

He grabbed her hand and they dashed for the stairs, joining the cops rushing to get out of the clinic before the bomb Eberhardt had assumed was there went off. One of them was talking into his radio, requesting that the bomb squad be dispatched.

When they reached the entrance, Rhys wrapped an arm around her waist and lifted her over the safety glass littering the floor.

"Do you know where it is?" he said.

"In the computer center."

He set her down in the grass and turned to yell for Eberhardt, who had apparently stayed to make sure everybody else got out, and was bringing up the rear.

"It's not here," Rhys said when the agent joined them. "It's in the hospital, in the central computer room."

Eberhardt's eyes narrowed. He glanced from one of them to the other. "This is something else you just *know,* right?"

Rhys tucked their linked hands behind him and gave Faith's a hard squeeze. "Right."

The FBI agent hesitated a moment. Then he turned away and hot-footed it over to the officer with the radio, telling him to order the bomb disposal unit sent to the hospital instead of the clinic.

Faith tugged at Rhys's hand. "Come on, we have to hurry."

He didn't question her, or suggest that they let the bomb disposal squad take over from here. He ran with her, across the clinic property and then the street, taking out his badge and holding it in front of him as they raced up the hospital drive. Somebody had picked up the radio transmission; the security staff was already clearing the area in front of the hospital, dispersing the crowd. But when they reached the foyer, a private rent-a-cop wearing a gray uniform planted himself solidly in their path.

"Louisville PD," Rhys snapped at him. "There's a bomb in the computer center. Where is it?"

"The bomb squad is on the way," the guard said firmly. "They'll handle it. I'm sorry, but you'll have to—"

Faith grabbed his arm with both hands. *"Please!* It's set to go off at three o'clock! Where's the computer center?"

Evidently the desperation in her voice impressed the man more than Rhys's badge had. He swiveled to look at a large sunburst clock above the information desk. The clock read 2:55.

"It's over by the emergency room. Come on, I'll take you."

"The emergency room," Rhys said heavily as they followed the guard down a series of corridors. They had to jog to keep up with him. "I brought you here the night of the fire, remember?"

She nodded, picking up the image that sprang to his mind. "It's the waiting room from my dream."

"Damn, I spent an hour there that night—I even got a soda from the machine across the hall—but it didn't hit me till just now."

"Don't beat yourself up over it," Faith said. *"I* should have realized Leon might be the bomber. I should have thought of him as soon as I heard your cyberphobe theory."

The guard stopped in front of a pristine white door with a brass plate that said Systems Management and yanked it open. "This is it. If you're looking for the mainframe, it's on the other side of the office."

"Thanks," Rhys said. "You'd better get everybody out."

The guard nodded brusquely. As Rhys hurried toward another door on the far side of the spacious office, he started shepherding the bewildered employees out into the hall. Two almost identical fresh-faced young men wearing white smocks and wire-rimmed glasses were the only human occupants of the large room behind the door. Virtually every inch of floor space was taken up by the mainframe computer and its peripheral units. Rhys stopped, scanning the equipment in dismay. Dear God, Leon could have put the bomb anywhere.

One of the young men noticed him and asked, "Can I help you, sir?" in a tone that added an unspoken, "You're not supposed to be in here."

Rhys flashed his badge. "There's a strong possibility that a bomb has been concealed somewhere in this room."

"What!" both young men exclaimed in unison.

He ignored the interruption. "I need to know the most likely places to look. If one of you wanted to hide a bomb in here, where would you put it?"

"What you're suggesting isn't possible," one of the young men told him flatly.

His clone pushed his glasses up his nose and declared, "Obviously you've been given incorrect information."

Rhys couldn't resist the urge to glance at his watch. It was 2:57. "Listen, we've got about three minutes before all these expensive toys of yours get blown to smithereens, and us with them. I don't want to hear that there's no bomb, dammit! Just tell me where the hell it could be."

"Maybe out there in one of the desks," dweeb no. 1 said, nodding at the door to the office. "Or a filing cabinet, or something. But it isn't in here. Nobody could have brought it in without being seen. There are always at least two programmers on duty."

"Always," dweeb no. 2 confirmed. "At least two. Twenty-four hours a day."

Their unshakable certainty was beginning to give Rhys

a bad feeling. "A janitor, one of the housekeeping staff, would have brought it in."

"That proves it can't be here," dweeb no. 2 said. "This room is strictly *verboten* to the housekeeping crews. We do the cleaning ourselves. Can't risk having any harsh detergents or solvents around this equipment. One spill could bring down the entire system."

"Oh, Jesus," Rhys muttered. He checked his watch again. Another ninety seconds had elapsed. He glanced over his shoulder, instinctively turning to Faith, thinking if they ran like hell, maybe they could get out through the emergency entrance before the bomb went off. She wasn't there.

"Rhys," she called from the office.

He bolted back through the door and then stopped dead in surprise. She was sitting on the floor in one corner, in front of a photocopy machine. She'd been a busy girl. All the drawers in two filing cabinets had been emptied onto the floor, along with several desk drawers. Nobody could have conducted such a thorough search by hand in a minute and a half.

"I found it," she said. She didn't look up. She was staring into the space provided for storing paper and toner drums under the copy machine.

Rhys fell to his knees behind her and peered into the small compartment. An ordinary shoebox—which had once contained a pair of size thirteen men's athletic shoes—sat on the bottom shelf. A digital watch was fastened to the top, the cheap plastic watchband secured with black electrical tape wrapped completely around the box and lid. A couple of thin wires ran from the back of the watch through two small holes punched in the box's lid. There was a little bell in the top left corner of the face, indicating that the watch's alarm function had been set. The time displayed beside the bell was 3:00P. The larger LCD numerals below showed the current time as 2:59:16.

"Can you disarm it?" he asked, his heart in his throat.

"I don't know," she said in a small, frightened voice.

He put his hands on her shoulders and squeezed. "You have to try." Bending down, he pressed his cheek against hers. "Remember the fire, when you knew there was going to be an explosion? Do what you did then."

Her uncertainty filled his mind, a dark, dampening fog that made him want to roar with frustration. The two programmers came up behind him to see what they were staring at. One of them said, "Shit!" his voice cracking in fear.

The clock's display showed 2:59:42.

"Faith!" Rhys said hoarsely, giving her a little shake. "Don't think about it, for God's sake, just do it!"

She leaned back against him and he wrapped both arms around her, bracing her, remembering how she'd jerked backward in the street outside the photographic equipment store. The clock showed 2:59:53.

He felt . . . something. A gathering. No, more like a *summoning*. He sat back on his heels, tightening his embrace. A soft, fizzing sound that seemed to come from the shoebox made the hairs on his arms and the back of his neck stand at attention.

The next thing he knew, his shoulder blades were slamming into a desk four feet behind him and one of the programmers had fallen across his right leg, which felt dislocated at both knee and hip. The young man dazedly pushed himself to hands and knees and crawled across the floor to retrieve his glasses. Rhys gritted his teeth and straightened his leg, and in the process became aware of the dead weight in his arms.

"Faith!"

Her name was ripped from him in a voice that wasn't his own. He half turned her, laying her back against his left arm. When he saw that her eyes were open, he breathed again. But she didn't stir, and when he probed her mind, it was like trying to read a blank sheet of paper. Fear gripped him, blacker and colder than anything he'd ever known. God, no. Had she saved everyone else only to lose herself?

"Faith, please," he murmured. "Come back to me." He curled his body around her, tucking her face under his chin, unconsciously rocking back and forth as if she were a colicky infant. "You can't leave me. I need you. I love you. Please, come back."

Her eyelashes fluttered against his neck. The sensation was so faint, so barely there, that he was afraid he'd only imagined it. He pulled back to look at her. She smiled.

"I love you, too."

Rhys make a choked sound that was part relief and part unbridled joy as he crushed her to his chest and buried his face in her hair. Neither of them noticed that the bomb disposal team had arrived.

Faith tried unsuccessfully to stifle a yawn. It had been late when she and Rhys finally got home Tuesday night, and then she'd had to get up earlier than usual this morning to accompany a bunch of Louisville cops and ATF and FBI agents to the clinic. They'd wanted her to describe, in detail, what had happened in the PT department before Rhys and Agent Eberhardt arrived. Specifically, how the records area and waiting room had come to look as if two warring armies and a tornado had passed through.

After quite a bit of wrangling—which was frequently interrupted by demonstrations of affection—Rhys had finally convinced her that, in this case, complete honesty wouldn't be the best policy. It was ironic that, now that she'd embraced her psychic abilities and was eager to exercise them openly, he was urging caution and restraint. They weren't ready for the truth, he argued. They wouldn't accept it if she gave it to them gift-wrapped. They'd end up inventing some explanation that would account for what had happened and at the same time let them hold fast to their narrow-minded beliefs.

Faith didn't like admitting it, but she knew he was right. So in the end she gave in and invented the explanation for them. They were busy men. Why not do what she could to lighten their workload?

By the time she finished leading them through those ten minutes or so of terror, Leon Perry had acquired superhuman strength and cunning. Faith didn't enjoy lying about another person; but considering that this particular person had tried to murder her (and, conveniently, wasn't around to contradict her story), she decided her conscience could tolerate a little mendacity.

Agent Gonzales of the Bureau of Alcohol, Tobacco and Firearms stood in the middle of the waiting room and scratched his chin.

"I still don't understand why he moved all the furniture away from the walls."

Faith shrugged. "I guess he was hoping I'd trip over it. And it worked because I did, a couple of times."

"But *all* the furniture? That's going a little overboard. A couple of chairs and a table would have served the same purpose."

"Maybe it was some kind of ritual thing," Special Agent Eberhardt remarked. Everyone looked at him in surprise, which clearly made him uncomfortable. "Well, his delusions did have religious significance, at least in his own mind," he explained. Faith thought he sounded just a tad defensive. "Maybe he was trying to arrange some kind of symbol or something that only he understood."

"Or an altar," one of the junior ATF agents said. "Perry intended to stab Miss McRae. Maybe he thought of her death as some kind of sacrifice."

Faith resisted the urge to roll her eyes. Rhys had encouraged her to let them speculate all they wanted, but this was getting out of hand. "Don't you think that's pretty farfetched?" she murmured.

"Maybe not," Gonzales replied. His forehead creased in a thoughtful frown, he started circling the jumble of overturned chairs and tables, evidently attempting to detect some pattern in their arrangement. "Show me which pieces you think you might have tripped over or stumbled into."

Faith sighed and tried to decide on a few choices.

"This chair?" Eberhardt asked, indicating one that was lying on its side.

Something in his tone made her glance at him. His expression was solemn, but his eyes were practically boring holes in her. She frowned. Was he trying to send her some kind of message? Without a second's hesitation or guilt, she reached into his mind.

Say yes.

Faith felt her mouth drop open. "Yes," she blurted. "Yes, I believe that is one of the chairs I tripped over."

"And this table?" the young ATF agent asked excitedly. "Did you bump into it?"

He was pointing to the big table responsible for the bruise over her right pelvic ridge. "I wish I'd only bumped into it," she said dryly. "I fell on it when he tackled me. It nearly took off my hip."

"And you probably moved it a little in the process," the young man said.

"I guess I could have." She didn't point out that the table hadn't been sitting in the middle of the floor when she banged her hip on it.

"Do you see?" His excitement was increasing by leaps and bounds. "If the chair was upright, and the table was a few inches over this way, they'd be aligned to form a sort of . . . slab. A sacrificial altar. And these other chairs are arranged in an irregularly shaped circle. There's probably some significance to that, as well."

Faith pursed her lips to keep from smiling. This guy had a terrific imagination.

Gonzales nodded soberly. "I think you're on to something, Marks."

She slid an incredulous look at him from the corner of her eye, but she didn't say anything. Agent Eberhardt was studying the ceiling as if he expected to see a message in blood scrawled there. Faith picked up his silent chuckle.

Well I'll be damned, she thought in amazement.

"He set them up!" she told Rhys that evening, as they ate the hamburgers and potato salad he'd fixed. "To stop them questioning me. Why would he do that?"

Rhys shrugged. "I think he knows, or at least suspects, something of the truth. But he also knows Gonzales and his superiors would never buy it. The case is closed. There's no doubt in anyone's mind that Leon Perry was the bomber, even though he'll never be tried and convicted. Eberhardt probably wants things wrapped up so he can get back to Washington."

Faith had sat at the table while he mixed the potato salad and kept an eye on the burgers, and he'd filled her in on the information various agencies had collected in the past twenty-four hours. Horace Richmond's secretary had remembered that Leon was in her office last Friday afternoon, collecting her computer paper for recycling, when the director came in and instructed her to write the memo about Tuesday's early closing. That must have been when Leon got the idea to leave the phony message from Rhys, to keep Faith there after everyone else had left. And when FBI agents cleaned out Leon's locker at the janitorial service, they'd found a rambling, incoherent statement he'd apparently left behind to explain the bombings.

"I could've told them why he did it," Faith observed. "He once referred to computers as tools of the devil. That was one of the things that set me off. He was like my mother, in a way—scared to death of anything he didn't understand, or that threatened his beliefs. And I guess *his* mother was at least partly responsible for that fear. His twin brother's death—the *way* he died, I mean—must've pushed them both over the edge."

She propped an elbow on the table and rested her chin in her hand. "When you told me that Leon's mother died last night, for a second or two I felt . . . I don't know . . . regret, I suppose."

"The woman had had a major stroke," Rhys said gently.

"Her death had nothing to do with Leon's psychosis or his campaign against computer technology."

"But maybe it did. Who's to say the stress of her other son's death didn't contribute to the stroke?" She sighed. "I can't help thinking that if I hadn't reacted so strongly to Leon's sermonizing, I might have been able to change his opinions, and maybe none of this would have happened."

Rhys scowled at her. "The man was a raving lunatic, Faith. A walking time bomb. If you'd tried to argue with him or convert him, God knows what might have happened."

"You're probably right," she acknowledged with another sigh.

"You know damn well I'm right," he said flatly. "Now stop trying to make sense of what happened by playing that pointless 'if only' mind game and take another helping of potato salad. I made way too much. We'll be eating potato salad for the next week."

Faith smiled and spooned more onto her plate. "You know, after what Tommy Carver told me, I'd just about decided to try to patch things up with Leon. If he'd strolled into the PT department yesterday and been halfway approachable, he probably could have finished me off in ten seconds flat—no hassle, no trouble, no stumbling around in the dark. He could've held out his hand for me to shake and then nailed me with that screwdriver."

Rhys choked on a chunk of hamburger. "God in heaven," he croaked when he'd stopped coughing.

"Well, it's true."

They finished the meal in silence. After the dishes were washed, they settled on the living room sofa for some much needed snuggling. When Faith could tell that Rhys had recovered from the shock she'd given him, she murmured, "You haven't said anything about the bomb."

"Oh, yes, the bomb." His mouth quirked in a half smile, displaying one dimple. "Strangest thing about that bomb. Everything was there—timer, detonator, explosive charge—but the components weren't connected. Remember the two little wires that ran from the watch into the box?"

Faith nodded.

"Well, the guys from the bomb squad cut a hole in the side of the box and stuck one of their miniature cameras inside to see what they were dealing with. They discovered that the ends of the wires had melted."

"Melted?" Faith repeated.

"Mmm, they can't figure it out. They claim the wires *were* attached, but somehow they got so hot that they literally melted. A soldering gun could have done it, maybe, but the lid was taped to the box, and there were no scorch marks on the cardboard, inside or out. And the wires were so short they'd have pulled loose if somebody had cut the tape and removed the lid. Besides, if anybody *had* done that, there wouldn't have been any need to use a soldering gun. It's a real mystery. They're all completely baffled."

Faith grinned. "Don't you love a good mystery?" She was elated. She had done it—used the power with such controlled precision that only the two tiny little wires were affected.

"Mmm, I do," Rhys murmured as he nuzzled her throat. "That's why I'm such a good detective."

She laughed. "Okay, Mr. Ace Detective, see if you can detect what I'm thinking right now."

He lifted his head to look at her, the expression in his beautiful blue eyes warming her all the way to her toes.

"I'll accept that challenge." He eased her onto her back, taking care not to jar her sore right hip. "But you'll have to give me a few clues."

"Well, if I must." She reached out and slowly walked her fingers up the faded denim stretched tight over his thigh. "Is that the sort of clue you mean?"

"Darling," Rhys murmured with a wicked grin, "you read my mind."